DOROTHY L. SAYERS

HAVE
HIS
CARCASE

WITH A NEW INTRODUCTION
BY LEE CHILD

HODDER

First published in Great Britain in 1932 by Victor Gollancz Ltd
First published in paperback by New English Library in 1974

This edition published in 2016 by Hodder & Stoughton
An Hachette UK company

5

A CIP catalogue record for this title is available from the British Library

Paperback ISBN 978 1 473 62136 7
Ebook 978 1 848 94734 2

Typeset by Hewer Text UK Ltd, Edinburgh
Printed and bound by Clays Ltd, St Ives plc

Hodder & Stoughton policy is to use papers that are natural, renewable
and recyclable products and made from wood grown in sustainable
forests. The logging and manufacturing processes are expected to
conform to the environmental regulations of the country of origin.

Hodder & Stoughton Ltd
Carmelite House
50 Victoria Embankment
London EC4Y 0DZ

www.hodder.co.uk

NOTE

In *The Five Red Herrings*, the plot was invented to fit a real locality; in this book, the locality has been invented to fit the plot. Both places and people are entirely imaginary.

All the quotations at the chapter heads have been taken from T.L. Beddoes.

My grateful acknowledgements are due to Mr John Rhode, who gave me generous help with all the hard bits.

DOROTHY L. SAYERS

This novel can be counted two different ways: it's the seventh of eleven in the Peter Wimsey series, and it's the first of the last five. The distinction is significant. If you line up the original editions on your bookshelf, you'll notice this one is much fatter than the first six, as are the final four. A dendroarchaeologist, thinking in terms of tree rings, might conclude that in about 1931 something changed for the better in Dorothy Sayers' life, because tree rings get wider as the weather improves and conditions become more clement. But in fact the opposite was true. Life got worse.

Dorothy Sayers was a complicated person. She was christened in Christ Church Cathedral, was taught Latin from the age of six by her clergyman father, was confirmed in Salisbury Cathedral, and took an excellent first-class degree at Oxford University. She said her surname as if it rhymed with 'airs' – as in 'airs and graces', we're tempted to think. But she was also bawdy and profane, and intensely interested in sex, believing it should satisfy the woman as much as the man – even though she remained a virgin until the age of thirty. She smoked heavily and loved food and drank pints of beer. She swore and flirted and spent hours in the pub.

Those earthy interests required two components – money and men. Both were a problem. Unless she married, she would have to live alone, which she didn't want, and without a second household income, she would be poor, which she didn't want. But jobs and especially men were thin on the ground. Casualties in World War One had left a numerical imbalance between the sexes. Her first love affair – intense but chaste – was with the Russian Johann Gregorievitch Korshoon, who had immigrated to England via America and changed his name to John Cournos. He was a writer and a journalist, a pretentious, self-important and self-pitying man – and an affected bohemian who abjured marriage, until he didn't, when he married someone else. We will see a faint and surprisingly generous echo of him in this book.

Meanwhile, Sayers' initial employment possibilities were in practice limited to school teaching, which she tried but hated, so she quit, and like unemployed people everywhere, she wrote a book. She aimed to mine the evident public appetite for detective stories, and she invented Lord Peter Wimsey. He just came to her, she said later, 'complete with spats'. He had money because she didn't. To write 'rich' cost no more in fountain-pen ink than 'poor', and she said she enjoyed spending his wealth for him. He was a relative success, in a pinched 1920s-author kind of way. Financially, he kept her head above water, but only just.

Again meanwhile, her next romantic fling – and her first sexual relationship – was with a motorcycle mechanic named Bill. Inevitably, she got pregnant. Inevitably, Bill disappeared. She had the illegitimate child – a boy – and hid him with a cousin. She took the emotional repercussions in her stride, and seemed largely unaffected by them. By that point she was working at an advertising agency, professionally fulfilled, writing more Wimsey novels at the weekends, spending raucous evenings in the pub with her colleagues. She met a journalist named Mac Fleming. He was a veteran of World War One, alive, damaged by shell shock and gas, but functioning. They fell in love and got married, and lived in Bloomsbury as a 1920s-style two-income-no-kids couple. At that point, life for Sayers was about as good as it was likely to get. Accordingly, she decided to ditch Wimsey, who up until then she had seen only as a stop-gap financial necessity – a nice little earner when times had been tough, but never really her heart's desire. She planned to marry him off, after the fifth Wimsey novel, *Strong Poison* – to Harriet Vane, an arch version of herself – and then let him disappear to pipe and slippers.

But things went wrong. Mac's fragile health collapsed, both physically and mentally. He stopped earning, his morale evaporated, he became surly, violent, bad tempered, and resentful of her having to fund him. Presciently Sayers had written about such behavior – distressingly common after World War One – in the fourth Wimsey novel, *The Unpleasantness at the Bellona Club*. Now she was living it for real. Wimsey went back to the front burner, as a matter of renewed financial necessity, of course, but more deeply and urgently, I think, as a matter of simple emotional compensation. Her real-life man had proved a dud, so she would lose herself in her fictional man. Her own life was now a mess, so Harriet Vane's – her alter ego's – would blossom and flourish. Home life was now unbearable, so she would escape to an imagined life with new and unprecedented immersion and enthusiasm. Now Wimsey really was her heart's desire.

The result was this book, *Have His Carcase*, and it's

magnificent. It's a book about people more than plot. It's multi-layered, with delightful strands of romantic suspense between Harriet and Wimsey, with clever in-jokes about what it means to be a mystery writer, with perceptive social commentary, with a sharply drawn portrait of a lost England, with its tea dances and watering holes and itinerant barbers, all built around a classically intricate Golden Age story about time of death, and time and distance, and timetables and tide tables, with a final reveal as convincing and satisfying as any in the canon. Hours could be spent arguing between this and *The Nine Tailors* and *Gaudy Night* as the quintessential if-you-could-only-read-one Wimsey novel, and it's notable that all three were written after the tree rings widened. Dorothy Sayers' distress was of course tragic for her, but as so often in the literary world, we readers benefitted from it, enormously.

Lee Child, New York, 2016

CONTENTS

I

THE EVIDENCE OF THE CORPSE

'The track was slippery with spouting blood.'
Rodolph

THURSDAY, 18 JUNE

THE best remedy for a bruised heart is not, as so many people seem to think, repose upon a manly bosom. Much more efficacious are honest work, physical activity, and the sudden acquisition of wealth. After being acquitted of murdering her lover, and, indeed, in consequence of that acquittal, Harriet Vane found all three specifics abundantly at her disposal; and although Lord Peter Wimsey, with a touching faith in tradition, persisted day in and day out in presenting the bosom for her approval, she showed no inclination to recline upon it.

Work she had in abundance. To be tried for murder is a fairly good advertisement for a writer of detective fiction. Harriet Vane thrillers were booming. She had signed up sensational contracts in both continents, and found herself, consequently, a very much richer woman than she had ever dreamed of becoming. In the interval between finishing *Murder by Degrees* and embarking on *The Fountain-Pen Mystery*, she had started off on a solitary walking-tour: plenty of exercise, no responsibilities and no letters forwarded. The time was June, the weather, perfect; and if she now and again gave a thought to Lord Peter Wimsey diligently ringing up an empty flat, it did not trouble her, or cause her to alter her steady course along the south-west coast of England.

On the morning of the 18th June, she set out from Lesston Hoe with the intention of walking along the cliffs to Wilvercombe, sixteen miles away. Not that she particularly looked forward to Wilvercombe, with its seasonal population of old ladies and invalids and its subdued attempts at the gay life, seeming somehow themselves all a little invalid and old-ladyish. But the town made a convenient objective, and one could always choose some more rural spot for a night's lodging. The coast-road ran pleasantly at the top of a low range of cliffs, from which she could look down upon the long yellow stretch of the beach, broken here and there by scattered rocks, which rose successively, glistening in the sunlight, from the reluctant and withdrawing tide.

Overhead, the sky arched up to an immense dome of blue, just fretted here and there with faint white clouds, very high and filmy. The wind blew from the west, very softly, though the weather-wise might have detected in it a tendency to freshen. The road, narrow and in poor repair, was almost deserted, all the heavy traffic passing by the wider arterial road which ran importantly inland from town to town, despising the windings of the coast with its few scattered hamlets. Here and there a drover passed her with his dog, man and beast alike indifferent and preoccupied; here and there a couple of horses out at grass lifted shy and foolish eyes to look after her; here and there a herd of cows, rasping their jawbones upon a stone wall, greeted her with heavy snufflings. From time to time the white sail of a fishing-boat broke the seaward horizon. Except for an occasional tradesman's van, or a dilapidated Morris, and the intermittent appearance of white smoke from a distant railway-engine, the landscape was as rural and solitary as it might have been two hundred years before.

Harriet walked sturdily onwards, the light pack upon her shoulders interfering little with her progress. She was twenty-eight years old, dark, slight, with a skin naturally a little sallow, but now tanned to an agreeable biscuit-colour by sun and wind. Persons of this fortunate complexion are not troubled by midges and sunburn, and Harriet, though not too old to care for her personal appearance, was old enough to prefer convenience to outward display. Consequently, her luggage was not burdened by skin-creams, insect-lotion, silk frocks, portable electric irons or other impedimenta beloved of the 'Hikers' Column'. She was dressed sensibly in a short skirt and thin sweater and carried, in addition to a change of linen and an extra provision of footwear, little else beyond a pocket edition of *Tristram Shandy*, a vest-pocket camera, a small first-aid outfit and a sandwich lunch.

It was about a quarter to one when the matter of the lunch began to loom up importantly in Harriet's mind. She had come about eight miles on her way to Wilvercombe, having taken things easily and made a detour to inspect certain Roman remains declared by the guide-book to be 'of considerable interest'. She began to feel both weary and hungry, and looked about her for a suitable lunching-place.

The tide was nearly out now, and the wet beach shimmered golden and silvery in the lazy noonlight. It would be pleasant, she thought, to go down to the shore – possibly even to bathe, though she did not feel too certain about that, having a wholesome dread of unknown shores and eccentric currents. Still, there was no harm in going to see. She stepped over the low wall which bounded the road on the seaward side and set about looking for a way down. A short scramble among the rocks tufted with scabious and sea-pink brought her easily down to the beach. She found herself in a small cove, comfortably screened from the wind by an outstanding mass of cliff, and with a few convenient boulders against which to sit. She selected the cosiest spot, drew out her lunch and *Tristram Shandy*, and settled down.

There is no more powerful lure to slumber than hot sunshine on a sea-beach after lunch; nor is the pace of

Tristram Shandy so swift as to keep the faculties working at high pressure. Harriet found the book escaping from her fingers. Twice she caught it back with a jerk; the third time it eluded her altogether. Her head drooped over at an unbecoming angle. She dozed off.

She was awakened suddenly by what seemed to be a shout or cry almost in her ear. As she sat up, blinking, a gull swooped close over her head, squawking and hovering over a stray fragment of sandwich. She shook herself reprovingly and glanced at her wrist-watch. It was two o'clock. Realising with satisfaction that she could not have slept very long, she scrambled to her feet, and shook the crumbs from her lap. Even now, she did not feel very energetic, and there was plenty of time to make Wilvercombe before evening. She glanced out to sea, where a long belt of shingle and a narrow strip of virgin and shining sand stretched down to the edge of the water.

There is something about virgin sand which arouses all the worst instincts of the detective-story writer. One feels an irresistible impulse to go and make footprints all over it. The excuse which the professional mind makes to itself is that the sand affords a grand opportunity for observation and experiment. Harriet was no stranger to this impulse. She determined to walk out across that tempting strip of sand. She gathered her various belongings together and started off across the loose shingle, observing, as she had often observed before, that footsteps left no distinguishable traces in the arid region above high-water mark.

Soon, a little belt of broken shells and half-dry seaweed showed that the tide-mark had been reached.

'I wonder,' said Harriet to herself, 'whether I ought to be able to deduce something or other about the state of the tides. Let me see. When the tide is at neaps, it doesn't rise or fall so far as when it is at springs. Therefore, if that is the case, there ought to be two seaweedy marks – one quite dry and farther in, showing the highest point of spring tides, and one damper and farther down, showing today's best effort.' She glanced backwards and forwards. 'No; this is the only tide-mark. I deduce, therefore, that I have arrived somewhere about the top of springs, if that's the proper phrase. Perfectly simple, my dear Watson. Below tide-mark, I begin to make definite footprints. There are no others anywhere, so that I must be the only person who has patronised this beach since last high tide, which would be about – ah! yes, there's the difficulty. I know there should be about twelve hours between one high tide and the next, but I haven't the foggiest notion whether the sea is coming in or going out. Still, I do know it was going out most of the time as I came along, and it looks a long way off now. If I say that nobody has been here for the last five hours I shan't be far out. I'm making very pretty footprints now, and the sand is, naturally, getting wetter. I'll see how it looks when I run.'

She capered a few paces accordingly, noticing the greater depth of the toe-prints and the little spurt of sand thrown out at each step. This outburst of energy brought her round the point of the cliff and into a much larger bay, the only striking feature of which was a good-sized rock, standing down at the sea's edge, on the other side of the point. It was roughly triangular in shape, standing about ten feet out of the water, and seemed to be crowned with a curious lump of black seaweed.

A solitary rock is always attractive. All right-minded people feel an overwhelming desire to scale and sit upon it. Harriet made for it without any mental argument, trying to draw a few deductions as she went.

'Is that rock covered at high tide? Yes, of course, or it wouldn't have seaweed on top. Besides, the slope of the shore proves it. I wish I was better at distances and angles, but I should say it would be covered pretty deep. How odd that it should have seaweed only in that lump at the top.

You'd expect it to be at the foot, but the sides seem quite bare, nearly down to the water. I suppose it *is* seaweed. It's very peculiar. It looks almost more like a man lying down; is it possible for seaweed to be so very – well, so very localised?'

She gazed at the rock with a faint stirring of curiosity, and went on talking aloud to herself, as was her rather irritating habit.

'I'm dashed if it isn't a man lying down. What a silly place to choose. He must feel like a bannock on a hot girdle. I could understand it if he was a sun-bathing fan, but he seems to have got all his clothes on. A dark suit at that. He's very quiet. He's probably fallen asleep. If the tide comes in at all fast, he'll be cut off, like the people in the silly magazine stories. Well, I'm not going to rescue him. He'll have to take his socks off and paddle, that's all. There's plenty of time yet.'

She hesitated whether to go on down to the rock. She did not want to wake the sleeper and be beguiled into conversation. Not but that he would prove to be some perfectly harmless tripper. But he would certainly be somebody quite uninteresting. She went on, however, meditating, and drawing a few more deductions by way of practice.

'He must be a tripper. Local inhabitants don't take their siestas on rocks. They retire indoors and shut all the windows. And he can't be a fisherman or anything of that kind; they don't waste time snoozing. Only the black-coated brigade does that. Let's call him a tradesman or a bank-clerk. But then they usually take their holidays complete with family. This is a solitary sort of fowl. A schoolmaster? No. Schoolmasters don't get off the lead till the end of July. How about a college undergraduate? It's only *just* the end of term. A gentleman of no particular occupation, apparently. Possibly a walking tourist like myself – but the costume doesn't look right.' She had come nearer now and could see

6

the sleeper's dark blue suit quite plainly. 'Well, I can't place him, but no doubt Dr Thorndyke would do so at once. Oh, of course! How stupid! He must be a literary bloke of some kind. They moon about and don't let their families bother them.'

She was within a few yards of the rock now, gazing up at the sleeper. He lay uncomfortably bunched up on the extreme seaward edge of the rock, his knees drawn high and showing his pale mauve socks. The head, tucked closely down between the shoulders, was invisible.

'What a way to sleep,' said Harriet. 'More like a cat than a human being. It's not natural. His head must be almost hanging over the edge. It's enough to give him apoplexy. Now, if I had any luck, he'd be a corpse, and I should report him and get my name in the papers. That would be something like publicity. "Well-known Woman Detective-Writer Finds Mystery Corpse on Lonely Shore." But these things never happen to authors. It's always some placid labourer or night-watchman who finds corpses. . . .'

The rock lay tilted like a gigantic wedge of cake, its base standing steeply up to seaward, its surface sloping gently back to where its apex entered the sand. Harriet climbed up over its smooth, dry surface till she stood almost directly over the man. He did not move at all. Something impelled her to address him.

'Oy!' she said, protestingly.

There was neither movement nor reply.

'I'd just as soon he didn't wake up,' thought Harriet. 'I can't imagine what I'm shouting for. *Oy!*'

'Perhaps he's in a fit or a faint,' she said to herself. 'Or he's got sunstroke. That's quite likely. It's very hot.' She looked up, blinking, at the brazen sky, then stooped and laid one hand on the surface of the rock. It almost burnt her. She shouted again, and then, bending over the man, seized his shoulder.

'Are you all right?'

The man said nothing and she pulled upon the shoulder. It shifted slightly – a dead weight. She bent over and gently lifted the man's head.

Harriet's luck was in.

It *was* a corpse. Not the sort of corpse there would be any doubt about, either. Mr Samuel Weare of Lyons Inn, whose 'throat they cut from ear to ear', could not have been more indubitably a corpse. Indeed, if the head did not come off in Harriet's hands, it was only because the spine was intact, for the larynx and all the great vessels of the neck had been severed 'to the hause-bone', and a frightful stream, bright red and glistening, was running over the surface of the rock and dripping into a little hollow below.

Harriet put the head down again and felt suddenly sick. She had written often enough about this kind of corpse, but meeting the thing in the flesh was quite different. She had not realised how butchery the severed vessels would look, and she had not reckoned with the horrid halitus of blood, which streamed to her nostrils under the blazing sun. Her hands were red and wet. She looked down at her dress. That had escaped, thank goodness. Mechanically, she stepped down again from the rock and went round to the edge of the sea. There she washed her fingers over and over again, drying them with ridiculous care upon her handkerchief. She did not like the look of the red trickle that dripped down the face of the rock into the clear water. Retreating, she sat down rather hastily on some loose boulders.

'A dead body,' said Harriet, aloud to the sun and the seagulls. 'A dead body. How – how appropriate!' She laughed.

'The great thing,' Harriet found herself saying, after a pause, 'the great thing is to keep cool. Keep your head, my girl. What would Lord Peter Wimsey do in such a case? Or, of course, Robert Templeton?'

Robert Templeton was the hero who diligently detected between the covers of her own books. She dismissed the image of Lord Peter Wimsey from her mind, and concentrated on that of Robert Templeton. The latter was a gentleman of extraordinary scientific skill, combined with almost fabulous muscular development. He had arms like an orang-outang and an ugly but attractive face. She conjured up his phantom before her in the suit of rather loud plus-fours with which she was accustomed to invest him, and took counsel with him in spirit.

Robert Templeton, she felt, would at once ask himself, 'Is it Murder or Suicide?' He would immediately, she supposed, dismiss the idea of an accident. Accidents of that sort do not happen. Robert Templeton would carefully examine the body, and pronounce –

Quite so; Robert Templeton would examine the body. He was, indeed, notorious for the sang-froid with which he examined bodies of the most repulsive description. Bodies reduced to boneless jelly by falling from aeroplanes; bodies charred into 'unrecognisable lumps' by fire; bodies run over by heavy vehicles, and needing to be scraped from the road with shovels – Robert Templeton was accustomed to examine them all, without turning a hair. Harriet felt that she had never fully appreciated the superb nonchalance of her literary offspring.

Of course, any ordinary person, who was not a Robert Templeton, would leave the body alone and run for the police. But there were no police. There was not a man, woman or child within sight; only a small fishing-boat, standing out to sea some distance away. Harriet waved wildly in its direction, but its occupants either did not see her or supposed that she was merely doing some kind of reducing exercise. Probably their own sail cut off their view

9

of the shore, for they were tacking up into the wind, with the vessel lying well over. Harriet shouted, but her voice was lost amid the crying of the gulls.

As she stood, hopelessly calling, she felt a wet touch on her foot. The tide had undoubtedly turned, and was coming in fast. Quite suddenly, this fact registered itself in her mind and seemed to clear her brain completely.

She was, as she reckoned, at least eight miles from Wilvercombe, which was the nearest town. There might be a few scattered houses on the road, but they would probably belong to fishermen, and ten to one she would find nobody at home but women and children, who would be useless in the emergency. By the time she had hunted up the men and brought them down to the shore, the sea would very likely have covered the body. Whether this was suicide or murder, it was exceedingly necessary that the body should be examined, before everything was soaked with water or washed away. She pulled herself sharply together and walked firmly up to the body.

It was that of a young man, dressed in a neat suit of dark-blue serge, with rather over-elegant, narrow-soled brown shoes, mauve socks and a tie which had also been mauve before it had been horridly stained red. The hat, a grey soft felt, had fallen off – no, had been taken off and laid down upon the rock. She picked it up and looked inside, but saw nothing but the maker's name. She recognised it as that of a well-known, but not in the best sense, famous, firm of hatters.

The head which it had adorned was covered with a thick and slightly too-long crop of dark, curly hair, carefully trimmed and smelling of brilliantine. The complexion was, she thought, naturally rather white and showed no signs of sunburn. The eyes, fixed open in a disagreeable stare, were blue. The mouth had fallen open, showing two rows of carefully-tended and very white teeth. There were no gaps in the rows, but she noticed that one of the thirteen-year-old molars had been crowned. She tried to guess the exact age of the man. It was difficult, because he wore – very unexpectedly – a short, dark beard, trimmed to a neat point. This made him look older, besides giving him a somewhat foreign appearance, but it seemed to her that he was a very young man, nevertheless. Something immature about the lines of the nose and face suggested that he was not much more than twenty years old.

From the face she passed on to the hands, and here she was again surprised. Robert Templeton or no Robert Templeton, she had taken for granted that this elegantly-dressed youth had come to this incongruous and solitary spot to commit suicide. That being so, it was surely odd that he should be wearing gloves. He had lain doubled up with his arms beneath him, and the gloves were very much stained. Harriet began to draw off one of them, but was overcome by the old feeling of distaste. She saw that they were loose chamois gloves of good quality, suitable to the rest of the costume.

Suicide – with gloves on? Why had she been so certain that it was suicide? She felt sure she had a reason.

Well, of course. If it was not suicide, where had the murderer gone? She knew he had not come along the beach from the direction of Lesston Hoe, for she remembered that bare and shining strip of sand. There was her own solitary line of footprints leading across from the shingle. In the Wilvercombe direction, the sand was again bare except for a single track of footmarks – presumably those of the corpse.

The man, then, had come down to the beach, and he had come alone. Unless his murderer had come by sea, he had been alone when he died. How long had he been dead? The tide had only turned recently, and there were no keel-marks on the sand. No one, surely, would have climbed the seaward face of the rock. How long was it since there had been a sufficient depth of water to bring a boat within easy reach of the body?

Harriet wished she knew more about times and tides. If Robert Templeton had happened, in the course of his brilliant career, to investigate a sea-mystery, she would, of course, have had to look up information on this point. But she had always avoided sea-and-shore problems, just precisely on account of the labour involved. No doubt the perfect archetypal Robert Templeton knew all about it, but the knowledge was locked up within his shadowy and ideal brain. Well, how long had the man been dead, in any case?

This was a thing Robert Templeton would have known, too, for he had been through a course of medical studies among other things and, moreover, never went out without a clinical thermometer and other suitable apparatus for testing the freshness or otherwise of bodies. But Harriet had no thermometer, nor, if she had had one, would she have known how to use it for the purpose. Robert Templeton was accustomed to say, airily, 'Judging by the amount of rigor and the temperature of the body, I should put the time of death at such-and-such', without going into fiddling details about the degrees Fahrenheit registered by the instrument. As for rigor, there certainly was not a trace of it present – naturally; since rigor (Harriet did know this bit) does not usually set in till from four to ten hours after death. The blue suit and brown shoes showed no signs of having been wet by sea-water; that hat was still lying on the rock. But four hours earlier, the water must have been over the rock and over the footprints. The tragedy must be more recent than that. She put her hand on the body. It seemed quite warm. But anything would be warm on such a scorching day. The back and the top of the head were almost as hot as the surface of the rock. The under surface, being in shadow, felt cooler, but no cooler than her own hands which she had dipped in the sea-water.

Yes – but there was one criterion she *could* apply. The weapon. No weapon, no suicide – that was a law of the Medes and Persians. There was nothing in the hands – no signs of that obliging 'death-grip' which so frequently preserves evidence for the benefit of detectives. The man had slumped forward – one arm between his body and the rock, the other, the right, hanging over the rock-edge just beneath his face. It was directly below this hand that the stream of blood ran down so uninvitingly, streaking the water. If the weapon was any-where it would be here. Taking off her shoes and stockings, and turning her sleeve up to the elbow, Harriet groped cautiously in the water, which was about eighteen inches deep at the base of the rock. She stepped warily, for fear of treading on a knife-edge, and it was as well that she did, for presently her hand encountered something hard and sharp. At the cost of a slight cut on her finger, she drew up an open cut-throat razor, already partially buried in the sand.

The weapon was there, then; suicide seemed to be the solution after all. Harriet stood with the razor in her hand, wondering whether she was leaving finger-prints on the wet surface. The suicide, of course, would have left none, since he was wearing gloves. But once again, why that precau-tion? It is reasonable to wear gloves to commit a murder, but not to commit suicide. Harriet dismissed this problem for future consideration, and wrapped her handkerchief round the razor.

The tide was coming in inexorably. What else could she do? Ought she to search any pockets? She had not the strength of a Robert Tempeton to haul the body above high-water mark. That was really a business for the police, when the body was removed, but it was just possible that there might be papers, which the water would render illegible. She gingerly felt the jacket pockets, but the dead man had obviously attached too much importance to the set of his clothes to carry very much in them. She found only a silk handkerchief with a laundry-mark, and a thin gold cigarette-case in the right-hand pocket; the other was empty. The outside breast-pocket held a mauve silk handkerchief, obviously intended for display rather than for use; the hip-pocket was empty. She could not get at the trouser-pockets without lifting the corpse, which, for many reasons, she did not want to do. The inner breast-pocket, of course, was the one for papers, but Harriet felt a deep repugnance to handling the inner breast-pocket. It appeared to have received the full gush of blood from the throat. Harriet excused herself by thinking that any papers in *that* pocket would be illegible already. A cowardly excuse, possibly – but there it was. She could not bring herself to touch it.

She secured the handkerchief and the cigarette-case and once more looked around her. Sea and sand were as deserted as ever. The sun still shone brightly, but a mass of cloud was beginning to pile up on the seaward horizon. The wind, too, had hauled round to the south-west and was strengthening every moment. It looked as though the beauty of the day would not last.

She still had to look at the dead man's footprints, before the advancing water obliterated them. Then, suddenly, she remembered that she had a camera. It was a small one, but it did include a focusing adjustment for objects up to six feet from the lens. She extracted the camera from her pack, and took three snapshots of the rock and the body from different viewpoints. The dead man's head lay still as it had fallen when she moved it – canted over a little sideways, so that it was just possible to secure a photograph of the features. She expended a film on this, racking the camera out to the six-foot mark. She had now four films left in the camera. On one, she took a general view of the coast with the body in the foreground, stepping a little way back from the rock for the purpose. On the second, she took a closer view of the line of footprints, stretching from the rock across the sand in the direction of Wilvercombe. On the third, she made a close-up of one of the footprints, holding the camera, set to six feet, at arm's-length above her head and pointing the lens directly downwards to the best of her judgement.

She looked at her watch. All this had taken her about twenty minutes from the time that she first saw the body. She thought she had better, while she was about it, spare time to make sure that the footprints belonged to the body. She removed one shoe from the foot of the corpse, noticing as she did so that, though the sole bore traces of sand, there were no stains of sea-water upon the leather of the uppers. Inserting the shoe into one of the footprints, she observed that they corresponded perfectly. She did not care for the job of replacing the shoe, and therefore took it with her, pausing as she regained the shingle, to take a view of the rock from the landward side.

The day was certainly clouding over and the wind getting up. Looking out beyond the rock, she saw a line of little swirls and eddies, which broke from time to time into angry-looking spurts of foam, as though breaking about the tops of hidden rocks. The waves everywhere were showing feathers of foam, and dull yellow streaks reflected the gathering cloud-masses further out to sea. The fishing-boat was almost out of sight, making for Wilvercombe.

Not quite sure whether she had done the right thing or the wrong, Harriet gathered up her belongings, including the shoe, hat, razor, cigarette-case and handkerchief, and started to scramble up the face of the cliff. It was then just after half-past two.

II

THE EVIDENCE OF THE ROAD

'None sit in doors,
Except the babe, and his forgotten grandsire,
And such as, out of life, each side do lie
Against the shutter of the grave or womb.'

The Second Brother

THURSDAY, 18 JUNE

THE road, when Harriet reached it, seemed as solitary as before. She turned in the direction of Wilvercombe and strode along at a good, steady pace. Her instinct was to run, but she knew that she would gain nothing by pumping herself out. After about a mile, she was delighted by the sight of a fellow-traveller; a girl of about seventeen, driving a couple of cows. She stopped the girl and asked the way to the nearest house.

The girl stared at her. Harriet repeated her request.

The reply came in so strong a west-country accent that Harriet could make little of it, but at length she gathered that 'Will Coffin's, over to Brennerton', was the nearest habitation, and that it could be reached by following a winding lane on the right.

'How far is it?' asked Harriet.

The girl opined that it was a good piece, but declined to commit herself in yards or miles.

'Well, I'll try there,' said Harriet. 'And if you meet anybody on the road, will you tell them there's a dead man on the beach about a mile back and that the police ought to be told.'

The girl stared dumbly.

Harriet repeated the message, adding, 'Do you understand?'

'Yes, miss,' said the girl, in the tone of voice which makes it quite clear that the hearer understands nothing.

As Harriet hurried away up the lane, she saw the girl still staring after her.

Will Coffin's proved to be a small farmhouse. It took Harriet twenty minutes to reach it, and when she did reach it, it appeared to be deserted. She knocked at the door without result; pushed it open and shouted, still without result; then she went round to the back.

When she had again shouted several times, a woman in an apron emerged from an outbuilding and stood gazing at her.

'Are any of the men about?' asked Harriet.

The woman replied that they were all up to the seven-acre field, getting the hay in.

Harriet explained that there was a dead man lying on the shore and that the police ought to be informed.

'That do be terrible, surely,' said the woman. 'Will it be Joe Smith? He was out with his boat this morning and the rocks be very dangerous thereabouts. The Grinders, we call them.'

'No,' said Harriet; 'it isn't a fisherman – it looks like somebody from the town. And he isn't drowned. He's cut his throat.'

'Cut his throat?' said the woman, with relish. 'Well, now, what a terrible thing, to be sure.'

'I want to let the police know,' said Harriet, 'before the tide comes in and covers the body.'

'The police?' The woman considered this. 'Oh, yes,' she said, after mature thought. 'The police did ought to be told about it.'

Harriet asked if one of the men could be found and sent

with a message. The woman shook her head. They were getting in the hay and the weather did look to be changing. She doubted if anybody could be spared.

'You're not on the telephone, I suppose?' asked Harriet.

They were not on the telephone, but Mr Carey at the Red Farm, he was on the telephone. To get to the Red Farm, the woman added, under interrogation, you would have to go back to the road and take the next turning, and then it was about a mile or maybe two.

'Was there a car Harriet could borrow?

The woman was sorry, but there was no car. At least, there was one, but her daughter had gone over to Heathbury market and wouldn't be back till late.

'Then I must try and get to the Red Farm,' said Harriet, rather wearily. 'If you *do* see anybody who could take a message, would you tell them that there's a dead man on the shore near the Grinders, and that the police ought to be informed.'

'Oh, I'll tell them sure enough,' said the woman, brightly. 'It's a very terrible thing, isn't it? The police did ought to know about it. You're looking very tired, miss; would you like a cup of tea?'

Harriet refused the tea, and said she ought to be getting on. As she passed through the gate, the woman called her back. Harriet turned hopefully.

'Was it you that found him, miss?'

'Yes, I found him.'

'Lying there dead?'

'Yes.'

'With his throat cut?'

'Yes.'

'Dear, dear,' said the woman, ' 'Tis a terrible thing, to be sure.'

Back on the main road, Harriet hesitated. She had lost a good deal of time on this expedition. Would it be better to

18

turn aside again in search of the Red Farm, or to keep to the main road where there was more chance of meeting a passerby? While still undecided, she arrived at the turn. An aged man was hoeing turnips in a field close by. She hailed him.

'Is this the way to the Red Farm?'

He paid no attention, but went on hoeing turnips.

'He must be deaf,' muttered Harriet, hailing him again. He continued to hoe turnips. She was looking about for the gate into the field when the aged man paused to straighten his back and spit on his hands, and in so doing brought her into his line of vision.

Harriet beckoned to him, and he hobbled slowly up to the wall, supporting himself on the hoe as he went.

'Is this the way to the Red Farm?' She pointed up the lane.

'No,' said the old man, 'he ain't at home.'

'Has he got a telephone?' asked Harriet.

'Not till tonight,' replied the ancient. 'He's over to Heathbury market.'

'A telephone,' repeated Harriet, 'has he got a telephone?'

'Oh, ay,' said the old man, 'you'll find her somewhere about.' While Harriet was wondering whether the pronoun was the one usually applied in that county to telephones, he dashed her hopes by adding: 'Her leg's bad again.'

'How far is it to the farm?' shouted Harriet, desperately.

'I shouldn't wonder if 'twas,' said the old man, resting on the hoe, and lifting up his hat to admit the breeze to his head, 'I tell'd her o' Saturday night she hadn't no call to do it.'

Harriet, leaning far over the wall, advanced her mouth to within an inch of his ear.

'How *far* is it?' she bawled.

'There ain't no need to shout,' said the old man. 'I bain't deaf. Eighty-two come Michaelmas, and all my faculties, thank God.'

'How far—' began Harriet.

'I'm telling 'ee, amn't I? Mile and half by the lane, but if you was to take the short cut through the field where the old bull is—'

A car came suddenly down the road at considerable speed and vanished into the distance.

'Oh, bother!' muttered Harriet, 'I might have stopped that if I hadn't wasted my time on this old idiot.'

'You're quite right, miss,' agreed Old Father William, catching the last word with the usual perversity of the deaf. 'Madmen, I calls 'em. There ain't no sense in racketing along at that pace. My niece's young man—'

The glimpse of the car was a deciding factor in Harriet's mind. Far better to stick to the road. If once she began losing herself in by-ways on the chance of finding an elusive farm and a hypothetical telephone, she might wander about till dinner-time. She started off again, cutting Father William's story off abruptly in the middle, and did another dusty half-mile without further encounter.

It was odd, she thought. During the morning she had seen several people and quite a number (comparatively) of tradesmen's vans. What had happened to them all? Robert Templeton (or possibly even Lord Peter Wimsey, who had been brought up in the country) would have promptly enough found the answer to the riddle. It was market-day at Heathbury, and early-closing day at Wilvercombe and Lesston Hoe – the two phenomena being, indeed, interrelated so as to permit the inhabitants of the two watering-places to attend the important function at the market-town. Therefore there were no more tradesmen's deliveries along the coast-road. And therefore all the local traffic to Heathbury was already well away inland. Such of the aborigines as remained were at work in the hayfields. She did, indeed, discover a man and a youth at work with a two-horse hay-cutter, but they stared aghast at her suggestion that they should leave their work and their horses to look for the police. The farmer himself was (naturally) at Heathbury market. Harriet, rather hopelessly, left a message with them and trudged on.

Presently there came slogging into view a figure which appeared rather more hopeful; a man clad in shorts and carrying a pack on his back – a hiker, like herself. She hailed him imperiously.

'I say, can you tell me where I can get hold of somebody with a car or a telephone? It's frightfully important.'

The man, a weedy, sandy-haired person with a bulging brow and thick spectacles, gazed at her with courteous incompetence.

'I'm afraid I can't tell you. You see, I'm a stranger here myself.'

'Well, could you—?' began Harriet, and paused. After all, what could he do? He was in exactly the same boat as herself. With a foolish relic of Victorianism she had somehow imagined that a man would display superior energy and resourcefulness, but, after all, he was only a human being, with the usual outfit of legs and brains.

'You see,' she explained, 'there's a dead man on the beach over there.' She pointed vaguely behind her.

'No, really?' exclaimed the young man. 'I say, that's a bit thick, isn't it? Er – friend of yours?'

'Certainly not,' retorted Harriet. 'I don't know him from Adam. But the police ought to know about it.'

'The police? Oh, yes, of course, the police. Well, you'll find them in Wilvercombe, you know. There's a police-station there.'

'I know,' said Harriet, 'but the body's right down near low-water mark, and if I can't get somebody along pretty quick the tide may wash him away. In fact, it's probably done so already. Good lord! It's almost four o'clock.'

'The tide? Oh, yes. Yes, I suppose it would. If' – he

brightened up with a new thought – 'if it's coming in. But it might be going out, you know, mightn't it?'

'It might, but it isn't,' said Harriet, grimly. 'It's been coming in since two o'clock. Haven't you noticed?'

'Well, no, I can't say I have. I'm shortsighted. And I don't know much about it. I live in London, you see. I'm afraid I can't quite see what I can do about it. There don't seem to be any police about here, do there?'

He gazed round about, as though he expected to sight a constable on point-duty in the middle-distance.

'Have you passed any cottages lately?' asked Harriet.

'Cottages? Oh, yes – yes, I believe I did see some cottages a little way back. Oh, yes, I'm sure I did. You'll find somebody there.'

'I'll try there, then. And if you meet anybody would you mind telling them about it. A man on the beach – with his throat cut.'

'His throat?'

'Yes. Near some rocks they call the Grinders.'

'Who cut his throat?'

'How should I know? I should think he probably did it himself.'

'Yes – oh, naturally. Yes. Otherwise it would be murder, wouldn't it?'

'Well, it *may* be murder, of course.'

The hiker clutched his staff nervously.

'Oh! I shouldn't think so, should you?'

'You never know,' said Harriet, exasperated. 'If I were you, I'd be getting along quickly. The murderer may be somewhere about, you know.'

'Good heavens!' said the young man from London. 'But that would be awfully dangerous.'

'Wouldn't it? Well, I'll be pushing on. Don't forget, will you? A man with his throat cut near the Grinders.'

'The Grinders. Oh, yes. I'll remember. But, I say?'

'Yes?'

'Don't you think I'd better come along with you? To protect you, you know, and that sort of thing?'

Harriet laughed. She felt convinced that the young man was not keen on passing the Grinders.

'As you like,' she said indifferently, walking on.

'I could show you the cottages,' suggested the young man.

'Very well,' said Harriet. 'Come along. We'll have to be as quick as we can.'

A quarter of an hour's walk brought them to the cottages – two low thatched buildings standing on the right-hand side of the road. In front of them a high hedge had been planted, screening them from the sea-gales and, incidentally, helping to cut off all view of the shore. Opposite them, on the other side of the road, a narrow walled lane twisted down to the sea's edge. From Harriet's point of view the cottages were a disappointment. They were inhabited by an aged crone, two youngish women and some small children, but the men were all out fishing. They were late back today but were expected on the evening tide. Harriet's story was listened to with flattering interest and enthusiasm, and the wives promised to tell their husbands about it when they came in. They also offered refreshment which, this time, Harriet accepted. She felt pretty sure that the body would by now be covered by the tide and that half an hour could make no real difference. Excitement had made her weary. She drank the tea and was thankful.

The companions then resumed their walk, the gentleman from London, whose name was Perkins, complaining of a blistered heel. Harriet ignored him. Surely something would soon come along.

The only thing that came was a fast saloon car, which overtook them about half a mile further on. The proud chauffeur, seeing two dusty trampers signalling, as it appeared to him, for a lift, put his stern foot down on the accelerator and drove on.

'The beastly road-hog!' said Mr Perkins, pausing to caress his blistered heel.

'Saloons with chauffeurs are never any good,' said Harriet. 'What we want is a lorry, or a seven-year-old Ford. Oh, look! What's that?'

'That' was a pair of gates across the road and a little cottage standing beside it.

'A level-crossing, by all that's lucky!' Harriet's sinking courage revived. 'There *must* be somebody here.'

There was. There were, in fact, two people – a cripple and a small girl. Harriet eagerly asked where she could get hold of a car or a telephone.

'You'll find that all right in the village, miss,' said the cripple. 'Leastways, it ain't what you'd call a village, exactly, but Mr Hearn that keeps the grocery, he's got a telephone. This here's Darley Halt, and Darley is about ten minutes' walk. You'll find somebody there all right, miss, for certain. Excuse me a minute, miss. Liz! the gates!'

The child ran out to open the gates to let through a small boy leading an immense cart-horse.

'Is there a train coming through?' asked Harriet, idly, as the gates were pushed across the road again.

'Not for half an hour, miss. We keeps the gates shut most times. There ain't a deal of traffic along this road, and they keeps the cattle from straying on to the line. There's a good many trains in the day. It's the main line from Wilvercombe to Heathbury. Of course, the expresses don't stop here, only the locals, and they only stops twice a day, except market days.'

'No, I see.' Harriet wondered why she was asking about the trains, and then suddenly realised that, with her professional interest in time-tables, she was instinctively checking up the ways and means of approaching the Grinders. Train, car, boat – how had the dead man got there?

'What time—?'

No, it didn't matter. The police could check that up. She thanked the gate-keeper, pushed her way through the side-wickets and strode on, with Mr Perkins limping after her.

The road still ran beside the coast, but the cliffs were gradually sloped down almost to sea-level. They saw a clump of trees and a hedge and a little lane, curving away past the ruins of an abandoned cottage to a wide space of green on which stood a tent, close by the sandy beach, with smoke going up from a campers' fire beside it. As they passed the head of this lane a man emerged from it, carrying a petrol-tin. He wore a pair of old flannel slacks, and a khaki shirt with sleeves rolled up to the elbow. His soft hat was pulled down rather low over his eyes, which were further protected by a pair of dark spectacles.

Harriet stopped him and asked if they were anywhere near the village.

'A few minutes farther on,' he replied, briefly, but civilly enough.

'I want to telephone,' went on Harriet. 'I'm told I can do so at the grocer's. Is that right?'

'Oh, yes. Just across on the other side of the green. You can't mistake it. It's the only shop there is.'

'Thank you. Oh, by the way – I suppose there isn't a policeman in the village?'

The man halted as he was about to turn away and stared at her, shading his eyes from the sun's glare. She noticed a snake tattooed in red and blue upon his forearm, and wondered whether he might perhaps have been a sailor.

'No, there's no policeman living in Darley. We share a constable with the next village, I believe – he floats round on a bicycle occasionally. Anything wrong?'

'There's been an accident along the coast,' said Harriet. 'I've found a dead man.'

'Good lord! Well, you'd better telephone through to Wilvercombe.'

'Yes, I will, thanks. Come along, Mr Perkins. Oh! he's gone on.'

Harriet caught up her companion, rather annoyed by his patent eagerness to dissociate himself from her and her errand.

'There's no need to stop and speak to everybody,' complained Mr Perkins, peevishly. 'I don't like the look of that fellow, and we're quite near the place now. I came through here this morning, you know.'

'I only wanted to ask if there was a policeman,' explained Harriet, peaceably. She did not want to argue with Mr Perkins. She had other things to think of. Cottages had begun to appear, small, sturdy buildings, surrounded by little patches of gay garden. The road turned suddenly inland, and she observed with joy telegraph poles, more houses and at length a little green, with a smithy at one corner and children playing cricket on the grass. In the centre of the green stood an ancient elm, with a seat round it and an ancient man basking in the sunshine; and on the opposite side was a shop, with 'Geo. Hearn: Grocer', displayed on a sign above it.

'Thank goodness!' said Harriet.

She almost ran across the little green and into the village shop, which was festooned with boots and frying-pans, and appeared to sell everything from acid drops to corduroy trousers.

A bald-headed man advanced helpfully from behind a pyramid of canned goods.

'Can I use your telephone, please?'

'Certainly, miss; what number?'

'I want the Wilvercombe police-station.'

'The police-station?' The grocer looked puzzled – almost shocked. 'I'll have to look up the number for you,' he said, hesitatingly. 'Will you step into the parlour, miss – and sir?'

'Thank you,' said Mr Perkins. 'But really – I mean – it's the lady's business really. I mean to say – if there's any sort of hotel hereabouts, I think I'd better – that is to say – er – good-evening.'

He melted unobtrusively out of the shop. Harriet, who had already forgotten his existence, followed the grocer into the back room and watched him with impatience as he put on his spectacles and struggled with the telephone directory.

III

THE EVIDENCE OF THE HOTEL

'Little and grisly, or bony and big,
   White, and clattering, grassy and yellow;
The partners are waiting, so strike up a jig,
   Dance and be merry, for Death's a droll fellow.

. . . .

Where's Death and his sweetheart? We want to begin.'

Death's Jest-Book

THURSDAY, 18 JUNE

IT WAS a quarter-past five when the grocer announced that
Harriet's call was through. Allowing for stoppages and for
going out of her way to the Brennerton Farm, she had
covered rather more than four miles of the distance between
the Grinders and Wilvercombe in very nearly three hours.
True, she had actually walked six miles or more, but she felt
that a shocking amount of time had been wasted. Well, she
had done her best, but fate had been against her.

'Hullo!' she said, wearily.

'Hullo!' said an official voice.

'Is that the Wilvercombe police?'

'Speaking. Who are you?'

'I'm speaking from Mr Hearn's shop at Darley. I want to
tell you that this afternoon at about two o'clock I found the
dead body of a man lying on the beach near the Grinders.'

'Oh!' said the voice. 'One moment, please. Yes. The dead
body of a man at the Grinders. Yes?'

'He'd got his throat cut,' said Harriet.

'Throat cut,' said the official voice. 'Yes?'

'I also found a razor,' said Harriet.

'A razor?' The voice seemed rather pleased, she thought, by this detail. 'Who is it speaking?' it went on.

'My name is Vane, Miss Harriet Vane. I am on a walking-tour, and happened to find him. Can you send someone out to fetch me, or shall I—?'

'Just a moment. Name of Vane – V-A-N-E – yes. Found at two o'clock, you say. You're a bit late letting us know, aren't you?'

Harriet explained that she had had difficulty in getting through to them.

'I see,' said the voice. 'All right, miss, we'll be sending a car along. You just stay where you are till we come. You'll have to go along with us and show us the body.'

'I'm afraid there won't be any body by now,' said Harriet. 'You see, it was down quite close to the sea, on that big rock, you know, and the tide—'

'We'll see to that, miss,' replied the voice, confidently, as though the Nautical Almanack might be expected to conform to police regulations. 'The car'll be along in about ten minutes or so.'

The receiver clicked and was silent. Harriet replaced her end of the instrument and stood for a few minutes, hesitating. Then she took the receiver off again.

'Give me Ludgate 6000 – quick as ever you can. Urgent press call. I must have it within five minutes.'

The operator began to make objections.

'Listen – that's the number of the *Morning Star*. It's a priority call.'

'Well,' said the operator, dubiously, 'I'll see what I can do.'

Harriet waited.

Three minutes passed – four – five – six. Then the bell rang. Harriet snatched the receiver down.

'*Morning Star.*'

'Give me the news-room – quick.'

Buzz – click.

'*Morning Star* news-editor.'

Harriet gathered herself together to cram her story into the fewest and most telling words.

'I am speaking from Darley near Wilvercombe. The dead body of a man was found at two o'clock this afternoon – all right. Ready? – on the coast this afternoon with his throat cut from ear to ear. The discovery was made by Miss Harriet Vane, the well-known detective novelist. . . . Yes, that's right – the Harriet Vane who was tried for murder two years ago. . . . Yes. . . . The dead man appears to be about twenty years of age – blue eyes – short dark beard – dressed in a dark-blue lounge suit with brown shoes and chamois-leather gloves. . . . A razor was found near the body. . . . Probably suicide. . . . Oh, yes, it *might* be murder; or call it mysterious circumstances. . . . Yes. . . . Miss Vane, who is on a walking-tour, gathering material for her forthcoming book, *The Fountain-Pen Mystery*, was obliged to walk for several miles before getting help. . . . No, the police haven't seen the body yet . . . it's probably under water by now, but I suppose they'll get it at low tide. . . . I'll ring you later. . . . Yes. . . . What? . . . Oh, this *is* Miss Vane speaking. . . . Yes. . . . No, I'm giving you this exclusively. . . . Well, I suppose it will be all over the place presently, but I'm giving you *my* story exclusively . . . provided, of course, you give me a good show. . . . Yes, of course. . . . Oh! well, I suppose I shall be staying in Wilvercombe. . . . I don't know; I'll ring you up when I know where I'm staying. . . . Right . . . right. . . . Good-bye.'

As she rang off, she heard a car draw up to the door, and emerged through the little shop to encounter a large man in a grey suit, who began impatiently: 'I am Inspector Umpelty. What's all this about?'

'Oh, Inspector! I'm so glad to see you. I began to think I never *should* get hold of anybody with any common-sense about them. I've had a trunk-call, Mr Hearn. I don't know what it costs, but here's a ten-bob note. I'll call for the change another time. I've told my friends I shall be stuck in Wilvercombe for a few days, Inspector. I suppose that's right, isn't it?'

This was disingenuous, but novelists and police-inspectors do not always see eye to eye as regards publicity.

'That's right, miss. Have to ask you to stay on a bit while we look into this. Better jump into the car and we'll run out to where you say you saw this body. This gentleman is Dr Fenchurch. This is Sergeant Saunders.'

Harriet acknowledged the introduction.

'Why *I've* been brought along I *don't* know,' said the police-surgeon in an aggrieved voice. 'If this man was down near low-water mark at two o'clock, we shan't see much of him tonight. Tide's more than half-full now, and a strong wind blowing.'

'That's the devil of it,' agreed the Inspector.

'I know,' said Harriet, mournfully, 'but really I did my best.' She recounted the details of her odyssey, mentioning everything she had done at the rock and producing the shoe, the cigarette-case, the hat, the handkerchief and the razor.

'Well, there,' said the Inspector, 'you seem to have done a pretty tidy job, miss. Anybody'd think you'd made a study of it. Taking photographs and all. Not but what,' he added, sternly, 'if you'd started sooner you'd have been here before.'

'I didn't waste much time,' pleaded Harriet, 'and I thought, supposing the body got washed away, or anything, it would be better to have *some* record of it.'

'That's very true, miss, and I shouldn't wonder but what you did the right thing. Looks like a big wind rising, and that'll hold the tide up.'

'Due south-west it is' put in the policeman who was

driving the car. 'That there rock will be awash next low tide if it goes on like this, and with the sea running it'll be a bit of a job to get out there.'

'Yes,' said the Inspector. 'The current sets very strong round the bay, and you can't get a boat in past the Grinders – not without you want her bottom stove in.'

Indeed, when they arrived at 'Murder Bay', as Harriet had mentally christened it, there were no signs of the rock, still less of the body. The sea was half-way up the sand, rolling in heavily. The little line of breakers that had shown the hidden tops of the Grinders reef had disappeared. The wind was freshening still more, and the sun gleamed in spasms of brilliance between thickening banks of cloud.

'That's the place, miss, is it?' asked the Inspector.

'Oh, yes, that's the place,' replied Harriet, confidently.

The Inspector shook his head.

'There's seventeen feet of water over that rock by now,' he said. 'Tide'll be full in another hour. Can't do anything about it now. Have to wait for low tide. That'll be two ack emma, or thereabouts, Have to see if there's any chance of getting out to it then, but if you ask me, it's working up for roughish weather. There's the chance, of course, that the body may get washed off and come ashore somewhere. I'll run you up to Brennerton, Saunders; try and get some of the men there to keep a look-out up and down the shore, and I'll cut along back to Wilvercombe and see what I can arrange about getting a boat out. You'll have to come along with me, miss, and make a statement.'

'By all means,' said Harriet, rather faintly.

The Inspector turned round and took a look at her.

'I expect you're feeling a bit upset, miss,' he said, kindly, 'and no wonder. It's not a pleasant thing for a young lady to have to deal with. It's a miracle to me, the way you handled it. Why, most young ladies would have run away, let alone taking away all these boots and things.'

'Well, you see,' explained Harriet, 'I know what ought to be done. I write detective stories, you know,' she added, feeling as she spoke that this must appear to the Inspector an idle and foolish occupation.

'There now,' said the Inspector. 'It isn't often, I daresay, you get a chance of putting your own stories into practice, as you might say. What did you say your name was, miss? Not that I read those sort of books much, except it might be Edgar Wallace now and again, but I'll have to know your name, of course, in any case.'

Harriet gave her name and her London address. The Inspector seemed to come to attention rather suddenly.

'I fancy I've heard that name before,' he remarked.

'Yes,' said Harriet, a little grimly; 'I expect you have. I am—' she laughed rather uncomfortably – 'I'm the notorious Harriet Vane, who was tried for poisoning Philip Boyes two years ago.'

'Ah, just so!' replied the Inspector. 'Yes. They got the fellow who did it, too, didn't they? Arsenic case. Yes, of course. There was some very pretty medical evidence at the trial, if I remember rightly. Smart piece of work. Lord Peter Wimsey had something to do with it, didn't he?'

'Quite a lot,' said Harriet.

'He seems to be a clever gentleman,' observed the Inspector. 'One's always hearing of him doing something or other.'

'Yes,' agreed Harriet; 'he's – full of activities.'

'You'll know him very well, I expect?' pursued the Inspector, filled with what Harriet felt to be unnecessary curiosity.

'Oh, yes, quite well. Yes, of course.' It struck her that this sounded ungracious, seeing that Wimsey had undoubtedly saved her from a very disagreeable position, if not from an ignominious death, and she went on, hastily and stiltedly, 'I have a great deal to thank him for.'

'Naturally,' replied the Inspector. 'Not but what' (loyally)

'Scotland Yard would probably have got the right man in the end. Still' (here local patriotism seemed to take the upper hand), 'they haven't the advantages in some ways that we have. They can't know all the people in London same as we know everybody hereabouts. Stands to reason they couldn't. Now, in a case like this one here, ten to one we shall be able to find all about the young man in a turn of the hand, as you might say.'

'He may be a visitor,' said Harriet.

'Very likely,' said the Inspector, 'but I expect there'll be somebody that knows about him, all the same. This is where you get off, Saunders. Raise all the help you can, and get Mr Coffin to run you over to Wilvercombe when you're through. Now then, miss. What did you say this young chap was like?'

Harriet again described the corpse.

'Beard, eh?' said the Inspector. 'Sounds like a foreigner, doesn't it? I can't just place him for the moment, but there's not much doubt he'll be pretty easily traced. Now, here we are at the police-station, miss. If you'll just step in here a minute, the Superintendent would like to see you.'

Harriet accordingly stepped in and told her story once again, this time in minute detail, to Superintendent Glaisher, who received it with flattering interest. She handed over the various things taken from the body and her roll of film, and was then questioned exhaustively as to how she had spent the day, both before and after finding the body.

'By the way,' said the Superintendent, 'this young fellow you met on the road – what's become of him?'

Harriet stared about her as though she expected to find Mr Perkins still at her elbow.

'I haven't the slightest idea. I'd forgotten all about him. He must have gone off while I was ringing you up.'

'Odd,' said Glaisher, making a note to inquire after Mr Perkins.

'But he can't possibly know anything about it,' said Harriet. 'He was fearfully surprised – and frightened. That's why he came back with me.'

'We'll have to check up on him, though, as a matter of routine,' said the Superintendent. Harriet was about to protest that this was a waste of time, when she suddenly realised that in all probability it was her own story that was due to be 'checked up on'. She was silent, and the Superintendent went on:

'Well, now, Miss Vane. I'm afraid we shall have to ask you to stay within reach for a few days. What were you thinking of doing?'

'Oh, I quite understand that. I suppose I'd better put up somewhere in Wilvercombe. You needn't be afraid of *my* running away. I want to be in on this thing.'

The policeman looked a little disapproving. Everybody is, of course, only too delighted to take the limelight in a gruesome tragedy, but a lady ought, surely, to pretend the contrary. Inspector Umpelty, however, merely replied with the modest suggestion that Clegg's Temperance Hostel was generally reckoned to be as cheap and comfortable as you could require.

Harriet laughed, remembering suddenly that a novelist owes a duty to her newspaper reporters. 'Miss Harriet Vane, when interviewed by our correspondent at Clegg's Temperance Hostel—' That would never do.

'I don't care for Temperance Hostels,' she said, firmly. 'What's the best hotel in the town?'

'The Resplendent is the largest,' said Glaisher.

'Then you will find me at the Resplendent,' said Harriet, picking up her dusty knapsack and preparing for action.

'Inspector Umpelty will run you down there in the car,' said the Superintendent, with a little nod to Umpelty.

'Very good of him,' answered Harriet, amused.

Within a very few minutes the car deposited her at one of

those monster seaside palaces which look as though they had been designed by a German manufacturer of children's cardboard toys. Its glass porch was crowded with hothouse plants, and the lofty dome of its reception-hall was supported on gilt pilasters rising out of an ocean of blue plush. Harriet tramped heedlessly through its spacious splendours and demanded a large single bedroom with private bath, on the first floor, and overlooking the sea.

'Ai'm afraid,' said the receptionist, casting a languid glance of disfavour at Harriet's knapsack and shoes, 'that all our rooms are engaged.'

'Surely not,' said Harriet, 'so early in the season. Just ask the manager to come and speak to me for a moment.' She sat down with a determined air in the nearest well-stuffed armchair and, hailing a waiter, demanded a cocktail.

'Will you join me, Inspector?'

The Inspector thanked her, but explained that a certain discretion was due to his position.

'Another time, then,' said Harriet, smiling, and dropping a pound-note on the waiter's tray, with a somewhat ostentatious display of a well-filled note-case.

Inspector Umpelty grinned faintly as he saw the receptionist beckon to the water. Then he moved gently across to the desk and spoke a few words. Presently the assistant-receptionist approached Harriet with a deprecating smile.

'We find, madam, that we can efter all accommodate you. An American gentleman has informed us thet he is vacating his room on the first floor. It overlooks the Esplanade. Ai think you will find it quaite satisfactory.'

'Has it a private bath?' demanded Harriet, without enthusiasm.

'Oh, yes, madam. And a belcony.'

'All right,' said Harriet, 'What number? Twenty-three. It has a telephone, I suppose? Well, Inspector, you'll know where to find me, won't you?'

She grinned a friendly grin at him.

'Yes, miss,' said Inspector Umpelty, grinning also. He had his private cause for amusement. If Harriet's note-case had ensured her reception at the Resplendent, it was his own private whisper of 'friend of Lord Peter Wimsey' that had produced the view over the sea, the bath and the balcony. It was just as well that Harriet did not know this. It would have annoyed her.

Curiously enough, however, the image of Lord Peter kept intruding upon her mind while she was telephoning her address to the *Morning Star*, and even while she was working her way through the Resplendent's expensive and admirable dinner. If the relations between them had not been what they were, it would have been only fair to ring him up and tell him about the corpse with the cut throat. But under the circumstances, the action might be misinterpreted. And, in any case, the thing was probably only the dullest kind of suicide, not worth bringing to his attention. Not nearly so complicated and interesting a problem, for instance, as the central situation in *The Fountain-Pen Mystery*. In that absorbing mystery, the villain was at the moment engaged in committing a crime in Edinburgh, while constructing an ingenious alibi involving a steam-yacht, a wireless time-signal, five clocks and the change from summer to winter time. (Apparently the cut-throat gentleman had come from the Wilvercombe direction. By road? by train? Had he walked from Darley Halt? If not, who had brought him?) Really, she must try and concentrate on this alibi. The town-clock was the great difficulty. How could that be altered? And altered it must be, for the whole alibi depended on its being heard to strike midnight at the appropriate moment. Could the man who looked after it be made into an accomplice? Who did look after town-hall clocks? (Why gloves? And had she left her own finger-prints on the razor?) Was it, after all, going to be necessary to go to

Edinburgh? Perhaps there was no town-hall and no clock. A church-clock would do, of course. But church-clocks and bodies in belfries had been rather overdone lately. (It was odd about Mr Perkins. If the solution was murder after all, could not the murderer have walked through the water to some point? Perhaps she ought to have followed the shore and not the coast-road. Too late now, in any case.) And she had not properly worked out the speed of the steam-yacht. One ought to know about these things. Lord Peter would know, of course; he must have sailed in plenty of steam-yachts. It must be nice to be *really* rich. Anybody who married Lord Peter would be rich, of course. And he was amusing. Nobody could say he would be dull to live with. But the trouble was that you never knew what anybody was like to live with except by living with them. It wasn't worth it. Not even to know all about steam-yachts. A novelist couldn't possibly marry all the people from whom she wanted specialised information. Harriet pleased herself over the coffee with sketching out the career of an American detective-novelist who contracted a fresh marriage for each new book. For a book about poisons, she would marry an analytical chemist; for a book about somebody's will, a solicitor; for a book about strangling, a – a hangman, of course. There might be something in it. A spoof book, of course. And the villainess might do away with each husband by the method described in the book she was working on at the time. Too obvious? Well, perhaps.

She got up from the table and made her way into a kind of large lounge, where the middle space was cleared for dancing. A select orchestra occupied a platform at one end, and small tables were arranged all round the sides of the room, where visitors could drink coffee or liqueurs and watch the dancing. While she took her place and gave her order, the floor was occupied by a pair of obviously professional dancers, giving an exhibition waltz. The man was tall and fair, with sleek hair plastered closely to his head, and a queer, unhealthy face with a wide, melancholy mouth. The girl, in an exaggerated gown of petunia satin with an enormous bustle and a train, exhibited a mask of Victorian coyness as she revolved languidly in her partner's arms to the strains of the 'Blue Danube'. '*Autres temps, autres moeurs,*' thought Harriet. She looked about the room. Long skirts and costumes of the seventies were in evidence – and even ostrich feathers and fans. Even the coyness had its imitators. But it was so obvious an imitation. The slender-seeming waists were made so, not by savage tight-lacing, but by sheer expensive dressmaking. Tomorrow, on the tennis-court, the short, loose tunic-frock would reveal them as the waists of muscular young women of the day, despising all bonds. And the sidelong glances, the down-cast eyes, the mock-modesty – masks, only. If this was the 'return to womanliness' hailed by the fashion-correspondents, it was to a quite different kind of womanliness – set on a basis of economic independence. Were men really stupid enough to believe that the good old days of submissive womanhood could be brought back by milliners' fashions? 'Hardly,' thought Harriet, 'when they know perfectly well that one has only to remove the train and the bustle, get into a short skirt and walk off, with a job to do and money in one's pocket. Oh, well, it's a game, and presumably they all know the rules.'

The dancers twirled to a standstill with the conclusion of the waltz. The instrumentalists tweaked a string and tightened a peg here and there and rearranged their music, under cover of perfunctory applause. Then the male dancer selected a partner from one of the nearer tables, while the petunia-clad girl obeyed a summons from a stout manufacturer in tweeds on the other side of the room. Another girl, a blonde in pale blue, rose from her solitary table near the platform and led out an elderly man. Other visitors rose, accompanied by their own partners, and took the floor to the strains of another waltz. Harriet beckoned to the waiter and asked for more coffee.

Men, she thought, like the illusion that woman is dependent on their approbation and favour for her whole interest in life. But do they like the reality? Not, thought Harriet, bitterly, when one is past one's first youth. The girl over there, exercising S.A. on a group of rather possessive-looking males, will turn into a predatory hag like the woman at the next table, if she doesn't find something to occupy her mind, always supposing that she has a mind. Then the men will say she puts the wind up them.

The 'predatory hag' was a lean woman, pathetically made-up, dressed in an exaggeration of the fashion which it would have been difficult for a girl of nineteen to carry off successfully. She had caught Harriet's attention earlier by her look of radiant, almost bridal exaltation. She was alone, but seemed to be expecting somebody, for her gaze roamed incessantly about the room, concentrating itself chiefly on the professionals' table near the platform. Now she appeared to be getting anxious. Her ringed hands twitched nervously, and she lighted one cigarette after another, only to stub it out, half-smoked, snatch at the mirror in her handbag, readjust her make-up, fidget, and then begin the whole process again with another cigarette.

'Waiting for her gigolo,' diagnosed Harriet, with a kind of pitiful disgust. 'The frog-mouthed gentleman, I suppose. He seems to have better fish to fry.'

The waiter brought the coffee, and the woman at the next table caught him on his way back.

'Is Mr Alexis not here tonight?'

'No, madam.' The waiter looked a little nervous. 'No. He is unavoidably absent.'

'Is he ill?'

'I do not think so, madam. The manager has just said he will not be coming.'

'Did he send no message?'

'I could not say, madam.' The waiter was fidgeting with his feet. 'Mr Antoine will no doubt be happy . . .'

'No, never mind. I am accustomed to Mr Alexis. His step suits me. It does not matter.'

'No, madam, thank you, madam.'

The waiter escaped. Harriet saw him exchange a word and a shrug with the head waiter. Lips and eyebrows were eloquent. Harriet felt annoyed. Did one come to this, then, if one did not marry? Making a public scorn of one's self before the waiters? She glanced again at the woman, who was rising to leave the lounge. She wore a wedding-ring. Marriage did not save one, apparently. Single, married, widowed, divorced, one came to the same end. She shivered a little, and suddenly felt fed-up with the lounge and the dance-floor. She finished her coffee and retired to the smaller lounge, where three stout women were engaged in an interminable conversation about illness, children and servants. 'Poor Muriel – *quite* an invalid since the birth of her last baby. . . . I spoke quite firmly, I said, "Now you quite understand, if you leave before your month you will be liable to me for the money." . . . Twelve guineas a week, and the surgeon's fee was a hundred guineas. . . . Beautiful boys, both of them, but with Ronnie at Eton and Wilfred at Oxford. . . . They oughtn't to *let* boys run up these bills . . . my dear, *pounds* thinner, I hardly knew her, but I wouldn't care to . . . some kind of electric heat treatment, too marvellous . . . and what with rates and taxes and all this terrible unemployment. . . . You can't argue with nervous dyspepsia, but it makes things very difficult . . . left me high and dry with the house full of people, these girls have *no* gratitude.'

'And these,' thought Harriet, 'are the happy ones, I suppose. Well, dash it! How about that town-clock?'

IV

THE EVIDENCE OF THE RAZOR

'Well, thou art
A useful tool sometimes, thy tooth works quickly,
And if thou gnawest a secret from the heart
Thou tellest it not again.'

Death's Jest-Book

FRIDAY, 19 JUNE

IN SPITE of the horrors she had witnessed, which ought to
have driven all sleep away from the eyelids of any self-
respecting female, Harriet slept profoundly in her first-floor
bedroom (with bathroom, balcony and view over Esplanade) and came down to breakfast with a hearty appetite.

She secured a copy of the *Morning Star*, and was deep in
the perusal of her own interview (with photograph) on the
front page, when a familiar voice addressed her:

'Good morning, Sherlock. Where is the dressing-gown?
How many pipes of shag have you consumed? The hypo-
dermic is on the dressing-room table.'

'How in the world,' demanded Harriet, 'did *you* get
here?'

'Car,' said Lord Peter, briefly. 'Have they produced the
body?'

'Who told you about the body?'

'I nosed it from afar. Where the carcase is, there shall be
eagles gathered together. May I join you over the bacon-
and-eggs?'

'By all means,' said Harriet. 'Where did you come from?'

'From London – like a bird that hears the call of its mate.'

'I didn't—' began Harriet.

'I didn't mean you. I meant the corpse. But still, talking of mates, will you marry me?'

'Certainly not.'

'I thought not, but I felt I might as well ask the question. Did you say they had found the body?'

'Not that I know of.'

'I don't expect they will, then, for a bit. There's a regular sou'wester blowing great guns. Tiresome for them. Can't have an inquest without a body. You must produce the body, as it says in the Have-His-Carcase Act.'

'No, but really,' protested Harriet, 'how did you hear about it?'

'Salcombe Hardy rang me up from the *Morning Star*. Said "my Miss Vane" had found a corpse, and did I know anything about it. I said I knew nothing about it and that Miss Vane was unhappily not mine – yet. So I buzzed off, and here I am. I brought Sally Hardy down with me. I expect that's what he really rang me up for. Smart old bird, Sally – always on the spot.'

'He told you where to find me, I suppose.'

'Yes – he seemed to know all about it. I was rather hurt. Fancy having to ask the *Morning Star* where the pole-star of one's own heaven has gone to. Hardy seemed to know all about it. How do these things get into the papers?'

'I rang them up myself,' replied Harriet. 'First-class publicity, you know, and all that.'

'So it is,' agreed Wimsey, helping himself lavishly to butter. 'Rang 'em up, did you, with all the gory details?'

'Naturally; that was the first thing I thought of.'

'You're a woman of business. But does it not, pardon me, indicate a certain coarsening of the fibres?'

'Obviously,' said Harriet. 'My fibres at this moment resemble coconut matting.'

'Without even "Welcome" written across them. But, look here, beloved, bearing in mind that I'm a corpse-fan, don't you think you might, as man to man, have let me in on the ground-floor?'

'If you put it that way,' admitted Harriet, rather ashamed of herself, 'I certainly might. But I thought—'

'Women *will* let the personal element creep in,' said Wimsey, acutely. 'Well, all I can say is, you owe it to me to make up for it now. *All* the details, please.'

'I'm tired of giving details,' grumbled Harriet, perversely.

'You'll be tireder before the police and the newspaper lads have finished with you. I have been staving off Salcombe Hardy with the greatest difficulty. He is in the lounge. The *Banner* and the *Clarion* are in the smoking room. They had a fast car. The *Courier* is coming by train (it's a nice, respectable, old-fashioned paper), and the *Thunderer* and the *Comet* are hanging about outside the bar, hoping you may be persuaded to offer them something. The three people arguing with the commissionaire are, I fancy, local men. The photographic contingent have gone down en masse, packed in a single Morris, to record the place where the body was found, which, as the tide is well up, they will not see. Tell me all, here and now, and I will organise your publicity for you.'

'Very well,' said Harriet, 'I tell thee all, I can no more.' She pushed her plate aside and took up a clean knife.

'This,' she said, 'is the coast-road from Lesston Hoe to Wilvercombe. The shore bends about like this—' She took up the pepper-pot.

'Try salt,' suggested Wimsey. 'Less irritatin' to the nasal tissues.'

'Thank you. This line of salt is the beach. And this piece of bread is a rock at low-water level.'

Wimsey twitched his chair closer to the table.

'And this salt-spoon,' he said, with childlike enjoyment, 'can be the body.'

He made no comment while Harriet told her story, only interrupting once or twice with a question about times and distances. He sat drooping above the sketch-map she was laying out among the breakfast-things, his eyes invisible, his long nose seeming to twitch like a rabbit's with concentration. When she had finished, he sat silent for a moment and then said:

'Let's get this clear. You got to the place where you had lunch – when, exactly?'

'Just one o'clock. I looked at my watch.'

'As you came along the cliffs, you could see the whole shore, including the rock where you found the body.'

'Yes; I suppose I could.'

'Was anybody on the rock then?'

'I really don't know. I don't even specially remember noticing the rock. I was thinking about my grub, you see, and I was really looking about at the side of the road for a suitable spot to scramble down the cliff. My eyes weren't focused for distance.'

'I see. That's rather a pity, in a way.'

'Yes, it is; but I can tell you one thing. I'm quite sure there was nothing *moving* on the shore. I did give one glance round just before I decided to climb down. I distinctly remember thinking that the beach seemed absolutely and gloriously deserted – a perfect spot for a picnic. I hate picnicking in a crowd.'

'And a single person on a lonely beach would be a crowd?'

'For picnicking purposes, yes. You know what people are. The minute they see anyone having a peaceful feed they gather in from the four points of the compass and sit down beside one, and the place is like the Corner House in the rush hour.'

'So they do. That must be the symbolism of the Miss Muffet legend.'

'I'm positive there wasn't a living soul walking or standing or sitting anywhere within eyeshot. But as to the body's being already on the rock, I wouldn't swear one way or the other. It was a goodish way out, you know, and when I saw it from the beach I took the body for seaweed just at first. I shouldn't make a mental note of seaweed.'

'Good. Then at one o'clock the beach was deserted, except possibly for the body, which may have been there making a noise like seaweed. Then you got down the side of the cliff. Was the rock visible from where you had lunch?'

'No, not at all. There is a sort of little bay there – well, scarcely that. The cliff juts out a bit, and I was sitting close up against the foot of the rocks, so as to have something to lean against. I had my lunch – it took about half an hour altogether.'

'You heard nothing then? No footsteps or anything? No car?'

'Not a thing.'

'And then?'

'Then I'm afraid I dozed off.'

'What could be more natural? For how long?'

'About half an hour. When I woke I looked at my watch again.'

'What woke you?'

'A sea-gull squawking round after bits of my sandwich.'

'That makes it two o'clock.'

'Yes.'

'Just a minute. When I arrived here this morning it was a bit early for calling on one's lady friends, so I toddled down to the beach and made friends with one of the fishermen. He happened to mention that it was low tide off the Grinders yesterday afternoon at 1.15. Therefore when you arrived, the tide was practically out. When you woke, it had turned and had been coming in for about forty-five minutes. The foot of your rock – which, by the way, *is* locally named The Devil's Flat-Iron – is only uncovered for about half an hour between tide and tide, and that only at the top of springs, if you understand that expression.'

'I understand perfectly, but I don't see what that has to do with it.'

'Well, this – that if anybody had come walking along the edge of the water to the rock, he could have got there without leaving any footprints.'

'But he did leave footprints. Oh, I see. You're thinking of a possible murderer.'

'I should prefer it to be murder, naturally. Shouldn't you?'

'Yes, of course. Well, that's a fact. A murderer might have walked along from either direction, if he did it that way. If he came from Lesston Hoe he must have arrived after me, because I could see the shore as I walked along, and there was no one walking there then. But he could have come at any time from the Wilvercombe side.'

'No, he couldn't,' said Wimsey. 'He wasn't there, you said, at one o'clock.'

'He might have been standing on the seaward side of the Flat-Iron.'

'So he might. Now, how about the corpse? We can tell pretty close when *he* came.'

'How?'

'You said there were no wet stains on his shoes. Therefore he went dry-shod to the rock. We only have to find out exactly when the sand on the landward side of the rock is uncovered.'

'Of course. How stupid of me. Well, we can easily find that out. Where had I got to?'

'You had been awakened by the cry of a sea-gull.'

'Yes. Well, then, I walked round the point of the cliff and out to the rock, and there he was.'

'And at that moment there was nobody within sight?'

'Not a single soul, except a man in a boat.'

'Yes – the boat. Now, supposing the boat had come in when the tide was out, and the occupant had walked or waded up to the rock—'

'That's possible, of course. The boat was some way out.'

'It all seems to depend on when the corpse got there. We must find that out.'

'You're determined it should be murder.'

'Well, suicide seems so dull. And why go all that way to commit suicide?'

'Why not? Much tidier than doing it in your bedroom or anywhere like that. Aren't we beginning at the wrong end? If we knew who the man was, we might find he had left an explanatory note behind him to say why he was going to do it. I daresay the police know all about it by now.'

'Possibly,' said Wimsey in a dissatisfied tone.

'What's worrying you?'

'Two things. The gloves. Why should anybody cut his throat in gloves?'

'I know. That bothered me too. Perhaps he had some sort of skin disease and was accustomed to wearing gloves for everything. I ought to have looked. I did start to take the gloves off, but they were – messy.'

'Um! I see you still retain a few female frailties. The second point that troubles me is the weapon. Why should a gentleman with a beard sport a cut-throat razor?'

'Bought for the purpose.'

'Yes; after all, why not? My dear Harriet, I think you are right. The man cut his throat, and that's all there is to it. I am disappointed.'

'It is disappointing, but it can't be helped. Hallo! here's my friend the Inspector.'

It was indeed Inspector Umpelty who was threading his way between the tables. He was in mufti – a large, comfortable-looking tweed-clad figure. He greeted Harriet pleasantly.

'I thought you might like to see how your snaps have turned out, Miss Vane. And we've identified the man.'

'No? Have you? Good work. This is Inspector Umpelty – Lord Peter Wimsey.'

The Inspector appeared gratified by the introduction.

'You're early on the job, my lord. But I don't know that you'll find anything very mysterious about this case. Just a plain suicide, I fancy.'

'We had regretfully come to that conclusion,' admitted Wimsey.

'Though why he should have done it, I don't know. But you never can tell with these foreigners, can you?'

'I thought he looked rather foreign,' said Harriet.

'Yes. He's a Russian, or something of that sort. Paul Alexis Goldschmidt, his name is; known as Paul Alexis. Comes from this very hotel, as a matter of fact. One of the professional dancing-partners in the lounge here – you know the sort. They don't seem to know much about him. Turned up here just over a year ago and asked for a job. Seemed to be a good dancer and all that and they had a vacancy, so they took him on. Age twenty-two or thereabouts. Unmarried. Lived in rooms. Nothing known against him.'

'Papers in order?'

'Naturalised British subject. Said to have escaped from Russia at the Revolution. He must have been a kid of about nine, but we haven't found out yet who had charge of him. He was alone when he turned up here, and his landlady doesn't ever seem to have heard of anybody belonging to him. But we'll soon find out when we go through his stuff.'

'He didn't leave any letter for the coroner, or anything?'

'We've found nothing so far. And as regards the coroner, that's a bit of a bother, that is. I don't know how long it'll be, miss, before you're wanted. You see, we can't find the body.'

'You don't mean to tell me,' said Wimsey, 'that the evil-eyed doctor and the mysterious Chinaman have already conveyed it to the lone house on the moor?'

'You will have your fun, my lord, I see. No – it's a bit simpler than that. You see, the current sets northwards round the bay there, and with this sou'wester blowing, the body will have been washed off the Flat-Iron. It'll either come ashore somewhere off Sandy Point, or it'll have got carried out and caught up in the Grinders. If that's where it is, we'll have to wait till the wind goes down. You can't take a boat in there with this sea running, and you can't dive off the rocks – even supposing you knew whereabouts to dive. It's a nuisance, but it can't be helped.'

'H'm,' said Wimsey. 'Just as well you took those photographs, Sherlock, or we'd have no proof that there ever had been a body.'

'Coroner can't sit on a photograph, though,' said the Inspector, gloomily. 'Howsomever, it looks like a plain suicide, so it doesn't matter such a lot. Still, it's annoying. We like to get these things tidied up as we go along.'

'Naturally,' said Wimsey. 'Well, I'm sure if anybody can tidy up, you can, Inspector. You impress me as being a man with an essentially tidy mind. I will engage to prophesy, Sherlock, that before lunch-time. Inspector Umpelty will have sorted out the dead man's papers, got the entire story from the hotel-manager, identified the place where the razor was bought and explained the mysterious presence of the gloves.'

The Inspector laughed.

'I don't think there's much to be got out of the manager, my lord, and as for the razor, that's neither here nor there.'

'But the gloves?'

'Well, my lord, I expect the only person that could tell us

about that is the poor blighter himself, and he's dead. But as regards the papers, you're dead right. I'm looking along there now.' He paused, doubtfully, and looked from Harriet to Wimsey and back again.

'No,' said Wimsey. 'Set your mind at rest. We are not going to ask to come with you. I know that the amateur detective has a habit of embarrassing the police in the execution of their duty. We are going out to view the town like a perfect little lady and gentleman. There's only one thing I *should* like to have a look at, if it isn't troubling you too much – and that's the razor.'

The Inspector was very willing that Lord Peter should see the razor. 'And if you like to comerlongerme,' he added kindly, 'you'll dodge all these reporters.'

'Not me!' said Harriet. 'I've got to see them and tell them all about my new book. A razor is only a razor, but good advance publicity means sales. You two run along; I'll follow you down.'

She strolled away in search of the reporters. The Inspector grinned uneasily.

'No flies on that young lady,' he observed. 'But can she be trusted to hold her tongue?'

'Oh, she won't chuck away a good plot,' said Wimsey, lightly. 'Come and have a drink.'

'Too soon after breakfast,' objected the Inspector.

'Or a smoke,' suggested Wimsey.

The Inspector declined.

'Or a nice sit-down in the lounge,' said Wimsey, sitting down.

'Excuse me,' said Inspector Umpelty, 'I must be getting along. I'll tell them at the Station about you wanting to look at the razor. . . . Fair tied to that young woman's apron-strings,' he reflected, as he shouldered his bulky way through the revolving doors. 'The poor mutt!'

Harriet, escaping half an hour later from Salcombe

Hardy and his colleagues, found Wimsey faithfully in attendance.

'I've got rid of the Inspector,' observed that gentleman, cheerfully. 'Get your hat on and we'll go.'

Their simultaneous exit from the Resplendent was observed and recorded by the photographic contingent, who had just returned from the shore. Between an avenue of clicking shutters, they descended the marble steps, and climbed into Wimsey's Daimler.

'I feel,' said Harriet, maliciously, 'as if we had just been married at St George's, Hanover Square.'

'No, you don't,' retorted Wimsey. 'If we had, you would be trembling like a fluttered partridge. Being married to me is a tremendous experience – you've no idea. We'll be all right at the police-station, provided the Super doesn't turn sticky on us.'

Superintendent Glaisher was conveniently engaged, and Sergeant Saunders was deputed to show them the razor.

'Has it been examined for finger-prints?' asked Wimsey.

'Yes, my lord.'

'Any result?'

'I couldn't exactly say, my lord, but I believe not.'

'Well, anyway, one is allowed to handle it.' Wimsey turned it over in his fingers, inspecting it carefully, first with the naked eye and secondly with a watchmaker's lens. Beyond a very slight crack on the ivory handle, it showed no very striking peculiarities.

'If there's any blood left on it, it will be hanging about the joint,' he observed. 'But the sea seems to have done its work pretty thoroughly.'

'You aren't suggesting,' said Harriet, 'that the weapon isn't really the weapon after all?'

'I should like to,' said Wimsey. 'The weapon never is the weapon, is it?'

'Of course not; and the corpse is never the corpse. The body is, obviously, not that of Peter Alexis—'

'But of the Prime Minister of Ruritania—'

'It did not die of a cut throat—'

'But of an obscure poison, known only to the Bushmen of Central Australia—'

'And the throat was cut after death—'

'By a middle-aged man of short temper and careless habits, with a stiff beard and expensive tastes—'

'Recently returned from China,' finished up Harriet, triumphantly.

The sergeant, who had gaped in astonishment at the beginning of this exchange, now burst into a hearty guffaw.

'That's very good,' he said, indulgently. 'Comic, ain't it, the stuff these writer-fellows put into their books? Would your lordship like to see the other exhibits?'

Wimsey replied gravely that he should, very much, and the hat, cigarette-case, shoe and handkerchief were produced.

'H'm,' said Wimsey. 'Hat fair to middling, but not exclusive. Cranial capacity on the small side. Brilliantine, ordinary stinking variety. Physical condition pretty fair—'

'The man was a dancer.'

'I thought we agreed he was a Prime Minister. Hair, dark, curly and rather on the long side. Last year's hat, reblocked, with new ribbon. Shape, a little more emphatic than is quite necessary. Deduction: not wealthy, but keen on his personal appearance. Do we conclude that the hat belongs to the corpse?'

'Yes, I think so. The brilliantine corresponds all right.'

'Cigarette-case – this is different. Fifteen-carat gold, plain and fairly new, with monogram P.A. and containing six de Reszkes. The case is pukka, all right. Probably a gift from some wealthy female admirer.'

'Or, of course, the cigarette-case appropriate to a Prime Minister.'

'As you say. Handkerchief – silk, but not from Burlington Arcade. Colour beastly. Laundry-mark—'

'Laundry-mark's all right,' put in the policeman. 'Wilvercombe Sanitary Steam Laundry; mark O.K. for this fellow Alexis.'

'Suspicious circumstance,' said Harriet, shaking her head. 'I've got three handkerchiefs in my pack with not only the laundry-marks but the initials of total strangers.'

'It's the Prime Minister, all right,' agreed Wimsey, with a doleful nod. 'Prime Ministers, especially Ruritanian ones, are notoriously careless about their laundry. Now the shoe. Oh, yes. Nearly new. Thin sole. Foul colour and worse shape. Hand-made, so that the horrid appearance is due to malice aforethought. Not the shoe of a man who does much walking. Made, I observe, in Wilvercombe.'

'That's O.K., too,' put in the sergeant. 'We've seen the man. He made that shoe for Mr Alexis all right. Knows him well.'

'And you took this actually off the foot of the corpse? These are deep waters, Watson. Another man's handkerchief is nothing, but a Prime Minister in another fellow's shoes—'

'You will have your joke, my lord,' said the sergeant, with another hoot of laughter.

'I never joke,' said Wimsey. He brought the lens to bear on the sole of the shoe. 'Slight traces of salt water here, but none on the uppers. Inference: he walked over the sand when it was very wet, but did not actually wade through salt water. Two or three scratches on the toe-cap, probably got when clambering up the rock. Well, thanks awfully, sergeant. You are quite at liberty to inform Inspector Umpelty of all the valuable deductions we have drawn. Have a drink.'

'Thank you very much, my lord.'

Wimsey said nothing more till they were in the car again.

'I'm sorry,' he then announced, as they threaded their way through the side-streets, 'to renounce our little programme of viewing the town. I should have enjoyed that simple pleasure. But unless I start at once, I shan't get to town and back tonight.'

Harriet, who had been preparing to say that she had work to do and could not waste time rubber-necking round Wilvercombe with Lord Peter, experienced an unreasonable feeling of having been cheated.

'To town?' she repeated.

'It will not have escaped your notice,' said Wimsey, skimming with horrible dexterity between a bath-chair and a butcher's van, 'that the matter of the razor requires investigation.'

'Of course – a visit to the Ruritanian Legation is indicated.'

'H'm – well; I don't know that I shall get any farther than Jermyn Street.'

'In search of the middle-aged man of careless habits?'

'Yes, ultimately.'

'He really exists, then?'

'Well, I wouldn't swear to his exact age.'

'Or his habits?'

'No, they might be the habits of his valet.'

'Or his stiff beard and short temper?'

'Well, I think one may be reasonably certain about the beard.'

'I give in,' said Harriet, meekly. 'Please explain.'

Wimsey drew up the car at the entrance to the Hotel Resplendent, and looked at his watch.

'I can give you ten minutes,' he remarked, in an aloof tone. 'Let us take a seat in the lounge and order some refreshment. It is a little early, to be sure, but I always drive more mellowly on a pint of beer. Good. Now, as to the razor. You will have observed that it is an instrument of excellent and expensive quality by a first-class maker, and that, in addition to the name of the manufacturer, it is engraved on the reverse side with the mystic word "Endicott".'

'Yes; what is Endicott?'

'Endicott is, or was, one of the most exclusive hairdressers in the West End. So fearfully exclusive and grand that he won't even call himself a hairdresser in the snobbish modern way, but prefers to be known by the old-world epithet of "barber". He will, or would, hardly condescend to shave anybody who has not been in Debrett for the last three hundred years. Other people, however rich or titled, have the misfortune to find his chairs always occupied and his basins engaged. His shop has the rarefied atmosphere of one of the more aristocratic mid-Victorian clubs. It is said of Endicott's that a certain peer, who made his money during the War by cornering bootlaces or buttons or something, was once accidentally admitted to one of the sacred chairs by a new assistant who had been most unfortunately taken on with insufficient West End experience during the temporary war-time shortage of barbers. After ten minutes in that dreadful atmosphere, his hair froze, his limbs became perfectly petrified, and he had to be removed to the Crystal Palace and placed among the antediluvian monsters.'

'Well?'

'Well! Consider first of all the anomaly of the man who buys his razor from Endicott's and yet wears the regrettable shoes and mass-production millinery found on the corpse. Mind you,' added Wimsey, 'it is not a question of expense, exactly. The shoes are hand-made – which merely proves that a dancer has to take care of his feet. But *could* a man who is shaved by Endicott possibly order – deliberately *order* – shoes of that colour and shape? A thing imagination boggles at.'

'I'm afraid,' admitted Harriet, 'that I have never managed

to learn all the subtle rules and regulations about male clothing. That's why I made Robert Templeton one of those untidy dressers.'

'Robert Templeton's clothes have always pained me,' confessed Wimsey. 'The one blot on your otherwise fascinating tales. But to leave that distressing subject and come back to the razor. That razor has seen a good deal of hard wear. It has been re-ground a considerable number of times, as you can tell by the edge. Now, a really first-class razor like that needs very little in the way of grinding and setting, provided it is mercifully used and kept carefully stropped. Therefore, either the man who used it was very clumsy and careless about using the strop, or his beard was abnormally stiff, or both – probably both. I visualise him as one of those men who are heavy-handed with tools – you know the kind. Their fountain pens always make blots and their watches get over-wound. They neglect to strop their razors until the strop gets hard and dry, and then they strop them ferociously and jag the edge of the blade. Then they lose their tempers and curse the razor and send it away to be ground and set. The new edge only lasts them for a few weeks and then back the razor goes again, accompanied by a rude message.'

'I see. Well, I didn't know all that. But why did you say the man was middle-aged?'

'That was rather guess-work. But I suggest that a young man who had so much difficulty with his razor would be more likely to change over to a safety and use a new blade every few days. But a man of middle-age would not be so likely to change his habits. In any case, I'm sure that razor has had more than three years' hard wear. And if the dead man is only twenty-two now, and has a full beard, then I don't see how he could very well have worn the blade down to that extent, with any amount of grinding and setting. We must find out from the hotel manager here whether he was already wearing the beard when he came a year ago. That would narrow the time down still further. But the first thing to do is to trace old Endicott and find out from him whether it was possible for one of his razors to have been sold later than 1925.'

'Why 1925?'

'Because that was the date at which old Endicott sold his premises and retired with varicose veins and a small fortune.'

'And who kept on the business?'

'Nobody. The shop is now a place where you buy the most recherché kind of hams and potted meats. There were no sons to carry on – the only young Endicott was killed in the Salient, poor chap. Old Endicott said he wouldn't sell his name to anybody. And anyhow, Endicott's without an Endicott wouldn't be Endicott's. So that was that.'

'But he might have sold the stock?'

'That's what I want to find out. I'll have to be off now. I'll try and be back tonight, so don't worry.'

'I'm not worrying,' retorted Harriet, indignantly. 'I'm perfectly happy.'

'Splendid. Oh! While I'm about it, shall I see about getting a marriage-licence?'

'Don't trouble, thank you.'

'Very well; I just thought I'd ask. I say, while I'm away, how would it be if you put in some good work with the other professional dancers here? You might get hold of some gossip about Paul Alexis.'

'There's something in that. But I'll have to get a decent frock if there is such a thing in Wilvercombe.'

'Well, get a wine-coloured one, then. I've always wanted to see you in wine-colour. It suits people with honey-coloured skin. (What an ugly word "skin" is.) "Blossoms of the honey-sweet and honey-coloured menuphar" – I always have a quotation for everything – it saves original thinking.'

'Blast the man!' said Harriet, left abruptly alone in the blue-plush lounge. Then she suddenly ran out down the steps and leapt upon the Daimler's running-board.

'Port or sherry?' she demanded.

'What?' said Wimsey, taken aback.

'The frock – port or sherry?'

'Claret,' said Wimsey. 'Château Margaux 1893 or thereabouts. I'm not particular to a year or two.'

He raised his hat and slipped in the clutch. As Harriet turned back, a voice, faintly familiar, accosted her:

'Miss – er – Miss Vane? Might I speak to you for a moment?'

It was the 'predatory hag' whom she had seen the evening before in the dance-lounge of the Resplendent.

V

THE EVIDENCE OF THE BETROTHED

'He said, dear mother, I should be his countess;
Today he'd come to fetch me, but with day
I've laid my expectation in its grave.'

The Bride's Tragedy

FRIDAY, 19 JUNE

HARRIET had almost forgotten the woman's existence, but now the whole of the little episode came back to her, and she wondered how she could have been so stupid. The nervous waiting; the vague, enraptured look, changing gradually to peevish impatience; the inquiry for Mr Alexis; the hasty and chagrined departure from the room. Glancing at the woman's face now, she saw it so old, so ravaged with grief and fear, that a kind of awkward delicacy made her avert her eyes and answer rather brusquely:

'Yes, certainly. Come up to my room.'

'It is very good of you,' said the woman. She paused a moment and then added, as they walked across to the lift:

'My name is Weldon – Mrs Weldon. I've been staying here some time. Mr Greely – the manager, that is – knows me very well.'

'That's all right,' said Harriet. She realised that Mrs Weldon was trying to explain that she was not a confidence-trickster or an hotel-crook or a white-slave agent, and was herself trying to make it clear that she did not suppose Mrs Weldon to be any of these things. She felt shy and this made her speak gruffly. She saw a 'scene' looming ahead, and she was not one of those women who enjoy 'scenes'. She led the way in a glum silence to Number 23, and begged her visitor to sit down.

'It's about,' said Mrs Weldon, sinking into an armchair and clasping her lean hands over her expensive handbag – 'it's about – Mr Alexis. The chamber-maid told me a horrible story – I went to the manager – he wouldn't tell me anything – I saw you with the police – and all those reporters were talking – they pointed you out – oh, Miss Vane, *please* tell me what has happened.'

Harriet cleared her throat and began searching her pockets instinctively for cigarettes.

'I'm awfully sorry,' she began. 'I'm afraid something rather beastly has happened. You see – I happened to be down on the shore yesterday afternoon, and I found a man lying there – dead. And from what they say, I'm dreadfully afraid it was Mr Alexis.'

No use beating about the bush. This forlorn creature with the dyed hair and haggard, painted face would have to know the truth. She struck a match and kept her eye on the flame.

'That's what I heard. Was it, do you know, was it a heart attack?'

'Afraid not. No. They – seem to think he' – (what was the gentlest form of words?) – 'did it himself.' (At any rate that avoided the word 'suicide'.)

'Oh, he couldn't have! he couldn't have! Indeed, Miss Vane, there must be a mistake. He must have had an accident.'

Harriet shook her head.

'But you don't know – how could you? – how impossible it all is. But people shouldn't say such cruel things. He was so perfectly happy – he *couldn't* have done anything like that. Why, he—' Mrs Weldon stopped, searching Harriet's face with her famished eyes. 'I heard them saying something about a razor – Miss Vane! What killed him?'

There were no kindly words for this – not even a long, scientific, Latin name.

'His throat was cut, Mrs Weldon.'

(Brutal Saxon monosyllables.)

'Oh!' Mrs Weldon seemed to shrink into a mere set of eyes and bones. 'Yes – they said – they said – I couldn't hear properly – I didn't like to ask – and they all seemed so pleased about it.'

'I know,' said Harriet. 'You see – these newspaper men – it's what they live by. They don't mean anything. It's bread-and-butter to them. They can't help it. And they couldn't possibly know that it meant anything to you.'

'No – but it does. But you – *you* don't want to make it out worse than it is. I can trust *you*.'

'You can trust me,' said Harriet slowly, 'but really and truly it could not have been an accident. I don't want to give you the details, but believe me, there's no possibility of accident.'

'Then it can't be Mr Alexis. Where is he? Can I see him?'

Harriet explained that the body had not been recovered.

'Then it must be somebody else! How do they know it is Paul?'

Harriet reluctantly mentioned the photograph, knowing what the next request would be.

'Show me the photograph.'

'It isn't very pleasant to look at.'

'Show me the photograph. *I* couldn't be deceived about it.'

Better, perhaps, to set all doubt at rest. Harriet slowly produced the print. Mrs Weldon snatched it from her hand.

'Oh, God! Oh, God! . . .'

Harriet rang the bell and, stepping out into the corridor, caught the waiter and asked for a stiff whisky-and-soda. When it came, she took it in herself and made Mrs Weldon drink it. Then she fetched a clean handkerchief and waited for the storm to subside. She sat on the arm of the chair and patted Mrs Weldon rather helplessly on the shoulder. Mercifully, the crisis took the form of violent sobbing and not of hysterics. She felt an increased respect for Mrs Weldon. When the sobs had subsided a little, and the groping fingers began to fumble with the handbag, Harriet pushed the handkerchief into them.

'Thank you, my dear,' said Mrs Weldon, meekly. She began to wipe her eyes, daubing the linen with red and black streaks from her make-up. Then she blew her nose and sat up.

'I'm sorry,' she began, forlornly.

'That's all right,' said Harriet, again. 'I'm afraid you've had rather a shock. Perhaps you'd like to bathe your eyes a bit. It'll make you feel better, don't you think?'

She supplied a sponge and towel. Mrs Weldon removed the grotesque traces of her grief and made her appearance from within the folds of the towel as a sallow-faced woman of between fifty and sixty, infinitely more dignified in her natural complexion. She made an instinctive movement towards her handbag, and then abandoned it.

'I look awful,' she said, with a dreary little laugh, 'but – what's it matter, now?'

'I shouldn't mind about it,' said Harriet. 'You look quite nice. Really and truly. Come and sit down. Have a cigarette. And let me give you a phenacetin or something. I expect you've got a bit of a headache.'

'Thank you. You're very kind. I won't be stupid again. I'm giving you a lot of trouble.'

'Not a bit. I only wish I could help you.'

'You can. If you only would. I'm sure you're clever. You look clever. I'm not clever. I do wish I was. I think I should have been happier if I'd been clever. It must be nice to *do* things. I've so often thought that if I could have painted pictures or ridden a motor-cycle or something, I should have got more out of life.'

Harriet agreed, gravely, that it was perhaps a good thing to have an occupation of some sort.

'But of course,' said Mrs Weldon, 'I was never brought up to that. I have lived for my emotions. I can't help it. I suppose I am made that way. Of course, my married life was a tragedy. But that's all over now. And my son – you might not think I was old enough to have a grown-up son, my dear, but I was married scandalously young – my son has been a sad disappointment to me. He has no heart – and that does seem strange, seeing that I am really all heart myself. I am *devoted* to my son, dear Miss Vane, but young people are so unsympathetic. If only he had been kinder to me, I could have lived *in* and *for* him. Everybody always said what a wonderful mother I was. But it's terribly lonely when one's own child deserts one, and one can't be blamed for snatching a little happiness, can one?'

'I know that,' said Harriet. 'I've tried snatching. It didn't work, though.'

'Didn't it?'

'No. We quarrelled, and then – well, he died and they thought I'd murdered him. I didn't, as a matter of fact. Somebody else did; but it was all very disagreeable.'

'You poor thing. But, of course, you are clever. You *do* things. That must make it easier. But what am I to do? I don't even know how to set about clearing up all this terrible business about Paul. But you are clever and you will help me – won't you?'

'Suppose you tell me just exactly what you want done.'

'Yes, of course. I'm so stupid – I can't even explain things properly. But you see, Miss Vane, I *know*, I know absolutely, that poor Paul couldn't have – done anything rash. He couldn't. He was so utterly happy with me, and looking forward to it all.'

'To what?' asked Harriet.

'Why, to our marriage,' said Mrs Weldon, as though the matter was self-evident.

'Oh, I see. I'm so sorry. I didn't realise you were going to be married. When?'

'In a fortnight's time. As soon as I could be ready for it. We were so happy – like children—'

Tears gathered again in Mrs Weldon's eyes.

'I will tell you all about it. I came here last January. I had been very ill and the doctor said I needed a mild climate, and I was so tired of the Riviera. I thought I'd try Wilvercombe just for a change. I came here. It really is a very nice hotel, you know, and I'd been here once before with Lady Hartlepool – but she died last year, you know. The very first night I was here, Paul came over and asked me to dance. We seemed to be drawn together. From the moment our eyes met, we knew we had found one another. He was lonely, too. We danced together every night. We went for long drives together and he told me all about his sad life. We were both exiles in our own way.'

'Oh yes – he came from Russia.'

'Yes, as a tiny boy. Poor little soul. He was really a prince, you know – but he never liked to say too much about that. Just a hint here and there. He felt it very much, being reduced to being a professional dancer. I told him – when we got to know one another better – that he was a prince in my heart now, and he said that that was better to him than an Imperial crown, poor boy. He loved me terribly. He quite frightened me sometimes. Russians are so passionate, you know.'

'Of course, of course,' said Harriet. 'You didn't have any misunderstanding or anything that might have led him—?'

'Oh, *no*! We were too marvellously at one together. We danced together that last night, and he whispered to me that there was a *great* and wonderful change coming into his life.

He was all eagerness and excitement. He used to get terribly excited over the least little thing, of course – but this was a real, big excitement and happiness. He danced so wonderfully that night. He told me it was because his heart was so full of joy that he felt as if he was dancing on air. He said: "I may have to go away tomorrow – but I can't tell you yet where or why." I didn't ask him anything more, because that would have spoilt it, but naturally I knew what he meant. He had been getting the licence, and we should be married in a fortnight after that.'

'Where were you going to be married?'

'In London. In church, of course, because I think a registrar's office is *so* depressing. Don't you? Of course he'd have to go and stay in the parish – that was what he meant by going away. We didn't want anybody here to know our secret beforehand, because there might have been unkind talk. You see, I'm a little bit older than he was, and people say such horrid things. I was a little worried about it myself, but Paul always said, "It is the heart that counts, Little Flower" – he called me that, because my name is Flora – such a dreadful name, I can't think how my poor dear parents came to choose it – "It is the heart that counts, and your heart is just seventeen." It was beautiful of him, but quite true. I felt seventeen when I was with him.'

Harriet murmured something inaudible. This conversation was dreadful to her. It was nauseating, pitiful, artificial yet horribly real; grotesquely comic and worse than tragic. She wanted to stop it at all costs, and she wanted at all costs to go on and disentangle the few threads of fact from the gaudy tangle of absurdity.

'He had never loved anybody till he met me,' went on Mrs Weldon. 'There is something so fresh and sacred in a young man's first love. One feels – well, almost reverent. He was jealous of my former marriage, but I told him he need not be. I was such a child when I married John Weldon, *far* too young to realise what love meant. I was utterly unawakened till I met Paul. There had been other men, I don't say there hadn't, who wanted to marry me (I was left a widow very early), but they meant nothing to me – nothing at all. "The heart of a girl with the experience of a woman" – that was Paul's lovely way of putting it. And it was true, my dear, indeed it was.'

'I'm sure it was,' said Harriet, trying to put conviction into her tone.

'Paul – he was so handsome and so graceful – if you could have seen him as he was! And he was very modest and not the least bit spoilt, though *all* the women ran after him. He was afraid to speak to me for a long time – to tell me how he felt about me, I mean. As a matter of fact, I had to take the first step, or he never would have dared to speak, though it was quite obvious how he felt. In fact, though we got engaged in February, he suggested putting the wedding off till June. He felt – so sweet and thoughtful of him – that we ought to wait and try to overcome my son's opposition. Of course, Paul's position made him very sensitive. You see, I'm rather well off, and of course, he hadn't a penny, poor boy, and he always refused to take any presents from me before we were married. He'd had to make his own way all alone, because those horrible Bolsheviks didn't leave him anything.'

'Who looked after him when he first came to England?'

'The woman who brought him over. He called her "old Natasha", and said she was a peasant-woman and absolutely devoted to him. But she died very soon, and then a Jewish tailor and his family were kind to him. They adopted him and made him a British subject, and gave him their own name of Goldschmidt. After that, their business failed somehow, and they were terribly poor. Paul had to run errands and sell newspapers. Then they tried emigrating to New York, but that was still worse. Then they died, and

Paul had to look after himself. Paul didn't like to say very much about that part of his life. It was all so terrible to him – like a bad dream.'

'I suppose he went to school somewhere.'

'Oh, yes – he went to the ordinary State school with all poor little East-side children. But he hated it. They used to laugh at him because he was delicate. They were rough with him and once he got knocked down in the playground and was ill for a long time. And he was terribly lonely.'

'What did he do when he left school?'

'He got work at a night-club, washing up glasses. He says the girls were kind to him, but of course, he never talked much about that time. He was sensitive, you see. He thought people would look down on him if they knew he had done that kind of work.'

'I suppose that was where he learnt to dance,' said Harriet, thoughtfully.

'Oh, yes – he was a marvellous dancer. It was in his blood, you know. When he was old enough, he got work as a professional partner and did very well, though of course it wasn't the kind of life he wanted.'

'He managed to make quite a good living at it,' said Harriet, thoughtfully, thinking of the too-smart clothes and the hand-made shoes.

'Yes; he worked very hard. But he never was strong, and he told me that he wouldn't be able to keep on much longer with the dancing. He had some trouble in one of his knees – arthritis or something, and he was afraid it would get worse and cripple him. Isn't it all terribly pathetic? Paul was so romantic, you know, and he wrote beautiful poetry. He loved everything that was beautiful.'

'What brought him to Wilvercombe?'

'Oh, he came back to England when he was seventeen, and got work in London. But the place went bankrupt, or got shut up by the police, or something, and he came here for a little holiday on what he had saved. Then he found they wanted a dancer here and he took the job temporarily, and he was so brilliant that the management kept him on.'

'I see,' Harriet reflected that it was going to be too difficult to trace these movements of Alexis through the Ghetto of New York and the mushroom clubs of the West End.

'Yes – Paul used to say it was the hand of Destiny that brought him and me here together. It does seem strange, doesn't it? We both just happened to come – by accident – just as though we were fated to meet. And now—'

The tears ran down Mrs Weldon's cheeks, and she gazed up helplessly at Harriet.

'We were both so sad and lonely; and we were going to be happy together.'

'It's frightfully sad,' said Harriet, inadequately. 'I suppose Mr Alexis was rather temperamental.'

'If you mean,' said Mrs Weldon, 'that he did this awful thing himself – no, never! I know he didn't. He was temperamental, of course, but he was radiantly happy with me. I'll never believe he just went away like that, without even saying good-bye to me. It isn't possible, Miss Vane. You've got to *prove* that it wasn't possible. You're so clever, I know you can do it. That's why I wanted to see you and tell you about Paul.'

'You realise,' said Harriet, slowly, 'that if he didn't do it himself, somebody else must have done it.'

'Why not?' cried Mrs Weldon, eagerly. 'Somebody must have envied our happiness. Paul was so handsome and romantic – there must have been people who were jealous of us. Or it may have been the Bolsheviks. Those horrible men would do anything, and I was only reading in the paper yesterday that England was simply swarming with them. They say all this business about passports isn't a bit of good to keep them out. I call it absolutely wicked, the way we let them come over here and plot against everybody's safety and this Government simply encourages them. They've killed Paul, and I shouldn't wonder if they started throwing bombs at the King and Queen next. It ought to be stopped, or we shall have a revolution. Why, they even distribute their disgusting pamphlets to the Navy.'

'Well,' said Harriet, 'we must wait and see what they find out. I'm afraid you may have to tell the police about some of this. It won't be very pleasant for you, I'm afraid, but they'll want to know everything they can.'

'I'm sure I don't mind what I have to go through,' said Mrs Weldon, wiping her eyes resolutely, 'if only I can help to clear Paul's memory. Thank you *very* much, Miss Vane. I'm afraid I've taken up your time. You've been very kind.'

'Not at all,' said Harriet. 'We'll do our best.'

She escorted her visitor to the door, and then returned to an armchair and a thoughtful cigarette. Was the imminent prospect of matrimony with Mrs Weldon a sufficient motive for suicide? She was inclined to think not. One can always take flight from these things. But with temperamental people, of course, you never can tell.

VI

THE EVIDENCE OF THE FIRST BARBER

'Old, benevolent man.'
The Second Brother

FRIDAY, 19 JUNE – AFTERNOON AND EVENING

'CAN you tell me,' inquired Lord Peter, 'what has become of old Mr Endicott these days?'

The manager of the ham-shop, who liked to attend personally to distinguished customers, arrested his skewer in the very act of thrusting it into the interior of a ham.

'Oh, yes, my lord. He has a house at Ealing. He occasionally looks in here for a jar of our Gentleman's Special Pickle. A very remarkable old gentleman, Mr Endicott.'

'Yes, indeed. I hadn't seen him about lately. I was afraid perhaps something had happened to him.'

'Oh, dear no, my lord. He keeps his health wonderfully. He has taken up golf at seventy-six and collects papier-mâché articles. Nothing like an interest in life, he says, to keep you hearty.'

'Very true,' replied Wimsey. 'I must run out and see him some time. What is his address?'

The manager gave the information, and then, returning to the matter in hand, plunged the skewer into the ham close to the bone, twirled it expertly and, withdrawing it, presented it politely by the handle. Wimsey sniffed it gravely, said 'Ah!' with appropriate relish, and pronounced a solemn benediction upon the ham.

'Thank you, my lord. I think you will find it very tasty. Shall I send it?'

'I will take it with me.'

The manager waved forward an attendant, who swathed the article impressively in various layers of grease-proof paper, white paper and brown paper, corded it up with best-quality string, worked the free end of the string into an ingenious handle and stood, dandling the parcel, like a nurse with a swaddled princeling.

'My car is outside,' said Wimsey. The assistant beamed gratification. A little ritual procession streamed out into Jermyn Street, comprising: The Assistant, carrying the ham; Lord Peter, drawing on his driving-gloves; the Manager, murmuring a ceremonial formula; the Second Assistant, opening the door and emerging from behind it to bow upon the threshold; and eventually the car glided away amid the reverent murmurings of a congregation of persons gathered in the street to admire its stream-lining and dispute about the number of its cylinders.

Mr Endicott's house at Ealing was easily found. The owner was at home, and the presentation of the ham and reciprocal offer of a glass of old sherry proceeded with the cheerful dignity suitable to an exchange of gifts among equal, but friendly potentates. Lord Peter inspected the collection of papier-mâché trays, conversed agreeably about golf-handicaps and then, without unseemly haste, opened up the subject of his inquiry.

'I've just come across one of your razors, Endicott, in rather peculiar circumstances. I wonder if you could tell me anything about it?'

Mr Endicott, with a gracious smile upon his rosy countenance, poured out another glass of the sherry and said he would be happy to assist if he could.

Wimsey described the make and appearance of the razor, and asked if it would be possible to trace the buyer.

'Ah!' said Mr Endicott. 'With an ivory handle, you say. Well, now, it's rather fortunate it should be one of that lot, because we only had the three dozen of them, most of our customers preferring black handles. Yes; I can tell you a bit about them. That particular razor came in during the War – 1916, I think it was. It wasn't too easy to get a first-class blade just then, but these were very good. Still, the white handle was against them, and I remember we were glad when we were able to send off a dozen of them to an old customer in Bombay. Captain Francis Egerton, that was. He asked us to send some out for himself and friends. That would be in 1920.'

'Bombay? That's a bit far off. But you never know. How about the rest?'

Mr Endicott, who seemed to have a memory like an encyclopaedia, plunged his thoughts into the past and said:

'Well, there was Commander Mellon; he had two of them. But it wouldn't be him, because his ship was blown up and sank with all hands and his kit went down with him. In 1917, that would be. A very gallant gentleman, was the Commander, and of good family. One of the Dorset Mellons. The Duke of Wetherby: he had one, and he was telling me the other day that he still had it; it wouldn't be him. And Mr Pritchard: he had a remarkable experience with his; his personal man went off his head and attacked him with his own razor, but fortunately Mr Pritchard was able to overpower him. They brought him in guilty of attempted murder but insane, and the razor was an exhibit at the trial. I know Mr Pritchard came in afterwards and bought a new razor, a black one, because the other had struck the back of a chair during the struggle and had a piece chipped out of the edge, and he said he was going to keep it as a memento of the narrowest shave of his life. That was very good, I thought. Mr Pritchard was always a very amusing gentleman. Colonel Grimes: he had one, but he had to abandon all his kit in the Retreat over the Marne – I couldn't say what happened to that one. He liked that razor and came back for another one similar, and he has it yet. That makes six out of the second dozen. What happened to the others? – Oh, I know! There was a very funny story about one of them. Young Mr Ratcliffe – the Hon. Henry Ratcliffe – he came in one day in a great state. "Endicott," he said, "just you look at my razor!" "Bless me, sir!" I said, "it looks as if somebody had been sawing wood with it." "That's a very near guess, Endicott," he said. "My sister-in-law and some of that bright crowd of hers in her studio got the idea that they'd have some private theatricals and used my best razor to cut out the scenery with." My goodness, he was wild about it! Of course the blade was ruined for ever; he had a different one after that, a very fine French razor which we were trying out at the time. Then, ah, yes! There was poor Lord Blackfriars. A sad business that was. He married one of these film-stars, and she ran through his money and went off with a dago – you'll remember that, my lord. Blew his brains out, poor gentleman. He left his pair of razors to his personal man, who wouldn't part with them on any account. Major Hartley had two and so did Colonel Belfridge. They've left Town and gone to live in the country. I could give you their addresses. Sir John Westlock – well, now, I couldn't say for certain about him. There was some sort of trouble and he went abroad, at the time of the Megatherium Scandal. Early in the twenties, wasn't it? My memory isn't what it was. He had a pair of razors. Very fond of a good blade, he was, and looked after it very carefully. Mr Alec Baring – that was sad, too. They said it was in the family, but I always thought that flying crash had something to do with it. I suppose they wouldn't let him have razors where he is now. He only had one of that set, as a replacement for one he left in an hotel. How many does that make? Sixteen altogether, not counting the dozen that went to Bombay.

Well, that's nearly the lot, because I gave a round half-dozen to my late head-assistant when we broke up the business. He has an establishment of his own in Eastbourne, and is doing very well there, I'm told. Twenty-two. Now, what about the last pair?'

Mr Endicott scratched his head with a pained look.

'Sometimes I think I'm beginning to fail a bit,' he said, 'though my handicap is getting shorter and my wind's as good as ever it was. Now, who *did* have that pair of razors? Well, there! Could it have been Sir William Jones? No, it couldn't. Or the Marquis of – ? No. Stop a minute. That was the pair Sir Harry Ringwood bought for his son – young Mr Ringwood up at Magdalen College. I knew I hadn't seen them about. He had them in 1925, and the young gentleman went out to British East Africa under the Colonial Office when he left the University. There! I knew I should get it in time. That's the lot, my lord.'

'Endicott,' said Lord Peter, 'I think you're marvellous. You're the youngest man of your age I ever struck, and I should like to meet your wine-merchant.'

Mr Endicott, gratified, pushed the decanter across the table and mentioned the name of the vendor.

'A lot of these people we can dismiss at once,' said Lord Peter. 'Colonel Grimes is a problem – goodness knows what happened to the kit he left in France, but I expect somebody out there got hold of it. The razor may have returned to this country. He's a possibility. Major Hartley and Colonel Belfridge will have to be traced. I shouldn't think it would be Sir John Westlock. If he was a careful sort of blighter, he probably took his razors with him and cherished them. We'll have to inquire about poor Baring. His razor may have been sold or given away. And we might just ask about young Ringwood, though we can probably count him out. Then there's your head-assistant. Would he be likely to have sold any of them, do you think?'

'Well, no, my lord; I shouldn't think he would. He told me that he should keep them for his own use and for use on his own premises. He liked having the old name on them, you see. But for sale to his customers, he would have his razors marked with his own name. That has a certain value, you see, my lord. It's only if you're in a good way of business and can order in razors in three-dozen lots that you get your own name put on them. He started off very well with a new three dozen Kropp blades, for he told me all about it, and, things being equal, those are what he would supply his customers with.'

'Quite. Any likelihood of his selling the others second-hand?'

'That,' said Mr Endicott, 'I could not say. There isn't a great deal of business done in second-hand razors, without it's one of these tramp-hairdressers now and again.'

'What's a tramp-hairdresser?'

'Well, my lord, they're hairdressers out of a job, and they go about from place to place looking to be taken on as extra hands when there's a press of work. We didn't see much of them in *our* place, of course. They're not first-class men as a rule, and I wouldn't have taken it upon me to engage any but a first-class man for *my* gentlemen. But in a place like Eastbourne, where there's a big seasonal custom, you would have them round pretty frequently. It might be worth while asking my late assistant. Plumer, his name is, in Belvedere Road. If you like, I will send him a line.'

'Don't bother; I'll run down and see him. Just one other thing. Was any of the customers you've mentioned a clumsy-handed fellow who took a lot out of his razor and was always sending it back to be re-set?'

Mr Endicott chuckled.

'Ah! now you're talking,' he said. 'Colonel Belfridge – oh, dear! oh, dear! He was a terribly hard man on his razors – is

76

still, for all I know. Time and again he'd say to me, " 'Pon my word, Endicott, I don't know what you *do* to my razors. They won't keep their edge a week. Steel isn't what it was before the War." But it wasn't the steel, or the War either. He was always the same. I think he took the edge off with the strop, instead of putting it on; I do indeed. He didn't keep a man, you know. The Colonel belongs to one of our best families, but not a wealthy man, by any means. A very fine soldier, I believe.'

'One of the old school, eh?' said Wimsey. 'Good-hearted but peppery. I know. Where did you say he was living now?'

'Stamford,' replied Mr Endicott, promptly. 'He sent me a card last Christmas. Very kind of him, I thought it, to remember me. But my old customers are very thoughtful in those ways. They know I value their kind remembrance. Well, my lord, I am exceedingly pleased to have seen you,' he added, as Wimsey rose and took up his hat, 'and I'm sure I hope I may have been of some assistance to you. You keep very fit, I hope. You're looking well.'

'I'm getting old,' said Lord Peter. 'My hair is turning grey over the temples.'

Mr Endicott emitted a concerned cluck.

'But that's nothing,' he hastened to assure his visitor. 'Many ladies think it looks more distinguished that way. Not getting thin on top, I hope and trust.'

'Not that I know of. Take a look at it.'

Mr Endicott pushed the straw-coloured thatch apart and peered earnestly at the roots.

'No sign of it,' he pronounced, confidently. 'Never saw a healthier scalp. At the same time, my lord, if you *should* notice any slight weakening or falling-off, let me know. I should be proud to advise you. I've still got the recipe for Endicott's Special Tonic, and though I say so myself, I've never found anything to beat it.'

Wimsey laughed, and promised to call on Mr Endicott for help at the first symptom of trouble. The old barber saw him to the door, clasping his hand affectionately and begging him to come again. Mrs Endicott would be so sorry to have missed him.

Seated behind the steering-wheel, Wimsey debated the three courses open to him. He could go to Eastbourne; he could go to Stamford; he could return to Wilvercombe. A natural inclination pointed to Wilvercombe. It was, surely, only justifiable to return at once to the scene of the crime, if it was a crime. The fact that Harriet was also there was a purely accidental complication. On the other hand, his obvious duty was to clear up this razor business as quickly as possible. Musing, he drove to his own flat in Piccadilly, where he found his man, Bunter, mounting photographs in a large album.

To Bunter he laid bare his problem, requesting his advice. Bunter, revolving the matter in his mind, took a little time for consideration and then delivered himself respectfully of his opinion.

'In your lordship's place, my lord, I fancy I should be inclined to go to Stamford. For a variety of reasons.'

'You would, would you?'

'Yes, my lord.'

'Well, perhaps you are right, Bunter.'

'Yes, thank you, my lord. Would your lordship wish me to accompany you?'

'No,' said Wimsey. 'You can go down to Eastbourne.'

'Very good, my lord.'

'Tomorrow morning. I shall stay the night in Town. You might send off a telegram for me – no, on second thoughts, I'll send it myself.'

Telegram from Lord Peter Wimsey to Miss Harriet Vane:

FOLLOWING RAZOR CLUE TO STAMFORD REFUSE
RESEMBLE THRILLER HERO WHO HANGS ROUND HEROINE
TO NEGLECT OF DUTY BUT WILL YOU MARRY ME – PETER.

Telegram from Miss Harriet Vane to Lord Peter Wimsey:

GOOD HUNTING CERTAINLY NOT SOME DEVELOPMENTS
HERE – VANE.

VII

THE EVIDENCE OF THE GIGOLOS

'A worthless life,
A life ridiculous.'
Death's Jest-Book

FRIDAY, 19 JUNE – EVENING

MISS HARRIET VANE, in a claret-coloured frock, swayed round the dance-lounge of the Hotel Resplendent in the arms of Mr Antoine, the fair-haired gigolo.

'I'm afraid I am not a very good dancer,' she remarked, apologetically.

Mr Antoine, who was, rather surprisingly, neither Jew nor South-American dago, nor Central European mongrel, but French, clasped her a very little more firmly in his competent professional arm, and replied:

'You dance very correctly, mademoiselle. It is only the *entrain* that is a little lacking. It is possible that you are awaiting the perfect partner. When the heart dances with the feet, then it will be *à merveille*.' He met her eyes with a delicately calculated expression of encouragement.

'Is that the kind of thing you have to say to all these old ladies?' asked Harriet, smiling.

Antoine opened his eyes a trifle and then, mocking back to her mockery, said:

'I am afraid so. That is part of our job, you know.'

'It must be very tedious.'

Antoine contrived to shrug his exquisite shoulders without in any way affecting the lithe grace of his motion.

'*Que voulez-vous?* All work has its tedious moments, which are repaid by those that are more agreeable. One may say truthfully to mademoiselle what might in another case be a mere politeness.'

'Don't bother about me,' said Harriet. 'There's something else I want to talk about. I wanted to ask you about Mr Alexis.'

'*Ce pauvre Alexis!* It was mademoiselle who found him, I understand?'

'Yes. I just wondered what sort of person he was, and why he should have – done away with himself like that.'

'Ah! that is what we are all wondering. It is, no doubt, the Russian temperament.'

'I had heard' – Harriet felt that she must tread cautiously here – 'that he was engaged to be married.'

'Oh, yes – to the English lady. That was understood.'

'Was he happy about it?'

'Mademoiselle, Alexis was poor and the English lady is very rich. It was advantageous to him to marry her. At first, no doubt, it might offer a little *désagrément*, but afterwards – you understand, mademoiselle, these matters arrange themselves.'

'You don't think that he suddenly felt he couldn't face it, and took this way out?'

'That is difficult to say, but – no, I do not think so. He had, after all, only to go away. He was a very good dancer and very popular. He would easily have found another situation, provided his health would permit him to continue.'

'I wondered whether there was any other attachment to make things more difficult.'

'From what he said to us, mademoiselle, I know of nothing which could not easily have been arranged.'

'Women like him, I suppose?' demanded Harriet, bluntly.

Antoine's smile was a sufficient answer.

'There wasn't any disappointment of any kind?'

'I did not hear of any. But of course, one does not tell one's friends everything.'

'Of course not. I don't mean to be inquisitive, but it all seems to me rather odd.'

The music stopped.

'What is the arrangement?' asked Harriet. 'Do we go on or have you other engagements?'

'There is no reason why we should not continue for the next dance. After that, unless mademoiselle wishes to make a special arrangement with the management, I am expected to attend to my other patrons.'

'No,' said Harriet, 'I don't want to upset things. Is there any reason why you and the two young ladies should not have a little supper with me later on?'

'None at all. It is very kind; very amiable. Leave it to me, mademoiselle. I will arrange it all. It is natural that mademoiselle should take an interest.'

'Yes, but I don't want the manager to think that I'm interrogating his staff behind his back.'

'N'ayez pas peur, je m'en charge. I will ask you to dance again in a little time, and then I will tell you what I have contrived.'

He handed her back to her table with a smile, and she saw him gather up a vast and billowy lady in a tightly fitting gown and move smoothly away with her, the eternal semi-sensuous smile fixed upon his lips as though it was painted there.

About six dances later, the smile reappeared beside her, and Antoine, guiding her steps through a waltz, informed her that if, at 11.30, when the dancing was over, she would be good enough to seek out a small restaurant a few streets away, he, with Doris and Charis, would be there to meet her. It was only a small restaurant, but very good, and the proprietor knew them very well; moreover, Antoine himself lodged in the little hotel attached to the restaurant and would give himself the pleasure of offering mademoiselle a glass of wine. They would be private there, and could speak quite freely. Harriet assented, with the proviso that she should pay for the supper, and accordingly, shortly before midnight, found herself seated on a red-plush settee beneath a row of gilded mirrors, over a pleasant little supper of the Continental sort.

Doris the blonde and Charis the brunette were only too delighted to discuss the affairs of the late Mr Alexis. Doris appeared to be the official confidante; she could give inside information about her late partner's affairs of the heart. He had had a girl – oh, yes; but some weeks earlier this connection had come to an end rather mysteriously. It was nothing to do with Mrs Weldon. *That* matter had been, in Mr Micawber's phrase, already 'provided for'. No; it was apparently a breaking-off by mutual consent, and nobody seemed to have been much upset by it. Certainly not Alexis, who, though expressing a great deal of conventional regret, had seemed to be rather pleased about it, as though he had brought off a smart piece of business. And since then, the young lady in question had been seen going about with another man, who was supposed to be a friend of Alexis.

'And if you ask me,' said Doris, in a voice whose fundamental cockney was overlaid by a veneer of intense refinement, 'Alexis pushed her off on to this chap on purpose, to get her out of the way of his other little plans.'

'What other little plans?'

'I'm sure I don't know. But he had something up his sleeve these last few weeks. Very grand he was about it; I'm sure one was almost afraid to speak to his high-mightiness. "You'll see," he said, "just you wait a little bit." "Well, I'm sure," I said, "I have no wish to intrude. You can keep your secrets," I said, "for I don't want to know them." It's my belief he was up to some game or other. Whatever it was, he was like a dog with two tails about it.'

Mrs Weldon too, thought Harriet, had said the same thing. Alexis was going to have some news for her – though Mrs Weldon had put her own interpretation on the remark. Harriet put out another feeler of inquiry.

'Marriage-licence?' said Charis. 'Oh, no! he wouldn't be putting up any flags about that. He couldn't very well *like* the idea of marrying that dreadful old woman. Well, it serves her right now. She's got left. I think that sort of thing is disgusting.'

'I am sorry for her,' said Antoine.

'Oh, you are always sorry for people. I do think it's beastly. I think these horrible fat men are beastly, too, always pawing a girl about. If Greely wasn't a decent sort, I'd chuck the whole thing, but I will say he does see to it that they behave themselves. But an old *woman*—' Charis, superb in her vigorous youth, expressed contempt by voice and gesture.

'I suppose,' suggested Harriet, 'that Alexis wanted to feel safe and settled financially. I mean, a dancer can't go on dancing all his life, can he? Particularly if he isn't very strong.'

She spoke with hesitation, but to her relief Antoine immediately and emphatically agreed with her.

'You are right. While we are young and gay it is all very good. But presently the head grows bald, the legs grow stiff, and – finish! The manager says, "It is all very well, you are a good dancer, but my clients prefer a younger man, *hein*? Then good-bye the first-class establishment. We go, what you call, down the hill. I tell you, it is a great temptation when somebody comes and says, "Look! You have only to marry me and I will make you rich and comfortable for life." And what is it? Only to tell lies to one's wife every night instead of to twenty or thirty silly old ladies. Both are done for money – where is the difference?'

'Yes, I suppose we shall all come to it,' said Charis, with a grimace. 'Only, from the way Alexis talked, you'd think he'd have wanted a little more poetry about it. All that rubbish about his noble birth and fallen fortunes — like something out of those stories he was so potty about. Quite a hero of romance, according to him. Always wanted to take the spot-light, did Mr Paul Alexis. You'd think he did the floor a favour by dancing on it. And then the fairy prince comes down to marrying an old woman for her money.'

'Oh, he wasn't so bad,' protested Doris. 'You oughtn't to talk that way, dear. It's not so easy for we dancers, the way everybody treats us like dirt. Though they're willing enough to take advantage of you if you give them half a chance. Why shouldn't Alexis, or any of us, get a bit of our own back? Anyhow, he's dead, poor boy, and you oughtn't to run him down.'

'Ah, *voilà!*' said Antoine. 'He is dead. Why is he dead? One does not cut one's throat *pour s'amuser.*'

'That's another thing,' said Charis, 'that I can't quite make out. The minute I heard about it, I said to myself, "That's not like Alexis," He hadn't the nerve to do a thing like that. Why, he was terrified of pricking his little finger. You needn't frown, dear, Alexis was a regular namby-pamby, and if he was dead ten times over it wouldn't make any difference. You used to laugh at him yourself. "I cannot climb that step-ladder, I am afraid to fall." "I do not like to go to the dentist, he might pull my teeth out." "Do not shake me when I am cutting the bread, I might cut my fingers." "Really, Mr Alexis," I used to say to him, "anybody would thing you were made of glass." '

'I know what mademoiselle is thinking,' said Antoine, his melancholy mouth curling. 'She thinks: "*Voilà!* that is the gigolo. He is not a man, he is a doll stuffed with sawdust." He is bought, he is sold, and sometimes there is an un-pleasantness. Then the English husband, he say, "Well, what can you expect? This fellow, he is a nasty piece of work. He lives on foolish women and he does not play the cricket." Sometimes it is not very nice, but one must live. *Que voulez-vous? Ce n'ast pas rigolo que d'être gigolo.*'

Harriet blushed.

'I wasn't thinking that,' she said.

'But you were, mademoiselle, and it is very natural.'

'Antoine doesn't play cricket,' put in Doris, kindly, 'but he plays tennis and swims very well.'

'It is not me that is in question,' said Antoine. 'And truly, I cannot understand this business of throat-cutting. It is not reasonable. Why did Alexis go all that distance away? He never walked; he found the walking fatigued him. If he had decided to suicide himself, he would have done it at home.'

'And he'd have taken some sleeping-stuff,' said Doris, nodding her golden head. 'I know that, because he showed it to me once, when he was in one of his blue fits. "That is my way out of the bad world," he said, and he talked a lot of poetry. I told him not to be silly – and of course, in half an hour he had got over it. He was like that. But cutting his throat with a razor – no!'

'That's awfully interesting,' said Harriet. 'By the way,' she went on, remembering her conversation with Wimsey, 'did he have anything the matter with his skin? I mean, did he always have to wear gloves, or anything of that sort?'

'Oh, no,' said Antoine. 'The gigolo must not have things the matter with his skin. That would not do at all. Alexis had very elegant hands. He was vain of them.'

'He said his skin was sensitive, and that's why he didn't shave,' put in Doris.

'Ah, yes! I can tell you about that,' Antoine took up his cue. 'When he came here about a year ago he asked for a job. Mr Greely he say to me, "See him dance." Because, you see, mademoiselle, the other dancer had just left us, all of a sudden, *comme ça* – without the proper notice. I see him dance and I say to Mr Greely, "That is very good." The manager say, "Very well, I take you on trial for a little time, but I must not have the beard. The ladies will not like it. It is unheard of, a gigolo with a beard," Alexis say, "But if I shave the beard I come out all over buttons."'

'Pimples?' suggested Harriet.

'Yes, pardon, pimples. Well, the gigolo with the pimples, that is unheard of also, you understand. "Well," say the manager, "you can come a little time with the beard till we are suited, but if you want to stay, you remove the beard." Very well, Alexis come and dance, and the ladies are delighted. The beard is so distinguished, so romantic, so unusual. They come a very long distance express to dance with the beard. Mr Greely say, "It is good. I was mistaken. You stay and the beard stay too. My God! What will these ladies want next? The long whiskers, perhaps? Antoine," he say to me, "you grow the long whiskers and maybe you get off still better." But me, no! God has not given me the hair to make whiskers.'

'Did Alexis have a razor at all?'

'How should I know? If he knew that the shaving made the pimples, he must have tried to shave, *n'est-ce pas*? But as to the razor, I cannot tell. Do you know, Doris?'

'Me? I like that. Alexis never was my fancy-man. But I'll ask Leila Garland. She ought to know.'

'*Sa maîtresse*,' explained Antoine. 'Yes, ask her, Doris. Because evidently that is of a considerable importance. I have not thought of that, *mon dieu!*'

'You've told me a lot of interesting things,' said Harriet. 'I'm very much obliged to you. And I'd be still more obliged if you didn't mention that I'd been asking you, because, what with the newspaper reporters and so on—'

'Oh!' said Antoine. 'Listen, mademoiselle, you must not think that because we are the dolls that are bought and sold we have neither eyes nor ears. This gentleman that arrived this morning – do you think we do not know who he is? This Lord Peter, so celebrated, he does not come here for nothing, *hein*? It is not for nothing he talks to you and asks questions. He is not interested because a foreign dancer has cut his throat in a tantrum. No. But, equally, we know how to be discreet. *Ma foi*, if we did not, we should not keep our jobs, you understand. We tell you what we know, and the lady who writes the *romans-policiers* and the lord who is *connaisseur* in mysteries, they make the investigations. But we say nothing. It is our business to say nothing. That is understood.'

'That's right,' said Charis. 'We won't let on. Not that there's a great deal to tell anybody. We've had the police asking questions, of course, but they never believe anything one says. I'm sure they all think it's something to do with Leila. These policemen always think that if anything happens to a fellow, there must be a girl at the bottom of it.'

'But that,' said Antoine, 'is a compliment.'

VIII

THE EVIDENCE OF THE SECOND BARBER

'Send him back again,
An unmasked braggart to his bankrupt den.'
Letter from Göttingen

SATURDAY, 20 JUNE
SUNDAY, 21 JUNE

WIMSEY, sleek with breakfast, sunshine and sentiment, strolled peacefully upon the close-clipped lawn of the George at Stamford, pausing now and again to inhale the scent of a crimson rose, or to marvel at the age and extent of the wisteria, trailing its lacy tendrils along the grey stone wall. He had covenanted with himself to interview Colonel Belfridge at eleven o'clock. By that time, both of them would have digested their breakfasts and be ready for a small, companionable spot of something. He had a pleasurable interior certainty that he was on the track of a nice, difficult, meaty problem, investigated under agreeable conditions. He lit up a well-seasoned pipe. Life felt good to him.

At ten minutes past eleven, life felt slightly less good. Colonel Belfridge, who looked as though he had been designed by H. M. Bateman in a moment of more than ordinary inspiration, was extremely indignant. It seemed to him that it was an ungentlemanly action to go and interrogate a man's barber, hr'rm, about a man's personal belongings, and he resented the insinuation that a man could possibly be mixed up, hr'rm, in the decease of a damned dago, hr'rm, in an adjectival four-by-three watering-place like Wilvercombe. Wimsey ought to be ashamed, hr'rm, woof! of interfering in what was properly the business of the police, dammit, sir! If the police didn't know their own damned business, what did we pay rates and taxes for, tell me that, sir!

Wimsey apologised for worrying Colonel Belfridge, and protested that a man must take up some sort of hobby.

The Colonel intimated that golf, or, hr'rm, breeding spaniels would be a more seemly amusement for a gentleman.

Wimsey said that, having engaged in a spot of intelligence work during the War, he had acquired a kind of taste for that kind of thing.

The Colonel pounced on this remark immediately, turned Wimsey's war-record inside out, discovered a number of military experiences common to both of them, and presently found himself walking with his visitor down the pansy-edged path of his little garden to display a litter of puppies.

'My dear boy,' said Colonel Belfridge, 'I shall only be too happy to help you in any way I can. You're not in a hurry, are you? Stay to lunch, and we can talk it over afterwards. Mabel!' – in a stentorian shout.

A middle-aged woman appeared in the back doorway and waddled hastily down the path towards them.

'Gentleman for lunch!' bawled the Colonel. 'And decant a bottle of the '04. Carefully now, dammit! I wonder, now,' he added, turning to Wimsey, 'if you recollect a fellow called Stokes.'

It was with very great difficulty that Wimsey detached the Colonel's mind from the events of the Great War and led it back to the subject of razors. Once his attention was captured, however, Colonel Belfridge proved to be a good and reliable witness.

He remembered the pair of razors perfectly. Had a lot of trouble with those razors, hr'rm, woof! Razors were not what they had been in his young days. Nothing was, sir, dammit! Steel wouldn't stand up to the work. What with these damned foreigners and mass-production, our industries were going to the dogs. He remembered, during the Boer War –

Wimsey, after a quarter of an hour, mentioned the subject of razors.

'Ha! yes,' said the Colonel, smoothing his vast white moustache down and up at the ends with a vast, curving gesture. 'Ha, hr'rm, yes! The razors, of course. Now, what do you want to know about them?'

'Have you still got them, sir?'

'No, sir, I have not. I got rid of them, sir. A poor lot they were, too. I told Endicott I was surprised at his stocking such inferior stuff. Wanted re-setting every other week. But it's the same story with all of 'em. Can't get a decent blade anywhere nowadays. And we shan't sir, we shan't, unless we get a strong Conservative Government – I say, a *strong* Government, sir, that will have the guts to protect the iron and steel industry. But will they do it? No, damme, sir – they're afraid of losing their miserable votes. Flapper votes! How can you expect a pack of women to understand the importance of iron and steel? Tell me that, ha, hr'rm!'

Wimsey asked what he had done with the razors.

'Gave 'em to the gardener,' said the Colonel. 'Very decent man. Comes in twice a week. Wife and family. War pensioner with a game leg. Helps with the dogs. Quite a good man. Name of Summers.'

'When was that, sir?'

'What? Oh! when did I give 'em to him, you mean. Let me see, now, let me see. That was after Diana had whelped – near thing that – nearly lost her that time, poor bitch. She died two years ago – killed – run over by a damned motorcyclist. Best bitch I ever had. I had him up in court for it – made him pay. Careless young devil. No consideration for anybody. And now they've abolished the speed-limit—'

Wimsey reminded the Colonel that they were talking about razors.

After further consideration, the Colonel narrowed down the period to the year 1926. He was sure about it, because of the spaniel's illness, which had given Summers considerable trouble. He had made the man a present of money, and had added the razors, having just purchased a new pair for himself. Owing to the illness of the mother, only one puppy out of the litter had been successfully reared, and that was Stamford Royal, who had proved a very good dog. A reference to the stud-book clinched the date conclusively.

Wimsey thanked the Colonel, and asked whether he could interview Summers.

By all means. It was not one of Summers' days, but he lived in a little cottage near the bridge. Wimsey could go and see him and mention the Colonel's name. Should the Colonel walk down with Wimsey?

Lord Peter was grateful, but begged the Colonel would not take the trouble. (He felt, indeed, that Summers might be more communicative in Colonel Belfridge's absence.) With some trouble, he disengaged himself from the old soldier's offers of hospitality, and purred away through the picturesque streets of Stamford to the cottage by the bridge.

Summers was an easy man to question – alert, prompt and exact. It was very kind of Colonel Belfridge to give him the razors. He himself could not make use of them, preferring the safety instrument, but of course he had not told the Colonel that, not wishing to hurt his feelings. He had given the razors to his sister's husband, who kept a hair-dressing establishment in Seahampton.

Seahampton! Less than 50 miles from Wilvercombe! Had Wimsey struck it lucky with his very first shot? He was turning away, when it occurred to him to ask whether there was any special mark by which either of the razors might be recognised.

Yes, there was. One of them had been accidentally dropped on the stone floor of the cottage and there was a slight, a very slight crack across the ivory. You wouldn't hardly notice it without you looked closely. The other razor was, so far as Summers knew, quite perfect.

Wimsey thanked his informant and rewarded him suitably. He returned to the car and set his course southward. He had always thought Stamford a beautiful town and now, with its grey stone houses and oriel windows bathed in the mellow afternoon sunshine, it seemed to him the loveliest jewel in the English crown.

He slept that night in Seahampton, and on the Sunday morning set forth in search of Summers' brother-in-law, whose name was Merryweather – a name of happy omen. The shop turned out to be a small one, in the neighbourhood of the docks. Mr Merryweather lived above his premises, and was delighted to give Wimsey information about the razors.

He had had them in 1927, and they were good razors, though they had been badly treated and were considerably worn when they came into his hands. He had one of them still, and it was doing good service. Perhaps his lordship would like to look at it. Here it was.

Wimsey, with a beating heart, turned it over in his hands. It was the exact duplicate of the razor that Harriet had found on the shore. He examined it carefully, but found no crack in the ivory. But what, he asked, almost afraid to put the question for fear of disappointment, what had become of the fellow to it?

'Now that, my lord,' said Mr Merryweather, 'I unfortunately cannot show you. Had I known it would be wanted, I certainly would never have parted with it. I sold that razor, my lord, only a few weeks ago, to one of these tramping fellows that came here looking for a job. I had no work for him here, and to tell you the truth, my lord, I wouldn't have given it to him if I had. You'd be surprised, the number of these men who come round, and half of them are no more skilled hairdressers than my tom-cat. Just out for what they can pick up, that's what they are. We generally give them a few razors to set, just to see what they're made of, and the way they set about it, you can tell, nine times out of ten, that they've never set a razor in their lives. Well, this one was like that, and I told him he could push off. Then he asked me if I could sell him a second-hand razor, so I sold him this one to get rid of him. He paid for it and away he went, and that's the last I saw of him.'

'What was he like?'

'Oh, a little rat of a fellow. Sandy-haired and too smooth in his manner by half. Not so tall as your lordship, he wasn't, and if I remember rightly he was a bit – not deformed, but what I might call crooked. He might have had one shoulder a trifle higher than the other. Nothing very noticeable, but he gave me that impression. No, he wasn't lame or anything of that kind. Quite spry, he seemed, and quick in his movements. He had rather pale eyes, with sandy eyelashes – an ugly little devil, if you'll excuse me. Very well-kept hands – one notices that, because, of course, when a man asks for a job in this kind of establishment, that's one of the first things one looks for. Dirty or bitten nails, for instance, are what one couldn't stand for for a moment. Let me see, now. Oh, yes – he spoke very well. Spoke like a gentleman, very refined and quiet. That's a thing one notices, too. Not that it's of any great account in a neighbourhood like this. Our customers are sometimes a roughish lot. But one can't help notice, you see, when one's been used to it. Besides, it gives one an idea what kind of place a man has been used to.'

'Did this man say anything about where he had been employed previously?'

'Not that I remember. My impression of him was that he'd been out of employment for a goodish time, and wasn't too keen on giving details. He said he was on his own. There's plenty of them do that – want you to believe they had their own place in Bond Street and only lost their money through unexampled misfortunes. You know the sort, I expect, my lord. But I didn't pay a lot of attention to the man, not liking the look of him.'

'I suppose he gave a name.'

'I suppose he did, come to think of it, but I'm dashed if I know what it was. Henry! What did that sneaking little red-haired fellow that came here the other day say his name was? The man that bought that razor off me?'

Henry, a youth with a crest like a cocktaoo, who apparently lodged with his employer, laid aside the Sunday paper which he had been unsuccessfully pretending to read.

'Well, now,' he said, 'I don't remember, Mr Merryweather. Some ordinary name. Was it Brown, now? I think it was Brown.'

'No, it wasn't,' said Mr Merryweather, suddenly enlightened. 'It was Bright, that's what it was. Because don't you remember me saying he didn't act up to his name when it came to setting razors?'

'That's right,' said Henry. 'Of course. Bright. What's the matter with him? Been getting into trouble?'

'I shouldn't wonder if he had,' said Wimsey.

'Police?' suggested Henry, with a sparkling countenance.

'Now, Henry,' said Mr Merryweather. 'Does his lordship here look as if he was the police? I'm surprised at you. You'll never make your way in this profession if you don't know better than that.'

Henry blushed.

'I'm not the police,' said Wimsey, 'but I shouldn't be

surprised if the police did want to get hold of Mr Bright one of these days. But don't you say anything about that. Only, if you should happen to see Mr Bright again, at any time, you might let me know. I'm staying at Wilvercombe at the moment – at the Bellevue – but in case I'm not there, this address will always find me.'

He proffered a card, thanked Mr Merryweather and Henry, and withdrew, triumphant. He felt that he had made progress. Surely there could not be two white Endicott razors, bearing the same evidence of misuse and the same little crack in the ivory. Surely he had tracked the right one, and if so –

Well, then he had only to find Mr Bright. A tramp-barber with sandy hair and a crooked shoulder ought not to be so very difficult to find. But there was always the disagreeable possibility that Mr Bright had been a barber for that one performance only. In which case, his name was almost certainly not Bright.

He thought for a moment, then went into a telephone call-box and rang up the Wilvercombe police.

Superintendent Glaisher answered him. He was interested to hear that Wimsey had traced the early history of the razor. He had not personally observed the crack in the ivory, but if his lordship would hold the line for a moment. . . . Hullo! was Wimsey there? . . . Yes, his lordship was quite right. There was a crack. Almost indistinguishable, but it was there. Certainly it was an odd coincidence. It really looked as though it might bear investigation.

Wimsey spoke again.

Yes, by all means. The Seahampton police should be asked to trace Bright. No doubt it would turn out that Alexis had got the razor off Bright, but it was funny that he couldn't have bought one in Wilvercombe if he wanted one. About three weeks ago, was it? Very good. He would see what could be done. He would also find out whether Alexis had been to Seahampton within that period or whether, alternatively, Bright had been seen in Wilvercombe. He was obliged to Lord Peter for the trouble he had taken in the matter, and if his lordship thought of coming back to Wilvercombe, there had been recent developments which might interest him. It was now pretty certain that it was a case of suicide. Still, one had to go into these matters pretty carefully. Had the body been found? No. The body had not come ashore, and the wind was still holding the tide up and making it impossible to undertake any operations off the Grinders.

IX

THE EVIDENCE OF THE FLAT-IRON

> 'Come, tell me now,
> How sits this ring?'
> *The Bride's Tragedy*

SUNDAY, 21 JUNE

HARRIET VANE and Lord Peter Wimsey sat side by side on the beach, looking out towards the Devil's Flat-Iron. The fresh salt wind blew strongly in from the sea, ruffling Harriet's dark hair. The weather was fine, but the sunshine came only in brilliant bursts, as the driven clouds rolled tumultuously across the bellowing vault of the sky. Over the Grinders, the sea broke in furious patches of white. It was about three o'clock in the afternoon, and the tide was at its lowest, but even so, the Flat-Iron was hardly uncovered, and the Atlantic waves, roaring in, made a heavy breach against its foot. A basket of food lay between the pair, not yet unpacked. Wimsey was drawing plans in the damp sand.

'The thing we want to get,' he said, 'is the time of the death. The police are quite clear about how Alexis came here, and there doesn't seem to be any doubt in the matter, which is a blessing. There's a train from Wilvercombe that stops at Darley Halt on Thursdays at 10.15, to take people in to Heathbury market. Alexis travelled by that train and got out at the Halt. I think it must have been Alexis all right. He was pretty conspicuous with his black beard and his natty gent's outfitting. I think we can take that bit as proved. The guard on the train remembered him, and so did three or four of his fellow-travellers. What's more, his landlady says he left his rooms in time to catch the train, and the booking-clerk remembers him at Wilvercombe. *And*, dear Harriet, there is a first return-ticket from Wilvercombe to that Halt that was never given up and never accounted for.'

'A return-ticket?' asked Harriet.

'A return-ticket. And that, as you so acutely remark, Sherlock, seems to knock the suicide theory on the head. I said as much to the Super, and what was his reply? That suicides, let alone foreign suicides, were that inconsistent there was no accounting for them.'

'So they may be, in real life,' observed Harriet, thoughtfully. 'One wouldn't made an intending suicide take a return-ticket in a book, but real people are different. It might have been a slip, or just habit – or he may not have quite made up his mind to the suicide business.'

'I thought my friend Chief Inspector Parker was the most cautious beggar on the face of the earth, but you beat him. You can knock out habit. I refuse to believe that our dainty Alexis made a habit of travelling to the Halt in order to walk four and a half miles to weep by the sad sea waves. However, we'll just note the return half of the ticket as something that needs explainin'. Very good. Well, now, there was nobody else got off at the Halt, though quite a bunch of people got in, so we don't know what happened to Alexis; but if we allow that he could walk at the moderate rate of three miles an hour, he can't have got to the Flat-Iron later than, say, 11.45.'

'Stop a minute. How about the tide? When was low water on Thursday?'

'At 1.15. I've been into all that. At 11.45 there would be about five feet of water at the foot of the Flat-Iron, but the rock is ten feet high, and rises gradually from the landward side. At 11.45, or very shortly after, our friend could have walked out dry-shod to the rock and sat upon it.'

'Good. We know he did go out dry-shod, so that all fits in nicely. What next?'

'Well, what? Whether he cut his own throat or somebody cut it for him when did he die? It's an awful pity we've lost the body. Even if it turns up now, it won't tell us a thing. It wasn't stiff, of course, when you saw it, and you say you can't tell if it was cold.'

'If,' said Harriet, 'there had been a block of ice on that rock at that time, you could have boiled eggs on it.'

'Tiresome, tiresome. Wait a minute. The blood. How about that? Did you notice whether it was in thick red clots, or whether it was a sort of jelly of white serum, with the red part at the bottom, or anything?'

Harriet shook her head.

'It wasn't. It was liquid.'

'It was *what*?'

'Liquid. When I put my hand into it, it was quite wet.'

'Great Scott! Half a sec. Where was the blood? Splashed all over the place, I suppose.'

'Not exactly. There was a big pool of it underneath the body – just as though he had leaned over and cut his throat into a basin. It had collected in a sort of hollow in the rock.'

'Oh, I see. That explains it. I expect the hollow was full of sea-water left by the tide, and what looked like blood was a mixture of blood and water. I began to think—'

'But listen! It was quite liquid everywhere. It dripped out of his neck. And when I lifted his head up and disturbed the body, it dripped some more. Horrid!'

'But, my darling girl—'

'Yes, and listen again! When I tried to take his glove off, the leather wasn't stiff – it was soft and wet. His hands had been lying right under his throat.'

'Good lord! But—'

'That was the left hand. The right hand was hanging over the side of the rock and I couldn't get at it without

100

clambering over him, which I didn't fancy, somehow. Otherwise, I should have tried that. I was wondering, you see, why the gloves?'

'Yes, yes, I know. But we know there was nothing wrong with his hands. That doesn't matter now. It's the blood – do you realise that, if the blood was still liquid, he *can* only have been dead a few minutes?'

'Oh!' Harriet paused in consternation. 'What a fool I am! I *ought* to have known that. And I thought I was deducing things so nicely! He couldn't have been bleeding slowly to death for some time, I suppose?'

'With his throat cut to the neck-bone? Dear child, pull yourself together. Look here. Blood clots very quickly – more quickly, of course, on a cold surface. In the ordinary way it will clot almost instantaneously on exposure to the air. I daresay it might take a little longer on a hot surface like the rock you describe so graphically. But it couldn't take more than a few minutes. Say ten, to give it an outside limit.'

'Ten minutes. Oh, Peter!'

'Yes?'

'That noise that woke me up. I thought it was a sea-gull. They sound so human. But suppose it was—'

'It must have been. When was that?'

'Two o'clock. I looked at my watch. And I shouldn't think it took me more than ten minutes to reach the rock. But – I say!'

'Well?'

'How about your murder-theory? That's done it in absolutely. If Alexis was murdered at two o'clock, and I was there ten minutes after – *what became of the murderer?*'

Wimsey sat up as suddenly as though he had been stung.

'Oh, *hell!*' he exclaimed. 'Harriet; dear, sweet, beautiful Harriet, say you were mistaken. We *can't* be wrong about the murder. I've staked my reputation with Inspector Um-

101

pelty that it couldn't have been suicide. I shall have to leave the country. I shall never hold my head up again. I shall have to go and shoot tigers in fever-haunted jungles, and die, babbling of murder between my swollen and blackened lips. Say that the blood was clotted. Or say there were footprints you overlooked. Or that there was a boat within hail. Say something.'

'There *was* a boat, but not within hail; because I hailed it.'

'Thank God there was a boat! Perhaps I may leave my bones in Old England yet. What do you mean, not within hail because you hailed it? If the murderer was in the boat, naturally he wouldn't have put back if it had hailed sweet potatoes. I wish you wouldn't give me such shocks. My nerves are not what they were.'

'I don't know much about boats, but this one looked to me a pretty good way out. The wind was blowing in-shore, you know.'

'It doesn't matter. So long as there was a good stiff wind, and he could sail close enough to it, he might have made quite a good way in ten minutes. What sort of boat was it?'

Here Harriet's knowledge failed her. She had put it down as a fishing-boat – not because she could scientifically distinguish a fishing-boat from a 5-metre yacht, but because one naturally, when visiting the seaside, puts down all boats as fishing-boats until otherwise instructed. She thought it had a pointed sort of sail – or sails – she couldn't be sure. She was sure it was not, for example, a fully rigged four-masted schooner, but otherwise one sailing-boat was to her exactly like any other; as it is to most town-bred persons, especially to literary young women.

'Never mind,' said Wimsey. 'We'll be able to trace it all right, All boats must come to shore somewhere, thank goodness. And they're all well known to people along the coast. I only wanted to know what sort of draught the boat was likely to have. You see, if the boat couldn't come right in to the rock, the fellow would have had to row himself in, or swim for it, and that would delay him a good bit. And he'd have to have somebody standing on and off with the boat while he did it, unless he stopped to take in sail, and all that. I mean, you can't just stop a sailing boat and step out of it like a motor-car, leaving it on its own all ready to start. You'd get into difficulties. But that makes no odds. Why shouldn't the murderer have an accomplice? It has frequently happened before. We'd better assume that there were at least two men in a small boat with a very light draught. Then they could bring her close in, and one of the men would bring her round to the wind, while the other waded or rowed alone, did the murder and got back, so that they could make off again without wasting a moment. You see, they've got to do the murder, get back to the boat and clear out to where you saw them within the ten minutes between the cry you heard and the time of your arrival. So we can't allow a lot of time for pulling the boat to shore and making fast and pushing off again and setting sail and all that. Hence I suggest the accomplice.'

'But how about the Grinders?' asked Harriet, rather diffidently. 'I thought it was very dangerous to bring boats close to shore at that point.'

'Blow it! So it is. Well, they must have been very skilful sailors. But *that* would mean further to row or wade, as the case may be. Bother it! I wish we could allow them rather more time.'

'You don't think—' began Harriet. A very unpleasant idea had just struck her. 'You don't think the murderer could have been there, quite close, all the time, swimming under water, or something?'

'He'd have had to come up to breathe.'

'Yes, but I might not have noticed him. There were lots of times when I wasn't looking at the sea at all. He would have heard me coming, and he might have ducked down close under the rock and waited there till I came down to look for the razor. Then he might have dived and swum away while my back was turned. I don't know if it's possible, and I hope it isn't, because I should hate to think he was there all the time – watching me!'

'It's a nasty thought,' said Wimsey. 'I rather hope he was there, though. It would give him a beast of a shock to see you hopping round taking photographs and things. I wonder if there is any cleft in the Flat-Iron where he might have hidden himself. Curse the rock! Why can't it come out and show itself like a man? I say, I'm going down to have a look at it. Turn your modest eyes seawards till I have climbed into a bathing-suit, and I'll go down and explore.'

Not content with this programme, unsuited to a person of her active temperament, Harriet removed, not only her glance, but her person, to the shelter of a handy rock, and emerged, bathing-suited, in time to catch Wimsey as he ran down over the sand.

'And he strips better than I should have expected,' she admitted candidly to herself. 'Better shoulders than I realised, and, thank Heaven, calves to his legs.' Wimsey, who was rather proud of his figure, would hardly have been flattered could he have heard this modified rapture, but for the moment he was happily unconcerned about himself. He entered the sea near the Flat-Iron with caution, not knowing what bumps and boulders he might encounter, swam a few strokes to encourage himself, and then popped his head out to remark that the water was beastly cold and that it would do Harriet good to come in.

Harriet came in, and agreed that the water was cold and the wind icy. Agreed on this point, they returned to the Flat-Iron, and felt their way carefully round it. Presently Wimsey, who had been doing some under-water investigation on the Wilvercombe side of the rock, came out, spluttering, and asked if Harriet had come down on that side or on the other to hunt for the razor.

'On the other,' said Harriet. 'It was like this, I was up on top of the rock with the body, like this.' She climbed out, walked up to the top of the rock, and stood shivering in the wind. 'I looked round on both sides of me like this.'

'You didn't look down in this direction, by any chance?' inquired Wimsey's head, standing up sleek as a seal's out of the water.

'No, I don't think so. Then, after I'd fussed about with the corpse a bit, I got down this way. I sat on something just about here and took my shoes and stockings off and tucked my things up. Then I came round in this direction and groped about under the rock. There was about eighteen inches of water then. There are about five feet now, I should think.'

'Can you—?' began Wimsey. A wave slopped suddenly over his head and extinguished him. Harriet laughed.

'Can you see me?' he went on, blowing the water out of his nostrils.

'I can't. But I heard you. It was very amusing.'

'Well, restrain your sense of humour. You can't see me.'

'No. There's a bulge in the rock. Where, exactly, are you, by the way?'

'Standing in a nice little niche, like a saint over a cathedral door. It's just about the size of a coffin. Six feet high or thereabouts, with a pretty little roof and room to squeeze in rather tightly sideways, if you're not what the Leopard called "too vulgar big". Come round and try it for yourself.'

'What a sweet little spot,' said Harriet, scrambling round and taking Wimsey's place in the niche. 'Beautifully screened from all sides, except from the sea. Even at quite low tide one couldn't be seen, unless, of course, somebody happened to come round and stand just opposite the opening. I certainly didn't do that. How horrible! The man must have been in here all the time.'

'Yes, I think it's more plausible than the boat idea.'

'Bright!' said Harriet.

'I'm so glad you think so.'

'I didn't mean that – and it was my idea in the first place. I meant Bright, the man who bought the razor. Didn't the hairdresser person say he was a small man – smaller than you, anyway?'

'So he did. One up to you. I wish we could get hold of Bright. I wonder – Oh, I say! I've found something!'

'Oh, what?'

'It's a ring – the sort of thing you tie boats up to, driven right into the rock. It's under water and I can't see it properly, but it's about five feet off the ground and it feels smooth and new, not corroded. Does that help with our boat-theory at all, I wonder?'

'Well,' said Harriet, looking round at the lonely sea and shore, 'there doesn't seem to be much reason why anyone should habitually tie a boat up here.'

'There doesn't. In that case the murderer, if there was one—'

'We're taking him for granted, aren't we?'

'Yes. He may have put this here for his own private use. Either he tied a boat up, or he—'

'Or he didn't.'

'I was going to say, used it for something else, but I'm dashed if I know what.'

'Well, that's fearfully helpful. I say, I'm getting cold. Let's swim about a bit, and then get dressed and discuss it.'

Whether it was the swim or the subsequent race over the sands to get warm that stimulated Harriet's brain is not certain, but when they were again sitting by the lunch-basket, she found herself full of ideas.

'Look here! If you were a murderer, and you saw an interfering woman pottering about among the evidence and then going off in search of help, what would you do?'

'Leg it in the opposite direction.'

'I wonder. Would you? Wouldn't you like to keep an eye on her? Or possibly even do away with her? You know, it would have been fearfully easy for Bright – if we may call him so for the moment – to slaughter me then and there.'

'But why should he? Of course he wouldn't. He was trying to make the murder look like suicide. In fact, you were a very valuable witness for him. You'd seen the body and you could prove that there really was a body, in case of its subsequently getting lost. And you could prove that there actually was a weapon there and that therefore suicide was more likely than not. And you could swear to the absence of footprints – another point in favour of suicide. No, my dear girl, the murderer would cherish you as the apple of his eye.'

'You're right; he would. Always supposing he wanted the body found. Of course there are lots of reasons why he should want it found. If he inherited under a will, for instance, and had to prove the death.'

'I don't fancy friend Alexis will have left much in his will. In fact, I'm pretty sure he didn't. And there might be other reasons for wanting to tell the world he was dead.'

'Then you think that when I'd gone, the murderer just trotted off home to Lesston Hoe? He can't have gone the other way, unless he deliberately kept behind me. Do you think he did that? He may have followed me up to see what I was going to do about it.'

'He might. You can't say he didn't. Especially as you left the main road quite soon after, to go up to the farm.'

'Suppose he missed me there and went on ahead of me along the road to Wilvercombe. Would it be possible to find out if he had passed over the level-crossing at the Halt, for instance? Or – I say! Suppose he'd gone along the main road and then turned back again, so as to pretend he'd come from Wilvercombe?'

'Then you'd have met him.'

'Well, suppose I did?'

'But – oh! lord, yes – Mr What's-his-name from London! By Jove!'

'Perkins. Yes. I wonder. Could anybody be genuinely as foolish as Perkins appeared? He was a rat of a man, too, quite small, and he *was* sandy-haired.'

'He was short-sighted, didn't you say, and wore glasses. Merryweather didn't say anything about Bright's wearing them.'

'It may have been a disguise. They may have been quite plain glass – I didn't examine them, à la Dr Thorndyke, to see whether they reflected a candle-flame upside-down or right way up. And, you know, I do think it's awfully funny the way Mr Perkins simply evaporated when we got to the village shops. He was keen enough to come with me before, and then, just as I'd got into touch with civilisation, he went and vanished. It does look queer. If it was Bright, he might just have hung round to get some idea of what I was going to say to the police, and then removed himself before the inquiry. Good lord! Fancy me, meekly trotting along for a mile and a half hand in hand with a murderer!'

'Juicy,' said Wimsey, 'very juicy! We'll have to look more carefully into Mr Perkins. (Can that name be real? It seems almost too suitable.) You know where he went?'

'No.'

'He hired a car in the village and got himself driven to Wilvercombe railway station. He is thought to have taken a train to somewhere, but the place was full of hikers and trampers and trippers that day, and so far they haven't traced him further. They'll have to try again. This thing is getting to look almost too neat. Let's see how it goes. First of all, Alexis arrives by the 10.15 at the Halt and proceeds on foot or otherwise, to the Flat-Iron. Why, by the way?'

'To keep an appointment with Perkins, presumably.

Alexis wasn't the sort to take a long country walk for the intoxicating pleasure of sitting on a rock.'

'True, O Queen. Live for ever. He went to keep an appointment with Perkins at two o'clock.'

'Earlier, surely; or why arrive by the 10.15?'

'That's easy. The 10.15 is the only train that stops there during the morning.'

'Then why not go by car?'

'Yes, indeed. Why not? I imagine it was because he had no car of his own and didn't want anybody to know where he was going.'

'Then why didn't he hire a car and drive it himself?'

'Couldn't drive a car. Or his credit is bad in Wilvercombe. Or – no!'

'What?'

'I was going to say: because he didn't intend to come back. But that won't work, because of the return-ticket. Unless he took the ticket absentmindedly, he *did* mean to come back. Or perhaps he just wasn't certain about it. He might take a return-ticket on the off-chance – it would only be a matter of a few pence one way or the other. But he couldn't very well just take a hired car and leave it there.'

'N-no. Well, he could, if he wasn't particular about other people's property. But I can think of another reason for it. He'd have to leave the car on top of the cliff where it could be seen. Perhaps he didn't want people to know that anybody was down on the Flat-Iron at all.'

'That won't do. Two people having a chat on the Flat-Iron would be conspicuous objects from the cliff, car or no car.'

'Yes, but unless you went down close to them, you wouldn't know who they were; whereas you can always check up on a car by the number-plates.'

'That's a fact – but it seems to me rather a thin explanation, all the same. Still, let it stand. For some reason Alexis thought he would attract less attention if he went by train. In that case, I suppose he walked along the road – he wouldn't want to invite inquiry by taking a lift from anybody.'

'Certainly not. Only why in the world he should have picked on such an exposed place for the appointment—'

'You think they ought to have had their chat behind a rock, or under some trees, or in a disused shed or a chalk quarry or something like that?'

'Wouldn't it seem more natural?'

'No. Not if you didn't want to be overheard. If you ever need to talk secrets, be sure you avoid the blasted oak, the privet hedge and the old summer-house in the Italian garden – all the places where people can stealthily creep up under cover with their ears flapping. You choose the middle of a nice open field, or the centre of a lake – or a rock like the Flat-Iron, where you can have half-an-hour's notice of anyone's arrival. And that reminds me, in one of your books—'

'Bother my books! I quite see what you mean. Well, then, some time or the other, Bright arrives to keep his appointment. How? And when?'

'By walking through the edge of the water, from any point you like to suggest. As for the time, I can only suggest that it was while you, my child, were snoozing over *Tristram Shandy*; and I fancy he must have come from the Wilvercombe side, otherwise he would have seen you. He'd hardly have taken the risk of committing a murder if he knew positively that somebody was lying within a few yards of him.'

'I think it was pretty careless of him not to take a look round the rocks in any case.'

'True; but apparently he didn't do it. He commits the murder, anyhow, and the time of that is fixed at two o'clock. So he must have reached the Flat-Iron between

1.30 and 2 – or possibly between one o'clock and two o'clock – because, if you were lunching and reading in your cosy corner, you probably wouldn't have seen or heard him come. It couldn't be earlier than 1 p.m., because you looked along the shore then and were positive that there wasn't a living soul visible from the cliffs.'

'Quite right.'

'Good. He commits the murder. Poor old Alexis lets out a yell when he sees the razor, and you wake up. Did you shout then, or anything?'

'No.'

'Or burst into song?'

'No.'

'Or run about with little ripples of girlish laughter?'

'No. At least, I ran about a few minutes later, but I wasn't making a loud noise.'

'I wonder why the murderer didn't start off home again at once. If he had, you'd have seen him. Let me see. Ah, I was forgetting the papers! He had to get the papers!'

'What papers?'

'Well, I won't swear it was papers. It may have been the Rajah's diamond or something. He wanted something off the body, of course. And just as he was stooping over his victim, he heard you skipping about among the shingle. Sound carries a long way by the water. The baffled villain pauses, and then, as the sounds come nearer, he hurries down to the seaward side of the Flat-Iron and hides there.'

'With all his clothes on?'

'I'd forgotten that. He'd be a bit damp-looking when he came out, wouldn't he? No. Without his clothes on. He left his clothes at wherever it was he started to walk along the shore. He probably put on a bathing-dress, so that if anybody saw him he would just be a harmless sun-bather paddling about in the surf.'

'Did he put the razor in the pocket of his regulation suit?'

111

'No; he had it in his hand, or slung round his neck. Don't ask silly questions. He'd wait in his little niche until you'd gone; then he'd hurry back along the shore—'

'Not in the direction of Wilvercombe.'

'Blow! Obviously, you'd have seen him. But not if he kept close to the cliff. He wouldn't have to bother so much about footprints when the tide was coming in. He could manage that all right. Then he'd come up the cliff at the point where he originally got down, follow the main road towards Wilvercombe, turn back at some point or other, and meet you on the way back. How's that?'

'It's very neat.'

'The more I look at it, the more I like it. I adore the thought of Bright's being Perkins. I say, though, how about this lop-sided, hunch-backed business. Was Perkins upright as a willow-wand, or how?'

'Not by any means. But I shouldn't have called him actually crooked. More sloppy and round-shouldered. He had a rucksack on his back, and he was walking a bit lame, because he said he had a blister on his foot.'

'That would be a good way of disguising any one-sidedness in his appearance. You're always apt to hunch up a bit on the lame side. Bright-Perkins is our man. We ought to get the police on to this right away, only I do so want my lunch. What time is it? *Four* o'clock. I'll slip along in the car and telephone to Glaisher, and then come back. Why should we give up our picnic for any number of murderers?'

X

THE EVIDENCE OF THE POLICE-INSPECTOR

> 'My life upon 't some miser,
> Who in the secret hour creeps to his hoard,
> And, kneeling at the altar of his love,
> Worships that yellow devil, gold.'
>
> *The Bride's Tragedy*

MONDAY, 22 JUNE

'YOU may say what you like, my lord,' said Inspector Umpelty, 'and I don't mind admitting that the Super is a bit inclined to your way of thinking, but it was suicide for all that, and if I was a sporting man, I wouldn't mind having a bet on it. There's no harm done by tracing this fellow Bright, because, if the identification of the razor is correct, that's who this Alexis must have brought it from, but there's no doubt in my mind that when the poor chap left his lodgings on Thursday, he never meant to come back. You've only got to look at the place. Everything tidied away, bills all paid up, papers burnt in the grate – you might say he'd regular said good-bye and kissed his hand to everything.'

'Did he take his latch-key with him?' asked Wimsey.

'Yes, he did. But that's nothing. A man keeps his key in his pocket and he mightn't think to put it out. But he left pretty well everything else in order. You'd be surprised. Not so much as an envelope, there wasn't. Must have had a regular old bonfire there. Not a photograph, not a line that would tell you anything about who he was or where he came from. Clean sweep of the lot.'

'No hope of recovering anything from the ashes?'

'Not a thing. Naturally, Mrs Lefranc – that's the landlady – had had the grate cleaned out on the Thursday morning, but she told me that everything had been broken down into black flinders and dust. And there was a rare old lot of it. I know, because she showed it me in the dust-bin. There certainly was nothing there you could have made out with a microscope. As you know, my lord, generally these folk aren't thorough – they leave a few bits half-burnt, maybe, but this chap had gone the right way about it and no mistake. He must have torn everything into small scraps first, and burnt it on a hot fire and beaten it into atoms with the poker. "Well," I said to Mrs Lefranc, "this is a nice set-out, this is!" And so it was, too.'

'Any books or anything with writing in the fly-leaves?'

'Just a few novels, with "Paul Alexis" inside, and some with nothing at all, and one or two paper-backed books written in Chinese.'

'Chinese?'

'Well, it looked like it. Russian, maybe. Not in proper letters, anyhow. You can see them any time you like, but I don't expect you'll get much out of them. One or two history-books there was, mostly about Russia and that. But no writing of any kind.'

'Any money?'

'No.'

'Had he a banking account?'

'Yes; he had a small account with Lloyds. Matter of a little over three hundred pounds. But he drew the whole lot out three weeks ago.'

'Did he? Whatever for? It wouldn't cost him all that to buy a razor.'

'No, but I said he'd been settling his debts.'

'Three hundred pounds worth of them?'

'I don't say that. Fact is we can't trace more than twenty

pounds odd. But he may have owed money in lots of places, As he's burnt all his papers, you see, it's a bit difficult to tell. We shall make inquiries, naturally. But I shouldn't be surprised if those hundred pounds had gone to some girl or other. There's that Leila Garland – a hard-boiled little piece if ever there was one. *She* could tell a lot if she liked, I daresay, but we aren't allowed to ask anybody any questions these days. If they say they won't answer, they won't and there's an end of it. You can't force 'em.'

'Leila Garland – that's the girl he used to go with?'

'That's it, my lord, and from what I can make out she turned Mister Alexis down good and hard. Terrible cut up he was about it, too, according to her. She's got another fellow now – sort of friend of Alexis, but a cut above him, as far as I can make out. Sort of dago fellow; leads the orchestra down at the Winter Gardens, and makes a pretty good thing out of it, I fancy. You know the sort, all la-di-dah and snake-skin shoes. Nothing wrong with him, though, as far as that goes. He was quite frank about it, and so was the girl. Alexis introduced them, and presently the young woman got the idea that she could do better with the dago than with Alexis. She says Alexis was getting very close with his money, and didn't seem to have his mind as much on Miss Leila as he might have. Possibly he had his eye on somebody else all the time and that was where the money went. Anyhow, Leila makes up her mind to give him the push and takes up with the dago, Luis da Soto, instead. Of course there was a scene, and Alexis threatens to make away with himself—'

'Did he say anything about throat-cutting?'

'Well, no, he didn't. Said he'd take poison. But what's the odds? He said he'd make away with himself and he's done it, and here we are.'

'Did you, by any chance, find any poison – you know, sleepy stuff or anything of that sort – in his room?'

'Not a thing,' said the Inspector, triumphantly.

'H'm.'

'But Inspector,' put in Harriet, who had been listening to this conversation in becoming silence, 'if you think Alexis had another girl in tow, why should he commit suicide when Leila Garland turned him down?'

'I couldn't say, I'm sure, miss. Maybe the other one turned him down as well.'

'And left him a low, lorn crittur, with all the world contrairy with him,' said Wimsey.

'Yes, and then there was this Mrs Weldon. We found out about her through these other girls. Wouldn't you say a prospect like that was enough to make any young fellow cut his throat?'

'He could have gone away,' said Harriet.

'And suppose he owed her money and she turned crusty and threatened to put him in court? What about that?'

'Perhaps the three hundred pounds—' began Wimsey.

'Oh, no, *no!*' cried Harriet indignantly. 'You mustn't think that. It's absolutely ridiculous. Why, the poor woman was infatuated with him. He could have turned her round his little finger. She'd have given him anything he wanted. Besides, she told me he wouldn't take her money.'

'Ah! But supposing he'd have given her the go-by, miss. She might have cut up rough about that.'

'*She* would have been the one to kill herself then,' said Harriet, firmly. 'She wouldn't have harmed him for the world, poor soul. Put him in court? Nonsense!'

'Now you know very well, miss,' said Inspector Umpelty, 'that it says in the Bible that the infernal regions, begging your pardon, knows no fury like a woman scorned. I've always remembered that from my school-days, and I find it gives a very useful line to follow in our way of business. If this Mrs Weldon—'

'Rubbish!' said Harriet. 'She'd never have done anything of the sort. I *know* she wouldn't.'

'Ah!' Inspector Umpelty winked in a friendly manner at Wimsey. 'When the ladies get to knowing things by this feminine intuition and all that, there's no arguing with it. But what I say is, let's suppose it, just for the moment.'

'I won't suppose it,' retorted Harriet.

'We seem to have reached a no-thoroughfare,' remarked Wimsey. 'Let's leave that for the time being, Inspector. You can come and suppose it in the bar, quietly, later on. Though I don't think it very likely myself. It's our turn to suppose something. Suppose a fishing-boat had wanted to come in at the Flat-Iron just about low tide on Thursday – could she do it?'

'Easy, my lord. Some of these boats don't draw more than a foot of water. You could bring her in beautifully, provided you kept clear of the Grinders, and remembered to reckon with the current.'

'A stranger might get into difficulties, perhaps.'

'He might, but not if he was a good seaman and could read a chart. He could bring a small boat up within a dozen feet of the Flat-Iron any day, unless the wind was setting with the current across the bay, when he might get driven on to the rocks if he wasn't careful.'

'I see. That makes it all very interesting. We are supposing a murder, you see, Inspector, and we've thought out two ways of doing it. We'd be glad to have your opinion.'

Inspector Umpelty listened with an indulgent smile to the rival theories of the Man in the Fishing-boat and the Man in the Niche, and then said:

'Well, miss, all I can say is, I'd like to read some of those books of yours. It's wonderful, the way you work it all in. But about that boat. That's queer, that is. We've been trying to get a line on that, because whoever was in it must have seen something. Most of the fishing-boats were out off

Shelly Point, but there's a few of them I haven't checked up on, and of course, it might be some of the visitors from Wilvercombe or Lesston Hoe. We're always warning these amateurs to keep from the Grinders, but do they? No. You'd think some of them was out for a day's suicide, the way they go on. But I've got an idea who it was, all the same.'

'How about those cottages along the coast, where I went to try and get help?' asked Harriet. 'Surely they must have seen the boat? I thought those sort of people knew every boat in the place by sight.'

'That's just it,' replied the Inspector. 'We've asked them and they're all struck blind and dumb, seemingly. That's why I say I think I could put a name to the boat. But we'll find a way to make them come across with it, never fear. They're a surly lot, those Pollocks and Moggeridges, and up to no good, in my opinion. They're not popular with the other fishers, and when you find a whole family boycotted by the rest of them, there's usually something at the back of it.'

'At any rate,' said Wimsey, 'I think we've got the actual time of the death pretty well fixed by now. That ought to help.'

'Yes,' admitted Inspector Umpelty, 'if what you and the lady tell me is correct, that does seem to settle it. Not but what I'd like a doctor's opinion on it, no offence to you. But I think you're right, all the same. It's a great pity you happened to fall asleep when you did, miss.' He looked reproachfully at Harriet.

'But wasn't it lucky I was there at all?'

The Inspector agreed that it was.

'And taking this question of the time as settled,' he went on, 'we've got some information to hand now that may clear matters up a bit. At least, from all I can see, it just goes to show that this murder-stuff is clean impossible, as I've said it was all along. But if we prove that, then we're all right, aren't we?'

The conference was taking place in the Inspector's cosy little villa in the suburbs of the town. Rising, Mr Umpelty went to a cupboard and extracted a large sheaf of official reports.

'You see, my lord, we haven't been idle, even though suicide looks more probable than anything else on the face of things. We had to take all the possibilities into account, and we've gone over the district with, as you might say, a magnifying glass.'

After an inspection of the reports, Wimsey was obliged to admit that this boast seemed justified. Chance had helped the police very considerably. An application had recently been made by the local authorities to the County Council to have the coast-road between Lesston Hoe and Wilvercombe put into better repair. The County Council, conscious that times were bad and that money was tight, had courteously replied that it did not think there was sufficient traffic along the said coast-road to justify the proposed expenditure. As a result of these negotiations, persons had been appointed (at a modest wage) by the County Council to take a census of the vehicular traffic passing along the said road, and one of these watchers had been stationed, during the whole of Thursday, 18 June, at the junction formed by the coast-road and the high road from Lesston Hoe to Heathbury. At the other end of the twelve miles or so which interested the detectives was Darley Halt, where, as Harriet had already discovered for herself, the gates were always shut unless particularly summoned to be opened for a passing vehicle. On either side of the railway gates was a wicket for foot passengers, but this was of the kind that does not admit anything so large even as a push-cycle. It was clear, therefore, that unless the hypothetical murderer had come on foot, he must have been seen at one end or other of the road, or else have come from some intermediate farm. During the past four days, the police had carefully investigated the bona fides of every traveller over this section of the road, Every car, motor-cycle, push-cycle, van, lorry, wagon and beast had been laboriously checked up and accounted for. Nothing had been unearthed to suggest suspicion of any kind. Indeed, all the persons using the road were local inhabitants, well known to all the police officers, and each one of them had been able to give an exact account of his or her movements during the day. This was not so surprising as it may appear, since nearly all of them were either tradesmen, accomplishing a given round in a given time, or farmers with business on their land or in the adjacent towns, who had witnesses to prove their departure and arrival. The only persons whose times could not very well be checked were those who loitered attendance upon cows and sheep in transit; but, apart from the extreme improbability of these rustics having gone out of their way to cut a gentleman's throat with an Endicott razor, Inspector Umpelty was quite ready to vouch personally for all of them.

'In fact, my lord,' he said, 'you may take it from me that all these people we have checked up are all right. You can put them right out of your mind. The only possibility left now for your murderer is that he came by sea, or else on foot along the shore from either Wilvercombe or Lesston Hoe, and, as this young lady says, Wilvercombe is the more probable direction of the two, because anybody coming from Lesston Hoe would have seen her and put his crime off to a more convenient season, as Shakespeare says.'

'Very well,' said Wimsey. 'All right. We'll admit that. The murderer didn't take any sort of wheeled conveyance for any part of the journey. Still, that leaves a lot of possibilities open. We'll wash out the Lesston Hoe side altogether and only take the Wilvercombe direction. We now have at least three suggestions. One: the murderer walked by the road from Wilvercombe or Darley, came down on to the beach at some point out of view from the Flat-Iron, and thence proceeded by the shore. Two: he came from one of those two cottages where the fishermen live (Pollock and Moggeridge, I think you said the names were). You don't mean to say you'll answer personally for those men, do you, Inspector?'

'No, I don't – only they weren't there,' retorted the Inspector, with spirit. 'Moggeridge and his two sons were over in Wilvercombe, buying some stuff there – I've got witnesses to that. Old Pollock was out in his boat, because Freddy Baines saw him, and his eldest boy was probably with him. We're going to pull those two in, and that's why I said the murderer might have come by sea. The only other Pollock is a boy of about fourteen, and you can't suppose it was him that did it, nor yet any of the women and children.'

'I see. Well then. Three: the murderer walked the whole way along the coast from Darley or Wilvercombe. By the way, didn't you say there was somebody camping out along there, just beyond Darley Halt.'

'Yes,' said Harriet, 'a square-built sort of man, who spoke – well, not quite like a countryman – like a gentleman of the country sort.'

'If anybody had passed that way, he might have seen him.'

'So he might,' replied the Inspector, 'but unfortunately we haven't laid hands on that particular gentleman, though we've got inquiries out after him. He packed up and departed early on Friday morning, taking his belongings in a Morgan. He'd been camping at the bottom of Hinks's Lane since Tuesday, and gave the name of Martin.'

'Is that so? And he disappeared immediately after the crime. Isn't that a trifle suspicious?'

'Not a bit.' Inspector Umpelty was quite triumphant. 'He was having his lunch at the Three Feathers in Darley at one o'clock and he didn't leave till 1.30. If you'll tell me how a man could walk four and a half miles in half-an-hour, I'll get a warrant made out for Mr Martin's arrest.'

'Your trick, Inspector. Well – let's see. Murder at two o'clock – four and a half miles to go. That means that the murderer can't have passed through Darley later than 12.50 at the very outside. That's allowing him to do four miles an hour, and since he would have to do at least part of the distance along the sand it's probably an over-estimate. On the other hand, he wouldn't be likely to do less than three miles an hour. That gives 12.30 as his earliest time – unless, of course, he sat and talked to Alexis for some time before he cut his throat.'

'That's just it, my lord. It's all so vague. In any case, Mr Martin isn't much good to us, because he spent Thursday morning in Wilvercombe – or so he mentioned to the landlord of the Feathers.'

'What a pity! He might have been a valuable witness. I suppose you'll go on looking for him, though it doesn't seem as if he'd be very much good to us. Did anybody notice the number of his Morgan?'

'Yes; it belongs to a London garage, where they hire out cars to be driven by the hirers. Mr Martin came in there last Thursday week, paid his deposit in cash and returned the 'bus on Sunday night. He said he had given up his house and had no fixed address, but gave a reference to a Cambridge banker. His driving-licence was made out in the name of Martin all right. There was no trouble about the insurance, because the garage uses a form of policy that covers all their cars irrespective of who is driving them.'

'But wasn't there an address on the driving-licence?'

'Yes; but that was the address of the house he'd given up, so they took no notice of that.'

'Do garage-owners usually ask to see people's driving licences?'

'I don't know that they do. Apparently this fellow showed it to them without being asked.'

'Curious. You'd almost think he was going out of his way to forestall criticism. How about the bank?'

'That's all right. Mr Haviland Martin has been a depositor there for five years. Introduced by another client. No irregularity.'

'I suppose they didn't mention the name of his referee nor the amount of his deposit.'

'Well, no. Banks don't care about giving away information. You see, we've absolutely nothing against this fellow Martin.'

'Exactly. All the same, I'd rather like to have a chat with him. There are points about him which seem to me suggestive, as Sherlock Holmes would say. What do you think, my dear Robert Templeton?'

'I think,' replied Harriet, promptly, 'that if I had been inventing a way for a murderer to reach an appointed spot and leave it again, complete with bag and baggage and without leaving more trail than was absolutely unavoidable, I should have made him act very much as Mr Martin has acted. He would open an account under a false name at a bank, giving the bank's address to the garage-proprietor as sole reference, hire a car and pay cash and probably close the account again in the near future.'

'As you say. Still, the dismal fact remains that Mr Martin obviously did not do the murder, always supposing that the Feathers' clock can be relied on. A little further investigation is indicated, I fancy. Five years seems a longish time to premeditate a crime. You might, perhaps, keep an eye on that bank – only don't make a row about it, or you may frighten the bird away.'

'That's so, my lord. All the same, I'd feel more enthusiastic, I don't mind saying, if I had any sort of proof that there really was a murder committed. Just at present it's a bit thin, you'll allow.'

'So it is; but there are quite a lot of small things that point that way. Taken separately, they aren't important, but taken together, they have a funny look. There's the razor, and the gloves, and the return-ticket, and the good spirits Alexis was in on the day before his death. And now there's this funny story of the mysterious gentleman who arrived at Darley in time to take a front seat for the crime, and then cleared off with such remarkable precautions to obscure his name and address.'

Inspector Umpelty's reply was cut short by the ringing of his telephone. He listened for a moment to its mysterious cluckings, said 'I'll be along at once, sir,' and rang off.

'Something else funny seems to have turned up,' he said. 'You'll excuse me if I rush off; I'm wanted down at the Station.'

XI

THE EVIDENCE OF THE FISHERMAN

> 'There's a fellow
> With twisting root-like hair up to his eyes,
> And they are streaked with red and starting out
> Under their bristling brows; his crooked tusks
> Part, like a hungry wolf's, his cursing mouth;
> His head is frontless, and a swinish mane
> Grows o'er his shoulders: brown and warty hands,
> Like roots, with pointed nails – He is the man.'
>
> *Fragment*

MONDAY, 22 JUNE

WIMSEY had not very long to wait before hearing the latest development. He had returned to the Bellevue for lunch, and was having a preliminary refresher in the bar, when he felt a smart tap on his shoulder.

'Lord, Inspector! How you startled me! All right, it's a fair cop. What's it for this time?'

'I just dropped along to tell you the latest, my lord. I thought you'd like to hear it. It's given us something to think about, I don't mind telling you.'

'Has it? You look quite agitated. I expect you're out of practice. It is exhausting when you're not used to it. Have one?'

'Thank you, my lord. I don't mind if I do. Now, look here – you remember about our young friend's banking account and the three hundred pounds?'

'Sure thing.'

'Well' – the Inspector dropped his voice to a hoarse whisper – 'we've found out what he did with it.'

Wimsey registered expectation, but this was not enough. Inspector Umpelty evidently felt that he had got hold of a really choice morsel, and was not going to let it go without full dramatic honours.

'I'll buy it, Inspector. *What* did he do with it?'

'Guess, my lord. You can have three guesses, and I bet you anything you like you don't hit on it. Not in twenty guesses.'

'Then I mustn't waste your valuable time. Go on. Have a heart. Don't keep me in such ghastly suspense. What *did* he do with it?'

'He went,' said the Inspector, lusciously, 'and turned it into gold.'

'Into WHAT?'

'Three hundred golden sovereigns – that's what he turned it into. Three hundred round, golden jimmy o' goblins.'

Wimsey stared blankly at him.

'Three hundred – oh, look here, Inspector, a shock like this is more than frail flesh and blood can stand. There isn't so much gold in the country. I haven't seen more than ten gold sovereigns together since I fought at my grandpapa's side at the Battle of Waterloo. Gold! How did he get it? How did he wangle it? They don't hand it out to you at the banks nowadays. Did he rob the Mint?'

'No, he didn't. He changed notes for it quite honestly. But it's a queer tale for all that. I'll tell you how it was, and how we come to know of it. You may remember that there was a photograph of Alexis published in the newspapers last week?'

'Yes, enlarged from that hotel group they took at the Gala Night last Christmas. I saw it.'

'That's right. Only one we could find; Alexis didn't leave anything about. Well, yesterday we had a quaint old bird calling at the Station – Gladstone sort of collar, whiskery bits, four-in-hand tie, cotton gloves, square-crowned bowler, big green gamp – all complete. Said he lived up Princemoor way. He pulls a newspaper out of his pocket and points to the photograph. "I hear you want information about this poor young man," he pipes up. "Yes, we do," says the Super, "you know anything about it, Dad?" "Nothing at all about his death," says the old boy, "but I had a very curious little transaction with him three weeks ago," he says, "and I thought you perhaps ought to know about it," he says. "Quite right, Dad," says the Super. "Go ahead." So he went ahead and told us all about it.

'It seems it was like this. You may remember seeing a while ago – not more than a month or so back – a bit in the papers about a queer old girl who lived all alone in a house in Seahampton with no companion except about a hundred cats. A Miss Ann Bennett – but the name don't matter. Well, one day the usual thing happens. Blinds left down, no smoke from kitchen chimney, milk not taken in, cats yowling fit to break your heart. Constable goes in with a ladder and finds the old lady dead in her bed. Inquest verdict is "death from natural causes", which means old age and semi-starvation with neglected pneumonia on top of it. And of course plenty of money in the house, including four hundred gold sovereigns in the matterss. It's always happening.'

Wimsey nodded.

'Yes. Well, then, the long-lost next-of-kin turns up and who should it be but this old chap from Princemoor, Abel Bennett. There's a will found, leaving everything to him, and begging him to look after the poor pussies. He's the executor, and he steps in and takes charge. Very good. On the day after the inquest, along comes our young friend Paul Alexis – name correctly given and person identified by the photograph. He tells old Bennett a rambling kind of story about wanting gold sovereigns for some purpose or other. Something about wanting to buy a diamond from a foreign rajah who didn't understand bank-notes – some bosh of that kind.'

'He got that out of a book, I expect,' said Wimsey. 'I've seen something like it somewhere.'

'Very likely. Old Bennett, who seems to have had more wits than his sister, didn't swallow the tale altogether, because, as he said, the young fellow didn't look to him like a person who would be buying diamonds off rajahs, but after all it's not criminal to want gold, and it was none of his business what it was wanted for. He put up a few objections, and Alexis offered him three hundred pounds in Bank of England notes, plus a twenty-pound bonus, in exchange for three hundred sovereigns. Old Abel wasn't adverse to a buckshee twenty quid and was willing to hand over, on condition he might have the notes vetted for him at a Seahampton bank. Alexis was agreeable and pulled out the notes then and there. To cut a long story short, they went to the Seahampton branch of the London & Westminster and got the O.K. on the notes, after which Bennett handed over the gold and Alexis took it away in a leather hand-bag. And that's all there is to it. But we've checked up the dates with the bank-people, and it's quite clear that Alexis drew his money out here for the purpose of changing it into gold as soon as ever he saw the account of Ann Bennett's death in the papers. But why he wanted it or what he did with it, I can't tell you, no more than the Man in the Moon.'

'Well,' said Wimsey, 'I always knew there were one or two oddities about this case, but I don't mind admitting that this beats me. Why on earth should anybody want to clutter himself up with all that gold? I suppose we can dismiss the story of the Rajah's Diamond. A £300 diamond is nothing very out of the way, and if you wanted one you could buy it in Bond street, without paying in gold or dragging in Indian potentates.'

'That's a fact. Besides, where are you going to find a rajah who doesn't understand Bank of England notes? These fellers aren't savages, not by any means. Why, lots of them have been to Oxford.'

Wimsey made suitable acknowledgement of this tribute to his own university.

'The only explanation that suggests itself to me,' he said, 'is that Alexis was contemplating a flitting to some place where Bank of England notes wouldn't pass current. But I hardly know where that could be at this time of day. Central Asia?'

'It may not be that, my lord. From the way he burnt everything before he left, it looks as though he didn't mean to leave any trace of where he was going. Now, you can't very well lose a Bank of England note. The numbers are bound to turn up somewhere or other, if you wait long enough. Currency notes are safe, but it is quite possible that you might have difficulty in exchanging them in foreign parts, once you were off the beaten track. It's my opinion Alexis meant to get away, and he took the gold because it was the only form of money that will pass everywhere and tell no tale. He probably wouldn't be asked about it at the Customs, and if he was, they would be very unlikely to search him.'

'True. I think you're right, Inspector. But, I say, you realise this knocks the suicide theory on the head all right?'

'It's beginning to look like it, my lord,' admitted Mr Umpelty, handsomely. 'Unless, of course, the stuff was paid out to some party in this country. For instance, suppose Alexis was being blackmailed by someone who wanted to skip. That party might be wanting gold for the very reasons we've been talking about, and he might get Alexis to do the job of getting it for him, so that he shouldn't appear in it himself. Alexis pays up, and goes off the deep end and cuts his throat.'

'You're very ingenious,' said Wimsey. 'But I still believe I'm right, though if it is a case of murder, it's been so neatly worked out that there doesn't seem to be much of a loophole in it. Unless it's the razor. Look here, Inspector, I've got an idea about that razor, if you'll let me carry it out. Our one hope is to tempt the murderer, if there is one, into making a mistake by trying to be too clever.'

He pushed the glasses aside and whispered into the Inspector's ear.

'There's something in that,' said Inspector Umpelty. 'I don't see why it shouldn't be tried. It may clinch the matter straight off, one way or another. You'd better ask the Super, but if he's got no objection, I'd say, go ahead. Why not come round and put it to him straight away?'

On arriving at the police-station, Wimsey and the Inspector found the Superintendent engaged with a crabbed old gentleman in a fisherman's jersey and boots, who appeared to be suffering under a sense of grievance.

'Can't a man take 'is own boat out when he likes and where he likes? Sea's free to all, ain't it?'

'Of course it is, Pollock. But if you were up to no mischief, why take that tone about it? You aren't denying you were there at the same time, are you? Freddy Baines swears he saw you.'

'Them Bainses!' grumbled Mr Pollock. 'A nasty, peerin', pryin' lot. What's it got to do with them where I was?'

'Well, you admit it anyhow. What time did you get to the Flat-Iron?'

'Per'aps Freddy Baines can tell you that, too. 'E zeems to be bloody free with his information.'

'Never mind that. What time do *you* say it was?'

'That ain't no business of yours. Perlice 'ere, perlice there

– there ain't no freedom in this blasted country. 'Ave I or 'ave I not the right to go where I like? Answer me that.'

'Look here, Pollock. All we want from you is some information. If you've got nothing to hide, why not answer a plain question?'

'Well, what is the question? Were I off the Flat-Iron on Thursday? Yes, I were. Wot about it?'

'You came along from your own place, I suppose?'

'Well, I did, if you want to know. Where's the 'arm in that?'

'None whatever. What time did you set out?'

'About one o'clock. Maybe more; maybe less. Round about the slack.'

'And you got to the Flat-Iron about two.'

'Well, and where's the 'arm in that?'

'Did you see anybody on the shore at that time?'

'Yus, I did.'

'You did?'

'Yus. I've got eyes in me 'ed, 'aven't I?'

'Yes. And you may as well have a civil tongue in your head. Where did you see this person?'

'On the shore by the Vlat-Iron – round about two o'clock.'

'Were you close enough in to see who it was?'

'No, I weren't. Not to come into your bleedin' court and swear to a pimple, I wasn't; and you can put that in your pipe, Mr Cocky Superintendent, and smoke it.'

'Well, what did you see?'

'I zee a vule of a woman, caperin' about on the beach, goin' on as if she was loony. She runs a bit an' stops a bit, an' pokes in the sand and then runs on a bit. That's what I zee.'

'I must tell Miss Vane that,' said Wimsey to the Inspector. 'It will appeal to her sense of humour.'

'Oh, you saw a woman, did you? Did you see what she did after that?'

'She runs up to the Vlat-Iron an' starts messin' about there.'

'Was there anybody else on the Flat-Iron?'

'There was a chap lyin' down. At least, it looked so.'

'And then?'

'Then she starts a-yowlin' an' wavin' her arms.'

'Well?'

'Well, what? I didn't take no notice. I never takes no notice of vemayles.'

'Now, Pollock, did you see anybody else at all on the shore that morning?'

'Not a zoul.'

'Were you within sight of shore all the time?'

'Yes, I were.'

'And you saw nobody except this woman and the man lying down?'

'Ain't I tellin' you? I zee nobody.'

'About this man on the Flat-Iron? Was he lying down when you first saw him?'

'Yes, he were.'

'And when did you first see him?'

'Soon as I come in zight of'un, I zee un.'

'When was that?'

''Ow can I tell to a minute. Might be a quarter to two, might be ten minutes to. I wasn't takin' perticklers for the perlice. I were attendin' to my own business, same as I wish other folks would.'

'What business?'

'Zailin' the bloody boat. That's my business.'

'At any rate, you saw the man some time before you saw the woman, and he was then lying on the rock. Was he dead, do you think, when you first saw him?'

''Ow wur I to know if 'e wur dead or alive? 'E didn't kiss 'is 'and to me. And if 'e 'ad, I shouldn't a' seen un, d'ye zee? I wur too far out.'

'But you said you were within sight of shore the whole time.'

'Zo I wur. But shore's a big thing. A man couldn't very well miss it. But that's not to zay I could zee every vule on it playin' at kiss-me-'and.'

'I see. Were you right out on the Grinders, then?'

'Wot's it matter where I wur? I weren't speckylatin' about corpses, nor yet what vemayles was after with their young men. I've got zummat more to do than zit about watchin' bathin' parties.'

'What had you to do?'

'That's my business.'

'Well, whatever your business was, it was out in the deep water off the Grinders?'

Mr Pollock was obstinately silent.

'Was anybody with you in the boat?'

'No, there weren't.'

'Then what was that grandson of yours doing?'

'Oh, him? He was with me. I thought you meant was there somebody else, that didn't ought to have been there.'

'What do you mean by that?'

'Nothing, only perlicemen is a pack of vules, mostly.'

'Where is your grandson?'

'Over to Cork. Went last Zatterday, he did.'

'Cork, eh? Smuggling goods into Ireland?'

Mr Pollock spat profusely.

''Course not. Business. My business.'

'Your business seems to be rather mysterious, Pollock. You'd better be careful. We'll want to see that young man when he gets back. Anyway, you say that when the young lady saw you, you had come in, and were putting out again.'

'Why not?'

'What did you come in for?'

'That's my business, ain't it?'

The Superintendent gave it up.

133

'At any rate, are you in a position to say whether you saw anybody walking along the shore between your cottage and the Flat-Iron?'

'Yes, I am. I zee nobody. Not up to quarter to two, anyway. After that, I couldn't swear one way nor t'other, 'avin' my own business to mind, like I zaid.'

'Did you see any other boat in the neighbourhood?'

'No, I didn't.'

'Very well. If your memory should improve in the next few days, you'd better let us know.'

Mr Pollock muttered something uncomplimentary, and removed himself.

'Not an agreeable old gentleman,' said Wimsey.

'An old scoundrel,' said Superintendent Glaisher. 'And the worst of it is, you can't believe a word he says. I'd like to know what he was really up to.'

'Murdering Paul Alexis, perhaps?' suggested the Inspector.

'Or conveying the murderer to the scene of the crime for a consideration,' added Wimsey. 'That's more likely, really. What motive should he have for murdering Alexis?'

'There's the three hundred pounds, my lord. We mustn't forget that. I know I said it was suicide, and I still think so, but we've got a much better motive for a murder than we had before.'

'Always supposing Pollock knew about the £300. But how should he?'

'See here,' said the Superintendent. 'Suppose Alexis was wanting to leave England.'

'That's what I say,' interjected Umpelty.

'And suppose he had hired Pollock to meet him somewhere off-shore with his boat and take him across to a yacht or something. And suppose, in paying Pollock, he'd happened to show him the rest of the money. Couldn't Pollock have put him ashore and cut his throat for him and made away with the gold?'

'But why?' objected Umpelty. 'Why put him ashore? Wouldn't it have been easier to cut his throat aboard the boat and drop the body into the sea?'

'No, it wouldn't,' said Wimsey, eagerly. 'Ever seen 'em stick a pig, Inspector? Ever reckoned how much blood there was to the job? If Pollock had cut Alexis' throat on board, it would take a devil of a lot of swabbing to get the boat properly clean again.'

'That's quite true,' said the Superintendent. 'But in any case, how about Pollock's clothes? I'm afraid we haven't got evidence enough to get a warrant and search his place for bloodstains.'

'You could wash 'em off oil-skins pretty easily, too,' remarked Wimsey.

The two policemen acquiesced gloomily.

'And if you stood behind your man and cut his throat that way, you'd stand a reasonable chance of not getting so very heavily splashed. It's my belief the man was killed in the place where he was found, murder or no murder. And if you don't mind, Superintendent, I've got a little suggestion which might work and tell us definitely whether it really was murder or suicide.'

He again outlined the suggestion, and the Superintendent nodded.

'I see no objection whatever, my lord. Something might quite well come of it. In fact,' said Mr Glaisher, 'something of the same kind had passed through my own mind, as you might say. But I don't mind it's appearing to come from your lordship. Not at all.'

Wimsey grinned and went in search of Salcombe Hardy, the *Morning Star* reporter, whom he found, as he expected, taking refreshment in the hotel bar. Most of the pressmen had withdrawn by this time, but Hardy, with a touching faith in Lord Peter, had clung to his post.

'Though you're treating me damn badly, old man,' he said, raising his mournful violet eyes to Wimsey's grey ones, 'I *know* you must have something up your sleeve, or you wouldn't be hanging round the scene of the crime like this. Unless it's the girl. For God's sake, Wimsey, say it isn't the girl. You wouldn't play such a shabby trick on a poor, hardworking journalist. Or, look here! If there's nothing else doing, give me a story about the girl. Anything'll do, so long as it's a story. "Romantic Engagement of Peer's Son" – that'd be better than nothing. But I must have a story.'

'Pull yourself together, Sally,' said his lordship, 'and keep your inky paws off my private affairs. Come right away out of this haunt of vice and sit down quietly in a corner of the lounge and I'll give you a nice, pretty story all to yourself.'

'That's right,' said Mr Hardy, in a burst of emotion. 'That's what I expected from a dear old friend. Never let down a pal, even if he's only a poor bloody journalist. Noblesse oblige. That's what I said to those other blighters. "I'm sticking to old Peter," I said, "Peter's the man for my money. He won't see a hardworking man lose a job for want of a good news story." But these new men – they've no push, no guts. Fleet Street's going to the dogs, curse it. There's nobody left now of the old gang except me. I know where the news is, and I know how to get it. I said to myself, You hang on to old Peter, I said, and one of these days he'll give you a story.'

'Splendid fellow!' said Wimsey. 'May we ne'er lack a friend or a story to give him. Are you reasonably sober, Sally?'

'Sober?' exclaimed the journalist indignantly. 'J'ever know a pressman who wasn't sober when somebody had a story to give him? I may not be a blasted pussyfoot, but my legs are always steady enough to go after a story, and what more could anybody want?'

Wimsey pushed his friend gently into position before a table in the lounge.

'Here you are, then,' he said. 'You take this stuff down and see that it gets a good show in your beastly rag. You can put in trimmings to suit yourself.'

Hardy glanced up sharply.

'Oh!' said he. 'Ulterior motive, eh? Not all pure friendship. Patriotism is not enough. Oh, well! as long as it's exclusive and news, the motive is imma – imma – damn the word – immaterial.'

'Quite,' said Wimsey. 'Now then, take this down. "The mystery surrounding the horrible tragedy at the Flat-Iron deepens steadily with every effort made to solve it. Far from being a simple case of suicide, as at first seemed probable, the horrible death—"'

'All right,' interjected Hardy. 'I can do that part on my head. What I want is the story.'

'Yes; but work up the mystery part of it. Go on, now: "Lord Peter Wimsey, the celebrated amateur of crime-detection, interviewed by our special correspondent in his pleasant sitting-room at the Hotel Bellevue—"'

'Is the sitting-room important?'

'The address is. I want them to know where to find me.'

'Right you are. Go ahead.'

'– "at the Hotel Bellevue, Wilvercombe, said that while the police still held strongly to the suicide theory, he himself was by no means satisfied. The point that particularly troubled him was that, whereas the deceased wore a full beard and had never been known to shave, the crime was committed—"'

'Crime?'

'Suicide is a crime.'

'So it is. Well?'

'– "committed with an ordinary cut-throat razor, which shows signs of considerable previous hard wear." Rub that

137

in well, Sally. "The history of this razor has been traced up to a point—"'

'Who traced it?'

'I did.'

'Can I say that?'

'If you like.'

'That makes it better. "Lord Peter Wimsey explained, with his characteristically modest smile, that he had himself been at pains to trace the previous history of the razor, a search which led him—" Where did it lead you, Wimsey?'

'I don't want to tell 'em that. Say that the search covered many hundred miles.'

'All right. I can make that sound very important. Anything else?'

'Yes. This is the important bit. Get 'em to put it in black lettering – you know.'

'Not my business. Sub-editor. But I'll try. Carry on. "Leaning over the table and emphasising the point with an eloquent gesture of his artistic hands, Lord Peter said—"'

'"The trail,"' dictated Wimsey, '"breaks off at the crucial point. *How did the razor get into the hands of Paul Alexis?* If once I could be satisfied of that, the answer might at once set at rest all my doubts. *If Paul Alexis can be proved to have bought the razor, I shall consider the suicide theory to have been proved up to the hilt.* But until that missing link in the chain of evidence is reconstructed, *I shall hold that Paul Alexis was foully and brutally murdered,* and I shall spare no efforts to bring the murderer to the judgement he has so richly deserved," How's that, Sally?'

'Not too bad. I can work that up into something. I shall add, of course, that you, knowing the enormous circulation of the *Morning Star*, are relying on the wide publicity it will give to this statement to etcetera, etcetera. I might even get them to offer a reward.'

'Why not? Anyway, pitch it to 'em hot and strong, Sally.'

'I will – for better, for worse, for richer, for poorer. Between you and me, *would* you be satisfied that it was suicide if the reward was claimed?'

'I don't know,' said Wimsey. 'Probably not. In fact, I am never satisfied.'

XII

THE EVIDENCE OF THE BRIDE'S SON

'How I despise
All such mere men of muscle!'
Death's Jest-Book

MONDAY, 22 JUNE

WIMSEY looked at his watch. It was half-past one, and he had had no lunch. He remedied the omission, took the car and drove out to Darley. He had to wait for a few moments while the gates were opened at the Halt, and took the opportunity to check up on the police inquiry. He found that the lame gate-keeper knew the mysterious Mr Martin by sight – had, in fact, met him one evening in the bar of the Feathers. A pleasant gentleman, with a hearty way with him. Suffered from some trouble with his eyes, which obliged him to wear dark glasses, but a very nice gentleman for all that. The gate-keeper was quite positive that Mr Martin had not passed through the railway-gates at any time on Thursday – not in any car or cart or on a cycle, that was to say. As for passing on foot, he couldn't swear to it, and you couldn't expect it of him.

Here, however, a new witness suddenly came forward. The gate-keeper's little daughter, Rosie, 'just going on for five, and a wonderful quick girl for her age,' as her father proudly remarked, was emphatic that 'the nasty man with the black glasses' had not been seen at the railway-gates during the critical period on the Thursday. Rosie knew him and disliked him, for she had seen him in the village the day before and his horrid black glasses had frightened her. She and a small friend had been 'playing Bluebeard' at the railway-gates on Thursday. She knew it was Thursday, because it was market day, when the 10.15 stopped there. She had been Sister Anne on her tower, and had called out to her companion when she saw anybody coming along the road. They had played there from after dinner (12.30 according to the gate-keeper) till nearly tea-time (four o'clock). She was absolutely sure the nasty man had not come through the railway-wickets. If he had, she would have run away.

This seemed to dispose of the last lingering possibility that the mysterious Mr Martin might have left the Feathers rather earlier than he was supposed to have done, walked to the crossing and been picked up by a car on the other side. Wimsey thanked Rosie with grave courtesy, gave her sixpence and drove on.

His next port of call was, of course, the Feathers. The landlord, Mr Lundy, was ready enough with his information. What he had told the inspector was quite right. He had first seen Mr Martin on Tuesday – the 16th, that would be. He had arrived about six o'clock and left his Morgan parked on the village green while he came in and took a glass of mild and bitter and asked the way to Mr Goodrich's house. Who was Mr Goodrich? Why, Mr Goodrich was the gentleman that owned the land down by Hinks's Lane, where Mr Martin had been camping. All the land thereabouts belonged to Mr Goodrich.

'I want to be clear about this,' said Wimsey. 'Did Mr Martin come here from the direction of Hinks's Lane, or which way did he come?'

'No, sir; he drove in along the Heathbury Road and left his car on the green, same as I said.'

'Did he come straight in here?'

'Straight as a swaller to its nest,' replied Mr Lundy, picturesquely. 'We was open, you see, sir.'

'And did he ask anybody about where he could camp? Or did he ask at once for Mr Goodrich?'

'He didn't ask no questions at all sir, only that: Where was Mr Goodrich's house?'

'He knew Mr Goodrich's name, then?'

'Seemingly he did, sir.'

'Did he say why he wanted to see Mr Goodrich?'

'No, sir. Just asked the way and drank up his beer and off in the car again.'

'I understand he had lunch here last Thursday?'

'That's right, sir. Came in a big open car with a lady. She set him down here and drove off again, and he came in and set down to lunch.' He thought it would be about one o'clock, but the girl could tell better than he could.

The girl knew all about it. Yes, as she had already told Inspector Umpelty, Mr Martin had come in about ten minutes to one. He mentioned to her that he had been to Wilvercombe, and thought he would make a change by lunching at the inn. His car, it seemed, had got something the matter with it, and a passing car had picked him up and taken him to Wilvercombe and back. Yes, he had lunched heartily: roast leg of mutton with potatoes and boiled cabbage and a rhubarb pie to follow.

Wimsey shuddered at the thought of roast mutton and cabbage on a red-hot June day, and asked when Mr Martin had left the inn.

'It would be half-past one, sir, by the right time. Our clocks are all ten minutes fast, same as the clock in the bar, that's set by the wireless every day. I couldn't say but what Mr Martin might have stopped in the bar on his way out, but half-past one was when he paid me for his lunch. I couldn't be mistaken about that, sir, because it was my day off and my young man was taking me over to Heathbury on his motor-cycle, and I was watching the clock, as you might say, to see how soon I'd get my work finished with. There wasn't nobody come in after Mr Martin, so I was able to clear away and get dressed and very pleased I was about it.'

This was clear enough. Mr Martin had certainly not left the Three Feathers earlier than 1.30. Undoubtedly he was not the murderer of Paul Alexis. Nevertheless, having begun his investigation, Wimsey determined to carry it through to the bitter end. Alibis, he reminded himself, were made to be broken. He would suppose that, by means of a magic carpet or other device, Mr Martin had been miraculously wafted from Darley to the Flat-Iron between 1.30 and two o'clock. In that case, did he come back that afternoon, and if so, when? and how?

There were not a great many houses in Darley, and a door-to-door inquiry, though laborious, seemed to be a fairly safe and certain method of answering these questions. He pulled up his socks and set to work. He had no difficulty in getting the villagers to talk. The death of Paul Alexis was a local event of an importance that almost swamped last Saturday's cricket match, and the revolutionary proposal to turn the disused Quaker meeting-house into a cinema; while the arrival of the Wilvercombe police to make inquiries about the movements of Mr Martin had raised the excitement to fever pitch. Darley felt strongly that, if this kind of thing was going to happen, it might get into the papers again. Darley had actually been in the papers that year already, when Mr Gubbins, the vicar's warden, had drawn a consolation prize in the Grand National sweep. The sporting half of Darley had been delighted, but envious; the pious half had been quite unable to understand why the vicar had not immediately dismissed Mr Gubbins from his privilege of handing round the plate and sitting on the Church Council, and thought that Mr Gubbins's action in devoting a tithe of his winnings to the Restoration Fund merely piled hypocrisy on the head of debauchery. But now, with the hope that they might be found to have entertained an angel of darkness unawares, they foresaw all manner of publicity. Wimsey discovered several people who thought that Mr Martin's manner odd and had not liked his face and who said so, at considerable length. It was, however, only after nearly two hours' patient research that he discovered somebody who had actually seen Mr Martin on Thursday afternoon. This was, of course, the most obvious person in the village – namely the proprietor of the little tin bungalow that did duty for a garage, and the only reason why Wimsey did not get this information a great deal sooner was that the said proprietor – one, Mr Polwhistle – had gone out when he first called upon him, to tackle the internals of a sick petrol-gas engine at a neighbouring farm, leaving behind him only a young woman to attend to the pump.

Mr Polwhistle, when he returned in company of a youthful mechanic, was most discouragingly informative. Mr Martin? – oh, yes. He (Mr Polwhistle) had seen him on Thursday afternoon all right. Mr Martin had come in – just upon three o'clock, weren't it, Tom? Yes, three o'clock – and asked them to come and have a look at his Morgan. They had gone round, and found that the Morgan wouldn't start, not for toffee. After prolonged investigation and exercise on the starting-handle, they had diagnosed trouble with the ignition. They had taken everything out and looked at it, and eventually it had occurred to Mr Polwhistle that the fault might be in the H.T. lead. On their removing this and putting in a new one, the engine had started up at once, sweet as a nut. There could be no doubt about the time, because Tom had entered it upon his time-sheet; 3 p.m. till 4 p.m.

It was now nearly half-past four, and Wimsey felt that he had a good chance of finding Mr Goodrich at home. He was directed to his house – the big place up the first turning off the Wilvercombe Road – and found the good gentleman and his family gathered about a table well

144

spread with bread and cakes and honey and Devonshire cream.

Mr Goodrich, a stout and hearty squire of the old school, was delighted to give any assistance in his power. Mr Martin had turned up at the house at about seven o'clock on the Tuesday evening and had asked permission to camp at the bottom of Hinks's Lane. Why Hinks's Lane, by the way? Well, there used to be a cottage there that belonged to an old fellow called Hinks – a regular character – used to read the Bible through regularly every year, and it was to be hoped it did him good, for a graceless old scamp he was and always had been. But that was donkey's years ago, and the cottage had fallen into disrepair. Nobody ever went down there now, except campers. Mr Martin had not asked for information about camping-grounds; he had asked straight out for permission to camp in Hinks's Lane, calling it by that name. Mr Goodrich had never set eyes on Mr Martin before, and he (Mr Goodrich) knew pretty well everything that went on in the village. He was almost certain that Mr Martin had never been in Darley before. No doubt somebody had told him about Hinks's Lane – it was a regular place for campers. They were out of the way down there, and there were no crops for them to damage and no gates for them to leave open, unless they were to go out of their way to trespass on Farmer Newcombe's pasture on the other side of the hedge. But there was no necessity for them to do so, as it didn't lead anywhere. The stream that ran through the pasture came out on to the beach only fifty yards away from the camping-ground and was fresh, except, of course, at flood-tide, when it was brackish. Now Mr Goodrich came to think about it, he believed there had been some complaint from Mr Newcombe about a broken hedge, but the story only came through Geary the blacksmith, who was a notorious talker and he (Mr Goodrich) didn't see that it had anything to do with Mr Martin. Mr

Newcombe was not altogether a satisfactory tenant in the matter of repairs to hedges and when there were gaps, animals would sometimes stray through them. Apart from this, he (Mr Goodrich) knew nothing to Mr Martin's discredit. He seemed to have been quiet enough, and in any case, Hinks's Lane being out of sight and sound of the village, campers couldn't make nuisances of themselves down there. Some of them brought gramophones or concertinas or ukuleles, according to their taste and social position, but Mr Goodrich had no objection to their amusing themselves, so long as they didn't disturb anybody. He never made any charge for camping on his ground – it didn't hurt *him*, and he didn't see why he should take payment for letting the poor devils who lived in town help themselves to a mouthful of fresh air and a drink of water. He usually asked them to leave the place as tidy as they could, and as a rule he had found them pretty decent in this respect.

Wimsey thanked Mr Goodrich and accepted his hospitable invitation to tea. He left at six o'clock, full of buns and cream, with just nice time to pay a visit to the camping-ground and so round off the chapter of Mr Martin. He drove down the stony little lane, and soon found signs of Mr Martin's recent presence. The land led out upon a flat expanse of rough turf, beyond which a belt of heavy stones and shingle sloped down to the edge of, the sea. The tide was about a quarter-full, and the beach became progressively less rough as it neared the water; presumably at low tide there would be a narrow strip of sand left uncovered.

The tracks of the Morgan's wheels were still faintly visible upon the coarse grass, and there was a patch of oily drippings to show where it had been parked. Close by, there were the holes where the pole and pegs of a small bell-tent had been driven in. There were the ashes of a burnt-out wood fire, and, among them, a ball of greasy newspaper, which had obviously been used to scrub out a frying-pan.

Rather reluctantly, Wimsey unfolded the distasteful sheets and glanced at the heading. Thursday's *Morning Star*; nothing particularly exciting about that. Careful search among the ashes of the fire revealed no blood-stained fragments of clothing – not so much as a button of a garment – no half-burnt scraps of paper which might have contained a clue to Mr Martin's real name and address. The only thing that was in any way remarkable was a piece of thinnish rope about three inches long, heavily blackened by the fire. Wimsey pocketed this, for lack of better occupation, and searched further.

Mr Martin had been a tidy camper on the whole, leaving no obviously offensive débris. On the right-hand side of the camping-ground there was, however, the remains of a stunted thorn hedge, surrounding the battered remnants of Hinks's Cottage. Half buried at the foot of this hedge, Wimsey discovered a repulsive cache, containing a great number of old tins and bottles, some recent and some obviously abandoned by previous campers, the heels of some loaves, the bones from a neck of mutton, an old dixie with a hole in the bottom, half a neck-tie, a safety-razor blade (still sharp enough to cut one's fingers on) and a very dead gull. An elaborate and back-aching crawl over the whole surface of the camping-ground rewarded the earnest sleuth further with an immoderate quantity of burnt matches, six empty match-boxes of foreign make, the dottles of several pipes, three oat-grains, a broken bootlace (brown), the stalks of about a pound of strawberries, six plum-stones, the stub of a pencil, a drawing-pin business end up, fifteen beer-corks, and an instrument for removing the patent caps of other beer-bottles. The rough grass showed no identifiable footprints.

Weary and hot, Lord Peter gathered his loot together and stretched his cramped limbs. The wind, still blowing heavily in from seaward, was grateful to his perspiring brow, however much it might hold up the Inspector's salvage operations. The sky was cloudy, but so long as the wind held, there was, he felt, not much likelihood of rain, and he was glad, for he didn't want rain. A vague possibility was forming itself in his mind, and he wanted to take a walk next day with Harriet Vane. At the moment, he could do no more. He would go back and change and eat and be normal.

He drove back to Wilvercombe.

After a hot bath and the putting-on of a boiled shirt and dinner-jacket, he felt better and telephoned to the Resplendent to ask Harriet to dine with him.

'I'm sorry, I'm afraid I can't. I'm dining with Mrs Weldon and her son.'

'Her son?'

'Yes; he's just arrived. Why not come round here after grub and be introduced?'

'Dunno. What sort of bloke is he?'

'Oh, yes – he's here, and would like to meet you very much.'

'Oh, I see. We are being overheard. I suppose I'd better come and look the blighter over. Is he handsome?'

'Yes, rather! Come along about a quarter to nine.'

'Well, you'd better tell him we're engaged, and then I shan't be obliged to assassinate him.'

'You will? That's splendid.'

'Will you marry me?'

'Of course not. We'll expect you at 8.45.'

'All right, and I hope your rabbit dies.'

Wimsey ate his solitary dinner thoughtfully. So this was the son, was it? The one who was out of sympathy with his mother. What was he doing here? Had he suddenly become sympathetic? Or had she sent for him and compelled him to come in, by financial or other pressure? Was he perhaps a new factor in the problem? He was the only son of his mother and she a rich widow. Here at last was a person to whom the removal of Paul Alexis might appear in the light of a god-send. Undoubtedly the man must be looked into.

He went round to the Resplendent after dinner and found the party waiting for him in the lounge. Mrs Weldon, who wore a plain black semi-evening dress and looked her full age in it, greeted Wimsey effusively.

'My dear Lord Peter! I am *so* glad to see you. May I introduce my son Henry? I wrote asking him to come and help us through this terrible time, and he has *most* kindly put his own business aside and come to me. So very sweet of you, Henry dear. I have just been telling Henry how good Miss Vane has been to me, and how *hard* you and she are working to clear poor Paul's memory.'

Harriet had merely been mischievous. Henry was certainly not handsome, though he was a good, sturdy specimen of his type. He stood about five foot eleven – a strongly built, heavyish man with a brick-red all-weather face. Evening dress did not suit him, for the breadth of his shoulders and the shortness of his legs gave him a rather top-heavy appearance; one would expect him to look his best in country tweeds and leggings. His hair, rather rough and dull in texture, was mouse-coloured, and offered a pregnant suggestion of what his mother's might once have looked like before it knew the touch of peroxide; indeed, he was, in a curious way, very like his mother, having the same low, narrow forehead and the same long and obstinate chin; though, in the mother the expression was that of a weak, fanciful obstinacy, and, in the son, of stubborn and unimaginative obstinacy. Looking at him, Wimsey felt that he was hardly the sort of man to take kindly to a Paul Alexis for a step-father; he would not sympathise with the sterile romance of any woman who was past the age of child-bearing. Wimsey, summing him up with the man of the world's experienced eye, placed him at once as a gentleman-farmer, who was not quite a gentleman and not much of a farmer.

At the moment, the understanding between Henry Weldon and his mother seemed, nevertheless, to be excellent.

'Henry is so delighted,' said Mrs Weldon, 'that you are here to help us, Lord Peter. That policeman is so stupid. He doesn't seem to believe a word I tell him. Of course, he's a very well-meaning, honest man, and *most* polite, but how can a person like that possibly understand a nature like Paul's. I *knew* Paul. So did Henry, didn't you, dear?'

'Oh, yes,' said Henry, 'certainly. Very pleasant fellow.'

'Henry knows how utterly devoted Paul was to me. *You* know, don't you, dear, that he *never* would have taken his own life and left me like that without a word. It hurts me so when people say such things – I feel I could –'

'There, there, Mother,' muttered Henry, embarrassed by the prospect of emotion and possible break-down in a public place. 'You must try to bear up. Of course we know Alexis was all right. Damned fond of you – of course, of course. Police are always silly fools. Don't let 'em worry you.'

'No dear, I'm sorry,' said Mrs Weldon, dabbing her eyes apologetically with a small handkerchief. 'It's all been such a shock to me. But I mustn't be weak and silly. We must all be courageous and work hard to *do* something about it.'

Wimsey suggested that a spot of something or other might do them all good, and, further, that he and Henry might make a concerted masculine raid on the bar, instructing the waiter to attend upon the ladies. He felt that he could dissect Henry more conveniently in a private interview.

As the two men's backs disappeared in the direction of the bar, Mrs Weldon turned her anxious eyes on Harriet.

'How nice Lord Peter is,' she said, 'and what a comforting thing it is for us both to have a man to rely on.'

This sentiment was not very well received; Harriet averted her gaze from Lord Peter's back, on which it had been absentmindedly and unaccountably fixed, and frowned; but Mrs Weldon bleated on, unheeding.

'It's beautiful how kind everybody is when one is in trouble. Henry and I haven't always been as close to one another as a mother and son should be. He takes after his father in a great many ways, though people say he is like me to look at, and when he was a little boy he had the dearest golden curls – just like mine. But he loves sport and out-door life – you can tell that by his looks, can't you? He's always out and about, seeing after his farm, and that's what makes him look a little older than his years. He's really quite a young man – I was a mere child when I married, as I told you before. But though, as I say, we haven't always been as much in harmony as one would have liked, he has been perfectly *sweet* to me about this sad affair. When I wrote to him and told him how much I *felt* the dreadful things they were saying about Paul, he came at *once* to help me, though I know he must be terribly busy just now. I really feel that poor Paul's death has brought us closer together.'

Harriet said that that must be a great comfort to Mrs Weldon. It was the only possible answer.

Henry, meanwhile, had his own view of the matter to put before Lord Peter.

'Bit of a staggerer for the old lady, this,' he observed over a glass of Scotch. 'Takes it hard. Between you and me, it's all for the best. How's a woman of her age going to be happy with a feller like that? Eh? Don't like these Popoffsky blighters, anyway, and she's fifty-seven if she's a day. I'm thirty-six myself. Consider I'm well out of it. Makes a chap look a bit of a fool when his mother proposes to give him a twenty-year-old lounge lizard for a step-papa. Suppose it's all over the place now. Bet everybody's grinning at me behind my back. Let 'em grin. All over now, anyway. Suppose the chappie did do himself in, didn't he?'

'It looks like it,' admitted Wimsey.

'Couldn't face the prospect, eh? All his own fault. Hard-up, I suppose, poor devil! The old girl's not a bad sort, really. She'd have given the feller a damn good time if he'd stuck to his bargain. But you can't trust these foreigners. Like collies – lick your boots one minute and bite you the next. Don't like collies, myself. Give me a good bull-terrier any day.'

'Oh, yes – so frightfully British and all that, what?'

'Thought I'd better push along and cheer Mother up. Stop all this nonsense about Bolsheviks. Won't do to have her wasting her time with these tom-fool notions. Enough to send the old dear clean off her rocker, you know. Once they get those notions in their heads it's a job to get rid of 'em. Form of mania, don't you think, like women's rights and crystal-gazing?'

Wimsey agreed cautiously that an unreasonable conviction might, in process of time, amount to an obsession.

'That's just what I mean. You've got the word – obsession, that's it. Well, I don't want the old lady to go wasting her time and money on an obsession. Look here, Wimsey, you're a sound sort of fellow – brainy and all that – can't you put her off this Bolshevik idea? She's taken a notion that you and that Vane girl are encouraging her. Now, take it from me, old man, that kind of thing won't do at all.'

Lord Peter delicately raised his eyebrows.

'Of course,' pursued Mr Weldon, 'I see your game all right. You're nuts on this kind of thing and it's all a darn good advertisement, and it gives you a jolly good excuse for barging round with the girl. That's quite all right. But it's not quite the game to go playing my mother up, if you see what I mean. So I thought I'd just give you a hint. You won't take offence?'

'I am quite ready,' said Lord Peter, 'to take anything I am offered.'

Mr Weldon looked puzzled for a moment and then burst into a hearty laugh.

'That's good,' he said, 'dashed good. What was yours? Martell Three-Star? Here, Johnnie, same again for this gentleman.'

'Thank you, no,' said Wimsey. 'You misunderstood me.'

'Oh, come – another little spot won't do you any harm. No? Oh, well, if you won't, you won't. Mine's a Scotch-and-soda. Well, now, we understand one another, eh?'

'Oh, yes. I think I understand you perfectly.'

'Good. Glad to have this chance of putting you wise. Whole thing's a nuisance, of course. Suppose we shall be stuck here now till they've found the body and held an inquest. Don't like these beastly watering-places. Suits you all right, I daresay. I like a bit more open air and none of this jazz and dinner-jackets.'

'Quite right,' said Wimsey.

'You think so, eh? I was putting you down for something more in the West End line. But I suppose you're a bit of a sportsman, too? Huntin', fishin', that sort of thing, eh?'

'I hunted pretty regularly with the Quorn and the Pytchley at one time, and I shoot and fish a bit,' said Wimsey. 'After all, I was brought up in the country, you know. My people have a place in the shires, and our headquarters is down in Norfolk – Duke's Denver, on the borders of the Fen country.'

'Oh, yes, of course. You're Denver's brother. Never seen the place, but I live in that part of the world myself – Huntingdonshire, not far from Ely.'

'Oh, yes; I know that part pretty well. Fruit-farming country and all that. Flattish, of course, but uncommonly good sort of soil.'

'Nothing in farming these days,' grumbled Mr Weldon.

'Look at all this Russian wheat they're dumpin' in. As if things weren't bad enough already, with wages what they are, and taxes, and rates and tithe and insurance. I've got fifty acres of wheat. By the time it's harvested I daresay it'll have cost me £9 an acre. And what shall I get for it? Lucky if I get five. How this damned Government expects the farmer to carry on, I don't know. Damned if I don't feel like chucking it altogether sometimes and clearing out of this bloody country. Nothing much to stick round here for. I'm not married, thank God! Too much sense. If you take my advice you'll do likewise. You must be pretty smart to have escaped so long. Look as if you did yourself pretty well, too. Lucky your brother's still a youngish man. Death-duties and all that. Cripple a place, don't they? But I always thought he was a pretty warm man, for a duke. How's he manage it?'

Wimsey explained that the Denver income was not derived from the Denver estate, which was a liability rather than an asset.

'Oh, I see. Well, you're lucky. Takes a man all he can do to get his living off the land these days.'

'Yes; I suppose you have to stick to it uncommonly closely. Up early and late. Nothing escapes the master's eye. That sort of thing, what?'

'Oh, yes – yes.'

'It must be trying to be obliged to leave things and come down to Wilvercombe. How long do you think you'll be here?'

'Eh? Oh, I don't know. Depends on this inquest, doesn't it? I've left a man in charge, of course.'

'Just so. Hadn't we better get back and join the ladies?'

'Ah!' Mr Weldon dug his elbow into Lord Peter's ribs. 'Ladies, eh? You be careful, my boy. Getting to the dangerous age, aren't you? If you ain't careful, you'll find yourself booked one of these days.'

'Oh, I daresay I shall manage to keep *my* head out of the noose.'

'Out of the – oh, yes – the matrimonial noose. Yes. Ha, ha! All right. I suppose we'd better go.'

Mr Weldon turned away from the bar rather abruptly. Wimsey, reflecting that the ability to swallow insult is a necessary part of the detective's make-up, restrained the temptation to connect his toe with Mr Weldon's rather massive hinder-end, and followed, ruminating.

A message from the waiter informed him that the ladies had adjourned into the dance-lounge. Henry growled, but was relieved to find that his mother was, after all, not dancing. She was watching Harriet who, clad in claret-colour, was revolving smoothly in the practised arms of Antoine. Wimsey politely begged Mrs Weldon to favour him, but she shook her head.

'I couldn't. Not so soon. In fact, never again – now that Paul – But I begged Miss Vane to enjoy herself and not mind about me. It is such a delight to watch her looking so happy.'

Wimsey sat down and did his best to enjoy the spectacle of Harriet's happiness. As the quick-step came to an end, Antoine, with professional tact, contrived to end his progress in the neighbourhood of their table and then, bowing gracefully, melted away. Harriet, a little flushed, smiled amiably upon Lord Peter.

'Oh, there you are,' said his lordship.

Harriet became suddenly conscious that every woman in the room was gazing furtively or with frank interest at Wimsey and herself, and the knowledge exhilarated her.

'Yes,' she said, 'here I am. Frivolling. You didn't know I could do it, did you?'

'I have always taken it for granted that you could do everything.'

'Oh, no. I can only do what I like doing.'

'We'll see about that.'

The orchestra swung gently into a dreamy tune. Wimsey advanced upon Harriet and steered her competently out into the centre of the room. For the first few bars of the music they had the floor to themselves.

'At last,' said Wimsey, 'we are alone. That is not an original remark, but I am in no condition to invent epigrams. I have been suffering agonies, and my soul is raw. Now that for a brief moment I have you all to myself –'

'Well?' said Harriet. She was aware that the wine-coloured frock became her.

'What,' said Wimsey, 'do you make of Mr Henry Weldon?'

'Oh!'

This was not quite the question Harriet had expected. She hastily collected her ideas. It was very necessary that she should be the perfect unemotional sleuth.

'His manners are dreadful,' she said, 'and I don't think his brains are much to write home about.'

'No, that's just it.'

'Just what?'

Wimsey countered the question with another.

'Why is he here?'

'She sent for him.'

'Yes, but why is he here. Sudden spasm of filial affection?'

'She thinks so.'

'Do *you* think so?'

'Possibly. Or, more likely, he doesn't want to get on the wrong side of her. It's her money, you know.'

'Quite. Yes. It's funny that that should only just have occurred to him. He's very like her, isn't he?'

'Very. So much so that he gave me an odd feeling just at first, as though I'd met him somewhere. Do you mean that they are too much alike to hit it off together?'

'They seem to be getting along all right at present.'

'I expect he's glad to be relieved from the prospect of Paul Alexis, and can't help showing it. He's not very subtle.'

'That's what feminine intuition makes of it, is it?'

'Bother feminine intuition. Do *you* find him romantic or obscure?'

'No; I wish I did. I only find him offensive.'

'Oh?'

'And I'd like to know why.'

Silence for a few moments. Harriet felt that Wimsey ought to be saying, 'How well you dance.' Since he did not say it, she became convinced that she was dancing like a wax doll with sawdust legs. Wimsey had never danced with her, never held her in his arms before. It should have been an epoch-making moment for him. But his mind appeared to be concentrated upon the dull personality of an East Anglian farmer. She fell a victim to an inferiority complex, and tripped over her partner's feet.

'Sorry,' said Wimsey, accepting responsibility like a gentleman.

'It's my fault,' said Harriet. 'I'm a rotten dancer. Don't bother about me. Let's stop. You haven't got to be polite to me, you know.'

Worse and worse. She was being peevish and egotistical. Wimsey glanced down at her in surprise and then suddenly smiled.

'Darling, if you danced like an elderly elephant with arthritis, I would dance the sun and moon into the sea with you. I have waited a thousand years to see you dance in that frock.'

'Idiot' said Harriet.

They made the circuit of the room in silence and harmony. Antoine, guiding an enormous person in jade-green and diamonds, swam comet-like into their orbit and murmured into Harriet's ear across an expanse of fat white shoulder:

'*Qu'est-ce que je vous ai dit? L'élan, c'est trouvé.*'

He slid away dexterously, leaving Harriet flushed.

'What did that blighter say?'

'He said I danced better with you than with him.'

'Curse his impudence!' Wimsey scowled over the heads of the intervening couples at Antoine's elegant back.

'Tell me now,' said Harriet. The ending of the dance had found them on the opposite side of the room from the Weldons, and it seemed natural to sit down at the nearest table. 'Tell me, what is biting you about Henry Weldon?'

'Henry Weldon?' Wimsey jerked his mind back from an immense distance. 'Yes, of course. Why is he here? Not to worm himself into his mother's good graces, surely?'

'Why not? Now is his time. Alexis is disposed of and he sees his opportunity. Now that he has nothing to lose by it, he can afford to come along and be frightfully sympathetic and help to investigate things and be filial and affectionate and so on.'

'Then why is he trying to drive me out of the place?'

'You?'

'Me.'

'How do you mean?'

'Weldon went out of his way in the bar this evening to be as offensive as he possibly could, without using actual violence or bad language. He informed me, in an indirect but unmistakable manner, that I was poking my nose in where I was not wanted, exploiting his mother for my private ends and probably sucking up to her for her money. In fact, he drove me to the indescribable vulgarity of reminding him who I was and why I did not require anybody's money.'

'Why didn't you sock him one over the jaw?'

'It was a temptation. I felt that you would love me better if I did. But you would not, in your calmer moments, really wish me to put my love before my detective principles.'

'Certainly not. But what's his idea?'

'Oh, that's clear enough. He made it very clear. He wants it to be understood that this detecting business is to stop, and that Mrs Weldon is to be restrained from lavishing time and money in pursuit of non-existent Bolsheviks.'

'I can understand that. He's looking to inherit the money.'

'Of course. But if I were to go and tell Mrs Weldon the things he's been saying to me, she'd probably disinherit him. And where would be the use of all this display of sympathy then?'

'I knew he was a stupid man.'

'He evidently thinks it very important to stop all these inquiries. So much so that he's prepared, not only to risk my splitting on him, but also to spend an indefinite time here hanging round his mother to see that she doesn't make inquiries on her own.'

'Well, I daresay he has nothing else to do.'

'Nothing else to do? My dear girl, he's a farmer.'

'Well?'

'And this is June.'

'What about it?'

'Why isn't he attending to his hay-making?'

'I didn't think of that.'

'About the last weeks of the year that any decent farmer would be willing to waste are the weeks from hay to harvest. I can understand his running over for a day, but he seems to be prepared to make a session of it. This Alexis business has become so important that he's ready to chuck everything, come down to a place he detests and hang about interminably in a hotel in attendance on a mother with whom he has never had very much in common. I think it's funny.'

'Yes, it is rather funny.'

'Has he ever been here before?'

'No. I asked him when we met. It's the kind of thing one does ask people. He said he hadn't. I expect he kept away while all the Alexis business was going on – he'd hate it.'

'And content himself with forbidding the banns at a distance?'

'Yes – though it doesn't seem the most effective way.'

'No? But the banns have been fairly effectively forbidden, haven't they?'

'Yes. But – are you casting Henry for the part of the murderer?'

'I should like to. But I don't feel I can, somehow.'

'No?'

'No. That's why I wanted to find out whether you thought Henry was subtle. You don't, and I agree with you. I don't think Henry has the brains to have murdered Paul Alexis.'

XIII

EVIDENCE OF TROUBLE SOMEWHERE

'Fool, would thy virtue shame and crush me down;
And make a grateful blushing bond-slave of me?'

Death's Jest-Book

TUESDAY, 23 JUNE

LORD PETER WIMSEY, reading his *Morning Star* over
the eggs and bacon, felt better than he had done for
some weeks. The *Morning Star* had come up to
scratch nobly, and was offering £100 reward for
information about the razor that had slain Paul Alexis.
Bunter, returning from his fruitless journey to Eastbourne, had come on to join his master at Wilvercombe, bringing with him a fresh supply of shirts,
collars, and other garments. Harriet Vane had danced
with Lord Peter in a wine-coloured frock. Wimsey
considered, rightly, that when a woman takes a man's
advice about the purchase of clothes, it is a sign that
she is not indifferent to his opinion. Various women,
at various times and in various quarters of the globe,
had clothed themselves by Wimsey's advice and sometimes also at his expense – but then, he had fully
expected them to do so. He had not expected it of
Harriet, and was as disproportionately surprised and
pleased as if he had picked up a sovereign in the
streets of Aberdeen. Like all male creatures, Wimsey
was a simple soul at bottom.

Not only had he this satisfactory past and present to

contemplate; he anticipated an interesting day. Harriet had consented to walk with him that afternoon from the Flat-Iron to Darley in search of clues. Low water being billed to take place at 4.45, they had arranged to drive out to the Flat-Iron, arriving there at 3.30. After a little light refreshment, the expedition would set out, searching conscientiously for whatever the shore might have to show them, while Bunter brought the car back by the road to Hinks's Lane; after which all three would return to their base at Wilvercombe in their original formation. It was all very clear, except that Harriet did not see – and said as much – what clues were likely to remain on the open shore after nearly a week of exceptionally high tides. She admitted, however, that she needed exercise and that walking was better exercise than most.

And – most immediate of pleasant things to look forward to – Harriet had further agreed to receive Lord Peter Wimsey after breakfast at the Resplendent, for a conference. It was necessary, in Wimsey's opinion, that the progress made so far should be tabulated and brought into some sort of order. Ten o'clock was the hour fixed for this meeting, and Wimsey was lingering lovingly over his bacon and eggs, so as to leave no restless and unfilled moment in his morning. By which it may be seen that his lordship had reached that time of life when a man can extract an Epicurean enjoyment even from his own passions – the halcyon period between the self-tormenting exuberance of youth and the fretful *carpe diem* of approaching senility.

The great wind had fallen at last. It had rained a little during the night, but now the sky was fair again, with only the gentlest of breezes ruffling the blue expanse of sea that was visible from the Bellevue's dining-room windows. Inspector Umpelty had been out with his helpers to explore the Grinders at four o'clock that morning, and had just looked in on Wimsey to say that they had found nothing yet.

'And why it hasn't come ashore somewhere before this, I don't know,' he grumbled. 'We've had a look-out kept all along the coast from Fishy Ness right up to Seahampton and on both sides of the estuary. Must have got hooked up with something. If we don't get it within another week, we'll have to give it up. Can't waste public money fishing for drowned dagoes. The ratepayers grumble enough as it is, and we can't keep the witnesses hanging round here for ever. Well, so long. We shall have another shot at low tide.'

At ten o'clock Wimsey and his collaborator sat down before a neat pile of scribbling paper. Harriet was inclined to be brief and businesslike.

'What system are we going to adopt about this? Do you favour the Michael Finsbury method by double entry as in *The Wrong Box*? Or one of those charts made out in columns, with headings for "Suspect", "Alibi", "Witnesses", "Motive" and so on, worked out in percentages?'

'Oh, don't let's have anything that means ruling a lot of lines and doing arithmetic. Let's behave like your Robert Templeton, and make a schedule of Things to be Noted and Things to be Done. That only means two columns.'

'Very well, I'm glad you approve of it. I always make Templeton start with the corpse.'

'Right. Here goes –'

PAUL ALEXIS (GOLDSCHMIDT)

Things to be Noted	*Things to be Done*
1. Russian by birth; English by adoption, partly American by education. Early history unknown, but claimed to be War refugee of noble descent.	1. Investigate origin. (N.B. The only people who knew much about him are dead, and anyway, this is a job for the police. And does it really matter? Probably not, unless Mrs Weldon's Bolshevik theory is correct.)
2. Personal characteristics: Said to be delicate (arthritis?); good dancer; vain of his appearance; wore beard on account of tendency to pimples; careful of his dress, but flamboyant in taste. Said to be romantic and emotional.	2. Had he the temperament to commit suicide? Find out if possible from colleagues and/or his mistress.
3. In February last, engaged himself to marry Mrs Weldon, a rich widow. Apparently desirous to secure himself against loss of profession consequent on increasing ill-health. Not anxious to push on marriage on account of opposition put forward by widow's son (or possibly on account of personal reluctance). Marriage fixed for fortnight or so after time of P. A.'s death.	3. Find out if Alexis really took any steps about the marriage at all.

Things to be Noted	*Things to be Done*
4. Poor, but not mercenary or dishonest, since he refused to soak Mrs W. Had balance of £320, which he changed into gold about three weeks ago. (N.B. He was only able to do so as result of curious accident. Can we say it was *essential* to any scheme he had in mind?)	4. Find the £300 in gold. Its destination will throw light on his intentions. N.B. – I think I know where it is. (P. W.) Do you? Where? (H. V.) Think it out for yourself. (P. W.)
5. About time of above transaction, his mistress left him for another man. (N.B. He affected distress, but his colleagues seem to think he was an assenting party. If so, did he intend (a) to facilitate his marriage with Mrs W.? (b) to start a new liaison with someone else? (c) to provide for his mistress in the event of his own disappearance or suicide?)	5. Interview the girl Leila Garland and her new man.
6. Shortly before his death he hinted to Mrs W. that something pleasing and mysterious was about to happen to him.	6. Find out if he mentioned this to anyone else. (Query: How does the turning of the £300 into gold bear on this point? It is suggestive of departure from the country rather than of suicide.)

Things to be Noted	*Things to be Done*
7. On the day preceding his death he paid all his bills and burnt his papers. Does this suggest suicide? Or an intention to leave the country?	7. Find out if he had a passport and visas. (Police.)
8. On the morning of his death he took a *return-*ticket to Darley Halt, and thence walked (or, just possibly, was conveyed) to the Flat-Iron Rock. (N.B. He packed no clothes and took his latchkey with him.)	8. I think we may take it for granted that none of the persons interviewed by the police took P. A. to the Flat-Iron. Find out whether anybody passed him on the road. He may not have walked alone. (Police.)
9. At 2.10 p.m. on Thursday, 18 June, he was found dead on the rock with his throat cut. A loud cry was heard at two o'clock, and the condition of the body when found showed that life had been only a few minutes extinct. A razor (which he never used) was found by the body, and he was wearing gloves.	9. FIND THE BODY.

'How professional it looks,' said Harriet. 'A nice little set of problems for Robert Templeton. The only thing I can do much about is interviewing this Leila person and her new young man. I fancy I might get more out of them than the police could.'

'There's nothing I can do that the police can't do better,' said Wimsey, mournfully. 'We'd better go on to the next.'

MRS WELDON

Things to be Noted	*Things to be Done*
1. Personal characteristics: Aged fifty-seven; silly; obstinate; genuinely attached to Alexis; incurably romantic.	1. Nothing to be done about it.
2. Rich widow; one son; formerly on cool terms with him and complained of lack of sympathy; now has summoned him to her side and seems full of affection for him.	2. Find out where her money came from; whether it is at her sole disposal; what she proposed to do with it (*a*) before meeting Alexis, (*b*) after marrying Alexis; what she means to do with it now.
3. She attributes death of Alexis to Bolshevik plot.	3. Get information from Scotland Yard about Bolshevik agents. No theory is too silly to be dismissed without investigation.

HENRY WELDON

Things to be Noted	*Things to be Done*
1. Personal characteristics: Tallish, broad, powerful, resembles his mother facially; obstinate, ill-mannered, countrified; apparently not very intelligent.	1. Kick him. (P. W.) Well, no, that wouldn't be politic. String him along and see if he is really as stupid as he makes out. (H. V.) All right, but kick him afterwards. (P. W.)

Things to be Noted	Things to be Done
2. He has suddenly left his farm at the busiest time to suck up to his mother and pretend to help her clear P. A.'s memory. But actually he is doing his best to drive P. W. to chucking up the investigation.	2. Find out what the state of his finances is, and what his farm is like. Also his local reputation. (Query: Why not give Bunter something to do?)
3. The news of P. A.'s death was in the papers on Friday morning; H. W. arrived Wilvercombe Monday evening, in answer to letter presumably sent by Mrs W. on Friday, and addressed to Huntingdonshire.	3. Find out where Henry Weldon was on Thursday.

ESDRAS POLLOCK

Things to be Noted	Things to be Done
1. Personal characteristics: Aged seventy or more, sturdy for his age; bent, grey, smells of fish; manners none and customs beastly; unpopular with the fishing population.	1. Pump fishing population.
2. He was in his boat off the Flat-Iron at 2.10 p.m. on Thursday, with his grandson.	2. A fact.

Things to be Noted	*Things to be Done*
3. He is reluctant to say what he was doing there, and the grandson has disappeared to Cork.	3. Trace grandson. (Police.)
4. He states that he hugged the shore between his cottage and the Flat-Iron and saw nobody along the shore; but when questioned about events at the Flat-Iron at two o'clock, contradicts himself and says that he was then in deep water. (N.B. He saw what H. V. was doing all right at 2.10.)	4. Try the grandson on this when traced. (Police.)
5. When pressed, says he first saw P. A. on rock about two o'clock, and that he was then alone and already lying down.	5. How about a little Third Degree? Once again, trace and interrogate grandson. (Police.)
6. Curiously enough, when asked if anyone was with him in the boat, says 'Nobody' – but when grandson is mentioned, admits grandson. Who did he think was meant?	6. Find out whether P. A. could have reached Flat-Iron in Pollock's boat. Find out what has happened to the £300 in gold. Search boat for bloodstains. (Police.)

– PERKINS (of London)

Things to be Noted	Things to be Done
1. Personal characteristics: Small, weakish, round-shouldered. Wore spectacles and was apparently shortsighted. Complained of blistered heel. Cockney accent. Appeared to be of timid disposition.	1. Find him.
2. Met H. V. on road at 4.15 about half-a-mile on the far side of Pollock's cottage, i.e. about one and a half miles from Flat-Iron and three miles from Darley. Said he had walked from Wilvercombe.	2. Find out if anybody noticed him on the way. Note: it is only seven miles from Wilvercombe to the place where H. V. met him. When did he start out? Where did he sleep Tuesday night? (Police must have done something about this – ask Umpelty.)
3. On hearing from H. V. about body, turned back and accompanied her, ostensibly to protect her (but was about as useful as a rain-coat under machine-gun fire).	3. Find him and see what he's made of.
4. Went willingly to Pollock's cottage, but was annoyed with H. V. for addressing Martin.	4. Find him! Find Martin!
5. Disappeared mysteriously while H. V. was telephoning police, took car to Wilvercombe station and undiscoverable.	5. Find him! find him! find him, curse you! (Meaning the police.)

Wimsey put his head to one side.

'Really, every character seems more suspicious than the last. Who else is there? How about the cast-off Leila Garland, for instance? Or this chap Antoine? Or Leila's new man?'

'We can't do much about them till we've seen them.'

'No; but either Leila or the man – what's his name – da Soto – might have a motive for getting rid of Alexis.'

'Well. We've already put down that they've got to be looked into. Is that all? Oh, no!'

'No. We now come to my own pet particular prize suspect, the sinister Mr Martin.'

HAVILAND MARTIN

Things to be Noted	*Things to be Done*
1. Personal characteristics: Tall, massive, dark hair; black spectacles; tattoo-mark on right wrist; dressed in khaki shirt and shorts, with wide-brimmed soft hat.	1. Keep your mind on the tattoo-mark! You can fake them, you know. (H. V.) Bah! (P. W.)
2. Arrived Darley six o'clock Tuesday, 16th, with hired Morgan, coming from Heathbury direction.	2. A fact. Why a Morgan?
3. Though no one had ever seen him in the village before, knew all about Hinks's Lane and Mr Goodrich.	3. Find out if anyone saw him in Heathbury or anywhere else and told him.
4. Seen at Three Feathers about one o'clock on Thursday, 18th, and lunched there.	4. A fact, apparently.

Things to be Noted	Things to be Done
5. Left Feathers not earlier than 1.30.	5. Also a fact, alas!
6. Seen by Mr Polwhistle and Tom at garage and in Hinks's Lane from 3 p.m. to 4 p.m.	6. Yet another fact, unless they are abominable liars!
7. Obtained car from London garage on previous Friday by means of reference to Cambridge bank. No settled address. Cambridge bank confirms he has had account there for five years.	7. Watch bank. Try to get information out of manager somehow.
8. It is certain that he did not reach the Flat-Iron by road on Thursday. He had not time to walk by the shore before two o'clock. (Aeroplanes are not practical politics.)	8. Bust this alibi if you can, Sherlock!!
9. Search at his camping-ground revealed a number of miscellaneous objects (see the Wimsey Collection). No complaints about him, except that Farmer Newcombe complains of gap made in his fence.	9. Walk along shore from Flat-Iron to Darley this afternoon – nice little job for H. V. and P. W.

'And that,' said Wimsey, triumphantly adding a flourish at the foot of this schedule, 'rounds off the inquiry charmingly.'

'It does.' Harriet frowned. Then –

'Have you ever considered this?' she asked, with a not too steady voice. She scribbled for a moment.

HARRIET VANE
Things to be Noted
1. Personal characteristics: Once tried for murder of her lover, and acquitted by the skin of her teeth.
2. May have known Paul Alexis in London.
3. Says she found Alexis dead at 2.10, but can bring no evidence to prove that she did not see him alive.
4. Took an unconscionable time getting to the Flat-Iron from Lesston Hoe.
5. Took three hours to walk four and a half miles to inform the police.
6. Is the sole witness to the finding of the razor, the time of the death and the conditions at the Flat-Iron.
7. Was immediately suspected by Perkins, and is probably still suspected by the police, who have been searching her room.

Wimsey's face darkened.

'Have they, by God?'

'Yes. Don't look like that. They couldn't very well do anything else, could they?'

'I'll have something to say to Umpelty.'

'No. You can spare me that.'

'But it's absurd.'

'It is not. Do you think I have no wits? Do you think I don't know why you came galloping down here at five minutes' notice? Of course it's very nice of you, and I ought to be grateful, but do you think I like it?'

Wimsey, with a grey face, got up and walked to the window.

'You thought I was pretty brazen, I expect, when you found me getting publicity out of the thing. So I was. There's no choice for a person like me to be anything but brazen. Would it have been better to wait till the papers dragged the juicy bits out of the dust-bin for themselves? I can't hide my name – it's what I live by. If I did hide it, that would only be another suspicious circumstance, wouldn't it? But do you think it makes matters any more agreeable to know that it is only the patronage of Lord Peter Wimsey that prevent men like Umpelty from being openly hostile?'

'I have been afraid of this,' said Wimsey.

'Then why did you come?'

'So that you might not have to send for me.'

'*Oh!*'

There was a strained pause, while Wimsey painfully recalled the terms of the message that had originally reached him from Salcombe Hardy of the *Morning Star* – Hardy, a little drunk and wholly derisory, announcing over the telephone, 'I say, Wimsey, that Vane woman of yours has got herself mixed up in another queer story.' Then his own furious and terrified irruption into Fleet Street, and the violent bullying of a repentant and sentimental Hardy, till the *Morning Star* report was hammered into a form that set the tone for the comments of the press. Then the return home to find that the Wilvercombe police were already besieging him, in the politest and most restrained manner, for information as to Miss Harriet Vane's recent movements and behaviour. And finally, the certainty that the best way out of a bad situation was to brazen it out – Harriet's word – even if it meant making a public exhibition of his feelings, and the annihilation of all the delicate structure of confidence which he had been so cautiously toiling to build up between this scathed and embittered woman and himself.

He said nothing, but watched the wreck of his fortune in Harriet's stormy eyes.

Harriet, meanwhile, having worked herself up into committing an act of what she obscurely felt to be injustice, was seized by an unreasonable hatred against the injured party. The fact that, until five minutes earlier, she had felt perfectly happy and at ease with this man, before she had placed both him and herself in an intolerable position, she felt somehow as one more added to the list of his offences. She looked round for something really savage to do to him.

'I suppose you think I haven't been humiliated enough already, without all this parade of chivalry. You think you can sit up there all day like King Cophetua being noble and generous and expecting people to be brought to your feet. Of course everybody will say, "Look what he did for that woman – isn't it marvellous of him!" Isn't that nice for you? You think if you go on long enough I ought to be touched and softened. Well, you're mistaken, that's all. I suppose every man thinks he's only got to go on being superior and any woman will come tumbling into his arms. It's disgusting.'

'Thank you,' said Wimsey. 'I may be everything you say – patronising, interfering, conceited, intolerable and all the rest of it. But do give me credit for a little intelligence. Do you think I don't know all that? Do you think it's pleasant for any man who feels about a woman as I do about you, to have to fight his way along under this detestable burden of gratitude? Damn it, do you think I don't know perfectly well that I'd have a better chance if I was deaf, blind, maimed, starving, drunken or dissolute, so that *you* could have the fun of being magnanimous? Why do you suppose I treat my own sincerest feelings like something out of a comic opera, if it isn't to save myself the bitter humiliation of seeing you try not to be utterly nauseated by them? Can't you understand that this damned dirty trick of fate has robbed me of the common man's right to be serious about his own passions? Is that a position for any man to be proud of?'

'Don't talk like that.'

'I wouldn't, if you didn't force me. And you might have the justice to remember that you can hurt me a damned sight more than I can possibly hurt you.'

'I know I'm being horribly ungrateful –'

'Hell!'

All endurance has its limits, and Wimsey had reached his.

'Grateful! Good God! Am I never to get away from the bleat of that filthy adjective? I don't want gratitude. I don't want kindness. I don't want sentimentality. I don't even want love – I could make you give me that – of a sort. I want common honesty.'

'Do you? But that's what I've always wanted – I don't think it's to be got.'

'Listen, Harriet. I do understand. I know you don't want either to give or to take. You've tried being the giver, and you've found that the giver is always fooled. And you won't be the taker, because that's very difficult, and because you know that the taker always ends by hating the giver. You don't want ever again to have to depend for happiness on another person.'

'That's true. That's the truest thing you ever said.'

'All right. I can respect that. Only you've got to play the game. Don't force an emotional situation and then blame me for it.'

'But I don't want any situation. I want to be left in peace.'

'Oh! but you are not a peaceful person. You'll always make trouble. Why not fight it out on equal terms and enjoy it? Like Alan Breck, I'm a bonny fighter.'

'And you think you're sure to win.'

'Not with my hands tied.'

'Oh! – well, all right. But it all sounds so dreary and exhausting,' said Harriet, and burst idiotically into tears.

'Good Heavens!' said Wimsey, aghast. 'Harriet! darling! angel! beast! vixen! don't say that.' He flung himself on his knees in a frenzy of remorse and agitation. 'Call me anything you like, but not dreary! Not one of those things you find in clubs! Have this one, darling, it's much larger and quite clean. Say you didn't mean it! Great Scott! Have I been boring you interminably for eighteen months on end? A thing any right-minded woman would shudder at. I know you once said that if anybody ever married me it would be for the sake of hearing me piffle on, but I expect that kind of thing palls after a bit. I'm babbling – I know I'm babbling. What on earth am I to do about it?'

'Ass! Oh, it's not fair. You always make me laugh. I can't fight – I'm so tired. You don't seem to know what being tired is. Stop. Let go. I won't be bullied. Thank God! there's the telephone.'

'Damn the telephone!'

'It's probably something very important.'

She got up and went to the instrument, leaving Wimsey on his knees, looking, and feeling, sufficiently absurd.

'It's you. Somebody wants you over at the Bellevue.'

'Let him want.'

'Somebody come in answer to the thing in the *Morning Star.*'

'Good lord!'

Wimsey shot across the room and snatched the receiver.

'That you, Wimsey? Thought I'd know where to get you. This is Sally Hardy. There's a fellow here claiming the reward. Hurry up! He won't come across without you, and I've got my story to think of. I've got him here in your sitting-room.'

'Who is he, and where's he come from?'

'Seahampton. Says his name's Bright.'

'Bright? By jove, yes, I'll come along right away. Hear that, my child? The man Bright has materialised! See you this afternoon at 3.30.'

He bolted out like a cat that hears the cry of 'Meat, meat!'

'Oh! what a fool I am,' said Harriet. 'What an utter, drivelling fool! And I haven't done a stroke of work since Wednesday.'

She pulled out the manuscript of *The Fountain-Pen Mystery*, unscrewed her own pen, and sank into an idle reverie.

XIV

THE EVIDENCE OF THE THIRD BARBER

'Not for him
Blooms my dark Nightshade, nor doth Hemlock brew
Murder for cups within her cavernous root.
Not him is the metal blessed to kill,
Nor lets the poppy her leaves fall for him.
To heroes such are sacred. He may live,
As long as 'tis the Gout and Dropsy's pleasure.
He wished to play at suicide.'

Death's Jest-Book

TUESDAY, 23 JUNE

On the doorstep of the Hotel Bellevue, Wimsey encountered Bunter.

'The person that was asking for your lordship is in your lordship's sitting-room,' said Bunter. 'I had the opportunity of observing him when he was inquiring for your lordship at the reception-counter, but I did not introduce myself to his notice.'

'You didn't, eh?'

'No, my lord. I contented myself with privately informing Mr Hardy of his presence. Mr Hardy is with him at present, my lord.'

'You always have a good reason for your actions, Bunter. May I ask why you have adopted this policy of modest self-effacement?'

'In case of your lordship's subsequently desiring to have the person placed under surveillance,' suggested Bunter, 'it

179

appeared to me to be preferable that he should not be in a position to recognise me.'

'Oh!' said Wimsey. 'Am I to infer that the person presents a suspicious appearance? Or is this merely your native caution breaking out in an acute form? Well, perhaps you're right. I'd better go up and interview the bloke. How about the police, by the way? We can't very well keep this from them, can we?'

He reflected for a moment.

'Better hear the story first. If I want you, I'll 'phone down to the office. Have any drinks gone up?'

'I fancy not, my lord.'

'Strange self-restraint on Mr Hardy's part. Tell them to bring up a bottle of Scotch and a siphon and some beer, for malt does more than Milton can to justify God's ways to man. At the moment there seem to be a good many things that call for justification, but perhaps I shall feel better about them when I've heard what Mr Bright has to tell me. Have at it!'

The moment Wimsey's eyes fell upon the visitor in his sitting-room he felt an interior conviction that his hopes were in a fair way to be realised. Whatever the result, he had, at any rate, been upon the right track in the matter of the razor. Here were the sandy hair, the small stature, the indefinite crookedness of shoulder so graphically described by the Seahampton hairdresser. The man was dressed in a shabby reach-me-down suit of blue serge, and held in his hands a limp felt hat, considerably the worse for wear. Wimsey noticed the soft skin and well-kept finger-nails, and the general air of poverty-stricken gentility.

'Well, Mr Bright,' said Hardy, as Wimsey entered, 'here is the gentleman you want to see. Mr Bright won't come across with his story to anybody but you, Wimsey, though, as I have explained to him, if he's thinking of claiming the *Morning Star* reward, he'll have to let me in on it.'

Mr Bright glanced nervously from one man to the other, and passed the tip of his tongue once or twice across his pallid lips.

'I suppose that's only fair,' he said, in a subdued tone, 'and I can assure you that the money is a consideration. But I am in a painful position, though I haven't done any wilful harm. I'm sure if I had ever thought what the poor gentleman was going to do with the razor –'

'Suppose we begin from the beginning,' said Wimsey, throwing his hat upon a table and himself into a chair. 'Come in! Oh, yes, drinks. What will you take, Mr Bright?'

'It is very kind of your lordship,' murmured Mr Bright, with humility, 'but I'm afraid I – the fact is, when I saw that piece in the paper I came away rather hurriedly. In fact, without my breakfast. I – that is to say – I am rather sensitive to alcohol taken upon an empty stomach.'

'Bring up some sandwiches,' said Wimsey to the waiter. 'It is very good of you, Mr Bright, to have put yourself to so much inconvenience in the interests of justice.'

'Justice?'

'I mean, in order to help us with this inquiry. And of course, you must allow us to refund your expenses.'

'Thank you, my lord. I won't say no. In fact, I am not in a position to refuse. I won't disguise that my means are very limited. As a matter of fact,' went on Mr Bright, with more frankness in the absence of the waiter, 'as a matter of fact, I had to go without any food in order to pay for my ticket. I don't like making this confession. It's very humiliating for a man who once had a flourishing business of his own. I hope you won't think, gentlemen, that I have been accustomed to this kind of thing.'

'Of course not,' said Wimsey. 'Bad times may happen to

anybody. Nobody thinks anything of that nowadays. Now, about this razor. By the way, your full name is –?'

'William Bright, my lord. I'm a hairdresser by profession. I used to have a business up Manchester way. But I lost money by an unfortunate speculation –'

'Whereabouts in Manchester?' put in Salcombe Hardy.

'In Massingbird Street. But it's all been pulled down now. I don't know if anybody would remember about it, I'm sure. It was before the War.'

'Any War record?' asked Hardy.

'No.' The hairdresser blushed painfully. 'I'm not a robust man. I couldn't get passed for active service.'

'All right,' said Wimsey. 'About the razor. What are you doing now?'

'Well, my lord, I am, as you might say, an itinerant hairdresser. I go from one place to the other, especially seaside towns during the season, and take temporary posts.'

'Where did you work last?'

The man glanced up at him with his hunted eyes.

'I haven't had anything, really, for a long time. I tried to get work in Seahampton. In fact, I'm still trying. I went back there last Wednesday after trying Wilvercombe and Lesston Hoe. I had a week's employment in Lesston Hoe. Ramage's is the name of the place. I had to leave there –'

'What for?' Hardy was brusque.

'There was trouble with a customer –'

'Theft?'

'Certainly not. He was a very quick-tempered gentleman. I had the misfortune to cut him slightly.'

'Drunk and incompetent, eh?' said Hardy.

The small man seemed to shrink together.

'They said so, but on my word of honour –'

'What name were you going by there?'

'Walters.'

'Is Bright your real name?'

Under the lash of Hardy's brutality, the story came out in all its sordid triviality. Alias after alias. A week's trial here and there, and then dismissal on the same humiliating grounds. Not his fault. A glass of spirits affected him more than it did the ordinary person. Simpson was his real name, but he had used a great many since then. But to each name, the same reputation had stuck. It was his sad weakness, which he had tried hard to overcome.

Hardy poured himself out a second glass of whisky, and carelessly left the bottle on the window-sill, out of Mr Bright's reach.

'In the matter of the razor,' said Wimsey, patiently.

'Yes, my lord. I got that razor in Seahampton, from the place where I tried to get work. Merryweather, the name was. I needed a new razor, and he was willing to sell this one cheap.'

'You'd better describe the razor,' suggested Hardy.

'Yes, sir. It was a Sheffeld blade with a white handle, and it came originally from a retailer in Jermyn Street. It was a good razor, but a bit worn. I came on to Wilvercombe, but there was nothing doing here, except that Moreton, down on the Esplanade, said he might be requiring help later on. Then I went to Lesston Hoe. I told you about that. After trying one or two other places there, I came back here and tried Moreton again, but he had just engaged somebody. He would tell you about it if you asked him. There was nothing doing anywhere else. I grew very low in my spirits.'

Mr Bright paused and licked his lips again.

'This was last Monday week, gentlemen. On the Tuesday night, I went down to the sea – just over there, at the end of the town, and sat on a seat to think things over. It was getting on for midnight.' The words were coming more fluently now, the glass of whisky having no doubt done its work. 'I looked at the sea and I felt the razor in my pocket and I wondered whether it was worth while struggling on. I was terribly depressed. I had come quite to the end of my resources. There was the sea, and there was the razor. You might think that the use of a razor would come natural to a hairdresser, but I can assure you gentlemen that the idea of using it for that purpose seems just as horrible to us as it would to you. But the sea – washing up against the wall of the Esplanade – it seemed to call me, if you can understand what I mean. It sounded as if it was saying: "Chuck it, chuck it, chuck it up, Bill Simpson." Fascinating and frightening at the same time, as you might say. All the same, I've always had a horror of drowning. Helpless and choking, and the green water in your eyes – we all have our special night-mares, and that one's mine. Well, I'd sat there for a bit, trying to make up my mind, when I heard somebody walking along, and presently this young fellow came and sat down on the seat beside me. He was in evening dress, I remember, with an overcoat and a soft hat. He had a black beard – that was about the first thing I noticed, because it's not very usual on a young man in this country, except he might be an artist, perhaps. Well, we got into conversation – I think he started it by offering me a cigarette. It was one of those Russian ones, with a paper tube to it. He spoke friendly, and, I don't know how it was, I found myself telling him all about the fix I was in. You know how it is, my lord. Sometimes you'll get talking to a stranger where you wouldn't to anybody you knew. It struck me he didn't feel so very happy himself, and we had a long talk about the general damnableness of life. He said he was a Russian and an exile and told me about the hard times he'd had as a kid, and a lot of stuff about "Holy Russia" and the Soviet. Seems as if he took it to heart a lot. And women and all that – seemed as though he'd had some trouble with his best girl. And then he said he only wished his difficulties could be solved as easy as mine, and how I ought to pull myself together and make a fresh start. "You give me that razor," he said, "and go away and think it over." So I said the razor was my livelihood, such as it was, and he laughed and said, "In the mood you're in, it's more likely to be your death-lihood." A funny way he had of talking, quick and sort of poetic, you know. So he gave me some money – five pounds it was, in Treasury notes – and I gave him the razor. "What'll you do with that, sir?" I said, "it's no good to you." "I'll find a use for it," he said, "never you fear." And he laughed and put it away in his pocket. Then he got up and said, "Funny we should drop across one another to-night," and something about "two minds with but a single thought". And he clapped me on the shoulder and told me to buck up and gave me a pleasant nod and away he went, and that's the last I saw of him. I wish I'd known what he wanted with the razor, or I wouldn't have given it to him, but there! how was I to know, I ask you, gentlemen?'

'Sounds like Paul Alexis, right enough,' said Wimsey, thoughtfully.

'He didn't actually say who he was, I suppose?' suggested Hardy.

'No, he didn't; but he said he was a professional dancing-partner at one of the hotels, and wasn't it one hell of a life for a man that ought to be a prince in his own country – making love to ugly old women at twopence-halfpenny a time. Very bitter he sounded.'

'Well,' said Wimsey, 'we're very much obliged to you, Mr Bright. That seems to clear the whole thing up quite satisfac-torily. I think you'll have to let the police know about it.'

Mr Bright looked uneasy at the mention of the police.

'Better come along now and get it over,' said Wimsey, jumping to his feet. 'You can't very well get out of it, and, hang it all, man! there's nothing in it for anybody to worry you about.'

The hairdresser agreed, reluctantly, and fastened his pale eyes on Sally Hardy.

'It all sounds O.K. to me,' said the latter, 'but we'll have to check up on your story, you know, old man. You might have invented it. But if the cops can prove what you say about yourself – it's their business, really – then there'll be a good, fat cheque for you, that ought to keep you going for some time, if you'll steer clear of that – er – little weakness of yours. The great thing,' added Sally, reaching for the whisky, 'is never to let weaknesses interfere with business.'

He poured himself out a stiff peg and, as an afterthought, mixed another for the hairdresser.

Superintendent Glaisher was delighted with Bright's story, and so was Inspector Umpelty, who had clung to the suicide theory all along.

'We'll soon get this business cleared up,' said the latter, confidently. 'We'll check up on this Bright lad's movements, but they're probably right enough. They fit in O.K. with what that man said at Seahampton. And we'll keep an eye on Bright. He's had to give us an address and his promise to stay in Wilvercombe, because, of course, he'll be wanted for the inquest – when we get an inquest. The body's bound to turn up soon. I can't understand why it's not been found before this. It's been five days in the water now, and it can't stay there for ever. They float first, you know, and then they sink, but they have to come up again when the gases start to form. I've seen 'em blown up like balloons. It must have got caught somewhere, that's about the way of it; but we'll be dragging the bay near the Grinders again this afternoon, and we're sure to get something before long. I'll be glad when we do. Makes one feel kind of foolish to be carrying on an investigation without a body to show for it.'

'Satisfied?' asked Hardy, as Wimsey returned from the police-station. He had telephoned his story to Town and was absorbing a little refreshment after his labours.

'I ought to be,' replied his lordship. 'The only thing that worries me, Sally, is that if I'd wanted to invent a story to fit this case, that is exactly the story I should have invented. I wonder where Mr Bright was at two o'clock on Thursday afternoon.'

'What an obstinate devil you are,' said Mr Hardy. 'Fact is, you're so damned keen on a murder, you smell murder everywhere. Forget it.'

Wimsey was silent, but when he had got rid of Sally Hardy, he drew out of his pocket a small leaflet entitled 'Tide Tables', and studied it carefully.

'I thought so,' he said.

He took a piece of paper and wrote out a schedule of Things to be noted and Things to be Done under the name of William Bright. It embodied the substance of Bright's story and of the conversation with the police; but the left-hand column ended with this observation:

> 'He states that the tide, lapping against the Esplanade, seemed to call him in a very convincing and poetic manner. But at midnight on Tuesday, 16 June the tide was not lapping against the Esplanade. It was the extreme bottom of the ebb.'

And in the right-hand column he wrote:

> 'Keep an eye on him.'

After a little more thought, he took a fresh sheet of paper and wrote a letter to Chief Inspector Parker of Scotland Yard, asking for information about Bolshevik agents. One never could tell. Queer things have happened before this – queerer things even than Bolshevik conspiracies. Incidentally, he mentioned Mr Haviland Martin and his banking account. Parker, with the Bolsheviks as an excuse, might find ways and means to unlock even a bank-manager's lips. Superintendent Glaisher might not like this horning in on his province – but Parker had married Lord Peter's sister, and may not a man write a private letter to his own brother-in-law?

XV

THE EVIDENCE OF THE
LADYLOVE AND THE LANDLADY

'You are an adept in these chamber-passions,
And have a heart that's Cupid's arrow-cushion
Worn out with use.'

Death's Jest-Book

'What's this? Did you not see a white convulsion
Rut through his cheek and fling his eyelids up?
There's mischief in the paper.'

Fragment

TUESDAY, 23 JUNE

IN THE meantime, Harriet's novel was not getting along very well. Not only was there the tiresomeness about the town-clock – or ought it to be called the Tolbooth clock? – but also she had arrived at the point where, according to the serial editor who was paying for the first rights, the heroine and the detective's friend were expected to indulge in a spot of love-making. Now, a person whose previous experience of love has been disappointing, and who has just been through a harassing scene with another suitor and is, further, busily engaged in investigating the rather sordid love-affairs of a third party who has been brought to a violent and blood-boltered end, is in no mood to sit down and deal competently with the raptures of two innocents holding hands in a rose-garden. Harriet shook her head impatiently, and plunged into her distasteful task.

'I say, Betty, I'm afraid you must think I'm a pretty average sort of idiot.'

'But I don't think you're an idiot at all, you idiot.'

Would even the readers of the *Daily Message* think that amusing? Harriet feared not. Well, better get on with it. The girl would have to say something encouraging now, or the stammering young imbecile would never come to the point.

'I think it's perfectly wonderful that you should be doing all this to help me.'

Here she was, remorselessly binding this hideous load of gratitude on the unfortunate girl. But Betty and Jack were a pair of hypocrites, anyway, because they both knew perfectly well that Robert Templeton was doing all the work. However.

'As if there was anything in the world I wouldn't try and do for you – Betty!'

'Well, Jack?'

'Betty – darling – I suppose you couldn't possibly –'

Harriet came to the conclusion that she couldn't – not possibly. She picked up the telephone, got put through to Telegrams, and dictated a brief, snappy message to her long-suffering agent. 'Tell Bootle I absolutely refuse induce love-interest – Vane.'

After that she felt better, but the novel was perfectly impossible. Wasn't there anything else she could do? Yes. She again seized the telephone and put an inquiry through to the office. Was it possible to get into touch with M. Antoine?

The management seemed quite used to putting clients in touch with M. Antoine. They had a telephone number which ought to find him. It did. Could M. Antoine put Miss Vane in touch with Miss Leila Garland and Mr da

Soto? Certainly. Nothing was more simple. Mr da Soto was playing at the Winter Gardens, and the morning concert would be just finishing. Miss Garland would probably be joining him for lunch. In any case, Antoine would charge himself with all that and would, if Miss Vane desired it, call for her and accompany her to the Winter Gardens. It was most good of M. Antoine. On the contrary, it was a pleasure; in a quarter of an hour's time, then? *Parfaitement.*

'Tell me, M. Antoine,' said Harriet, as their taxi rolled along the Esplanade. 'You who are a person of great experience, is love, in your opinion, a matter of the first importance?'

'It is, alas! of a great importance, mademoiselle, but of the first importance, no!'

'What is of the first importance?'

'Mademoiselle, I tell you frankly that to have a healthy mind in a healthy body is the greatest gift of *le bon Dieu*, and when I see so many people who have clean blood and strong bodies spoiling themselves and distorting their brains with drugs and drink and foolishness, it makes me angry. They should leave that to the people who cannot help themselves because to them life is without hope.'

Harriet hardly knew what to reply; the words were spoken with such personal and tragic significance. Rather fortunately, Antoine did not wait.

'*L'amour!* These ladies come and dance and excite themselves and want love and think it is happiness. And they tell me about their sorrows – me – and they have no sorrows at all, only that they are silly and selfish and lazy. Their husbands are unfaithful and their lovers run away and what do they say? Do they say, I have two hands, two feet, all my faculties, I will make a life for myself? No. They say, Give me cocaine, give me the cocktail, give me the thrill, give me my gigolo, give me *l'amo-o-ur*! Like a *mouton* bleating in a field. If they knew!

Harriet laughed.

'You're right, M. Antoine. I don't believe *l'amour* matters so terribly, after all.'

'But understand me,' said Antoine who, like most Frenchmen, was fundamentally serious and domestic, 'I do not say that love is not important. It is no doubt agreeable to love, and to marry an amiable person who will give you fine, healthy children. This Lord Peter Wimsey, *par example*, who is obviously a gentleman of the most perfect integrity –'

'Oh, never mind *him*!' broke in Harriet, hastily. 'I wasn't thinking about him. I was thinking about Paul Alexis and these people we are going to see.'

'Ah! *c'est différent*. Mademoiselle, I think you know very well the difference between love which is important and love which is not important. But you must remember that one may have an important love for an unimportant person. And you must remember also that where people are sick in their minds or their bodies it does not need even love to make them do foolish things. When I kill myself, for example, it may be out of boredom, or disgust, or because I have the headache or the stomach-ache or because I am no longer able to take a first-class position and do not want to be third-rate.'

'I hope you're not thinking of anything of the sort.'

'Oh, I shall kill myself one of these days,' said Antoine, cheerfully. 'But it will not be for love. No. I am not so *détraqué* as all that.'

The taxi drew up at the Winter Gardens. Harriet felt a certain delicacy about paying the fare, but soon realised that for Antoine the thing was a commonplace. She accompanied him to the orchestra entrance where, in a few minutes' time, they were joined by Leila Garland and Luis da Soto – the perfect platinum blonde and the perfect lounge-lizard. Both were perfectly self-possessed and incredibly polite; the only difficulty – as Harriet found when they were seated

191

together at a table – was to get any reliable information out of them. Leila had evidently taken up an attitude, and stuck to it. Paul Alexis was 'a terribly nice boy', but 'too romantic altogether'. Leila had been 'terribly grieved' to send him away, he 'took it so terribly hard' – but, after all, her feeling for him had been no more than pity – he had been 'so terribly timid and lonely'. When Luis came along, she realised at once where her affections really lay. She rolled her large periwinkle eyes at Mr da Soto, who responded by a languishing droop of his fringèd lids.

'I was all the more sorry about it,' said Leila, 'because poor darling Paul –'

'Not darling, honey.'

'Of course not, Luis – only the poor thing's dead. Anyway, I was sorry because poor Paul seemed to be so terribly worried about something. But he didn't confide in me, and what is a girl to do when a man won't confide in her? I sometimes used to wonder if he wasn't being blackmailed by somebody.'

'Why? Did he seem to be short of money?'

'Well, yes, he did. Of course, that wouldn't make any difference to me; I'm not that sort of girl. Still, it's not pleasant, you know, to think that one of your gentleman friends is being blackmailed. I mean, a girl never knows she may not get mixed up in something unpleasant. I mean, it isn't quite nice, is it?'

'Far from it. How long ago did he start being worried?'

'Let me see. I think it was about five months ago. Yes, it was. I mean, that was when the letters started coming.'

'Letters?'

'Yes; long letters with foreign stamps on them. I think they came from Czechoslovakia or one of those queer places. It wasn't Russia, anyway, because I asked him and he said no. I thought it was very funny, because he said he'd never been in any foreign country except Russia when he was quite a little boy, and in America, of course.'

'Have you told anybody else about these letters?'

'No. You see, Paul always said it would do him harm to have them mentioned. He said the Bolsheviks would kill him if anything got out. I said to him, "I don't know what you mean by that," I said, "I'm not a Bolshie," I said, "and I don't know any people of that sort, so what harm would it do to tell me about it?" But now he's dead it can't do any harm, can it? Besides, if you ask me, I don't believe it was Bolshies at all. I mean, it doesn't seem likely, does it? I said to him, "If you expect me to swallow *that* story, you're expecting a lot," I said. But he wouldn't tell me, and of course, that did make a little coolness between us. I mean to say, when a girl is friends with a man, like me and Paul, she does expect a little consideration.'

'Of course she does,' said Harriet, warmly. 'It was very wrong of him not to be perfectly frank with you. I really think, in your place, I'd have felt justified in trying to find out who the letters were from.'

Leila played delicately with a piece of bread.

'As a matter of fact,' she admitted, 'I did take a tiny peep once. I thought I owed it to myself. But they were all nonsense. You couldn't make a word of them.'

'Were they in a foreign language?'

'Well, I don't know. They were all in printing letters and some of the words hadn't any vowels in them at all. You couldn't possibly pronounce them.'

'It sounds like a cipher,' suggested Antoine.

'Yes, that's just what I thought. I did think it was terribly funny.'

'But surely,' said Harriet, 'an ordinary blackmailer wouldn't write letters in cipher.'

'Oh, but why shouldn't they? I mean, they might have been a gang, you know, like in that story, *The Trail of the*

Purple Python. Have you read it? The Purple Python was a Turkish millionaire, and he had a secret house full of steel-lined rooms and luxurious divans and obelisks–'

'Obelisks?'

'Well, you know. Ladies who weren't quite respectable. And he had agents in every country in Europe, who bought up compromising letters and he wrote to his victims in cipher and signed his missives with a squiggle in purple ink. Only the English detective's young lady found out his secret by disguising herself as an obelisk and the detective who was really Lord Humphrey Chillingfold arrived with the police just in time to rescue her from the loathsome embrace of the Purple Python. It was a terribly exciting book. Paul read lots of books like that – I expect he was trying to pick up ideas for getting the better of the gang. He liked the talkies too. Of course, in those stories, the hero always comes out on top, only poor dear Paul wasn't really a bit like a hero. I said to him one day, "It's all very well,' I said, "but I can't see *you* venturing into a Chinese opium den full of gangsters, with a pistol in your pocket, and being gassed and sandbagged and then throwing off your bonds and attacking the Underworld King with an electric lamp. You'd be afraid of getting hurt," I said to him. And so he would.'

Mr da Soto snickered appreciatively.

'You said a mouthful, honey. Poor Alexis was a friend of mine, but courage was just what he didn't have. I told him, if he didn't stand out of my way and let little Leila pick her own sweetie, I would give him a sock on the jaw. I give you my word, he was scared stiff.'

'So he was,' said Leila. 'Of course, a girl couldn't feel any respect for a man that didn't stand up for himself.'

'Remarkable!' said Antoine. 'And this young man, so timid, so complaisant, cuts his throat with a big, ugly gash because you turn him down. *C'est inoui.*'

'I suppose you believe his Bolshie story,' said Leila, offended.

'I? I believe nothing. I am agnostic. But I say that your portrait of Alexis is not very logical.'

'Antoine always talks about logic,' said Leila, 'but what I say is, people aren't logical. Look at all the funny things they do. Especially men. I always think men are terribly inconsistent.'

'You bet they are,' said Mr da Soto. 'You're just dead right, sweetest. They have to be, or they wouldn't be bothered with naughty little girlies like you.'

'Yes, but the letters,' said Harriet, sticking desperately to her point. 'How often did they come?'

'About once a week, sometimes oftener. He kept them locked up in a little box. He used to answer them, too. Sometimes when I went round to see him, he'd have his door locked, and old Ma Lefranc said he was writing letters and wasn't to be disturbed. Naturally, a girl doesn't like her gentleman friend to behave like that. I mean, you do expect him to pay a little attention to you and not shut himself up writing letters when you come to see him. I mean, it wasn't the sort of thing you could expect a girl to put up with.'

'Of course you couldn't baby,' said Mr da Soto.

Antoine smiled, and murmured unexpectedly:

'*Mais si quelqu'un venoit de la part de Cassandre,*
Ouvre-luy tost la porte, et ne le fais attendre,
Soudain entre dans ma chambre, et me vien accoustrer.'

Harriet smiled back at him and then, struck with an idea, asked Leila:

'When did the last of these letters arrive?'

'I don't know. I wasn't friends with him any more after I got friendly with Luis. But I expect Ma Lefranc would tell you. There isn't much goes on that Ma Lefranc doesn't know about.'

'Did you and Alexis live together when you were friendly?' demanded Harriet, bluntly.

'Of course not; what a dreadful thing to ask a girl.'

'I mean, in the same house.'

'Oh, no. We used to go and see each other quite often, but of course, after Luis and me became friends, I said to Paul that it would be better if we didn't see each other any more. You see, Paul was so fond of me, and Luis would have been imagining things – wouldn't you, Luis?'

'You bet your life I would, honey.'

'Haven't you told the police about these letters?'

'No, I have not,' replied Miss Garland, decidedly. 'I don't say I mightn't have told them if they had asked properly, but the way that fat Umpelty went on, you'd have thought I wasn't a respectable girl. So I said to him, "I know nothing about it," I said, "and you've got nothing against me," I said, "and you can't make me answer your silly questions unless you take me down to your dirty old police-station and charge me," I said.' Miss Garland's carefully modulated tones escaped from control and became shrill. 'And I said, "It wouldn't be a scrap of good if you did," I said, "because I know nothing about Paul Alexis and I haven't seen him for months," I said, "and you can ask anybody you like," I said, "and what's more, if you get bullying a respectable girl like this," I said, "you'll get yourself into trouble, Mr Rumpelty-Bumpelty," I said, "so now you know where you get off." That's what I said, and it's a good thing there's a law in this country to protect girls like I.'

'Ain't she the snail's ankles?' asked Mr da Soto admiringly.

There seemed to be no further information to be gathered from Leila Garland, whom Harriet put down in her own mind as 'a regular little gold-digger and as vain as a monkey'. As for da Soto, he looked harmless enough, and did not seem to have any pressing reason for doing away with Alexis. One never knew, of course, with these slinky people of confused nationality. Just as she was thinking this, da Soto drew out his watch.

'You will excuse me, ladies and gentlemen. I have a rehearsal at two o'clock. As always, Tuesdays and Thursdays.'

He bowed and left them, with his lithe walk, between a lounge and a swagger. Had he deliberately mentioned Thursdays in order to direct attention to an alibi for Thursday, 18th? And how did he know the time for which an alibi was required? That particular detail had not been allowed to get into the papers, and it was not likely to do so until the inquest. And yet – could one attach any importance to the remark? An alibi depending on an orchestra rehearsal was so easily established or refuted. Then an explanation occurred to her: the police would already have asked da Soto about his movements last Thursday. But surely they would not have emphasised the crucial time to that extent. They had agreed that the less anybody knew about the time the better – it would be helpful in the inquiry if anyone were to come forward ostentatiously flourishing an alibi for two o'clock.

Harriet returned with Antoine, still not quite knowing what to make of da Soto. It was still only a quarter past two; she had time to carry out a new plan which she had formed. She put some clothes in a suit-case and went round to interview Paul Alexis' landlady, Mrs Lefranc.

The door of the cheap-looking lodging-house was opened to her by an ample personage with brazen hair, who was dressed in a pink wrapper, much-laddered artificial silk stockings and green velvet mules, and wore about her heavily powdered neck a string of synthetic-amber beads like pigeon's eggs.

'Good morning,' said Harriet, 'I'm looking for a room.'

The lady eyed her shrewdly and said:

'Professional, dearie?'

To say 'Yes' was tempting but unsafe. Mrs Lefranc looked as though what she did not know about professionals could have been written on a threepenny bit. Besides, Harriet was becoming well-known in Wilvercombe – she could scarcely hope to hide her identity for ever.

'No,' she said. 'I write books. In fact, Mrs Lefranc, I'm the person who found poor Mr Alexis last week. I've been staying at the Resplendent, but it's terribly expensive, and I thought, if your room was still vacant, I might be able to take it.'

'Well, there!' said Mrs Lefranc. She opened the door a little wider, but seemed to be divided between suspicion and curiosity. 'Well, there! I hardly know what to say. You ain't one of these journalists?'

'Oh, dear, no,' replied Harriet.

'Because,' said Mrs Lefranc, 'with those fellers you never know where you are. Worried to death I've been with them, poking their long noses into my private affairs. But of course *you* can't help but feel an interest, dearie, can you, seeing it was you that found him, poor boy. Come along in. Excuse my negleegy, won't you? If I'm not up and down, up and down, keeping an eye on that girl, I don't know where we'd all be. I don't get time to posh myself up of a morning. How long would you be wanting the room for?'

'I don't quite know. It depends on when they have the inquest.'

'Ah, yes – and they've got to find him first, poor lamb, ain't they? You know, I've got such a warm heart, I can't sleep at nights for thinking of him washing about in all that nasty sea. Mind the coal-scuttle, dearie; the times I tell that girl not to leave it on the stairs. It's a lovely room on the first floor – quite the best in the house, and you'll find the bed comfortable. Poor Mr Alexis always said it was like a home to him and I'm sure he was like a son to me.'

Mrs Lefranc led the way up, her green mules flapping and displaying large holes in the heels of her stockings.

'There, dearie!' said Mrs Lefranc, throwing open the door. 'I'm sure you couldn't find better in Wilvercombe, and it's nice and quiet – you'll be able to do your writing beautiful. I've had it all cleaned up and his clothes and things put away – and if you was to dislike his books and bits of things about, I could easy put them to the one side. But there! I daresay you won't mind them. It's not as if he'd died in this room, is it, poor soul? And I'm sure Mr Alexis was far too much the gentleman to commit a rash act on anybody's premises. That kind of thing do give a place a bad name, there's no denying it, and one is apt to be blamed for things as aren't in any woman's control, try as she may to make her visitors happy. But as to the books, well, of course, if it had been anything infectious they'd have to have been destroyed, though as to who they belong to now I don't know, I'm sure and the police can't tell me either, and I daresay they've as much right here as anywhere, with me being like a mother to him this year past and more. But anything infectious there is not, for he never was subject to any such complaint, enjoying good health as a rule, barring the pain in his joints which he had to lay up for at times, and the agony he went through was cruel. I'm sure my heart bled for him, and the amount of antipyrin he took for it would surprise you and he never would have a doctor. But there! I don't blame him. My sister had the rheumatics something cruel and the amount she spent on doctors and electric treatment and nothing to show for it, except her knee swelled up like a pumpkin. And she lost the use of the limb altogether, which was a cruel thing for a woman in her profession. A trapeze-artist, she was; I've got her photograph in my room if you would like to see it one day, dearie, and the wreaths her old pals sent to her funeral was beautiful to see. Covered the hearse, they did, and they had to have an extra carriage on purpose for them. But as I was saying, if you don't care about the books I'll take them away. I'm not going to have that Weldon woman or Leila Garland – the little cat – coming here trying to get hold of them.'

The room was pleasant enough – large and airy and much cleaner than Harriet could have hoped from Mrs Lefranc's appearance. The furniture was, of course, hideous, but, though shabby, solid and in good order. The books were just as Inspector Umpelty had described them: mainly novels in cheap editions, with some Russian paper-backs and a few volumes of Russian Court memoirs. The only striking relic of the former tenant was a very beautiful little ikon hung at the head of the bed – certainly old and probably valuable.

For form's sake Harriet entered upon a long haggle with Mrs Lefranc about terms, emerging victorious with an inclusive charge of two and a half guineas per week, or twelve shillings and find yourself.

'And it's not everybody I'd do that for,' said Mrs Lefranc. 'Only I can see you're one of the quiet sort. If there's a thing I don't want in my house it's trouble. Though I'm sure all this dreadful business is trouble enough for anybody. The cruel shock it was to me,' said Mrs Lefranc, gasping a little and sitting down on the bed, as though to demonstrate that the shock had not yet spent its force. 'I was that fond of poor Mr Alexis.'

'I'm sure you must have been.'

'Such a thoughtful boy,' pursued Mrs Lefranc, 'and the manners of a prince, he had. I'm sure, many's the time when I was run off my feet with the girl and the lodgers and all, he'd say, "Cheer up, ma" – they all call me that, "cheer up, ma. Have a little cocktail with me and here's to better days." Just like a son he was to me, I'm sure.'

Whatever Harriet may have thought of this touching

reminiscence, which sounded quite unlike anything she had heard of Paul Alexis, she did not ignore the hint.

'How about a spot of something now?' she suggested.

'I'm sure,' said Mrs Lefranc, 'I wasn't meaning – well, there! It's no end sweet of you, dearie, but I couldn't touch anything this time in the day. Not but what there's the jug-and-bottle at the Dragon just round the corner, which comes very convenient, and there's no doubt as a drop of gin do help your dinner to settle.'

Harriet bent her energies to overcoming the resistance of Mrs Lefranc, who presently put her head over the staircase and called to 'the girl' to slip round to the Dragon for a suitable quantity of gin.

'They know me,' she added, with a wink. 'What with these ridiculous laws about bottles and half-bottles, if they don't know you, they'd get you all locked-up before you knew where you were. You'd think they wanted to make folks drunk by Act of Parliament, wouldn't you? What with one thing and another and the police sticking their noses in and asking questions – as though my house wasn't always as well-conducted as the Archbishop of Canterbury's – and they know it too, for I've been here twenty years and never a complaint – it's hard for a decent woman to keep her head above water these days. And one thing I can say – I've never stinted anybody. My house is just like home to 'em, and so you'll find it, dearie.'

Under the influence of gin-and-water, Mrs Lefranc became less and less guarded. She had her own version of the Leila Garland complication.

'What there might be between those two,' she observed, 'I couldn't tell you, dearie. It's not my business, so long as my visitors conducts themselves quietly. I always say to my girls, "I'm not against ladies seeing their gentlemen-friends and contrariwise, provided there's no trouble caused. We've all been young once," I say to them, "but you will please to remember we want no trouble here." That's what I say, and there's never been a mite of trouble in this house till now. But I must say I wasn't sorry when that little cat took herself off. No, I wasn't. Nor I didn't like that dago of hers, either. I hope she's making him pay through the nose. You couldn't give that girl enough. Not but what she didn't make herself pleasant enough, and bring me a bunch of flowers or a little present when she came to see Mr Alexis, though where the money came from I was not asking. But when poor Mr Alexis told me that she had taken up with this da Soto fellow, I said, "You're well rid of her." That's what I said, and if you ask me, he knew it well enough.'

'You don't think he killed himself on her account, then?'

'I do not,' said Mrs Lefranc. 'And I'm sure I've puzzled my head often enough wondering why he did it. It wasn't on account of the old lady he was engaged to – I know that. To tell you the truth, dearie, he never expected that to come off. Of course, a young man in his position has to humour his ladies, but her family never would have stood it. Mr Alexis as good as told me that would never come off – and not so long ago either. "You see, ma," he said to me no longer ago than last Sunday week, "one of these days I may do still better for myself." "Oh, yes," I says to him, "you will be marrying the Princess of China, you will, like Aladdin in the Panto." No. I've thought about it over and over again, and I'll tell you what I think. I think it was his speculations went wrong.'

'Speculations?'

'Yes – those speculations of his in foreign countries. The letters he used to get! All stuck over with foreign stamps and addressed in funny handwriting. I used to chaff him about them. Reports, he said they were, and if they came right, he'd be one of the biggest men in the world. He used to say, "Ma, when my ship comes in, I'll give you a tiara stuck full of diamonds and make you housekeeper to royalty." Oh, dear, many's the laugh we've had together over it. Not but what there was a time when I could have had tiaras and necklaces if I'd wanted 'em. One of these days I'll show you my newspaper critiques. Airy-fairy-Lilian they used to call me when I was principal boy in old Rosenbaum's shows, though you mightn't think it to look at me now, dearie, for my figure's spread a bit, there ain't no denying.'

Harriet admired and sympathised, and led Mrs Lefranc gently back to the subject of the foreign letters.

'Well, dearie, there was one of them come two days before this dreadful thing happened. It must have been a long one, for he was shut up hours and hours with it. Working out his position, he used to call it. Well *I* think there must have been bad news in it, though he didn't let on. But he was queer all that day and the next. Seemed as though he didn't see you or hear you when you spoke to him. And laughing – hysterical, I should call it, if he'd been a girl. He kissed me on the Wednesday night when he went up to his bed. Joking he was and talking wild, but I didn't pay attention. That was rather his way, you know. "One of these days," he said, "you'll find I've opened my wings and gone." Little did I think – oh, dear me! Poor boy! I can see now that was just his way of breaking it to me. I heard him about in his room all night. Burning his papers, he was, poor dear lad. He'd had a dreadful disappointment and he didn't want anybody to know. And in the morning he gave me his week's money. "I know it's a bit early," he said – because, of course, it wasn't due till Saturday, "but if I give it to you now, it'll be safe," he said. "If I took it out with me, I might spend it." Of course I know what was in his mind, poor dear. He knew he was going out and he didn't want me to suffer; he always was considerate. But when I think now that a word might have saved him –'

Mrs Lefranc burst into tears.

'I did think he might have been going away sudden to see

after his speculations, but he didn't pack up anything, so of course I put that out of my mind. And as for him doing what he did do – how could I have thought it? He seemed in such high spirits. But there! I *might* have guessed, if my mind hadn't been full of other things – only what with the girl giving notice as she did that morning and one thing and another, I didn't pay attention. But they often do seem to be in high spirits before they put an end to themselves. There was poor Billy Carnaby – he was just the same. Gave an oyster-and-champagne party to the whole cast on his last night with his last penny and him the life and soul of it, making us split our sides – and then went off and blew his brains out in the gentlemen's lavatory.'

Mrs Lefranc cried bitterly for a few moments.

'But there!' she exclaimed, suddenly pulling herself together and blowing her nose, 'life's a funny thing and you can't account for it, can you? Let's be happy while we can. We'll all be having a little white stone over us before long and it don't matter so much how or when. When was you wanting to take the room, dearie?'

'I'll be coming in tonight,' said Harriet. 'I don't know whether I'll want my board or not, but if I leave my suitcase and pay you the twelve shillings for the room in advance, that'll be all right, won't it?'

'That's O.K., dearie,' said Mrs Lefranc, obviously cheered. 'Just you come when you like, you'll be happy with Ma Lefranc. There, now, you'll think I've been talking enough to fetch the hind leg off a donkey, but what I say is, a good cry now and again does you good when the world ain't using you well. All my young people brings their troubles to me. I only wish poor Mr Alexis had told me all his worries and he'd be here now. But he was a foreigner, when all's said and done and they aren't like us, are they? Mind that dustpan, dearie. Time and again I tell them not to leave things on the stairs, but you might as well talk to the cat. Five mice she left on my door-mat yesterday morning, if you'll believe me, not that they ever come upstairs, dearie, and don't you think it, but the cellars is overrun with them, the dirty little beasts. Well, so long, dearie, and by the way, here's your latch-key. It's lucky I had a new one cut; poor Mr Alexis took his away with him when he went and goodness knows where it is now. I let my visitors come in when and how they like; you'll find yourself comfortable here.'

XVI

THE EVIDENCE OF THE SANDS

'This is the oft-wished hour, when we together
May walk upon the sea-shore.'
Death's Jest-Book

TUESDAY, 23 JUNE

IF EITHER Harriet Vane or Lord Peter Wimsey felt any embarrassment at meeting again after their burst of free speech, they did not show it. Both had a story to tell, and were thus spared the awkwardness of being gravelled for lack of matter.

'Cipher letters? Is it possible that Mrs Weldon is all right and that we are all wrong? It makes it look more like murder, anyhow, which is one up to us. I don't think much of Mrs Lefranc's suggestion about speculations, but it's perfectly obvious that Alexis had some scheme in hand, and it may be that the scheme went wrong. I don't know. . . . I don't know. . . . Were there, perhaps, two different sets of circumstances? Is it an accident that Alexis should have been killed just as his plans were maturing? He seems to have been surrounded by a bunch of curiously unpleasant people – liars and half-wits and prostitutes and dagoes.'

'Yes; I can't say we're moving in very exalted circles. Antoine is the decentest of them – but probably you don't approve of Antoine.'

'Is that meant for a challenge? I know all about Antoine. Vetted him last night.'

'To see if he was nice for me to know?'

'Not altogether. Part of the process of exploring the ground. He seems a modest, sensible fellow. It's not his fault that he suffers from lack of vitality and incipient melancholia. He's supporting a mother in an asylum and looks after an imbecile brother at home.'

'Does he?'

'Apparently; but that doesn't mean that his own wits are not quite reliable at the moment. He was a little more frank about Alexis' love-affairs than he could be to you. Alexis seems to have taken a fairly robust view of his association with Mrs Weldon, and to have got rid of Leila with more than ordinary tact and ability. Da Soto is a bad egg, of course, but good enough for Leila, and he is probably vain enough to believe quite sincerely that he took her from Alexis *vi et armis*. But *why* all this? Well, never mind; let's have our tea. Hullo! Great activity out at sea! Two boats stationed off the Grinders.'

'Fishermen?'

'Fishers of men, I fancy,' replied Wimsey, grimly. 'It's Umpelty and his merry men. Pass me the field-glasses, Bunter. Yes. They look very busy. They've got the drags out. Have a squint.'

He passed the glasses to Harriet, who exclaimed:

'They're hauling something up. It must be pretty heavy. The Inspector's lending a hand and one of the men is hanging on at the other end for dear life to trim the boat. Oh, oh! you didn't see that. What a pity! Something gave way suddenly, and Inspector Umpelty has gone head over heels backwards into the boat. Now he's sitting up and rubbing himself.'

'Dear Umpelty!' Wimsey helped himself to a sandwich.

'They're dragging again; he's left it to the fishermen this time. . . . They've got it – they're hauling – it's coming up!'

'Sit down and have your tea.'

'Don't be silly. They're pulling away like anything. There's something black just showing –'

'Here! Let's have a look.'

Harriet surrendered the glasses. They were Wimsey's, after all, though if he thought that she would be upset by a distant view of what she had once seen so unpleasantly close —

Wimsey looked and began to laugh.

'Here, take them, quick! It's a bit of old iron. It looks like a boiler or something. Don't miss Umpelty's face; it's worth seeing.'

'Yes; that's what it is – a sort of cylinder. I wonder how that got there. They're examining it very carefully. Perhaps they think they'll find the body inside it. No go. They've dropped it back again.'

'What a disappointment!'

'Poor Umpelty! I say, these are lovely sandwiches. Did Bunter make them? He's a genius.'

'Yes. Hurry up. I want to have another look at that cleft in the rock before we start.'

The cleft, however, remained an enigma. Wimsey's attention was concentrated on the ring-bolt.

'I'll swear,' he said, 'that this hasn't been here more than a fortnight. It looks perfectly new, and the ring isn't worn anywhere. What the devil he can have wanted that for – Well, let us be going. I'll take the high road and you take the low road; that is, I'll scramble among the loose stuff at high-water mark, and you walk along by the sea's edge, and we'll work to-and-fro between the two. Anybody who finds anything shouts and we compare notes.'

'Right-ho!'

To walk along a solitary shore with one's heart's idol in the calm of a summer's afternoon may be classed as an agreeable occupation; but it loses much of its charm when the couple have to proceed, separated by the whole width of the beach, searching with backs bent double and eyes fixed on the ground for something which neither can define and which in all probability is not there. Harriet, mystified, but resolutely believing that Wimsey had some idea in his mind, kept steady to her job; Wimsey, though he searched carefully, paused a good many times to scan sea and shore, and appeared to be computing distances and memorising landmarks. Each explorer carried a satchel in which to store treasure-trove, and the conversation, such as it was, rather resembled the dialogue of a Russian tragedy. Thus:

Harriet: Oy!

Peter: Hullo!

   (They meet, centre.)

Harriet: A boot! I've found a boot!

Peter: Alas! alas! What boots it to repeat.

Harriet: Hobnailed and frightfully ancient.

Peter: Only one boot!

Harriet: Yes; if it had been two boots, it might mark the place where the murderer started to paddle.

Peter: One foot on sea and one on shore. The tide has risen and fallen ten times since then. It isn't a good boot.

Harriet: No, it's a bad boot.

Peter: It's a rotten boot.

Harriet: Can I throw it away?

Peter: No; after all, it *is* a boot.

Harriet: It's an awfully heavy boot.

Peter: I can't help that; it's a *boot*. Dr Thorndyke likes boots.

Harriet: Oh, death! where is thy sting?

   (They separate, Harriet carrying the boot.)

Peter: Oy!

Harriet: Hullo!

   (They meet again.)

Peter: Here is an empty sardine-tin, and here is a broken bottle.

Harriet: Have you the pen of the gardener's aunt?

Peter: No; but my (female) cousin has (some) ink, (some) paper and (some) papers (use du, de la, des, de l' apostrophe).

Harriet: How long has the bottle been there?

Peter: The edges are much abraded by the action of the water.

Harriet: Do murderers eat sardines?

Peter: Do cats eat rats?

Harriet: I have cut my foot on a razor-shell; Paul Alexis had his throat cut with a razor.

Peter: The tide is going out.

(They separate.)

Harriet: (after a long and unproductive pause, meeting Peter with a sodden Gold Flake packet in one hand and half a Bible in the other): Dr Livingstone, I presume. Do murderers read the Bible?

Peter: Any book had served as well, Any book had stopped the bullet – that may be; I cannot tell.

Harriet (reading): 'Last of all the woman died also' – probably from backache.

Peter: My back aches, and a drowsy numbness stills My brain, as though of hemlock –

Harriet (suddenly practical): Look at the cigarette-card.

Peter: It belongs to the new series.

Harriet: Then it may be quite recent.

Peter (wearily): All right; keep it; we'll call it a clue. How about the Holy Writ?

Harriet (in a marked manner): *You* can keep that; it might be good for you.

Peter: Very well. (In a still more marked manner) Shall we begin with the Song of Songs.

Harriet: Get on with your job.

Peter: I am. How far have we come?

Harriet: How many leagues to Babylon?

Peter: We have walked a mile and a half, and we are still in full view of the Flat-Iron.

(*They separate.*)

Peter: Oy!

Harriet: Hullo!

Peter: I just wanted to ask whether you'd given any further thought to that suggestion about marrying me.

Harriet (sarcastically): I suppose you were thinking how delightful it would be to go through life like this together?

Peter: Well, not quite like this. Hand in hand was more my idea.

Harriet: What is that in your hand?

Peter: A dead starfish.

Harriet: Poor fish!

Peter: No ill-feeling, I trust.

Harriet: Oh, dear no.

They toiled along, presently coming abreast of the spot where the lane led down from Pollock's cottage. Here the beach became more shingly, with a number of biggish stones. Wimsey took the search more seriously here, scrutinising the stones above and around high-water mark very carefully, and even going part of the way up the lane. He seemed not to find anything of importance, and they went on, noticing that the high ground hid the cottages from sight of the beach.

A few hundred yards farther on, Harriet gave tongue again.

'Oy, oy, oy!'

'Hullo!'

'I really have found something this time.'

Peter came galloping down the sand.

'If you're pulling my leg, I'll wring your neck. Let your Uncle Peter look. . . . Ah! . . . we are interested, distinctly interested.'

'It ought to mean good luck, anyway.'

'You're holding it wrong way up; all the luck will drop

out if you're not careful, and a black day it will be for – somebody. Hand it over.'

He ran his fingers gently round the hoop of metal, clearing the sand away.

'It's a new shoe – and it hasn't been here very long. Perhaps a week, perhaps a little more. Belongs to a nice little cob, about fourteen hands. Pretty little animal, fairly well-bred, rather given to kicking her shoes off, pecks a little with the off-fore.'

'Holmes, this is wonderful! How do you do it?'

'Perfectly simple, my dear Watson. The shoe hasn't been worn thin by the 'ammer, 'ammer, 'ammer on the 'ard 'igh road, therefore it's reasonably new. It's a little rusty from lying in the water, but hardly at all rubbed by sand and stones, and not at all corroded, which suggests that it hasn't been here long. The size of the shoe gives the size of the nag, and the shape suggests a nice little round, well-bred hoof. Though newish, the shoe isn't fire-new, and it is worn down a little on the inner front edge, which shows that the wearer was disposed to peck a little; while the way the nails are placed and clinched indicates that the smith wanted to make the shoe extra secure – which is why I said that a lost shoe was a fairly common accident with this particular gee. Still, we needn't blame him or her too much. With all these stones about, a slight trip or knock might easily wrench a shoe away.'

'Him or her. Can't you go on and tell the sex and colour while you're about it?'

'I am afraid even I have my limitations, my dear Watson.'

'Do you think the shoe was lying where it fell? Or would the sea have moved it much? I found it just here, close by the water's edge, buried deep in sand.'

'Well, it wouldn't float, but the tide might drag it a bit one way or the other, and each successive tide would tend to bury it farther. It's very lucky you found it at all. But we can't tell exactly at what point the horse passed along, if you mean that. The shoe wouldn't just drop off. It would be thrown and would spin away on one side or other, according to the speed and direction and all that sort of thing.'

'So it would. Well, that's quite a pretty little piece of deduction. . . . *Peter!* Were you looking for a horse-shoe?'

'No; I was expecting the horse, but the shoe is a piece of pure, gorgeous luck.'

'And observation. I found it.'

'You did. And I could kiss you for it. You need not shrink and tremble. I am not going to do it. When I kiss you, it will be an important event – one of those things which stand out among their surroundings like the first time you tasted li-chee. It will not be an unimportant side-show attached to a detective investigation.'

'I think you are a little intoxicated by the excitement of the discovery,' said Harriet, coldly. 'You say you came here looking for a horse?'

'Naturally. Didn't you?'

'No – I never thought about it.'

'You miserable little cockney – no! You never thought of a horse except as something that holds up the traffic. Your knowledge of horses is comprised in the rhyme which says, "I know two things about the horse and one of them is rather coarse". Didn't it ever occur to you that a horse is made to R,U,N, *run*, and cover a given distance in a given time. Did you never even have a bob on the Derby? Wretched girl – wait till we are married. You shall fall off a horse every day till you learn to sit on it.'

Harriet was silent. She suddenly saw Wimsey in a new light. She knew him to be intelligent, clean, courteous, wealthy, well-read, amusing and enamoured, but he had not so far produced in her that crushing sense of utter inferiority which leads to prostration and hero-worship. But she now realised that there was, after all, something godlike about him. He could control a horse. She had a fleeting vision of him, very sleek, very smart, in a top-hat and pink coat and gleaming white breeches, loftily perched on an immense and fiery animal which pranced and jiggled about without even disturbing the lofty nonchalance of his de-meanour. Her imagination, making a terrific effort, promptly clothed her in a riding-habit of perfect cut, placed her on an animal still larger and fierier and set her at his side, amid the respectful admiration of the assembled no-bility and gentry. Then she laughed at this snobbish picture.

'I could do the falling-off part all right. Hadn't we better be getting on?'

'H'm. Yes. I think we'll do the rest by horse-power. I can't see the coast-road from here, but we shall probably find the faithful Bunter in attendance not very far off. We can't hope to find anything more along here. Two horse-shoes would be a work of supererogation.'

Harriet heartily welcomed this decision.

'We needn't crawl up the cliff,' Wimsey went on. 'We'll turn up and get to the road by the lane. We'll chuck the Bible and the boot – I don't think they'll get us anywhere.'

'Where are we going?'

'To Darley, to find the horse. I fancy we shall find that he belongs to Mr Newcombe, who had occasion to complain of gaps in his hedges. We shall see.'

The two or three miles to Darley were quickly covered, with only the necessary pause while the gates were opened at the Halt. At the top of Hinks's Lane they got out and walked down to the camping-place.

'I would draw your attention,' said Wimsey, 'to the three grains of oats found at this spot, and also to the two inches of burnt rope found in the ashes. Bunter, have you brought those things?'

'Yes, my lord.'

Bunter rummaged in the bowels of the car and brought

out a small paper bag and a halter. These he handed over to Wimsey, who immediately undid the bag and from it poured a couple of handfuls of oats into his hat.

'Well,' he said, 'we've got the halter – now we've only got to find a horse to put in it. Let's go round by the shore to look for the stream our friend Mr Goodrich spoke of.'

The stream was soon found – a small trickle of fresh water emerging through a bank beneath a hedge, some fifty yards from the encampment and wandering away across the sand towards the sea.

'No good looking for marks this side of the hedge – I fancy the tide comes pretty well up to the foot of the grass. Wait a minute, though. Here we are! Yes – on the very edge of the stream, right up against the hedge – a beauty, with nailmarks all complete. Lucky last night's rain didn't wash it out, but the grass overhangs it a bit. But there's no gap in the hedge here. He must – oh, of course, he would. Yes. Now, if we're right, this won't correspond to the shoe we've found – it'll be the other foot. Yes; this is the left fore. Our horse stood here to drink, which means that he (or she) was running loose around here about the ebb of the tide, horses not liking their water salt. The left fore was there – the right should be about here – it *is* here! Look! the print of the naked hoof, without shoe and rather light in the ground – lame, of course, after coming shoeless for nearly three miles over a stony beach. But where is the gap? Let us walk on, my dear Watson. Here, if I mistake not, is the place. Two new stakes driven in and a bunch of dead thorn shoved in and secured with wire. I agree that Mr Newcombe is not a good hand at mending hedges. Still, he has taken some precautions, so we will hope that our horse is still in the field. We scramble up the bank – we look over the hedge – one, two, three horses, by jove!'

Wimsey let his eye rove meditatively over the large field. At its far side was a thickish clump of spinney, from which the little stream emerged, meandering quietly through the coarse grass.

'Look how nicely those trees screen it from the road and the village. A pleasant, private spot for horse-stealing. How tiresome of Mr Newcombe to have filled this gap. Aha! What is this, Watson?'

'I'll buy it.'

'There is another gap a few yards down, which has been filled in a more workmanlike manner with posts and a rail. Nothing could be better. We approach it – we climb the rail, and we are in the field. Permit me – oh! you are over. Good! Now, which animal will you put your money on?'

'Not the black. He looks too big and heavy.'

'No, not the black, certainly. The chestnut might do, as regards size, but he has seen his best days and has hardly got class enough for our work. The jolly little bay cob rather takes my fancy. Coo-op, pretty,' said Wimsey, advancing delicately across the field, shaking the oats in the hat. 'Coo-op, coo-op.'

Harriet had often wondered how people ever managed to catch horses in large fields. It seemed so silly of the creatures to allow themselves to be taken – and indeed, she remembered distinctly having once stayed in a country rectory where it always took at least an hour for 'the boy' to catch the pony, with the result that the pony-trap frequently failed to catch the train. Possibly 'the boy' had not gone the right way about it, for, as by the miracle by which the needle turns to the pole, all three horses came lolloping steadily across the field to poke soft noses into the hatful of oats. Wimsey stroked the chestnut, patted the black, weeded out the bay from between them and stood for a little talking to it and running a hand gently over its neck and shoulders. Then he stooped, passing his palm down the off-fore leg. The hoof came obediently up into his hand, while the muzzle went round and gently nibbled his ear.

'Hi, you!' said Wimsey, 'that's mine. Look here, Harriet.'

Harriet edged round to his side and stared at the hoof.

'New shoe.' He put the foot down and reached in turn for the other legs. 'Better make sure they haven't made an all-round job of it. No; old shoes on three feet and new shoe on off-fore, corresponding exactly to the specimen picked up on the beach. You notice the special arrangement of the nails. The bay mare brings home the bacon all right. Wait a bit, my girl, we'll try your paces.'

He slipped the halter neatly over the bay mare's head and swung himself up.

'Come for a ride? Your toe on my foot, and up she comes! Shall we ride away into the sunset and never come back?'

'Better get on with it. Suppose the farmer comes.'

'How right you are!' He gave the halter a shake and cantered off. Harriet mechanically picked up his hat and stood squeezing the crown absently in and out, with her eyes on the flying figure.

'Allow me, miss.'

Bunter held out his hand for the hat; she relinquished it with a little start. Bunter shook out the remaining oats, dusted the hat with care inside and out and restored it to its proper shape.

'Handy to ride or drive,' said Wimsey, coming back and slipping down from his mount. 'Might do nine miles an hour on the road – on the shore, through shallow water, say eight. I'd like – my God! how I'd like – to take her along to the Flat-Iron. Better not. We're trespassing.'

He pulled the halter off and sent the mare off with a clap on the shoulder.

'It all looks so good,' he mourned, 'but it won't work. It simply won't work. You see the idea. Here's Martin. He comes and camps here; evidently he knows all about this place beforehand, and knows that horses are kept out in this field in summer. He arranges for Alexis to be at the Flat-Iron at two o'clock – I don't know how, but he works it some-how. At 1.30 he leaves the Feathers, comes down here, gets the mare and rides off along the shore. We see where he spilt the oats with which he got her to come to him and we see the gap he made getting her through the hedge. He rides along through the edge of the water, so as to leave no marks. He tethers the mare to the ring that he has driven into the rock; he kills Alexis and rides back in a deuce of a hurry. In crossing the rough pebbles below Pollock's cottage, the mare casts a shoe. That doesn't worry him, except that it lames the nag a bit and delays him. When he gets back, he doesn't return the mare to the field, but lets her run. Like that, it will look as though she broke out of the field on her own, and will easily explain the gap, the lameness, and the shoe, if anybody finds it. Also, if the horse should be found still blown and sweaty, it will appear perfectly natural. He is back at three o'clock, in time to go round to the garage about his car, and at some subsequent period he burns the halter. It's so convincing, so neat, and it's all wrong.'

'Why?'

'The time's too tight, for one thing. He left the inn at 1.30. After that, he had to come down here, catch the mare and ride four and a half miles. We can't very well allow him to do more than eight miles an hour under the conditions of the problem, yet at two o'clock you heard the scream. Are you sure your watch was right?'

'Positive. I compared it with the hotel clock when I got to Wilvercombe; it was dead right, and the hotel clock –'

'Is set by wireless time, naturally. Everything always is.'

'Worse than that; all the hotel clocks are controlled by a master-clock which is controlled directly from Greenwich. That was one of the first things I asked about.'

'Competent woman.'

'Suppose he had had the horse all ready before he went to the Feathers – tied up to the fence, or something?'

'Yes; but if these Darley people are right, he didn't go from here to the Feathers; he came by car from the Wil-vercombe side. And even if we allow that, he's still got to make rather over nine miles an hour to get to the Flat-Iron by two o'clock. I doubt if he could do it – though, of course, he *might*, if he leathered the poor beast like fury. That's why I said I'd like to do the ride.'

'And the scream I heard may not have been *the* scream. I thought it was a gull, you know – and perhaps it was. I took about five minutes to gather my stuff together and come out into view of the Flat-Iron. You might put the death at 2.5, I think, if you felt you had to.'

'All right. But that still leaves it all quite impossible. You see, *you* were there at 2.10 at the very latest. Where was the murderer?'

'In the cleft of the rock. Oh, ah – but not the horse. I see. There wouldn't be room for a horse too. How exasperating! If we put the murder too early, he wouldn't have time to get there, and if we put it too late, he wouldn't have time to get away. It's maddening.'

'Yes, and we can't really put the murder earlier than two o'clock because of the blood. Putting the horse's speed and the condition of the blood and the scream all together, we get two o'clock as the earliest possible and on the whole the most probable time for the murder. Right. You come on the scene, at latest, at 2.5. Allow (which is very unlikely) that the murderer dashed up at full gallop, cut Alexis' throat and dashed off again at full speed without wasting a second, and allow him (which is again most unlikely) to do as much as ten miles an hour *through water*. At 2.5 he will have done just under a mile on his way back. But we proved this afternoon that you have a clear view of over a mile and a half from the Flat-Iron in the direction of Darley. If he had been there, you couldn't have failed to see him. Or could you? You didn't start really *looking* till 2.10, when you found the body.'

'No, I didn't. But I've got *all* my faculties. If the murder was done at two o'clock, when the scream woke me, I couldn't possibly not have *heard* a horse galloping hell-for-leather along the shore. It would make a pretty good row, wouldn't it?'

'It certainly would. Tramp, tramp along the land they rode, Splash, splash along the sea. It won't do, my girl, it won't do. And yet, that mare went along that bit of beach not so very long ago, or I'll eat my hat. Eh? Oh, thanks, Bunter.'

He took the hat which Bunter gravely proffered him.

'And there's the ring-bolt in the rock. That didn't come there by chance. The horse was taken there, but when and why is a puzzle. Never mind. Let's check up on our facts, just as though the thing were coming out all right.'

They left the field and walked up Hinks's Lane.

'We won't take the car,' said Wimsey. 'We'll just wander along chewing straws and looking idle. Yonder is the village green, I fancy, where, as you once informed us, under a spreading chestnut tree the village smithy stands. Let us hope the smith is at work. Smiths, like electric drills, are made to be stared at.'

The smith was at work. The cheerful clink of his hammer fell cheerily on their ears as they crossed the green, and the huge dappled quarters of a cart-horse gleamed in the shaft of sunlight that fell across the open door.

Harriet and Wimsey lounged up, Wimsey dangling the horse-shoe in his hand.

'Afternoon, zur,' said the yokel in charge of the cart-horse, civilly.

' 'Noon,' replied Wimsey.

'Fine day, zur.'

'Ah!' said Wimsey.

The yokel looked Wimsey over thoroughly, and decided that he was a knowledgeable person and no foolish chatterer. He hitched his shoulder a little more comfortably against the door-post and fell into a reverie.

After about five minutes, Wimsey judged that the time had come when a further observation might be well received. He said, jerking his head in the direction of the anvil:

'Not so much of that as there used to be.'

'Ah!' said the man.

The smith, who had removed the dull shoe from the anvil and replaced it in the forge for re-heating, must have caught the remark, for he glanced towards the door. He said nothing, however, but put all his energy into working his bellows.

Presently, the shoe being once more on the anvil, the man with the horse shifted his shoulders again, pushed his cap back, scratched his head, replaced the cap, spat (but with perfect politeness), thrust his hand deep into the right-hand pocket of his breeches and addressed a brief word of encouragement to the horse.

Silence, punctuated only by the clink of the hammer, followed, till Wimsey remarked:

'You'll get the hay in all right, if this lasts.'

'Ah!' said the man, with satisfaction.

The smith, raising the shoe in the tongs and again returning it to the fire, wiped his brow with his leather apron and broke into the conversation. He followed Humpty-Dumpty's method of going back to the last remark but one.

'I recollect,' he said, 'when thur warn't none of these motor-cars, only the one Squire Goodrich had – what year would that be now, Jem?'

'Mafeking year, that wur.'

'Ah! zo it wur.'

Silence, while all meditated.

Then Wimsey said:

'I can remember when my father kept twenty-three horses, not counting the farm stock, of course.'

'Ah!' said the blacksmith. 'That 'ud be a big place, zur?'

'Yes; it was a big place. It was a treat for us kids to go down to the smithy and see them shod.'

'Ah!'

'I still know a good bit of work when I see one. This young lady and I picked up a cast shoe just now on the beach – you don't get as much of that sort of luck these days as you used to.'

He dangled the shoe on his fingers.

'Off-fore,' he added, casually; 'nice little well-bred cob about fourteen hands; kicks her shoes off, and pecks a bit on this foot – is that right?'

The smith extended a large hand, courteously wiping it first upon his apron.

'Ay,' he said. 'That's right enough. Bay cob – belongs to Mr Newcombe – I zhuld know it.'

'Your work?'

'Zartain zhure.'

'Ah!'

'Not been lying about very long, either.'

'No.' The smith licked his finger and rubbed the iron lovingly. 'What day wur that Mr Newcombe found the mare loose, Jem?'

Jem appeared to do a complicated arithmetical calculation, and replied:

'Vriday, ay, it did be Vriday morning. That's when it wur. Vriday.'

'Ah! to be zhure. So t'wur.'

The smith leaned on his hammer and considered the matter. By slow degrees he brought out the rest of the story. It was not much, but it confirmed Wimsey's deductions.

Farmer Newcombe always kept horses in that field during the summer months. No, he never mowed that meadow on account of the (agricultural and botanical detail of which

Harriet did not grasp the significance). No, Mr Newcombe wouldn't be about in that meadow much, no, nor yet the men, on account of it's lying a long way from the rest of his land (interminable historical detail dealing with the distribution of tenancies and glebe round about that district, in which Harriet became completely lost), nor they wouldn't need to, not to water the horses, on account of the stream (lengthy and rather disputatious account, to which Jem contributed, of the original course of the stream in Jem's grandfather's time, before Mr Grenfell made the pond over to Drake's Spinney), and it wasn't Mr Newcombe neither that see the mare running wild Friday morning, but Bessie Turvey's youngest, and he came and told Jem's uncle George and him and another of them got her in and terrible lame she were, but Mr Newcombe, he did ought to have mended that gap before (prolonged recital of humorous anecdote, ending 'and lord! how Old Parson did laugh, to be zhure!').

After which, the explorers drove back in state to Wilvercombe, to hear that the body had not turned up yet, but that Inspector Umpelty had a pretty good idea where it might be. And dinner. And dancing. And so to bed.

XVII

THE EVIDENCE OF THE MONEY

'O ho! here's royal booty, on my soul:
A draught of ducats!'

Fragment

WEDNESDAY, 24 JUNE

FAITHFUL to her self-imposed duty, Harriet next morning sought out Mrs Weldon. It was not altogether easy to get rid of Henry, whose filial affection seemed positively to tie him to his mother's apron-strings. A happy thought made Harriet suggest that she and Mrs Weldon might go and see what the Resplendent could do for them in the way of a Turkish bath. This was check-mate for Henry. He took himself off, murmuring that he would go and have a haircut.

In the mood of relaxation and confidence that follows on being parboiled, it was easy enough to pump Mrs Weldon. A little diplomacy was needed, so as not to betray the ulterior object of the inquiry, but no detective could have had a more unsuspecting victim. The matter proved to be very much as Harriet had supposed.

Mrs Weldon was the only daughter of a wealthy brewer, who had left her a very considerable fortune in her own right. Her parents having died when she was a child, she had been brought up by a strict Noncomformist aunt in the little town of St Ives in Huntingdonshire. She had been courted by a certain George Weldon, a prosperous farmer owning a considerable property at Leamhurst in the Isle of

Ely, and had married him at eighteen, chiefly in order to get away from the aunt. That rigid lady had not altogether opposed the marriage, which was reasonably suitable, though not brilliant; but she had shown sufficient business ability to insist that her niece's money should be tied up in such a manner that Weldon could not touch the capital. Weldon, to do him justice, had made no objection to this. He seemed to have been a perfectly honest, sober and industrious man, farming his land thriftily and well and having, so far as Harriet could make out, no drawbacks beyond a certain lack of imagination in matrimonial matters.

Henry was the only child of the marriage, and had been brought up from the beginning with the idea that he was to follow in his father's footsteps, and here again, Weldon senior took a very proper view of the matter. He would not have the boy brought up in idleness, or to ideas beyond his proper station in life. He was a farmer's son, and a farmer he should be, though Mrs Weldon herself had often pleaded that the boy should be brought up to one of the professions. But old Weldon was adamant, and indeed Mrs Weldon was obliged to admit that he had very likely been right after all. Henry showed no special aptitude for anything but the open-air life of the farm; the trouble was that he did not apply himself even to that as well as he should have done, and was inclined to run after girls and race-meetings, leaving his work to be done by his father and the farm-hands. Already, before the elder Weldon's death, there had been a good deal of antagonism between Henry and his mother, and this became intensified later on.

The farmer had died when Henry was twenty-five. He had left the farm and all his own savings to his son, knowing that his wife was well provided for. Under Henry's management the farm had begun to go down. Times had grown harder for farmers. More and more personal supervision was needed to make farming pay; Henry gave it less and less. There were experiments in horse-breeding, which had not turned out well, owing to lack of judgement in buying and handling the stock. Mrs Weldon had by this time left the farm, which she had always disliked, and was living a nomad life in spas and watering-places. Henry had several times come to her for loans, and had received them; but Mrs Weldon had steadily refused to make over any of her capital to him, although she might have done so, her trustees being now dead and the trust wound up. She had, after all, learnt something from the Noncomformist aunt. Finally, when she found out that Henry had got himself into rather disgraceful trouble with an innkeeper's wife in a neighbouring village, she quarrelled with Henry, loudly and finally. Since then, she had heard little from him. She understood, however, that the intrigue with the innkeeper's wife had come to an end, and in February of the current year she had told him about her forthcoming marriage to Alexis. Henry had come down to Wilvercombe, stayed for the weekend, met Alexis and expressed his disapproval of the whole business. This did not mend matters, and relations had been strained until the death of Alexis had urged the lonely woman to seek comfort in the ties of blood. Henry had come, expressed contrition for his former waywardness, received forgiveness and shown that he was, after all, her loving son.

Harriet mentioned Mrs Lefranc's theory that Alexis had committed suicide owing to the failure of unknown and important 'speculations'. Mrs Weldon scouted the theory.

'What could it matter to him, my dear? Paul knew perfectly well that when we were married I should settle my money on him – with the exception, of course, of a little provision for Henry. Of course, in the ordinary way, Henry would get everything, and I am afraid he was a little upset when he heard that I was going to get married, but, you know, it was not right that he should feel like that. His father left him very well off and always impressed upon him that he ought not to look for anything from me. After all, I was still quite a young woman when my husband died, and George – he was a very fair-minded man, I will say that for him – always said that I should be quite within my rights in spending my own father's money as I liked and marrying again if I chose. And I have lent Henry a great deal of money, which he has never repaid. I told Henry, when I got engaged to Alexis, that I should make him a free gift of everything that I had lent him, and make a will, giving him the life-interest in £30,000, the capital of which was to go to Henry's children, if he had any. If he hadn't any, then the money was to come back to Paul, if Paul outlived Henry, because, of course, Paul was the younger man.'

'Were you going to settle all the rest on Mr Alexis?'

'Why not, my dear? It was not as though I could have had any more children. But Paul didn't like that idea – he used to say, so charmingly and absurdly, that if I did that what would happen to me if he ran away and left me? No, what I was going to do was this. I was going to settle £30,000 on Paul when we were married. It would have been his, absolutely, of course – I shouldn't like my husband to have to come and ask me for permission if he wanted to alter the investments or anything. Then, at my death, Henry would have had the income from the other £30,000 and his debts washed out, and Paul would have had all the rest, which would have been about £100,000 altogether, including his own £30,000. Because, you see, Paul might have married again and had a family, and then he would need the money. I don't see that there was anything unfair about that, do you?'

Harriet felt that a great deal might be said about an arrangement which cut off the only son with the life-interest on £30,000, with reversion to a young step-father, and left full control of over three times that sum to the step-father;

and which also placed the hypothetical family of the son in a vastly inferior position to the equally hypothetical children of the step-father by a hypothetical new wife. Still, Mrs Weldon's money was her own, and Alexis had at least stood between her and the major folly of stripping herself of every farthing in his favour. One expression had caught her attention, and she returned to it.

'I think you showed considerable judgement,' she said – not specifying whether the judgement was good or bad – 'it would be much better for your son, if he is inclined to squander his money, only to have the life-interest in his share. Then he would always have something to fall back upon. I suppose that arrangement still holds good under your present will.'

'Oh, yes,' said Mrs Weldon. 'At least, it will do so. I must confess that I have been a little remiss up to the present. I haven't actually made a will. I have always enjoyed such wonderful health – but it will have to be done, of course. You know how one puts things off.'

The old story, thought Harriet. If all the wise wills projected in people's minds were actually executed, there would be fewer fortunes inherited only to be thrown away. She reflected that if Mrs Weldon died the next day, Henry would step into sole control of something over £130,000.

'You know,' she said, 'I think I should make that will if I were you. Even the youngest and healthiest people may get run over or something.'

'Yes, yes – you're so very right. But now that poor Paul is dead, I don't feel that I have the energy for business. It would matter more, of course, if Henry were married and had a family, but he says he doesn't mean to marry, and if so, he may as well have the money first as last. There's nobody else now. But I'm afraid I'm boring you, my dear, with all this chatter. You were asking about poor dear Paul, and I've been led away into telling you all these silly private affairs. What I was trying to say was that Paul simply *couldn't* have been worrying about speculations. He knew he was going to have plenty of money. Besides,' added Mrs Weldon, with perfect justice, 'you can't speculate much without capital, can you? Money breeds money, as a stock-broker I once knew used to say, and Paul never had any money to start with. I don't think he would have known anything about speculating either; he was too romantic and unworldly, poor dear boy.'

'Maybe,' said Harriet to herself, 'maybe. But he managed to get on the right side of the person who had it.' She was a little surprised. 'Wealthy' is a comparative term – she had imagined Mrs Weldon to possess about three thousand a year. But if her money was decently invested – and she spoke as if it was – she must have at least twice that amount. A pauper like Alexis might be excused for wedding £130,000 at whatever price in convenience and self-respect; had he really intended the marriage after all? And if, on the other hand, he had meant to forgo it and flee the country, what was the enormous threat or inducement which could make him abandon such a golden prospect for the much lesser glitter of three hundred sovereigns, genuine metal though they might be?

And Henry? Even when the death-duties had been subtracted, £130,000 was a pleasant sum, and men had done murder for less. Well, Lord Peter had undertaken to look into Henry's affairs. She became aware that Mrs Weldon was talking.

'What a curious face that Monsieur Antoine has,' she was saying, 'he seems to be a nice young man, though I'm sure he is far from robust. He spoke most kindly to me yesterday about Paul. He seems to have been very much attached to him, sincerely so.'

'Oh, Antoine!' thought Harriet, a little reproachfully. Then she remembered the mad mother and the imbecile brother and thought instead, 'Poor Antoine!' But the thought was still an unpleasant one.

'It's all very well for Lord Peter,' she grumbled to herself, '*he's* never wanted for anything.' Why Lord Peter should be brought into the matter, she could not explain, but there is undoubtedly something irritating about the favourites of fortune.

In the meantime, that wayward sprig of the nobility was trying not to be idle. He was, in fact, hanging round the police-station, bothering the Inspector. The reports about Bright were coming in, and they fully corroborated his story, so far as they went. He had come to Wilvercombe, as he said, from a lodging-house in Seahampton, and by the train specified, and he was now living peacefully in a cheap room in Wilvercombe, without seeing any strangers and without showing the least sign of wanting to disappear. He had been taken over to Seahampton by the police on the previous day, and had been identified by Merryweather as the man to whom the Endicott razor had been sold some time previously. In the course of a few hours, his movements for the last few weeks had been successfully checked, and were as follows:

May 28th. Arrived in Ilfracombe from London. Four days' employment. Dismissed as incompetent and intoxicated.

June 2nd. Arrived in Seahampton. Called at Merryweather's and purchased razor. Five days in that town looking for employment (details checked).

June 8th. Wilvercombe. Called on Moreton, the barber on the Esplanade. Told that there might be a job later. Recommended to try Ramage's in Lesston Hoe. Same day went on to Lesston Hoe; taken on by Ramage.

June 15th. Dismissed from Ramages – drunk and incompetent. Returned to Wilvercombe; informed by Moreton that post was now filled (which it was not; but his reputation had preceded him by telephone). Tried one or two other shops without success. Slept that night in free lodging-house.

June 16th (Tuesday). Again tried for work; no result. Slept that night in workmen's lodgings, where he arrived shortly after midnight. They were reluctant to admit him, but he showed a £1 note to prove that he could pay for his bed.

June 17th. Took 9.57 train to Seahampton. Called on hairdresser named Lyttleton and asked for work. Was told that Mr Lyttleton was away, but that he could call the following morning after 11.30. Visited two more hairdressers. Took a bed in lodging-house and spent the evening and night there in company with other residents.

June 18th (day of Alexis' death). Left the lodging-house at 10 a.m. and went directly to the Public Library, where he had sat for an hour in the Reading Room, studying the 'Situations Vacant' columns in various papers. The guardian of the Reading Room had identified him. He remembered Bright perfectly, on account of some questions he had asked about the dates of publication of the local papers, and also recollected showing him the shelf on which the local directory was kept. At eleven o'clock, Bright had asked whether the library clock was right, as he had an appointment at 11.30. At 11.15 he had left, presumably to keep his appointment.

The appointment was, of course, with Lyttleton, who also had no difficulty in identifying Bright. Lyttleton had returned to Seahampton by the 11.20 train, and, on reaching his shop, had found Bright waiting to see him. He told Bright that he could come and try his hand if he liked, and could start at once. Bright had worked in the toilet-saloon until one o'clock, when he had gone out to lunch. He had returned just after two o'clock and had remained at his job for the rest of the day. The proprietor had then decided that his work was not good enough, and paid him off. It was true that nobody was able to identify him at the small restaurant where he claimed to have lunched, but it was perfectly clear that nothing short of a magic carpet could have transported him forty miles to the Flat-Iron and back in order to commit a murder at two o'clock. Whatever part Bright had played in the tragedy, it was not that of First Murderer.

With regard to Bright's earlier history, they had made very little progress – principally because Bright himself did not even pretend to remember the various aliases under which he had passed from time to time in the last few years. The only statement they had so far succeeded in confirming – up to a point – was that there certainly had at one time been a hairdresser's establishment in Massingbird Street, Manchester. The proprietor's name had been Simpson, and this agreed with Bright's story; but Massingbird Street had long disappeared in the course of town-improvement and, as Bright himself had warned them, it was difficult to find anybody who remembered what Simpson the hairdresser had looked like.

'He must have lived in Manchester all right, some time or other,' was the Inspector's conclusion, 'or he wouldn't know all about Massingbird Street; and it's quite probable he may be Simpson as he says. But what he's been doing with himself between then and now is quite another matter.'

A further item of police information concerned old Pollock and his boat. A young constable, who had only recently joined the Wilvercombe force and was therefore likely to be unknown to the local fisher-folk, had been sent, disguised as a holiday-maker, to dawdle about the beach near Darley, in company with his young lady, and persuade Pollock to take them both out for a sail in his boat. The trip had been an uncomfortable one, owing, in the first place to the old fisherman's extreme surliness and, in the second, to the young lady's unfortunate tendency to *mal de mer*. They had asked to be taken out as near as possible to the seaward end of the Grinders reef, 'as the young lady was that keen to see them drag for the body'. Pollock had grumbled a good deal, but had taken them. They had kept the shore in view the whole way, but had finished their outward trip at a point too far from shore to make out clearly the movements of the search-party, who, at that particular moment, seemed to be engaged on shore in the immediate neighbourhood of the Flat-Iron. They had asked Pollock to put in close by the rock, but he had refused very definitely to do so. During the voyage, the constable had examined the boat as closely as he could for signs of anything unusual. He had gone so far as to lose a hypothetical half-crown and insist on having the bottom-boards up to see if it could have slipped below them. He had searched the musty space below thoroughly with a flash-light and seen no appearance of blood-stains. For the sake of verisimilitude he had pretended to find the half-crown, and for the sake of peace had handed it to Pollock by way of a tip. On the whole the expedition had been disappointing, having yielded nothing but sea-sickness and a close-up view of a considerable number of lobster-pots.

A question about Alexis' passport found the Inspector very much on his dignity. Did his lordship really suppose they had overlooked that obvious point? Alexis certainly had a passport, and, what was more, had had it visa'd within the last month. Where for? Why, for France, to be sure. But of course he could have got fresh visas from the Consul there, if he had wanted them.

'That offers some support for the theory that our young friend intended to flit, eh?'

'Yes, my lord. And if he was going to some remote place in Central Europe, I daresay he'd have found gold sovereigns a sight handier than notes. Though why he shouldn't have taken currency notes and changed them in Paris I don't know. Still, there it is, and he must have had *some* idea in his mind. I don't mind admitting, my lord, that I'm coming round a bit to your way of thinking. Here's a man with what I might call a purpose in view – and that purpose isn't suicide. And he had £300 in gold on him, and there's plenty as 'ud do murder for less than that. At least, we're supposing he had it on him. We can't tell till we find the body.'

'If he was murdered for the sake of the gold, you won't know even then,' said Wimsey.

'No, my lord, that's a fact. Unless we was to find the belt or what not he had it in. And even then, likely as not, the murderer would have taken belt and all.' The Inspector looked unhappy. 'But there might be papers or something to tell us – always supposing the murderer didn't take them as well or the salt water hasn't made pulp of them.'

'D'you know,' said Wimsey, 'I feel inspired to make a prophecy. I think you'll find that Alexis was murdered all right, but not for the sake of the money. I mean, not for the £300.'

'Why do you think that, my lord?'

'Because,' said Wimsey, 'you haven't found the body.'

The Inspector scratched his head.

'You don't mean that somebody came and took the body away? What should they want to do that for?'

'What indeed? If my idea's the right one, that's the last thing they would want to do. They'd want the body found.'

'Why?'

'Because the murder was not committed for the £300 in gold.'

'But you said that was why the body hadn't been found.'

'So it is.'

'Your proper walk in life,' said Inspector Umpelty, 'if you'll excuse me, my lord, is setting crossword puzzles. Say that again. They wanted the body found, because they didn't murder him for the £300. And *because* they didn't murder him for the £300, we can't find the body. Is that right?'

'That's right.'

The Inspector frowned heavily. Then a radiant smile illuminated his broad face. He smacked his hand jubilantly upon his thigh.

'Of course, my lord! By George, you're perfectly right. What mutts we were not to see that before. It's as clear as daylight. It was just your way of putting it that muddled me up. I must try that one on the Super. Bet you *he* won't see through it first go off. They didn't want the body found – no, that's wrong. They did want the body found because they did, didn't—'

'Try it in rhyme,' suggested Wimsey.

> *Why did they want the body found?*
> *They didn't want three hundred pound.*
> *They didn't want three hundred pound,*
> *And that's why the body wasn't found.*

'Very good, my lord,' said the Inspector. 'Why, you're quite a poet.' He drew out his note-book, and solemnly made an entry of the quatrain.

'You could sing it very nicely to the tune of "Here we go round the mulberry-bush",' suggested Wimsey, 'with the refrain, "All on a Thursday morning". Or it should be "Thursday afternoon", but that's just poetic licence. You have my permission to perform it at your next Police-concert. No fee.'

'You will have your joke, my lord.' The Inspector smiled indulgently, but as Wimsey left the police-station he heard a deep voice laboriously humming:

Why did they want the body found, body found, body found,
Why did they want the body found
All of a Thur-ursday morning?

Wimsey went back to the Bellevue and found a note from Harriet, containing the substance of her conversation with Mrs Weldon. He frowned over it for a moment and then abruptly summoned Bunter.

'Bunter, my man,' said he, 'I think it is time you took a trip to Huntingdonshire.'

'Very good, my lord.'

'You will go to a place called Leamhurst, and find out all about Mr Henry Weldon, who owns a farm there.'

'Certainly, my lord.'

'It's only a small village, so you must have some reason for going there. I suggest that you purchase or hire a car and are benighted, owing to some intricate kind of engine-trouble.'

'Precisely, my lord.'

'Here is £30. If you want more, let me know.'

'Very good, my lord.'

'You will, naturally, stay at the principal pub and pursue your inquiries in the bar.'

'Naturally, my lord.'

'You will find out everything you can about Mr Weldon, and, in particular, what his financial standing and reputation may be.'

'Quite so, my lord.'

'You will be as quick as you can about it, and return here as soon as possible.'

'Very good, my lord.'

'You will start immediately.'

'Very good, my lord.'

'Then be off!'

'Very good, my lord. Your lordship's dress-shirts are in the second drawer and the silk socks in the tray on the right-hand side of the wardrobe, with the dress-ties just above them.'

'Very good, Bunter,' said Wimsey, mechanically.

Ten minutes later, Mr Bunter, suit-case in hand, was on his way to the railway-station.

XVIII

THE EVIDENCE OF THE SNAKE

'There is a little, hairy, green-eyed snake,
Of voice like to the woody nightingale,
And ever singing pitifully sweet,
That nestles in the barry bones of Death,
And is his dearest friend and playfellow.'

Death's Jest-Book

WEDNESDAY, 24 JUNE

ON LEAVING the Turkish baths, Miss Harriet Vane went out on a shopping expedition. This was her second venture of the kind since her arrival in Wilvercombe, and on both occasions her purchases were dictated by the desire of pleasing a man. On this occasion, she wanted an afternoon frock. And why? She was going out for a picnic.

She had picnicked before, with Lord Peter; and for him the old tweed skirt and well-worn jumper had been good enough. But today, these garments would not do. Her appointment was with Mrs Weldon and Henry.

The curious inhibitions which caused her to be abrupt, harsh, and irritating with Lord Peter did not seem to trouble her in dealing with Henry Weldon. For him she produced a latent strain of sweet womanliness which would have surprised Wimsey. She now selected a slinky garment, composed of what male writers call 'some soft, clinging material', with a corsage which outlined the figure and a skirt which waved tempestuously about her ankles. She enhanced its appeal with an oversized hat of which one side

238

obscured her face and tickled her shoulder, while the other was turned back to reveal a bunch of black ringlets, skilfully curled into position by the head hairdresser at the Resplendent. High-heeled beige shoes and sheer silk stockings, with embroidered gloves and a hand-bag completed this alluring toilette, so eminently unsuitable for picnicking. In addition, she made up her face with just so much artful restraint as to suggest enormous experience aping an impossible innocence, and, thus embellished, presently took her place beside Henry in the driving-seat of Mrs Weldon's large saloon. Mrs Weldon sat at the back of the car, with a luxurious tea-basket at her feet and a case of liquid refreshment beside her.

Henry seemed gratified by the efforts made to please him, and by Miss Vane's openly expressed admiration of his driving. This was of a showy and ill-tempered kind, and involved 'putting the wind up' other users of the road. Harriet had herself driven cars, and suffered as all drivers do when being driven, but even when Henry rounded a corner very wide at fifty miles an hour and crammed a motor-cyclist into the ditch, she merely remarked (with some truth) that the speed made her feel quite nervous.

Mr Weldon, braking violently at the unexpected sight of a herd of cows nearly under his radiator, and crashing his gears as he changed down, smiled indulgently.

'No point in these damned machines of you don't make 'em move,' he said. 'Not like a horse – no life in 'em. Only useful for getting from one place to another.'

He waited while the cows dawdled by and then let his clutch in with a bang which nearly shot the liquid refreshment to the floor.

'You don't catch me motoring for pleasure,' said Mr Weldon. 'I like fresh air – none of these beastly stuffy boxes and stinking petrol. Used to breed gees once – but the bottom's dropped out of the market. Damned shame.'

Harriet agreed, and said she was so fond of horses. Life on a farm must be wonderful.

'All right if you don't have to make it pay,' growled Mr Weldon.

'I suppose it *is* rather hard nowadays.'

'Damned hard,' said Mr Weldon, adding, however, as though recollecting himself, 'not that I have a lot to grumble at as things go.'

'No? I'm glad of that. I mean, it's nice for you to be able to leave your work and come down here. I suppose a really well-managed farm runs itself, so to speak.'

Mr Weldon glanced at her almost as though he suspected her of some hidden meaning. She smiled innocently at him, and he said:

'Well – as a matter of fact, it's a beastly nuisance. But what can one do? Couldn't leave my mother all by herself in this hole.'

'Of *course* not; I think it's splendid of you to come and stand by her. And besides – well, I mean, it makes such a difference to have somebody really nice to talk to.'

'Jolly of you to say that.'

'I mean, it must make all the difference to your mother.'

'Not to you, eh? Dukes and lords are good enough for you?'

'Oh!' Harriet wriggled her shoulders, 'If you mean Lord Peter – he's all *right*, of course, but he's a little – you know what I mean.'

'La-di-dah!' said Mr Weldon. 'What's he want to wear that silly thing in his eye for?'

'That's just what I feel. It isn't manly, is it?'

'Lot of affected nonsense,' said Mr Weldon. 'Take that fellow away from his valet and his car and his evening togs, and where'd he be? Thinks he can ride, because he's pottered round with a fashionable hunt, trampling down people's crops and leaving the gates open. I'd like to see him –'

He broke off.

'See him what?'

'Oh, nothing. Don't want to be rude to a friend of yours. I say, what's he after down here?'

'Well!' Harriet smirked demurely behind the drooping brim of the preposterous hat. 'He *says* he's interested in this crime, or whatever it is.'

'But you know better, eh?' He nudged Harriet familiarly in the ribs. 'I don't blame the fellow for making the running while he can, but I do wish he wouldn't raise false hopes in the old lady. That's a dashed awkward hat of yours.'

'Don't you like it?'

'It's topping – suits you down to the ground, but it does keep a fellow at a distance. And I don't want to shout, because my mother can hear. I say, Miss Vane.'

'Yes?'

'Listen!' Henry pushed his face as far as possible under the guard of the hat and blew his confidence on to Harriet's cheek. 'I wish you'd do something for me.'

'Of course, I'd do anything I could.'

'That's nice of you. Do persuade this Wimsey fellow to drop it. As long as *she* thinks there's anything in that Bolshie idea of hers, she'll hang on here like grim death. It isn't good for her – morbid, you know. Besides, she's making an ass of herself. I want to get her away and go back to my work.'

'Yes, I see. I quite understand. I'll do my best.'

'Good girl!' Henry patted her encouragingly on the thigh. 'I knew you and I'd get on like a house on fire together.'

Harriet smiled.

'I don't know if I shall be able to persuade him. He doesn't like taking advice. You know what men are.'

'I bet *you* know all right. I don't suppose there's much you don't know, by jove!' Henry was obviously well aware that he was talking to a rather notorious young woman. He chuckled.

241

'Don't say I've said anything – just try what you can do. I bet you can twist him round your little finger if you try, eh?'

'Oh, Mr Weldon! I hope I'm not one of those managing sort of women!'

'You don't need to be. You know how to get your own way, I bet. I know you could do anything you liked with *me*.'

'You mustn't talk like that.'

'Mustn't I? Can't help it. You've got a way with you – haven't you, eh?'

Harriet wished that he would not say 'eh?' so often. And she disliked the grossness of his voice and the coarseness of his skin and the little tufts of hair in his ears.

'Don't drive with one hand like that – suppose anything came along suddenly.'

Henry laughed and patted her leg again.

'That's all right, don't you worry. I'll look after you, and you'll look after me, eh? Alliance, offensive and defensive – just between you and me, eh?'

'Oh, rather!'

'That's fine. And when all this stupid business is over, you must come and look Mother and me up. She's taken a great fancy to you. Get her to bring you along to my place. You'd like it. What about it?'

'That would be lovely!' (If Henry wanted to be vamped, she would vamp him.) 'One gets so tired of the kind of men one meets in London, and the stuffy, restricted, literary kind of surroundings. I don't suppose you ever come to London, Mr Weldon?'

'Not often. Don't care for the place.'

'Oh! Then it's no good asking you to call on me.'

'Isn't it, though? Of course I'd come and call on you like a shot. Some inducement, eh? Where do you live?'

'I've got a little flat in Bloomsbury.'

'All on your own?'

'Yes.'

'Isn't that a bit lonesome?'

'Oh! well, of course I have plenty of friends. And a woman who comes in for the day. I could give you tea if you cared to come along some time to cheer me up.'

'That would be sweet of you. We could go and do a show together or something.'

'I should enjoy that.'

No – Henry was really too easy. Surely even his colossal vanity could not suppose that he had really made a conquest. Yet there he sat, smiling away and almost audibly purring. No doubt he thought that Harriet Vane was any man's game. He really imagined that, placed between Lord Peter and himself, a woman could possibly – well, why not? How was he to know? It wouldn't be the first time that a woman had made a foolish choice. If anything, he was paying her the compliment of supposing that she was not mercenary. Or, horrid thought, did he expect her to be completely promiscuous?

That was it – he did! He was informing her now, in reasonably plain language, that somebody like himself would be a nice change for her and that he couldn't make out what a fine woman like herself could see in a fellow like Wimsey. Rage rendered her speechless for a moment; then she began to feel amused. If he thought that, he could be made to believe anything. She could twist men round her little finger, could she? Then she would twist *him*. She would fool him to the top of his bent.

She begged him not to talk so loudly; Mrs Weldon would overhear him.

This reminder had its effect, and Henry 'behaved himself' until their arrival at the spot selected for the picnic compelled him to return to his former attitude of ordinary politeness.

The picnic itself passed off without any remarkable

243

incident, and Henry did not succeed in getting Harriet to himself until the meal was over and they went to wash up the plates in a little brook that ran close by. Even then, Harriet was able to avoid his advances by sending him to do the washing while she stood by with a dish-cloth. She ordered him about prettily and he obeyed with delighted willingness, tucking up his sleeves and getting down to the job. However, the inevitable moment arrived when he returned with the clean plates and put them into her hands. Then, seizing his opportunity, he advanced upon her and clasped her with clumsy gallantry about the body. She dropped the plates and wriggled, pushing his arms away and bending her head down, so that the faithful and long-suffering hat was between them.

'Damn it!' said Henry. 'You might let a fellow –'

It was then that Harriet became really frightened. She gave a scream which was no mockery, but a really determined yell, and followed it up with a box on the ear that was no butterfly kiss. Henry, astonished, relaxed his grasp for a moment. She broke away from him – and at that moment Mrs Weldon, attracted by the scream, came running to the top of the bank.

'Whatever is the matter?'

'I saw a snake!' said Harriet, wildly. 'I'm sure it was a viper.'

She screamed again, and so did Mrs Weldon who was terrified of snakes. Henry, grunting, picked up the fallen plates and told his mother not to be silly.

'Come back to the car,' said Mrs Weldon. 'I won't stay another moment in this horrid place.'

They went back to the car. Henry looked glum and injured; he felt that he had been badly treated, as indeed he had. But Harriet's face was white enough to show that she had had a real shock, and she insisted on returning in the back of the car with Mrs Weldon, who made a great fuss over her with a smelling-bottle and ejaculations of horror and sympathy.

When they got back to Wilvercombe, Harriet was sufficiently recovered to thank Henry properly and apologise for having been so stupid. But she was still not quite herself, refused to come in to the hotel and insisted on walking back to her room at Mrs Lefranc's. She would not allow Henry to go with her – she wouldn't hear of it – she was quite all right – the walk would do her good. Henry, who was still offended, did not press the point. Harriet walked away, but not to Mrs Lefranc's. She hastened to the nearest telephone-cabinet and rang up the Bellevue. Was Lord Peter Wimsey there? No, he was out; could they take a message? Yes. Would he please come round and see Miss Vane at once, the minute he came in? It was frightfully urgent. Certainly they would tell him. No, they would not forget.

Harriet went home, sat down on Paul Alexis' chair and stared at Paul Alexis' ikon. She really felt quite upset.

She had sat there for an hour, without removing her hat and gloves – just thinking, when there was a commotion on the staircase. Feet came up two steps at a time and the door burst open so hard upon the preliminary knock as to make the knock superfluous.

'Hullo-ullo-ullo! Here we all are. What's up? Anything exciting? So sorry I was out – Here! I say! Hold up! It's all right, you know – at least, it *is* all right, isn't it?'

He gently extricated his arm from Harriet's frenzied grasp and shut the door.

'Now then! My dear, what's happened? You're all of a doodah!'

'Peter! I believe I've been kissed by a murderer.'

'Have you? Well, it serves you right for letting anybody kiss you but me. Good Heavens! You raise all sorts of objections to a perfectly amiable and reasonably virtuous man like myself, and the next thing I hear is that you are

245

wallowing in the disgusting embraces of a murderer. Upon my soul! I don't know what the modern girl is coming to.'

'He didn't actually kiss me – he only hugged me.'

'That's what I said – I said "disgusting embraces". And what is worse, you send urgent messages to my hotel, so that you can get me here to be gloated over. It is abominable. It is repulsive. Sit down. Take off that vulgar and idiotic hat and tell me who this low-down, bone-headed, bird-witted, dissipated murderer is who can't even keep his mind on his murdering, but rushes about the country embracing and hugging painted-faced females that don't belong to him.'

'Very well. Prepare for a shock. It was Haviland Martin.'

'Haviland Martin?'

'Haviland Martin.'

Wimsey walked very deliberately to a table near the window, laid down his hat and stick upon it, drew forward a chair, placed Harriet in it, drew up a second chair, sat down in it himself, and said:

'You win. I am astonished. I am thunderstruck. Kindly explain yourself. I thought you were out this afternoon with the Weldons.'

'I was.'

'Am I to understand that Haviland Martin is a friend of Henry Weldon's?'

'Haviland Martin is Henry Weldon.'

'You have been wallowing in the embraces of Henry Weldon?'

'Only in the interests of justice. Besides, I boxed his ears.'

'Go on. Begin from the beginning.'

Harriet began from the beginning. Wimsey bore fairly well the story of the vamping of Henry Weldon, merely interjecting that he hoped the man wouldn't make himself a nuisance later on, and listened patiently till she came to the incident of the plate-washing.

'I was sort of wriggling – because I didn't want him actually to kiss me, you know – and I looked down and saw his arm – it was round my waist, you understand –'

'Yes, I grasped that.'

'And I saw a snake tattooed all the way up his arm – just as it was up Martin's. And then I suddenly remembered how his face had seemed kind of familiar when I first saw him – and then I realised who he was.'

'Did you tell him so?'

'No. I just yelled, and Mrs Weldon came up and asked what was the matter. So I said I'd seen a snake – it was the only thing I could think of; and of course it was true.'

'What did Henry say?'

'Nothing. He was rather grumpy. Of course, he thought I was just making a fuss about his kissing me, only he couldn't tell his mother that.'

'No – but do you suppose he put two and two together?'

'I don't *think* he did. I hope not.'

'*I* hope not – or he may have bolted.'

'I know. I ought to have stuck to him like glue. But I couldn't. I couldn't, Peter. Honestly, I was frightened. It was silly, but I *saw* Alexis with his throat cut and the blood running all over the place – it was horrible. And the idea that – ugh!'

'Wait a moment. Let's think this thing out. You're sure you aren't mistaken about the snake and that Weldon really *is* Martin?'

'Yes. I'm sure he is. I can see it perfectly now. His profile's the same, now I come to think of it, and his height and size, and his voice too. The hair's different, of course, but he could easily have dyed that.'

'So he could. And his hair looks as if it had been dyed recently, for the matter of that, and re-bleached. I thought it looked funny and dead. Well, if Weldon is Martin, there's undoubtedly some funny business somewhere. But Harriet,

247

do put it out of your mind that he's a murderer. We've proved that Martin couldn't possibly have done it. He couldn't get to the place in time. Had you forgotten that?'

'Yes – I believe I had forgotten it. It seemed so obvious, somehow, that if he was there at Darley, in disguise, he must have been up to something or other.'

'Of course he was up to something or other. But what? He couldn't be in two places at once, even if he was disguised at Beelzebub.'

'No, he couldn't – could he? Oh, what an idiot I am! I've been sitting here having the horrors, and wondering how in the world we could ever break it to Mrs Weldon.'

'We may have to do that in any case, I'm afraid,' said Wimsey, gravely. 'It looks very much as if he had some hand in it, even if he didn't do the throat-cutting part of it. The only thing is, if he wasn't the actual murderer, why was he at Darley at all?'

'Goodness knows!'

'Something do do with the bay mare, that's a certainty. But what? What was the point of the bay mare at all? It beats me, Harriet; it beats me.'

'So it does me.'

'Well, there's only one thing to do.'

'What's that?'

'To ask him.'

'Ask him?'

'Yes. We'll ask him. It's just conceivable that there's some innocent explanation of the thing. And if we ask him about it, he'll have to commit himself one way or another.'

'Ye-es. That means open warfare.'

'Not necessarily. We needn't tell him all we suspect. I think you'd better leave this to me.'

'I rather think I had. I'm afraid I haven't handled Henry as well as I thought I was going to.'

'I don't know. You've got hold of a pretty valuable piece

of information, anyhow. Don't worry. We'll turn friend Henry inside-out before we've done with him. I'll just pop round to the Resplendent now, and see that he hasn't taken alarm.'

He popped round accordingly, only to find that Henry, so far from bolting, was dining and playing Bridge with a party of other residents. Should he break in on them with his question? Or should he wait? Better wait, perhaps, and let the matter crop up quietly in conversation the next morning. He made a private arrangement with the night porter to give him the tip if Mr Weldon showed any signs of departing during the night, and retired to his own quarters to do some hard thinking.

XIX

THE EVIDENCE OF THE DISGUISED MOTORIST

> 'Confess, or to the dungeon –
> Pause!'
> *Death's Jest-Book*

THURSDAY, 25 JUNE

MR WELDON did not bolt. Wimsey had no difficulty in catching him the following morning, and was rather glad he had waited, for in the meantime he had received a letter from Chief Inspector Parker.

'MY DEAR PETER,

'What will you want next? I have got a little preliminary information for you, and if anything fresh turns up I will keep you posted.

'First of all your Mr Haviland Martin is not a Bolshevik agent. He has had that account in Cambridge for quite a long time, and owns a small house, complete with lady, in the outskirts of the town. He took it, I believe, in 1925, and makes his appearance there from time to time, dark spectacles and all. He was recommended to the bank by one Mr Henry Weldon, of Leamhurst, Hunts, and there has never been any trouble with his account – a small one. He is thought to travel in something or other. All this suggests to me that the gentleman may be leading a double life, but you can put the Bolshevik theory out of your head.

'I got hold of Morris, the Bolshevik-wallah, this evening. He doesn't know of any Communist or Russian agent who might be knocking about Wilvercombe at the present time and thinks you have got hold of a mare's nest.

'By the way, the Cambridge police, from whom I had to wangle the Martin dope by telephone, want to know what is up. First Wilvercombe, then me! Fortunately, knowing their Super pretty well, I was able to get him to put pressure on the bank. I fancy I left them with the impression that it had something to do with bigamy!

'Talking of bigamy, Mary sends her love and wants to know whether you are any nearer committing monogamy yet. She says I am to recommend it to you out of my own experience, so I do so – acting strictly under orders.

'Affectionately yours,

'CHARLES.'

Thus armed, Wimsey descended on Henry Weldon, who greeted him with his usual offensive familiarity. Lord Peter bore with this as long as he thought advisable, and then said, carelessly:

'By the way, Weldon – you gave Miss Vane quite a turn yesterday afternoon.'

Henry looked at him rather unpleasantly.

'Oh! Did I? Well, I don't see why you need to come butting in.'

'I wasn't referring to your manners,' said Wimsey, 'though I admit they are a bit startling. But why didn't you mention that you and she had met before?'

'Met before? For the very simple reason that we never have met before.'

'Come, come, Weldon. How about last Thursday afternoon at the top of Hinks's Lane?'

He turned an ugly colour.

'I don't know what you're talking about.'

'Don't you? Well, it's your own business, of course, but if you want to go about the country incognito, you ought to get rid of that pattern on your arm. I understand that these things can be removed. Re-tattooing in flesh-colour is the simplest method, I believe.'

'Oh!' Henry stared for a few moments; then a slow grin spread itself over his face.

'So that's what the little hussy meant when she said she'd seen a snake. Sharp girl, that, Wimsey. Fancy her spotting that.'

'Manners, please!' said Wimsey. 'You will kindly refer to Miss Vane in a proper way and spare me the boring nuisance of pushing your teeth out at the back of your neck.'

'Oh, all right, just as you like. But I'd like to see you try.'

'You wouldn't see it. It would happen, that's all. But I've no time to waste in comparative physiology. I want to know what you were doing in Darley in disguise.'

'What affair is it of yours?'

'None; but the police might be interested. Anything that happened last Thursday interests them at the moment.'

'Oh! I see. You want to fix something on me. Well, just as it so happens, you can't, so you can put that in your pipe and smoke it. It's a fact that I came down here in another name. Why shouldn't I? I didn't want my mother to know I was here.'

'Why?'

'Well, you see, I didn't like this Alexis business at all. There's no harm in admitting that. I've said it already and I don't mind saying it again. I wanted to find out what was happening. If this marriage was really going through, I wanted to stop it.'

'But couldn't you have done that openly, without blacking your hair and dressing yourself up in dark spectacles?'

'Of course I could. I could have burst in on the lovebirds and made a hell of a row and frightened Alexis off, I dare say. And then what? Had a devil of a scene with my mother, and been cut off with a shilling, I suppose. No. My idea was to snoop around and see whether the job was really being put through, and, if it was, to get hold of the young blighter and buy him off privately.'

'You'd have needed some cash to do that,' said Wimsey, drily.

'I don't know about that. I'd heard some stories about a girl down here, don't you see, and if my mother got to know about that –'

'Ah, yes – a qualified form of blackmail. I begin to see the idea. You were going to pick up information in Wilvercombe about Alexis' previous entanglements, and then present him with the choice between having Mrs Weldon told about it and possibly getting nothing out of it, and taking your cash in hand and letting his credit as a faithful lover go. Is that it?'

'That's it.'

'And why Darley?'

'Because I didn't want to run into the old lady in Wilvercombe. A pair of specs and a bottle of hair-dye might be all right for the yokels, but to the sharp eye of mother-love, you understand, they might not be as impenetrable as a brick wall.'

'Quite so. Do you mind my asking whether you made any progress with this delicate investigation?'

'Not much. I only got to the place on Tuesday evening, and I spent most of Wednesday tinkering with the car. Those fools at the garage sent it out –'

'Ah, yes! One moment. Was it really necessary to hire a car with all that parade of secrecy?'

'It was, rather, because my mother would have recognised my own bus. It's rather an unusual colour.'

'You seem to have thought it all out very well. Did you have no difficulty about hiring it? – oh, no, how stupid of me! You could give your own name to the garage, naturally.'

'I could, but I didn't. To be perfectly frank – well! I don't mind saying that I had another name and address all ready to slip into. Sometimes I slip off to Cambridge on the quiet, see! To visit a lady there. *You* get me. Nice little woman – devoted and all that. Husband in the background somewhere. He won't divorce her, and I'm not worrying. Suits me all right as it is. Only there again, if my mother got to hear about it – there's been trouble, one way and another, and I didn't want to start it again. We're right as rain in Cambridge – Mr and Mrs Haviland Martin – all perfectly respectable, and all that, and it's easy enough to slip over when one wants a spot of domestic bliss and so on. You get me?'

'I get you. Do you also perambulate Cambridge in disguise?'

'I stick on the specs when I go to the bank. Some of my good neighbours keep an account there.'

'So you had this handy little disguise ready to slip into. I do congratulate you on the convenience of your arrangements. They really fill me with admiration, and I'm sure Mrs Martin must be a very happy woman. It really surprises me that you should be so anxious to pursue Miss Vane with your attentions.'

'Ah! But when a young lady asks for it – besides, I rather wanted to find out what the girl – the lady, that is, was after. When your mother's pretty well off, don't you see, you rather get the idea that people are looking out to make a bit out of her.'

Wimsey laughed.

'So you thought you'd vamp Miss Vane and find out. How great minds do think alike! She had rather the same idea about you. Wondered why you were so damned anxious to push her and me out of the place. I'm not surprised you each found the other so easy to talk to. Miss Vane said she was afraid you had seen through our little

254

plot and were pulling her leg. Well, well! So now we can come out into the open and be perfectly frank with one another. So much jollier and all that, what?'

Henry Weldon looked at Wimsey suspiciously. He had a dim notion that he had somehow been jockeyed into an absurd position. It was all very well – that damned girl and this chattering lunatic of an amateur detective seemed to be working hand in glove. But it did cross his mind that all this talk about frankness was a little one-sided.

'Oh yes, rather!' he replied, vaguely; adding rather anxiously: 'No need to tell my mother all about this, eh? She wouldn't like it.'

'Possibly not,' said Wimsey. 'But you see – the police, what? I don't quite see – British justice – duties of a citizen and all that, don't you know. I can't prevent Miss Vane from going to Inspector Umpelty, can I? Free agent and so on – and she's not over and above pleased with you, from what I can make out.'

'Oh, I don't mind the police.' Henry's face cleared. 'I've nothing to hide from *them*, you know. Not a bit. Rather not. Look here, old man – if I tell you all about it, couldn't you just tip them off and get 'em to leave me alone. You're damned thick with that Inspector fellow – if you tell him I'm all right he'll take it from you.'

'Oh, yes! Good fellow, the Inspector. Not his business to betray confidences. There's no reason whatever, so far as I can see, that Mrs Weldon should know anything about it. We men must stick together.'

'That's right!' Undeterred by experience, Mr Weldon instantly entered into another alliance, offensive and defensive. 'Well, look here. I came along to Darley on Tuesday evening and got permission to camp in Hinks's Lane.'

'You knew the place pretty well, I gather.'

'Never been there in my life; why?'

'Sorry – I thought you meant you knew about Hinks's Lane before you got there.'

'Eh? Oh! Oh, I see what you mean. I got it from some chap I met in a pub in Heathbury. Don't know his name.'

'Oh, quite!'

'I got in some stores and so on and settled in. Then, next day – that was Wednesday – I thought I'd better make a start on my inquiries. Stop a bit. That wasn't till the afternoon. I just loafed round in the morning – it was a grand day, and I was tired with trekking across country, especially as the car hadn't been going any too well. After lunch I had a go at it. It took me a devil of a time to start the bus, but I got her to go at last, and ran over to Wilvercombe. I went first of all to the registrar's and found that there was no marriage-notice put up there, so I followed that up by a round of the churches. There was nothing there either, but of course that proved nothing very much, because they might be going to get married in London or somewhere by licence or even by special licence.

'The next thing I did was to get the address of this chap Alexis from the people at the Resplendent. I took good care to dodge the old lady. I rang up the management with a story about a parcel that had gone to the wrong address, and got it out of them. Then I went round to the address they gave me, and tried to pump the old woman there, but she wasn't having any. However, she said I might find Alexis in a restaurant she told me about. I went round; he wasn't there, but I got talking with a fellow who dropped in – some dago, I don't know his name, and he said something which made me think I could find out what I wanted at the Winter Gardens.'

Henry paused.

'Of course,' he said, 'this must look pretty fishy to you – me hanging round there asking about Alexis, and then all this business happening next day, but that was exactly what

I did. Well, I went back to where I'd left the car, and had more trouble with it than ever – I began to curse the fool who'd hired it out to me, and I thought I'd better take it to a garage. Well, naturally, having once been started and warmed up, it went all right, and the garage people couldn't find anything wrong with it. They undid a few things and tightened a few things and charged me half a crown and that was all. By the time they'd finished, I was getting fed up, and thought I'd better take the beastly thing home while she was running. So I went back to Darley, with the engine missing all the way. After that, I went for a walk and that was the end of that day, except that I dropped in a bit later for a pint at the Feathers.'

'Which way did you walk?'

'Oh, along the beach for a bit. Why?'

'I just wondered if you'd rambled as far as the Flat-Iron?'

'Four and a half miles? Not likely. As a matter of fact, I haven't seen the place yet and I don't want to. Anyway, Thursday's the day you want to know about. All the details, as they say in the 'tec stories, eh? I had breakfast about nine o'clock – eggs and bacon, if you want to be particular – and then I thought I'd better see about getting along to Wilvercombe. So I went down to the village and flagged a passing car. That was – let me see – just after ten o'clock.'

'Whereabouts was this?'

'Where the main road enters Darley – the Wilvercombe side.'

'Why didn't you hire a car in the village?'

'Have you seen the cars you can hire in the village? If you had, you wouldn't ask.'

'Couldn't you have phoned up a Wilvercombe garage and got them to come out and pick you and the Morgan up?'

'I could have, but I didn't. The only garage I knew at Wilvercombe was the place I'd tried the night before, and I knew they weren't any good. Besides, what's wrong about taking a lift?'

'Nothing, if the driver isn't afraid about his insurance.'

'Oh! Well, this one wasn't. A very decent sort of woman she seemed to be. Drove a big red open Bentley. Made no bones about it at all.'

'You don't know her name, I suppose?'

'I never thought to ask. But I do remember the number of the car – it was a comic one: OI0101 – sort of thing you couldn't help remembering – Oi-oi-oi! I said to this woman what a funny one it was and we laughed about it a good bit.'

'Ha ha!' said Wimsey, 'that's a good one. Oi-oi-oi!'

'Yes – it made us both laugh. I remember saying it was a bit unfortunate having a number like that, because it 'ud stick in a bobby's mind. Oi-oi-oi!' Mr Weldon yodelled gleefully.

'So you got to Wilvercombe?'

'Yes.'

'And what did you do there?'

'The good lady put me down in the Market Square and asked me if I would like to be taken back. So I said that was very kind of her and when would she be leaving. She said she had to go just before one o'clock because she had an appointment in Heathbury, so I said that would do me all right, and she arranged to meet me in the Market Square again. So then I had a wander round and went down to the Winter Gardens. The chap I'd talked to said that this girl of Alexis' had something to do with the Winter Gardens – sang, or something.'

'She doesn't, as a matter of fact. Her present young man plays in the orchestra there.'

'Yes; I know that now. He'd got it all wrong. Anyhow, that's where I went, and I wasted a good bit of time listening to a tom-fool classical concert – my God! Bach and stuff at eleven in the morning! – and wondering when the real show began.'

'Were there many people there?'

'Lord, yes – packed with tabbies and invalids! I soon got fed-up and went round to the Resplendent. I wanted to get hold of the people there, only of course I had the luck to run slap-bang into my mother. She was just going out, and I dodged behind one of these silly palm-trees they have there so that she couldn't see me, and then I thought she might be going off to meet Alexis, so I padded after her.'

'And did she meet Alexis?'

'No; she went to some damned milliner's place.'

'How provoking!'

'I believe you. I waited a bit, and she came out and went to the Winter Gardens. "Hullo!" I said to myself, "what's all this? Is she on the same tack as I am?" So away I toddled again, and dash it! If it wasn't the same infernal concert, and if she didn't sit through it all by herself! I can tell you what they played, too. A thing called the Eroica Symphony. Such stuff!'

'Tut-tut! How wearisome.'

'Yes, I was wild, I can tell you. And the funny thing was, Mother looked as if she was waiting for somebody because she kept looking round and fidgeting. She sat on right through the programme, but when it came to God Save the King, she chucked it and went back to the Resplendent, looking as sick as a cat when you've taken its mouse away. Well, then I looked at my watch, and dashed if it wasn't twenty to one!'

'A sad waste of time! So I suppose you had to give up your drive home with the kindly lady in the Bentley?'

'What, me? Not a bit of it. She was a dashed fine woman. There wasn't such a devil of a hurry about Alexis. I went back to the Market Square, and there she was and we went home. I think that was all. No, it wasn't. I bought some collars at a shop near the War Memorial, and I believe I've got the bill about me somewhere, if that's evidence. Yes, here we are. One stuffs these things into one's pocket, you know. I've got one of the collars on now, if you'd like to look at it.'

'Oh, no – I believe you.'

'Good! Well, that's all, except that I went along and had some lunch at the Feathers. My good lady dropped me there and I think she went off up the Heathbury Road. After lunch, that is, at about 1.45, I went and had another go at the car, but couldn't get the slightest sign of a spark. So I thought I'd see if the local man could make anything of it. I went and got him and he came, and after a time they traced the trouble to a fault in the H.T. lead and put it right.'

'Well, that seems pretty clear. What time did you and the lady in the Bentley get to the Feathers?'

'Just on one o'clock. I remember hearing the church-clock strike and saying I hoped she wouldn't be late for her tennis-party.'

'And what time did you go to the garage?'

'Blest if I know. About three or half-past I should think. But they could probably tell you.'

'Oh, yes, they'll be able to check that up all right. It's very lucky you've got so many witnesses to your alibi, isn't it? Otherwise, as you say, it might have looked fishy. Now, here's another thing. While you were in Hinks's Lane on Thursday, did you happen to notice anybody or anything going along the shore?'

'Not a soul. But, as I've been trying to explain, I was only there up to ten o'clock and after 1.45, so it wasn't very likely I should see anything.'

'Nobody passed between 1.45 and three o'clock?'

'Oh! between 1.45 and three o'clock? I thought you meant earlier. Yes, there was a chap – a little pip-squeak of a fellow, in shorts, with horn-rimmed goggles on. He came down Hinks's Lane just after I got back – at 1.55, to be exact – and asked the time.'

'Did he? Where did he come from?'

'From the village. I mean, from the direction of the village; he seemed to be a stranger. I told him the time, and he went down to the shore and had his lunch on the beach. He cleared off later – at least, he wasn't there after I came back from the garage, and I think he went earlier than that. I didn't have much conversation with him. In fact, he wasn't keen for any, after I'd booted him one in the behind.'

'Great Scott! What for?'

'Nosey-parkering. I was struggling with the infernal car, and he stood about asking silly questions. I told him to clear out – standing there bleating "Won't it start?" Blasted little idiot!'

Wimsey laughed. 'He can't be our man, anyhow.'

'What man? The murderer? You still want to make out it's murder? Well, I'll swear that little shrimp had nothing to do with it. Sunday-school teacher, that's what he looked like.'

'And he was the only person you saw? Nothing else: neither man, woman nor child? Neither bird nor beast?'

'Why, no. No. Nothing.'

'H'm. Well, I'm much obliged to you for being so frank. I'll have to tell Umpelty about all this, but I don't imagine he'll bother you much – and I don't see the least need to inform Mrs Weldon.'

'I told you there was nothing in it.'

'Exactly. What time did you leave on Friday morning, by the way?'

'Eight o'clock.'

'Early start, wasn't it?'

'There was nothing to stay for.'

'Why?'

'Well, Alexis was dead, wasn't he?'

'How did you know that?'

Henry broke into a great guffaw.

'Thought you'd got something that time, didn't you? Well, I knew it because I was told. I went into the Feathers on Thursday night, and of course, they'd all heard about the dead man being found. Presently the local hobby came in – he doesn't live at Darley, but he comes through on his bike from time to time. He'd been over to Wilvercombe for something or other, and he told us they'd got a photo of the body and had just developed it up and identified it as a fellow called Alexis from the Resplendent. You ask the bobby, and he'll tell you. So I began to think I'd better pop off home, because that's where my mother would expect the condolences to come from. How's that, eh?'

'Overwhelming,' said Wimsey.

He left Henry Weldon and made for the police-station.

'Water-tight, water-tight, water-tight,' he muttered to himself. But why did he lie about the horse? He must have seen it, if it was running loose. Unless it broke out of the field after eight o'clock in the morning. And why shouldn't it? Water-tight, water-tight – damned suspiciously water-tight!

XX

THE EVIDENCE OF THE LADY IN THE CAR

'Madam, we're strangers:
And yet I knew some while ago a form
Like thine.'

The Bride's Tragedy

THURSDAY, 25 JUNE

THE Superintendent and the Inspector were perhaps even more surprised than pleased to hear of the identification of Mr Haviland Martin. They felt that the amateurs had somehow stolen a march on them, although, as they both hastened to point out, the case now remained as obscure as ever, if not more so. That is to say, considered as a murder, it was obscure; on the other hand, the evidence for suicide was perhaps a little strengthened, though only negatively. Instead of the sinister Martin, who might have been anybody, they now had merely Mr Henry Weldon, whom they knew. True, it was now extremely plain that Henry Weldon had a most cogent reason for wishing Paul Alexis out of the way. But his own explanation of his presence at Darley steemed plausible, if foolish, and there remained the absolute certainty that he could not possibly have been at the Flat-Iron at two o'clock. Moreover, the fact that he had been known for five years as the bespectacled Haviland Martin of the tinted glasses, robbed his latest masquerade of half its significance. The character of Martin had not been invented for the present purpose, and, since it already existed, it was natural enough that Weldon should have assumed it for the purpose of spying on his mother.

As to the outstanding points of Weldon's story, these could be easily checked. The bill for the collars was dated June 18th, and the date did not appear to have been altered in any way. A telephone-call to the shop confirmed it, and brought the additional information that the bill referred to was one of the last half-dozen made out on that day. Since Thursday had been early-closing day, when the shop closed at one o'clock, it was fairly evident that the purchase had been made shortly before that time.

Next, perhaps, in importance was the evidence of the Darley policeman. He was quickly found and interrogated. He admitted that Weldon's account of the matter was perfectly true. He had been in Wilvercombe that evening at about nine o'clock on a visit to his young lady (being then off duty) and had met one of the Wilvercombe Police, Rennie by name, outside the Resplendent. He had asked if there was any news about the body found at the Flat-Iron and Rennie had mentioned the identification. Rennie confirmed this, and there was no reason to doubt it; the photographs had been developed and printed within an hour of their arrival at the police-station; the hotels had been among the first places visited by the police; the identification had been made shortly before nine o'clock, and Rennie had been on duty with Inspector Umpelty while the manager of the Resplendent was being interrogated. The Darley constable further admitted having mentioned the identification in the bar at the Three Feathers. He had gone into the bar, quite legitimately, just before closing-time, in search of a man who was suspected of some trifling misdemeanour, and he distinctly remembered that 'Martin' was present at the time. Both constables were reprimanded for talking too freely; but the fact remained that Weldon had been told of the identification that night.

'So what have we got left?' inquired Superintendent Glaisher.

Wimsey shook his head.

'Nothing very much, but still, something. First: Weldon knows something about that horse – I'll swear he does. He hesitated when I asked him if he'd seen any person, thing, *or animal*, and I am almost certain he was wondering whether to say "No" or to make up a tarradiddle. Secondly: all this story is so thin. A child would know better than to set about his precious inquiries in the way he did. Why should he twice go into Wilvercombe and twice come away without really doing anything much? Thirdly: his story is so glib, and so full of exact times. Why, if he wasn't deliberately preparing an alibi? Fourthly: just at the most crucial moment of all, we get an account of his having been seen by an unknown person who asks the time. Why on earth should a man who had just passed through a village full of people and clocks, walk down Hinks's Lane to ask a casual camper for the time? The man who asks the time is part of the regular stock-in-trade of the alibimaker. The whole thing is so elaborate and fishy – don't you think so?'

Glaisher nodded.

'I agree with you. It is fishy. But what does it mean?'

'There you've got me. I can only suggest that, whatever Weldon was doing that morning in Wilvercombe, it wasn't what he said he was doing, and that he may somehow be in league with the actual murderer. How about this car OI 0101?'

'It's a —shire number, but that means nothing. Everybody buys second-hand cars these days. Still, naturally, we'll send out an inquiry. A wire to the —shire authorities will put us on the track. Not that that helps us very much about what Weldon was doing later in the day.'

'Not a bit, but there's no harm in getting hold of the lady. And have you asked at the Winter Gardens what the performance was last Thursday morning?'

'Yes: Constable Ormond is down there now – oh! here he is.'

Constable Ormond had inquired minutely. It was a classical concert, starting at 10.30. *Eine Kleine Nachtmusik*, by Mozart; two *Lieder ohne Worter* by Mendelssohn; Bach's *Air for G String*; Suite by Handel; Interval; Beethoven's *Eroica*. All present and correct, Bach and Beethoven as per statement and approximately at the correct times. No printed programme that anyone could have taken away or memorised. Further, the *Eroica* had been substituted at the last minute for the *Pastoral*, owing to some difficulty about mislaid band-parts. Each piece had been announced from the platform by the conductor. If anyone still nursed a suspicion that Mr Henry Weldon had not been present at that particular concert, it could only be out of surprise that he should have troubled to remember the items he had heard so exactly. Positive confirmation of his story there was none, though P.C. Ormond had carefully questioned the attendants. Persons in tinted spectacles were, alas! as common in the Winter Gardens as blackbeetles in a basement.

Some additional confirmation of Weldon's story was brought in a few minutes later by another constable. He had interviewed Mrs Lefranc and discovered that a gentleman in dark glasses really had called on Paul Alexis on the Wednesday and tried to get information about Leila Garland. Mrs Lefranc, scenting 'trouble', had packed him off with a flea in his ear to the restaurant where Alexis frequently lunched. Here the proprietor remembered him; yes, there had, he believed, been some talk about the Winter Gardens with a gentleman out of the orchestra who had happened to drop in – no, not Mr da Soto, but a much humbler gentleman, who played at the fourth desk of second violins. Finally, as sequel to a series of inquiries put round the principal Wilvercombe garages, a mechanic was found who remembered a gent calling on Wednesday evening with a Morgan and complaining of trouble in starting and feeble ignition. The mechanic had been able to find no fault beyond a certain amout of wear in the platinum points, which might have caused bad starting when the engine was cold.

All these things were of little importance as regarded the actual crime, if there was one; they served, however, to support the general accuracy of Weldon's statement.

One of the minor irritations of detective work is the delay which usually occurs in the putting-through of inquiries. Trunk-calls are held up; people urgently required for interviews are absent from home; letters take time to travel. It was, therefore, gratifying and surprising to find the identification of the owner of OI 0101 going along like oiled clockwork. Within an hour, a telegram arrived from the – shire County Council, stating that OI 0101 had been last transferred to a Mrs Morecambe, living at 17 Popcorn Street, Kensington. Within ten minutes, the Wilvercombe Telephone Exchange had put through a trunk-call. Within fifteen minutes the bell rang and Superintendent Glaisher was learning from Mrs Morecambe's maid that her mistress was staying at Heathbury Vicarage. A call to the vicarage received immediate attention. Yes, Mrs Morecambe was staying there; yes, she was at home; yes, they would fetch her; yes, this was Mrs Morecambe speaking; yes, she distinctly remembered driving a gentleman in dark glasses from Darley to Wilvercombe and back last Thursday; yes, she thought she could remember the times; she must have picked him up about ten o'clock, judging by the time she had started out from Heathbury, and she knew she had dropped him in Darley again at one o'clock, because she had consulted her watch to see if she would be in time for her luncheon and tennis-party at Colonel Cranton's, the other side of Heathbury. No, she had never seen the gentleman before and did not know his name, but she thought she could identify him if required. No trouble at all, thanks – she was only glad to know that the police had nothing against *her* (silvery laughter); when the maid said the Superintendent was on the phone she had been afraid she might have been trespassing on the white lines, or parking in the wrong place or something. She would be staying at the vicarage till next Monday and would he happy to assist the police in any way. She did hope she hadn't been helping a gangster to escape or anything of that sort.

The Superintendent scratched his head. 'It's uncanny,' he said. 'Here we are and we know all about it – not so much as a wrong number! But anyhow, if the lady's a friend of the Rev. Trevor's, she's O.K. He's lived here for fifteen years and is the nicest gentleman you could wish to meet – quite one of the old school. We'll just find out how well he knows this Mrs Morecambe, but I expect it's all right. As to this identification, I don't know that it's worth while.'

'You probably couldn't expect her to identify him without his dark hair and glasses,' said Wimsey. 'It's astonishing what a difference it makes having the eyes concealed. You could make him put the spectacles on, of course, or you could bring her over and get *him* to identify *her*. I'll tell you what. Ring up again and ask if she can come over here now. I'll get hold of Weldon and park him out on the verandah of the Resplendent, and you can fetch her along casually. If he spots her, all's well; if she spots him, we may feel differently about it.'

'I see,' said Glaisher. 'That's not a bad idea. We'll do that.' He rang up Heathbury Vicarage and spoke again.

'It's all right; she's coming.'

'Good. I'll toddle round and try to detach Weldon from

his mamma. If she's present at the interview the good Henry will be in the soup. If I can't get him, I'll ring you.'

Henry Weldon was readily found in the lounge. He was having tea with his mother, but excused himself when Wimsey came up and asked for a word in private. They selected a table about half-way along the verandah, and Weldon ordered drinks, while Wimsey embarked on a rather verbose account of his interview with the police that morning. He harped a good deal on the trouble he had taken to persuade Glaisher not to let the story come to Mrs Weldon's ears, and Henry expressed a proper sense of gratitude.

Presently a burly figure made his appearance, looking exactly like a police-constable out of uniform, and escorting a rather young-old lady, dressed in the extreme of fashion. They passed slowly along the verandah, which was well filled with people, making for an empty table at the far end. Wimsey watched the lady's glance roam over the assembly; it rested on him, passed on to Weldon and then, without a pause or sign of recognition, to a young man in blue glasses who was toying with a chocolate sundae at the next table. Here it paused for a moment – then it moved on again. At the same time Weldon gave quite a convulsive start.

'I beg your pardon,' said Wimsey, breaking off short in his monologue. 'Did you speak?'

'I – er – no,' said Weldon. 'I thought I recognised somebody, that's all. Probably a chance resemblance.' He followed Mrs Morecambe with his eyes as she approached them, and raised a tentative hand to his hat.

Mrs Morecambe saw the movement and looked at Weldon, with a faint expression of puzzlement. She opened her mouth as though to speak, but shut it again. Weldon completed the hat-raising gesture and stood up.

'Good afternoon,' he said. 'I'm afraid you don't–'

Mrs Morecambe stared with polite surprise.

'Surely I'm not mistaken,' said Weldon. 'You were good enough to give me a lift the other day.'

'Did I?' said Mrs Morecambe. She looked more closely and said:

'Yes, I believe I did – but weren't you wearing dark glasses that day?'

'I was – it makes rather a difference, doesn't it?'

'I really shouldn't have known you. But I recognise your voice now. Only I had an idea – But there! I'm not very observant. I carried away an impression that you were quite dark. Probably the glasses put it into my head. So stupid of me. I hope the Morgan has recovered itself.'

'Oh, yes, thanks. Fancy meeting you here. The world's a small place, isn't it?'

'Very. I hope you are having an enjoyable holiday.'

'Oh, very much so, thanks – now that my car is behaving itself again. I'm tremendously grateful to you for having taken compassion on me that day.'

'Not at all; it was a pleasure.'

Mrs Morecambe bowed politely and moved away with her companion. Wimsey grinned.

'So that was your attractive lady. Well, well. You're a gay dog, Weldon. Young or old, they all go down before you, spectacles or no spectacles.'

'Chuck it!' said Henry, not displeased. 'Lucky thing her turning up like that, wasn't it?'

'Remarkably so,' said Wimsey.

'Don't like the hick she's got with her, though,' pursued Henry. 'One of the local turnip-heads, I suppose.'

Wimsey grinned again. Could anybody be as slow-witted as Henry made himself out?

'I ought to have tried to find out who she was,' said Henry, 'but I thought it would look a bit pointed. Still, I daresay they'll be able to trace her, won't they? It's rather important to me, you know.'

'Yes, it is, isn't it? Very good-looking and well-off, too, from the looks of her. I congratulate you, Weldon. Shall I try and trace her for you? I'm a most skilful go-between and an accomplished gooseberry.'

'Don't be an ass, Wimsey. She's my alibi, you idiot.'

'So she is! Well, here goes!'

Wimsey slipped away, chuckling to himself.

'Well, that's all right,' said Glaisher, when all this was reported to him. 'We've got the lady taped now all right. She's the daughter of an old school-friend of Mrs Trevor's and stays with them every summer. Been at Heathbury for the last three weeks. Husband's something in the City; sometimes joins her for weekends, but hasn't been here this summer. Lunch and tennis at Colonel Cranton's all correct. No funny business there. Weldon's all right.'

'That will be a relief to his mind. He's been a bit nervy about this alibi of his. He skipped like a ram when he caught sight of Mrs Morecambe.'

'Did he? Skipping for joy, I expect. After all, you can't be surprised. How's he to know what time the alibi's wanted for? We've managed to keep that part of it out of the papers, and he probably still thinks, as we did at first, that Alexis was dead some time before Miss Vane found the body. He can't help knowing that he had a jolly good motive for killing Alexis, and that he was here under dashed suspicious circumstances. In any case, we've got to let him out, because, if he did the murder or helped to do it, he wouldn't make any mistake about the time. He's scared stiff, and I don't blame him. But his not knowing lets him out as surely and certainly as if he had a really cast-iron alibi for two o'clock.'

'Much more surely, my dear man. It's when I find people with cast-iron alibis that I begin to suspect them. Though Weldon's two o'clock alibi seems to be as nearly cast-iron as anything can be. But it's only when somebody comes along and swears himself black in the face that he saw Weldon behaving with perfect innocence at two o'clock precisely that I'll begin seriously to weave a hempen neck-tie for him. Unless, of course—'

'Well?'

'Unless, I was going to say, there was a conspiracy between Weldon and some other person to kill Alexis, and the actual killing was done by the other person. I mean, supposing, for example, Weldon and our friend Bright were both in it, and Bright was scheduled to do the dirty deed at eleven o'clock, for example, while Weldon established his own alibi, and suppose there was some hitch in the arrangements so that the murder didn't come off till two, and suppose Weldon didn't know that and was still sticking to the original time-table – how about that?'

'That's supposing a lot. Bright – or whoever it was – has had plenty of time to communicate with Weldon. He wouldn't be such a fool as not to let him know.'

'True; I'm not satisfied with that suggestion. It doesn't seem to fit Bright.'

'Besides, Bright really has a cast-iron alibi for two o'clock.'

'I know. That's why I suspect him. But what I mean is that Bright is a free agent. Even if it was too dangerous to meet Weldon he could always have written or telephoned, and so could Weldon. You haven't got anybody in jug who would fit the bill, I suppose? Or any sudden deaths? The only thing I can think of is that the accomplice may have been in some place where he couldn't communicate with anybody – quod, or six foot of elm with brass handles.'

'Or how about a hospital?'

'Or, as you say, a hospital.'

'That's an idea,' said Glaisher. 'We'll look into that, my lord.'

'It can't do any harm – though I haven't much faith in it. I seem to have lost my faith lately, as the good folks say. Well, thank Heaven! it's nearly dinner-time, and one can always eat. Hullo – ullo – ullo! What's all the excitement?'

Superintendent Glaisher looked out of the window. There was a noise of trampling feet.

'They're carrying something down to the mortuary. I wonder—'

The door burst open with scant ceremony and Inspector Umpelty surged in, damp and triumphant.

'Sorry, sir,' he said. 'Good-evening, my lord. We've got the body!'

XXI

THE EVIDENCE AT THE INQUEST

'At the word, "I'm murdered,"
The gaolers of the dead throw back the grave-stone,
Split the deep ocean, and unclose the mountain
To let the buried pass.'

Death's Jest-Book

FRIDAY, 26 JUNE

THE inquest upon the body of Paul Alexis was held on June 26th, to the undisguised relief and triumph of Inspector Umpelty. For years (it seemed to him) he had been trying to make an investigation about nothing tangible. But for Harriet's photographs, he might, in his more worried moments, have begun to think that the body was a myth. Now, however, here it definitely was: a real, solid – or comparatively solid – body. True, it was not quite so informative as he had hoped. It was not served out to him complete with a ticket, marked in plain figures: 'Suicide, with care', or 'This Year's Murder-Model; Body by Bright'. However, there was the corpse, and that was something gained. To quote Lord Peter (who seemed to be specialising in the provision of mnemonics), he might now say:

''T would make a man drink himself dead on gin-toddy
To have neither a corpus delicti *nor body;*
But now though by destiny scurvily tricked, I
At least have a corpse – though no corpus delicti.'

There was some little debate whether the whole matter should be thrashed out at the inquest or the complicated series of clues and suspicions suppressed and the inquest adjourned for further inquiries. In the end, however, it was decided to let matters take their course. Something useful might come out; one never knew. In any case, the possible suspects must know by this time pretty well where they stood. Certain clues – for example, the horseshoe – could, of course, be kept up the sleeves of the police.

The first witness to give evidence was Inspector Umpelty. He explained briefly that the body had been found tightly wedged into a deep crevice at the far end of the Grinders reef, from which it had been recovered with considerable difficulty by means of dredging-tackle and diving. It had apparently been washed into that position by the heavy seas of the previous week. When found, it was considerably distended by internal gases, but had not floated, being heavily weighted down by the presence of a cash-belt containing £300 in gold. (Sensation.)

The Inspector produced the belt and the gold (which the jury inspected with curiosity and awe), and also a passport found on the deceased; this had recently been visa'd for France. Two other items of interest had also been discovered in the dead man's breast-pocket. One was the unmounted photograph of a very beautiful girl of Russian type, wearing a tiara-shaped head-dress of pearls. The photograph was signed in a thin, foreign-looking hand with the name 'Feodora'. There was no mark of origin on the photograph, which either had never been mounted, or had been skilfully detached from its mount. It was in a fairly good state of preservation, having been kept in one of the compartments of a handsome leather note-case, which had protected it to some extent. The note-case contained nothing further but a few currency notes, some stamps, and the return half of a ticket from Wilvercombe to Darley Halt, dated 18th June.

The second item was more enigmatical. It was a sheet of quarto paper, covered with writing, but so stained with blood and sea-water that it was almost undecipherable. This paper had not been folded in the note-case, but tucked away behind it. Such writing as could be read was in printed capitals and in a purplish ink which, though it had run and smeared a good deal, had stood up reasonably well to its week's immersion. A few sentences could be made out, but they were not of an encouraging nature. There was, for instance, a passage which began musically 'SOLFA', but swiftly degenerated into 'TGMZ DXL LKKZM VXI' before being lost in a dirty crimson stain. Further down came 'AIL AXH NZMLF', 'NAGMJU KC KC' and 'MULBY MS SZLKO', while the concluding words, which might be the signature, were 'UFHA AKTS'.

The coroner asked Inspector Umpelty whether he could throw any light on this paper. Umpelty replied that he thought two of the witnesses might be able to do so, and stepped down to make way for Mrs Lefranc.

The lady of the lodgings, in a great state of nerves, tears and face-powder, was asked if she had identified the body. She replied that she had been able to do so by the clothes, the hair, the beard and by a ring which the deceased had always worn on his left hand.

'But as for his poor face,' sobbed Mrs Lefrane, 'I couldn't speak to it, not if I was his own mother, and I'm sure I loved him like a son. It's all been nibbled right away by those horrible creatures, and if ever I eat a crab or lobster again, I hope Heaven will strike me dead! Many's the lobster mayonnaise I've ate in the old days, not knowing, and I'm sure it's no wonder if they give you nightmare, knowing where they come from, the brutes!'

The court shuddered, and the managers of the Resplendent and the Bellevue, who were present, despatched hasty notes by messenger to the respective chefs, commanding them on no account whatever to put crab or lobster on the menu for at least a fortnight.

Mrs Lefranc deposed further that Alexis had been accustomed to receive letters from foreign parts which took him a long time to read and answer. That after receiving the last of these on the Tuesday morning he had become strange and excited in his manner. That on the Wednesday he had paid up all outstanding bills and burnt a quantity of papers, and that that night he had kissed her and referred mysteriously to a possible departure in the near future. That he had gone out on the Thursday morning after making rather a poor breakfast. He had not packed any clothes and had taken his latch-key as though he meant to return.

Shown the photograph: she had never seen it before; she had never seen the original of the portrait; she had never heard Alexis speak of anyone named Feodora; she knew of no ladies in his life except Leila Garland, with whom he had broken some time ago, and Mrs Weldon, the lady he was engaged to marry at the time of his death.

This, naturally, focused public attention on Mrs Weldon. Henry handed her a smelling-bottle and said something to her, and she responded by a faint smile.

The next witness was Harriet Vane, who gave a detailed account of the finding of the body. The coroner examined her particularly in the matter of the exact position of the body and the condition of the blood. Harriet was a good witness on these points, her training as a mystery-writer having taught her to assemble details of this kind coherently.

'The body was lying with the knees drawn up, as though it had crumpled together in that position as it fell. The clothes were not disarranged at all. The left arm was doubled so as to bring the hand and wrist directly beneath the throat. The right arm and hand hung over the edge of the rock immediately beneath the head of the corpse. Both hands and both arms, as well as the front part of the body were saturated with blood. The blood had collected in a pool in a hollow of the rock just under the throat, and was still dripping down the face of the rock when I saw it. I cannot say whether there might not have been sea-water as well as blood in the hollow. There was no blood on the upper surface of the rock, or on any part of the body except the front and on the hands and arms. The appearance presented was as though the throat of the deceased had been cut while he was bending forward – as, for example, a person might do over a sink or basin. When I shifted the body the blood flowed freely and copiously from the severed vessels. I did not observe whether any splashes of blood had been dried by the sun. I do not think so, because the pool of blood and the blood beneath the corpse were sheltered from the direct rays of the sun by the corpse itself. When I lifted the corpse, the blood gushed out, as I said before, and ran down the rock. It was quite liquid and ran freely.

'I handled the sleeves and breast of the coat and the gloves which the deceased was wearing. They were soaked in blood and felt limp and wet. They were not stiff at all. They were not sticky. They were limp and wet. I have seen bandages which had been soaked in blood some time previously and am acquainted with the stiffness and stickiness of clotted blood. The clothes were not like that at all. They appeared to have been soaked in fresh blood.

'The body felt warm to the touch. The surface of the rock was hot, as it was a hot day. I did not move the body, except when I turned it a little over and lifted the head at first. I am sorry now that I did not attempt to drag it further up the beach, but I did not think I was strong enough to make a good job of it, and supposed that I should be able to get help quickly.'

The coroner said he did not think the jury could possibly

blame Miss Vane for not having tried to remove the corpse, and complimented her on the presence of mind she had shown in taking photographs and carrying out investigations. The photographs were handed to the jury, and after Harriet had explained the various difficulties she had encountered before getting into communication with the police, she was allowed to step down.

The next witness was the police-surgeon, Dr Fenchurch. From his examination of the photographs and of the body he had formed the opinion that the throat of the deceased had been completely severed by a single blow with a sharp-bladed instrument. The lobsters and crabs had eaten away the greater part of the soft tissues, but the photographs were here of very great value, since they showed definitely that the throat had been cut at the first attempt, without any preliminary surface gashing. This was borne out by the condition of the muscular tissue, which showed no sign of any second cut. All the great vessels and muscles of the neck, including the carotid and jugular veins and the glottis, had been clearly cut through. The wound commenced high up under the left ear, and proceeded in a downward direction to the right side of the throat, extending backwards as far as the vertebral column, which had, however, not been nicked. He concluded that the cut had been made from left to right. This was characteristic of suicidal throat-cutting by a right-handed person; the same appearance would, however, be produced by a homicidal cut, provided the murderer were standing behind his victim at the time.

'Such a wound would, of course, produce a great effusion of blood?'

'It would.'

'In the case of a murderer, standing in the position you describe, his hands and clothes would necessarily be very much stained?'

'His right hand and arm, probably. His clothes might not

be stained at all, since they would be protected by the body of his victim.'

'Did you carry out a post-mortem on the body to ascertain if there was any other possible cause of death?'

The doctor, smiling slightly, said that he had, in the ordinary course of things, opened up the head and body, but had seen nothing of a suspicious nature.

'In your opinion, what was the cause of death?'

Dr Fenchurch, still smiling slightly, said that in his opinion the cause of death was acute haemorrhage, coupled with the severance of the respiratory canal. In fact, the deceased had died of having his throat cut.

The coroner, who was a lawyer and seemed unwilling to let the medical witness have his own way entirely, persisted.

'I am not trying to quibble over absurdities,' he remarked, acidly. 'I am asking you whether we are to understand that the death was actually caused by the wound in the throat, or whether there is any possibility that the deceased was killed in some other way, and the throat cut afterwards to produce the appearance of suicidal throat-cutting?'

'Oh, I see. Well, I can say this: that the throat-cutting was undoubtedly the immediate cause of death. That is, the man was undoubtedly alive when his throat was cut. The body was completely drained of blood. In fact, I have never seen a body drained so completely. There was some very slight clotting about the heart but it was remarkably little. This, however, is no more than one might expect from the great extent of the wound. If the man had been already dead when the wound was inflicted, there would, of course, have been little or no bleeding.'

'Quite so. It is as well to have that clear. You said that the throat-cutting was the *immediate* cause of death. What precisely did you mean by that?'

'I meant to exclude the bare possibility that the deceased might also have taken poison. It is not unusual to find suicides doubling their precautions in this way. As a matter of fact, however, the internal organs showed no signs of anything of this nature having taken place. If you wish, I can have an analysis made of the visceral contents.'

'Thank you; perhaps it would be as well. It would equally, I suppose, be possible that the man had been previously drugged by some other party before the delivery of the blow, or slash, that cut his throat?'

'Certainly. A soporific might have been administered beforehand in order to make the attack more easy.'

Here Inspector Umpelty rose and begged to draw the coroner's attention to the evidence of Harriet and the photographs that the deceased had walked to the rock on his own feet and alone.

'Thank you, Inspector; we shall come to that later. Permit me to finish with the medical evidence. You heard Miss Vane's account of her finding the body, Doctor, and her statement that at ten minutes past two the blood was still liquid. What inference do you draw as regards the time of the death?'

'I should say that it had occurred within a very few minutes of the finding of the body. Not earlier than two o'clock at the outside.'

'And would a person die quickly from the effects of having his throat cut in the manner described?'

'He would die immediately. The heart and arteries might continue to pump blood for a few seconds by spasmodic muscular contraction, but the man would be dead from the moment that the great vessels were severed.'

'So that we may take it that the wound was actually inflicted certainly not earlier than two o'clock?'

'That is so. Two o'clock is the extreme limit. I myself should incline to put it later.'

'Thank you. There is just one more question. You have heard that a razor was found in proximity to the body.

Inspector, would you kindly hand the exhibit to the witness. In your opinion, Doctor, is the appearance of the wound consistent with its having been inflicted by that weapon?'

'Decidedly so. This, or a similar razor, would be an ideal instrument for the purpose.'

'In your opinion, would great physical strength be required to deliver such a blow with that, or a similar weapon?'

'Considerable strength, yes. Exceptional strength, no. Much would depend upon the circumstances.'

'Will you explain what you mean by that?'

'In the case of a determined suicide, wounds of this kind have been known to be inflicted by persons of quite ordinary or even poor physique. In the case of homicide, much would depend on whether the victim was able to offer any effective resistance to the attack.'

'Did you find any other marks of violence on the body?'

'None whatever.'

'No signs of throttling or bruising?'

'None. There was nothing remarkable beyond the natural action of the water and the complete absence of postmortem staining. I attribute the latter to the small amount of blood present in the body and also to the circumstance that the body was not left lying in one position, but was washed from the rock shortly after death and tumbled about in the water.'

'In your opinion, does the condition of the body suggest suicide or homicide?'

'In my opinion, and taking all the circumstances into consideration, suicide appears rather more probable. The only point to set against it is the absence of surface cuts. It is rather rare for a suicide to be completely successful at the first attempt, though it is not by any means unknown.'

'Thank you.'

The next witness was Miss Leila Garland, who confirmed

the evidence of Mrs Lefranc with respect to the cipher letters. This naturally led to an inquiry into the relations between Miss Garland and Mr Alexis, from which it transpired that their acquaintance had been conducted on a footing of rigid, and even Victorian, propriety; that Mr Alexis had been terribly distressed when Miss Garland had put an end to the friendship; that Mr Alexis was not by any means a likely person to commit suicide; that (on the other hand) Miss Garland had been terribly upset to think of his having done anything rash on her account; that Miss Garland had never heard of anybody called Feodora, but did not, of course, know what follies Mr Alexis might not have committed in a despairing mood after the termination of their friendship; that Miss Garland had not so much as set eyes on Mr Alexis for ever so long and could not imagine why anybody should think this terrible business had anything to do with her. With regard to the letters, Miss Garland had thought that Mr Alexis was being blackmailed, but could produce no evidence to prove this.

It now became obvious that nothing on earth could keep Mrs Weldon out of the witness-box. Attired in near-widow's weeds, she indignantly protested against the suggestion that Alexis could possibly have made away with himself on Leila's account, or on any account whatever. She knew better than anybody that Alexis had had no genuine attachment to anyone but herself. She admitted that she could not explain the presence of the portrait signed 'Feodora', but asserted vehemently that, up to the last day of his life, Alexis had been radiant with happiness. She had last seen him on the Wednesday night, and had expected to see him again on the Thursday morning at the Winter Gardens. He had not arrived there, and she was perfectly sure that he must have been lured away to his death by some designing person. He had often said that he was afraid of Bolshevik plots, and in her opinion, the police ought to look for Bolsheviks.

This outburst produced some effect upon the jury, one of whom rose to inquire whether the police were taking any steps to comb out suspicious looking foreigners residing in, or hanging about, the vicinity. He himself had observed a number of disagreeable-looking tramps on the road. He also noticed with pain that at the very hotel where Alexis had worked, a Frenchman was employed as a professional dancer, and that there were also a number of foreigners in the orchestra at the Winter Gardens. The dead man was also a foreigner. He did not see that naturalisation papers made any difference. With two million British-born workers unemployed, he thought it a scandalous thing that this foreign riff-raff was allowed to land at all. He spoke as an Empire Free-Trader and member of the Public Health Committee.

Mr Pollock was then called. He admitted having been in the neighbourhood of the Grinders reef with his boat at about two o'clock on the day of the death, but insisted that he had been out in deep water and had seen nothing previous to Harriet's arrival on the scene. He was not looking in that direction; he had his own business to attend to. As to the nature of that business he remained evasive, but nothing could shake his obstinate assertion of complete ignorance. His grandson Jem (having now returned from Ireland) briefly confirmed this evidence, but added that he himself had surveyed the shore with a glass at, he thought, about 1.45. He had then seen someone on the Flat-Iron rock, either sitting or lying down, but whether dead or alive he could not say.

The last witness was William Bright, who told the story about the razor in almost exactly the same terms that he had used to Wimsey and the police. The coroner, glancing at a note handed up to him by Umpelty, allowed him to finish what he had to say, and then asked:

'You say this happened at midnight on Tuesday, 16 June?'

'Just after midnight. I heard the clock strike shortly before this man came up to me.'

'How was the tide at the time?'

For the first time, Bright faltered. He glanced about him as though he suspected a trap, licked his lips nervously, and replied:

'I know nothing about tides. I don't belong to this part of the country.'

'But you mentioned, in your very moving account of this interview, the noise made by the sea lapping against the wall of the Esplanade. That suggests, does it not, that the tide was then full?'

'I suppose so.'

'Would you be surprised to learn that at midnight on the 16th of this month the tide was actually at the lowest point of the ebb?'

'I may have sat there longer than I thought.'

'Did you sit there for six hours?'

No answer.

'Would it surprise you to know that the sea never comes up to the wall of the Esplanade except at the top of the spring tides which, on that particular date, would occur at about six o'clock in the evening?'

'I can only say that I must have been mistaken. You must allow for the effects of a morbid imagination.'

'You still say that the interview took place at midnight?'

'Yes; I am confident about that.'

The coroner dismissed Mr Bright with a warning to be more careful with statements he made in court, and recalled Inspector Umpelty with an inquiry into Bright's movements and character.

He then summed up the evidence. He did not attempt to disguise his own opinion, which was that deceased had taken his own life. (Incoherent protest from Mrs Weldon.) As to why he should have done so, it was not the jury's business to speculate. Various motives had been suggested, and the jury must bear in mind that deceased was a Russian by birth, and therefore excitable, and liable to be overcome by feelings of melancholy and despair. He himself had read a great deal of Russian literature and could assure the jury that suicide was of frequent occurrence among the members of that unhappy nation. We who enjoyed the blessing of being British might find that difficult to understand, but the jury could take it from him that it was so. They had before them clear evidence of how the razor came into the hands of Alexis, and he thought they need not lay too much stress on Bright's error about the tide. Since Alexis did not shave, what could he have needed a razor for, unless to commit suicide? He (the coroner) would, however, be perfectly fair and enumerate the one or two points which seemed to throw doubt on the hypothesis of suicide. There was the fact that Alexis had taken a return-ticket. There was the passport. There was the belt full of gold. They might perhaps think that the deceased had contemplated fleeing the country. Even so, was it not likely that he had lost heart at the last moment and taken the shortest way out of the country and out of life itself? There was the odd circumstance that the deceased had apparently committed suicide in gloves, but suicides were notoriously odd. And there was, of course, the evidence of Mrs Weldon (for whom they must all feel the deepest sympathy) as to the deceased's state of mind; but this was contradicted by the evidence of William Bright and Mrs Lefranc.

In short, here was a man of Russian birth and temperament, troubled by emotional entanglements and by the receipt of mysterious letters, and obviously in an unstable condition of mind. He had wound up his worldly affairs and procured a razor. He had been found in a lonely spot, to which he had obviously proceeded unaccompanied, and had been found dead, with the fatal weapon lying close under his hand. There were no footprints upon the sand but his own, and the person who had discovered the body had come upon it so closely after the time of the death as to preclude the possibility of any murderer having escaped from the scene of the crime by way of the shore. The witness Pollock had sworn that he was out in deep water at the time when the death occurred, and had seen no other boat in the neighbourhood, and his evidence was supported by that of Miss Vane. Further, there was no evidence that anybody had the slightest motive for doing away with the deceased, unless the jury chose to pay attention to the vague suggestions about blackmailers and Bolsheviks, which there was not an atom of testimony to support.

Wimsey grinned at Umpelty over this convenient summary, with its useful suppressions and assumptions. No mention of clefts in the rock or of horseshoes or of the disposal of Mrs Weldon's money. The jury whispered together. There was a pause. Harriet looked at Henry Weldon. He was frowning heavily and paying no attention to his mother, who was talking excitedly into his ear.

Presently the foreman rose to his feet – a stout person, who looked like a farmer.

'We're all agreed, for certain sure,' he said, 'as deceased come to his death by cutting of his throat, and most of us thinks he took his own life; but there's some' (he glared at the Empire Free-Trader) 'who will have it as it was Bolsheviks.'

'A majority verdict is sufficient,' said the coroner, 'Am I to understand that the majority is for suicide?'

'Yes, sir. I told you so, Jim Cobbley,' added the foreman, in a penetrating whisper.

'Then your verdict is that deceased came to his end by cutting his own throat.'

'Yes, sir.' (A further consultation.) 'We should like to add as we think the police regulations about foreigners did ought to be tightened up, like, deceased being a foreigner and suicides and murders being unpleasant in a place where so many visitors come in the summer.'

'I can't take that,' objected the harassed coroner. 'Deceased was a naturalised Englishman.'

'That don't make no difference,' said the juror, sturdily. 'We do think as the regulations ought to be tightened up none the more for that, and that's what we all say. Put it down, sir, as that's our opinion.'

'There you are,' said Wimsey, 'that's the breed that made the Empire. When empire comes in at the door, logic goes out at the window. Well, I suppose that's all. I say, Inspector.'

'My lord?'

'What are you doing with that scrap of paper?'

'I don't quite know, my lord. Do you think there's anything to be made of it?'

'Yes; send it up to Scotland Yard and ask them to get the photographic experts on to it. You can do a lot with coloured screens. Get hold of Chief Inspector Parker – he'll see that it's put into the right hands.'

The Inspector nodded.

'We'll do that. It's my belief there's something for us in that bit of paper, if we could only get at it. I don't know when I've seen a queerer business than this. It looks just about as clear a case of suicide as you could wish, if it wasn't for one or two things. And yet, when you look into those things separately, they seem to melt away, like. There's that Bright. I thought we'd got him on one point, anyhow. But there! I've noticed that these landsmen, nine times out of ten, haven't the least notion whether the tide's in or out or where it is. I think he was lying; so do you – but you couldn't expect a jury to hang a man for murder on the ground that he didn't know High Water from Low Water. We'll try to keep an eye on the fellow, but I don't see how we're going to detain him. The verdict's suicide (which suits us well enough in a way), and if Bright wants to move on, we can't stop him. Not unless we offer to pay for his board and lodging for an indefinite period, and *that* wouldn't suit the rate-payers. He's got no settled address, and seeing what his business is, we can't hardly expect it. We'll get out a general call to have him kept under observation, but that's about all we *can* do. And of course, he'll change his name again.'

'Isn't he on the dole?'

'No.' The Inspector snorted. 'Says he's got an independent spirit. That's a suspicious circumstance in itself, *I* should say. Besides – he'll be claiming this reward from the *Morning Star* and won't need any dole for a bit. But we can't force him to stay in Wilvercombe at his own expense, reward or no reward.'

'Get hold of Mr Hardy, and see if the paper can't hold the reward up a bit. Then, if he doesn't turn up to claim it, we'll know for a certainty that there's something wrong with him. A contempt for money, Inspector, is the root – or at any rate, the very definite sign – of all evil.'

The Inspector grinned.

'You and me think alike, my lord. There's something fishy about a bloke that doesn't take all he can get. Right you are. I'll speak to Mr Hardy. And I'll try and fix up with Bright to hang on here a couple of days. If he's up to anything queer, he won't try to bolt for fear of looking suspicious.'

'It'll look much more suspicious if he consents to stay.'

'Yes, my lord – but he won't reason that way. He won't want to make trouble. He'll stay for a bit, I daresay. Fact is, I was thinking, if we could pull him in over some other little matter . . . I don't know, but he's a slippery looking customer, and I shouldn't wonder but what we might find some excuse or other to detain him on.' He winked.

'Framing him, Inspector?'

'Good lord, no, my lord. Can't do that, in this country. But there's lots of little things a man may do in the way of breaking the law. There's street-betting, and drunk and disorderly, and buying stuff after closing-hours and so on – little odds-and-ends that come in handy at times.'

'My conscience!' said Wimsey. 'First time I've heard a good word for Dora! Well, I must be getting along. Hullo, Weldon! I didn't know you were there.'

'Funny business, all this.' Mr Weldon waved his hand vaguely. 'Lot of silly stuff people do talk, eh? You'd think the whole thing was plain as pie, but here's my mother still talking about Bolsheviks. Take more than a coroner's verdict to keep *her* quiet. Women! You can talk yourself black in the face reasoning with 'em and all they do is to go on bleating the same silly nonsense. You can't take any account of what they say, can you?'

'They're not all alike.'

'So they say. But that's all part of this equality nonsense. Now, take Miss Vane. Nice girl, and all that, and decent-looking when she takes the trouble to put her clothes on –'

'What about Miss Vane?' demanded Wimsey, sharply. Then he thought: 'Damn being in love! I'm losing my lightness of touch.' Weldon merely grinned.

'No offence,' he said. 'I only meant – take that evidence of hers. How's a girl like that to be expected to know about blood and all that – see what I mean? Women always get that idea of blood running about all over the place. Always reading novels. "Wallowing in gore." That kind of stuff. No good trying to persuade 'em. They see what they think they ought to see. Get me?'

'You seem to have studied feminine psychology,' said Wimsey, gravely.

'Oh, I know women pretty well,' said Mr Weldon, with solemn satisfaction.

'You mean,' went on Wimsey, 'that they think in clichés.'

'Eh?'

'Formulae. "There's nothing like a mother's instinct." "Dogs and children always know." "Kind hearts are more than coronets." "Suffering refines the character" – that sort of guff, despite all evidence to the contrary.'

'Ye-es,' replied Mr Weldon. 'What I mean is, you know, they think a thing ought to be so, and so they say it is so.'

'Yes; I grasped that that was what you meant.' Wimsey thought that if ever human being had the air of repeating a formula without a clear idea of its meaning, Mr Weldon was that human being; yet he pronounced the magic words with a kind of pride, taking credit to himself for a discovery.

'What you really mean,' went on Wimsey, 'is, I take it, that we can't rely on Miss Vane's evidence at all? You say: She hears a shriek, she finds a man with his throat cut and a razor beside him; it looks as though he'd that moment committed suicide, therefore she takes it for granted that he *has* that moment committed suicide. In that case the blood ought to be still flowing. Therefore she persuades herself that it *was* still flowing. Is that it?'

'That's it,' said Mr Weldon.

'Therefore the jury bring in a verdict of suicide. But you and I, who know all about women, know that the evidence about the blood was probably wrong, and that therefore it may quite well have been murder. Is *that* it?'

'Oh, no – I don't mean that,' protested Mr Weldon. 'I feel perfectly certain it was suicide.'

'Then what are you grumbling at? It seems so obvious. If the man was murdered after two o'clock, Miss Vane would have seen the murderer. She didn't see the murderer. Therefore it was suicide. The proof of the suicide really depends on Miss Vane's evidence, which shows that the man died after two o'clock. Doesn't it?'

Mr Weldon grappled for some moments with this surprising piece of logic, but failed to detect either the *petitio elenchi*, the undistributed middle or the inaccurate major premiss which is contrived to combine. His face cleared.

'Of course,' he said. 'Yes. I see that. Obviously it must have been suicide, and Miss Vane's evidence proves that it was. So she must be right after all.'

This was a syllogistic monstrosity even worse than the last, thought Wimsey. A man who could reason like that could not reason at all. He constructed a new syllogism for himself.

The man who committed this murder was not a fool.
Weldon is a fool.
Therefore Weldon did not commit this murder.

That appeared to be sound, so far as it went. But what was Weldon bothering about, in that case? One could only suppose that he was worried over having no perfect alibi for two o'clock. And indeed that was worrying Wimsey himself. All the best murderers have alibis for the time of the murder.

Then, suddenly, illumination came flooding, stabbing across the dark places of his mind like a searchlight. And, good God! if this was the true solution, Weldon was anything but a fool. He was one of the subtlest criminals a detective had ever encountered. Wimsey studied Weldon's obstinate profile – was it possible? Yes, it was possible – and the scheme might quite well have been successful, if only Harriet Vane had not turned up with her evidence.

Work it out this way; see how it looked. Weldon had murdered Alexis at the Flat-Iron at two o'clock. He had had the mare tethered ready somewhere, and, after leaving the Feathers at 1.30, he had gone down the Lane and got to horse without a moment's delay. Then he must have ridden hell-for-leather. Suppose he had somehow managed to do four miles in twenty-five minutes. That would leave him half a mile from the Flat-Iron at two o'clock. No, that would not do. Strain it a little farther. Let him start from Hinks's Lane at 1.32 and let him wallop a steady nine miles an hour out of the mare – that would almost do it. Let him, in any case, be within five minutes' quick walk of the rock at 1.55. Then what? *He sends the mare home.* Five minutes before Harriet woke, he could send the bay mare galloping back along the sands. Then he walks. He reaches the Flat-Iron at two o'clock. He kills. He hears Harriet coming. He hides in the cleft of the rock. And meanwhile, the bay mare has either run home, or, possibly, has reached the lane by the cottages and run up it, or –

Never mind the mare; she got back to her own field and stream somehow. The times were tight; the whole thing seemed absurdly elaborate, but it was not an absolute impossibility as he had thought at first. Suppose it had been so. Now, if Harriet had not been there, what would have happened? In a few hours the tide would have covered the body. Pause there, Morocco. If Weldon was the murderer, he would not want the body lost. He would want his mother to know that Alexis was dead. Yes; but under ordinary circumstances the body would have turned up sooner. It was the violent south-west wind and the three hundred sovereigns that had combined to keep the body hidden. And the body had been found, even so. Well, then. If Harriet had not found the body when she did, there would have been nothing to show that the death had not occurred earlier – say between 11 and 1.30 – the period for which there was the alibi. In fact, the victim's arrival at that early hour at Darley Halt made it look much more likely that the earlier hour was the right one. Why should you tempt your victim to a lonely spot at 11.30 a.m. and then wait two and a half hours before polishing him off – except in order to create a presumption that you had really killed him earlier? And then, too, there was that crusty pair,

Pollock and his grandson, with their grudging evidence that they had seen Alexis 'lying down' on the Flat-Iron at 1.45. They must be in it too. That was it. That must be it. The murder was meant to look like a morning murder – and that was why there had been that curious insistence on the alibi and the journey to Wilvercombe. 'Always suspect the man with the cast-iron alibi' – was not that the very first axiom in the detective's book of rules? And here it was – the cast-iron alibi which really was cast-iron; meant to be scrutinised; meant to stand every test – as how should it not, for it was truth! It looked queer – because it was intended to look queer. It was asking, clamouring for investigation. It existed simply and solely to distract attention from the crucial hour of two o'clock. And if only Harriet had not come upon that freshly slain corpse, how well the plan might have succeeded. But Harriet had been there, and the whole structure had collapsed under the shock of her evidence. That must have been a blow indeed. No wonder Weldon was doing his best to discredit that awkward testimony as to the time of the death. He knew better than anyone that death at two o'clock was no proof of suicide, whatever it might appear to a coroner's jury. He was not stupid; he was shamming stupid, and doing it damned well.

Wimsey was vaguely aware that Weldon was bidding him good-bye in some form of words or other. He let him go readily, eagerly. He wanted to think this thing over.

A little concentration in the privacy of his own room brought him to a point from which he could begin to work forward with some assurance.

The original scheme had been smashed to pieces by Harriet's evidence. What would Weldon do next?

He might do nothing. That would be the safest way of all. He might rely on the coroner's verdict and trust that the police and Wimsey and Harriet and everybody else would accept it. But would he have the deadly courage to do that?

He might – unless he knew of something in that cipher document which might prove the suicide to be murder. If so, or if he lost his head – then he would have to fall back on his second line of defence, which would be, what? Undoubtedly, an alibi for two o'clock – the real time of the murder.

What had he actually said about this? Wimsey looked up his notes, to which he had added considerably of late. Weldon had vaguely mentioned a possible witness, a man unknown who had been passing through Darley and had asked him the time.

Of course, yes. He had suspected this witness already – that stock character of detective fiction – the man who asks the time. Wimsey laughed. Now he felt sure about it. Everything was provided for and the way discreetly paved for the production of this useful witness in case of necessity. Now that the morning alibi had failed to draw the enemy's fire, the two o'clock alibi would be pushed to the front. Only, this time it would not be cast-iron. It would be a fake. Quite a good fake, very likely, but undoubtedly a fake. And then the shades of the prison-house would begin to close, darkly and coldly over the figure of Mr Henry Weldon.

'If it were done when it is done, then it were – Weldon,' said his lordship to himself. 'If I'm right, then that two o'clock witness will turn up pretty quickly now. And if he does turn up, I'll know I'm right.'

Which was logic after the manner of Mr Weldon.

XXII

THE EVIDENCE OF THE MANNEQUIN

'All honest men, good Melchior, like thyself –
For that thou art, I think, upon my life –
Believe thee too.'

Torrismond

SATURDAY, 27 JUNE
SUNDAY, 28 JUNE

HARRIET VANE found herself comfortable enough in the quarters of the late Paul Alexis. A polite letter from her literary agent asking 'whether the new book would be available for publication in the autumn' had driven her back to the problem of the town-clock, but she found herself giving it a very divided attention. Compared with the remarkable tangle of the Alexis affair, the plot seemed to be thin and obvious, while the ape-like Robert Templeton began to display a tiresome tendency to talk like Lord Peter Wimsey. Harriet continually found herself putting her work aside – 'to clear' (as though it were coffee). Novelists who have struck a snag in the working-out of the plot are rather given to handing the problem over in this way to the clarifying action of the sub-conscious. Unhappily, Harriet's sub-conscious had other coffee to clear and refused quite definitely to deal with the matter of the town-clock. Under such circumstances it is admittedly useless to ask the conscious to take any further steps. When she ought to have been writing, Harriet would sit comfortably in an armchair, reading a volume taken from Paul Alexis' bookshelf, with the idea of freeing the sub-conscious for its job. In this way, her conscious imbibed a remarkable amount of miscellaneous information about the Russian Imperial Court and a still more remarkable amount of romantic narrative about love and war in Ruritanian states. Paul Alexis had evidently had a well-defined taste in fiction. He liked stories about young men of lithe and alluring beauty who, blossoming into perfect gentlemen amid the most unpromising surroundings, turned out to be the heirs to monarchies and, in the last chapter, successfully headed the revolts of devoted loyalists, overthrew the machinations of sinister presidents, and appeared on balconies, dressed in blue-and-silver uniforms, to receive the plaudits of their rejoicing and emancipated subjects. Sometimes they were assisted by brave and beautiful English or American heiresses, who placed their wealth at the disposal of the loyalist party; sometimes they remained faithful despite temptation to brides of their own nationality, and rescued them at the last moment from marriages of inconvenience with the sinister presidents or their still more sinister advisers; now and again they were assisted by young Englishmen, Irishmen or Americans with clear-cut profiles and a superabundance of energy, and in every case they went through a series of hair-raising escapes and adventures by land, sea and air. Nobody but the sinister presidents ever thought of anything so sordid as raising money by the usual financial channels or indulging in political intrigue, nor did the greater European powers or the League of Nations ever have anything to say in the matter. The rise and fall of governments appeared to be a private arrangement, comfortably thrashed out among a selection of small Balkan States, vaguely situated and acknowledging no relationships outside the domestic circle. No literature could have been better suited for the release of the sub-conscious; nevertheless, the sub-conscious obstinately refused to work.

Harriet groaned in spirit and turned to crosswords, with the aid of Chambers' Dictionary – that Bible of the crossword fan – which she found wedged between a paper-covered book printed in Russian and *A Bid for the Throne*.

Lord Peter Wimsey had also found something to read, which was occupying both his conscious and sub-conscious very pleasantly. It was a letter, dated from Leamhurst in Huntingdonshire, and ran thus:

'MY LORD,

'Agreeably to your lordship's instructions I am residing here for a few days pending repairs to my magneto. I have established friendly relations with an individual called Hogben, who owns a reaper-and-binder, and is well acquainted with the principal farmers in this neighbour-hood.

'I understand from him that Mr Henry Weldon's affairs are considered to be in a somewhat involved condition, and that his farm (Fourways) is heavily mortgaged. He is popularly held to have raised a number of loans locally within the last year or two on the strength of his expecta-tions from his mother's estate, but, in view of the fact that Mrs Weldon has not visited him of late and that relations are rumoured to be somewhat strained between them, some uneasiness is felt as to the value of this security.

'The farm management is at present in the hands of a certain Walter Morrison, the head ploughman, a man of no great attainments, and, indeed, little better than an ordinary labourer, though with considerable experience in his own line. It is considered strange that Mr Weldon should have quitted the farm at this particular time. In view of your lordship's wire of last Wednesday evening, informing me of the identification of Mr Henry Weldon with Mr Haviland Martin, I need not tell your lordship that Mr Weldon left home on Sunday, 14th, returning on

Sunday, 21st, only to leave again early the next morning. There have been difficulties and delays of late in the payment of labourers' wages, and, owing partly to this cause, Morrison is finding it no easy matter to get the hay in.

'I heard also that there had been some trouble with the mortgagees over the upkeep of the farm-buildings, dykes, hedges, etc. Accordingly, I made an expedition to Four-ways, in order to inspect the property with my own eyes. I found the conditions to be as stated. Many of the walls and barns are in considerable disrepair, while the field-bound-aries display frequent gaps, due to insufficient attention to proper hedging and ditching. The drainage, also (which, as your lordship knows, is of paramount importance in this part of the country) is, in many places very defective. In particular a large field (known as the 16-acre) was allowed to remain (as I am informed) in a waterlogged condition all winter. Arrangements for the drainage of this piece of arable were commenced last summer, but proceeded no further than the purchase of the necessary quantities of pantiles, the cost of labour interfering with the progress of the work. In consequence, this piece of land (which adjoins the washes of the 100-foot level) is at present useless and sour.

'Personally, Mr Weldon appears to be fairly well liked in the neighbourhood, except that his manner is said to be somewhat too free with the ladies. He is reckoned as a sportsman, and is frequently seen at Newmarket. It is also rumoured that he supports a lady in a highly desirable little establishment in Cambridge. Mr Weldon is considered to have a very good knowledge of animals, but to be some-what ignorant or careless of the agricultural aspect of farming.

'His house is kept by an elderly man and his wife, who exercise the respective functions of cowman and dairymaid. They appear respectable and, from the conversation which I had with the woman when requesting the favour of a glass of milk, honest people with nothing to hide. She informed me that Mr Weldon lived quietly, when at home, keeping himself to himself. He receives few visitors, apart from the local farmers. During the six years that these people have been with him, his mother has visited him on three occasions (all within the first two years of this period). Also, on two occasions he has had a visitor from London, a small gentleman with a beard and said to be an invalid. This gentleman last stayed with him at the end of February this year. The woman (Mrs Sterne) preserved a perfect discretion on the subject of her employer's financial circumstances, but I have ascertained from Hogben that she and her husband have been privately inquiring after another situation.

'This is all that I have been able to discover in the short time at my disposal. (I should have mentioned that I proceeded by train to Cambridge, hiring an automobile there to sustain the character allotted to me and arriving here about Thursday noon.) If your lordship so desires, I can remain and pursue my inquiries further. Your lordship will forgive my reminding you that it is advisable to remove the links from the shirtcuffs before dispatching the garment to the laundry. It gives me great anxiety to feel that I may not be at hand to attend to the matter myself on Monday, and I should feel it deeply if there was any repetition of the disagreeable accident which occurred on the occasion of my last absence. I omitted to inform your lordship before leaving that the pin-stripe lounge suit must on no account be worn again until the slit in the right-hand pocket has been attended to. I cannot account for its presence, except by supposing that your lordship has inadvertently used the pocket for the transport of some heavy and sharp-edged article.

'I trust that your lordship is enjoying favourable climatic conditions and that the investigation is progressing according to expectation. My respectful compliments to Miss Vane, and believe me, my lord,

'Obediently yours,
'MERVYN BUNTER.'

This document reached Wimsey on the Saturday afternoon, and in the evening he received a visit from Inspector Umpelty, to whom he submitted it.

The Inspector nodded.

'We've received much the same information,' he observed. 'There's a bit more detail in your man's letter – what the deuce are pantiles? – but I think we may take it for granted that our friend Weldon is a bit up the pole financially. However, that's not what I came round about. The fact is, we've found the original of that photo.'

'You have? The fair Feodora?'

'Yes,' replied the Inspector, with modest triumph, and yet with a kind of mental reservation behind the triumph, 'the fair Feodora – only she says she isn't.'

Wimsey raised his eyebrows, or, to be more accurate, the one eyebrow which was not occupied in keeping his monocle in place.

'Then if she isn't herself, who is she?'

'She says she's Olga Kohn. I've got her letter here.' The Inspector rummaged in his breast pocket. 'Writes a good letter, and in a very pretty hand, I must say.'

Wimsey took the blue sheet of paper and cocked a knowing eye at it.

'Very dainty. As supplied by Mr Selfridge's fancy counter to the nobility and gentry. Ornate initial "O" on royal blue and gilt. A pretty hand, as you say, highly self-conscious. Intensely elegant envelope to match; posted in the Piccadilly district last post on Friday night, and addressed to the

Wilvercombe coroner. Well, well. Let us see what the lady has to say for herself.'

'159 Regent Square,
'Bloomsbury.

'DEAR SIR,

'I read the account of the inquest on Paul Alexis in tonight's paper and was very much surprised to see my photograph. I can assure you that I have nothing to do with the case and I cannot imagine how the photograph came to be on the dead body or signed with a name which is not mine. I never met anybody called Alexis that I know of and it is not my writing on the photograph. I am a mannequin by profession, so there are quite a lot of my photographs about, so I suppose somebody must have got hold of it. I am afraid I know nothing about this poor Mr Alexis so I cannot be of much help to you, but I thought I ought to write and tell you that it was my photograph which was in the paper.

'I cannot say at all how it can have got mixed up with the case, but of course I shall be glad to tell you anything I can. The photograph was taken about a year ago by Messrs Frith of Wardour Street. I enclose another copy so that you can see it is the same. It is one I used when applying for an engagement as mannequin, and I sent it to a great many heads of big firms, also to some theatrical agents. I am at present engaged as mannequin to Messrs Doré & Cie, of Hanover Square. I have been six months with them and they would give you references as to my character. I should be very glad to find out how the photograph got into Mr Alexis' hands, as the gentleman to whom I am engaged is very upset about it all. Excuse me for troubling you, but I thought it right to let you know, though I am afraid I cannot be of much help.

'Yours faithfully,
'OLGA KOHN.'

'And what do you make of that, my lord.'

'God knows. The young woman may be lying, of course, but somehow I don't think she is. I feel that the bit about the gentleman who is very upset rings true. Olga Kohn – who sounds like a Russian Jewess – is not precisely out of the top-drawer, as my mother would say, and was obviously not educated at Oxford or Cambridge, but though she repeats herself a good deal, she is businesslike, and her letter is full of useful facts. Also, if the photograph resembles her, she is easy to look at. What do you say to running up to Town and interviewing the lady? I will provide the transport, and tomorrow being Sunday, we shall probably find her at leisure. Shall we depart, like two gay bachelors, to find Olga Feodora and take her out to tea?'

The Inspector seemed to think that this was a good idea.

'We will ask her if she knows Mr Henry Weldon, that squire of dames. Have you a photograph of him, by the way?'

The Inspector had an excellent snapshot, taken at the inquest by a press photographer. A wire was sent to Miss Olga Kohn, warning her of the impending visit and, having made the necessary arrangements at the police-station, the Inspector heaved his large bulk into Wimsey's Daimler and was transported with perilous swiftness to London. They ran up that night, snatched a few hours of repose at Wimsey's flat and, in the morning, set out for Regent Square.

Regent Square is anything but a high-class locality, being chiefly populated by grubby infants and ladies of doubtful calling, but its rents are comparatively cheap for so central a situation. On mounting to the top of a rather dark and dirty stair, Wimsey and his companion were agreeably surprised to discover a freshly-painted green door with the name 'Miss O. Kohn' neatly written upon a white card and attached to the panel by drawing-pins. The brass knocker, representing the Lincoln Imp, was highly polished. At its summons the door was opened at once by a handsome young woman, the original of the photograph, who welcomed them in with a smile.

'Inspector Umpelty?'

'Yes, miss. You will be Miss Kohn, I take it? This is Lord Peter Wimsey, who has been kind enough to run me up to Town.'

'Very pleased to meet you,' said Miss Kohn. 'Come in.' She ushered them into a pleasantly furnished room, with orange window-curtains and bowls of roses placed here and there on low tables and a general air of semi-artistic refinement. Before the empty fireplace stood a dark-haired young man of Semitic appearance, who acknowledged the introductions with a scowl.

'Mr Simons, my fiancé,' explained Miss Kohn. 'Do sit down, and please smoke. Can I offer you any refreshment?'

Declining the refreshment, and heartily wishing Mr Simons out of the way, the Inspector embarked at once on the subject of the photograph, but it soon became obvious both to Wimsey and himself that Miss Kohn had told in her letter nothing more or less than the exact truth. Sincerity was stamped on every feature of her face as she assured them repeatedly that she had never known Paul Alexis and never given him a photograph under the name of Feodora or any other name. They showed her his photograph, but she shook her head.

'I am perfectly positive that I never saw him in my life.'

Wimsey suggested that he might have seen her at a mannequin parade and endeavoured to introduce himself.

'Of course, he may have seen me; so many people see me,' replied Miss Kohn, with artless self-importance. 'Some of them try to get off with one too, naturally. A girl in my position has to know how to look after herself. But I think I should remember this face if I had ever seen it. You see, a young man with a beard like that is rather noticeable, isn't he?'

She passed the photograph to Mr Simons, who bent his dark eyes on it disdainfully. Then his expression changed.

'You know, Olga,' he said, 'I think I have seen this man somewhere.'

'You, Lewis?'

'Yes. I don't know where. But there is something familiar about it.'

'You never saw him with me,' put in the girl, quickly.

'No. I don't know, now I come to think of it, that I ever saw him at all. It's an older face, the one I'm thinking of – it may be a picture I have seen and not a living person. I don't know.'

'The photograph has been published in the papers,' suggested Umpelty.

'I know; but it isn't that. I noticed a resemblance to – somebody or other, the first time I saw it. I don't know what it is. Something about the eyes, perhaps—'

He paused thoughtfully and the Inspector gazed at him as though he expected him to lay a golden egg there and then, but nothing came of it.

'No, I can't place it,' said Simons, finally. He handed the photograph back.

'Well, it means nothing to me,' said Olga Kohn. 'I do hope you all believe that.'

'I believe you,' said Wimsey, suddenly, 'and I'm going to hazard a suggestion. This Alexis fellow was a romantic sort of blighter. Do you think he can have seen the photograph somewhere and fallen in love with it, as you might say? What I mean is, he might have indulged in an imaginary thingmabob – an ideal passion, so to speak. Kind of fancied he was beloved and all the rest of it, and put a fancy name on to support the illusion if you get what I mean – what?'

'It is possible,' said Olga, 'but it seems very foolish.'

'Seems perfectly cock-eyed to me,' pronounced Umpelty with scorn. 'Besides, where did he get the picture from, that's what we want to know.'

'That wouldn't really be difficult,' said Olga. 'He was a dancer at a big hotel. He might easily have met many theatrical managers, and one of them might have given the photograph to him. They would get it, you know, from the agents.'

Inspector Umpelty asked for particulars of the agents and was supplied with the names of three men, all of whom had offices near Shaftesbury Avenue.

'But I don't suppose they'll remember much about it,' said Olga. 'They see so many people. Still, you could try. I should be terribly glad to have the thing cleared up. But you do believe me, don't you?'

'We believe in you, Miss Kohn,' said Wimsey, solemnly, 'as devoutly as in the second law of thermo-dynamics.'

'What are you getting at?' said Mr Simons, suspiciously.

'The second law of thermo-dynamics,' explained Wimsey, helpfully, 'which holds the universe in its path, and without which time would run backwards like a cinema film wound the wrong way.'

'No, would it?' exclaimed Miss Kohn, rather pleased.

'Altars may reel,' said Wimsey, 'Mr Thomas may abandon his dress-suit and Mr Snowden renounce Free Trade, but the second law of thermo-dynamics will endure while memory holds her seat in this distracted globe, by which Hamlet meant his head but which I, with a wider intellectual range, apply to the planet which we have the rapture of inhabiting. Inspector Umpelty appears shocked, but I assure you that I know no more impressive way of affirming my entire belief in your absolute integrity.' He grinned. 'What I like about your evidence, Miss Kohn, is that it adds the final touch of utter and impenetrable obscurity to the problem which the Inspector and I have undertaken to solve. It reduces it to the complete quintessence of incomprehensive nonsense. Therefore, by the second law of thermo-dynamics, which lays down that we are hourly and momently progressing to a state of more and more random-ness, we receive positive assurance that we are moving happily and securely in the right direction. You may not believe me,' added Wimsey, now merrily launched on a flight of fantasy, 'but I have got to the point now at which the slightest glimmer of common-sense imported into this preposterous case would not merely disconcert me but cut me to the heart. I have seen unpleasant cases, difficult cases, complicated cases and even contradictory cases, but a case founded on stark unreason I have never met before. It is a new experience and, blasé as I am, I confess that I am thrilled to the marrow.'

'Well,' said Inspector Umpelty, hoisting himself to his feet, 'I'm sure we're very much obliged to you, miss, for your information, though at the moment it doesn't seem to get us much farther. If anything should occur to you in connection with this Alexis, or if you, sir, should happen to call to mind where you saw Alexis before, we shall be very greatly obliged. And you mustn't take account of what his lordship here has been saying, because he's a gentleman that makes up poetry and talks a bit humorous at times.'

Having thus, as he supposed, restored confidence in the mind of Miss Olga Kohn, the Inspector shepherded his companion away, but it was to Wimsey that the girl turned while Umpelty was hunting in the little hall for his hat.

'That policeman doesn't believe a word I've been saying,' she whispered anxiously, 'but you do, don't you?'

'I do,' replied Wimsey. 'But you see, I can believe a thing without understanding it. It's all a matter of training.'

XXIII

THE EVIDENCE OF THE THEATRICAL AGENT

> 'Art honest, or a man of many deeds
> And many faces to them? Thou'rt a plotter,
> a politician.'
>
> *Death's Jest-Book*

MONDAY, 29 JUNE

WIMSEY and the Inspector spent Sunday in Town, and on the Monday started out for Shaftesbury Avenue. At the first two names on their list they drew blank; either the agent had given out no photographs of Olga Kohn or he could not remember anything of the circumstances. The third agent, a Mr Isaac J. Sullivan, had a smaller and dingier office than the other two. Its antechamber was thronged with the usual crowd, patiently waiting for notice. The Inspector sent his name by a mournful-eyed secretary, who looked as though he had spent all his life saying 'No' to people and taking the blame for it. Nothing happened. Wimsey seated himself philosophically on the extreme end of a bench already occupied by eight other people and began to work out a crossword in the morning paper. The Inspector fidgeted. The secretary, emerging from the inner door, was promptly besieged by a rush of applicants. He pushed them away firmly but not harshly, and returned to his desk.

'Look here, young man,' said the Inspector, 'I've got to see Mr Sullivan at once. This is a police matter.'

'Mr Sullivan's engaged,' said the secretary, impassively.

'He's got to be disengaged then,' said the Inspector.

'Presently,' said the secretary, copying something into a large book.

'I've no time to waste,' said the Inspector, and strode across to the inner door.

'Mr Sullivan's not there,' said the secretary, intercepting him with eel-like agility.

'Oh, yes, he is,' replied the Inspector. 'Now, don't you go obstructing me in the performance of my duty.' He put the secretary aside with one hand and flung the door open, revealing a young lady in the minimum of clothing, who was displaying her charms to a couple of stout gentlemen with large cigars.

'Shut the door, blast you,' said one gentleman, without looking around. 'Hell of a draught, and you'll let all that lot in.'

'Which of you is Mr Sullivan?' demanded the Inspector, standing his ground, and glaring at a second door on the opposite side of the room.

'Sullivan ain't here. Shut that door, will you?'

The Inspector retired, discomfited, amid loud applause from the ante-room.

'I say, old man,' said Wimsey, 'what do you think the blighter means by this: "Bright-eyed after swallowing a wingless biped?" Sounds like the tiger who conveyed the young lady of Riga.'

The Inspector snorted.

There was an interval. Presently the inner door opened again and the young lady emerged, clothed and apparently very much in her right mind, for she smiled round and observed to an acquaintance seated next to Wimsey:

'O.K. darling. "Aeroplane Girl," first row, song and dance, start next week.'

The acquaintance offered suitable congratulations, the two men with cigars came out with their hats on and the assembly surged towards the inner room.

'Now, ladies,' protested the secretary, 'it's not a bit of use. Mr Sullivan's engaged.'

'Look here,' said the Inspector.

At this moment the door opened a fraction of an inch and an impatient voice bellowed: 'Horrocks!'

'I'll tell him,' said the secretary, hastily, and wormed himself neatly through the crack of the door, frustrating the efforts of a golden-haired sylph to rush the barrier.

Presently the door opened again and the bellowing voice was heard to observe:

'I don't care if he's Godalmighty. He's got to wait. Send that girl in, and – oh, Horrocks –'

The secretary turned back – fatally. The sylph was under his guard in a moment. There was an altercation on the threshold. Then, suddenly, the door opened to its full extent and disgorged, all in a heap, the sylph, the secretary, and an immensely stout man, wearing a benevolent expression entirely at variance with his hectoring voice.

'Now, Grace, my girl, don't you get trying it on. There's nothing for you today. You're wasting my time. Be a good girl. I'll let you know when anything turns up. Hullo, Phyllis, back again? That's right. Might want you next week. No, Mammy, no grey-haired mommas wanted today. I – hullo!'

His eye fell on Wimsey, who had got stuck over his crossword and was gazing vaguely round in search of inspiration.

'Here, Horrocks! Why the hell didn't you tell me? What do you think I pay you for? Wasting my time. Here, you, what's your name? Never been here before, have you? I'm wanting your type. Hi! Rosencrantz!'

Another gentleman, slightly less bulky but also inclined to embonpoint, appeared in the doorway.

'Told you we should have something to suit you,' bellowed the first gentleman, excitedly.

'Vot for?' demanded Mr Rosencrantz, languidly.

'What for?' Indignation quivered in the tone. 'Why, for the *Worm that Turned*, to be sure! J'ever see such a perfect type? You've got the right thing here, my boy. Knock 'em flat, eh? The nose alone would carry the play for you.'

'That's all very well, Sullivan,' replied Mr Rosencrantz, 'but can he act?'

'Act?' exploded Mr Sullivan. 'He don't have to act. He's only got to walk on. Look at it! Ain't that the perfect Worm? Here, you, thingummy, speak up, can't you?'

'Well, really, don't you know.' Wimsey screwed his monocle more firmly into his eye. 'Really, old fellow, you make me feel all of a doo-dah, what?'

'There you are!' said Mr Sullivan, triumphantly. 'Voice like a plum. Carries his clothes well, eh! I wouldn't sell you a feller that wasn't the goods, Rosencrantz, you know that.'

'Pretty fair,' admitted Mr Rosencrantz, grudgingly. 'Walk a bit, will you?'

Wimsey obliged by mincing delicately in the direction of the inner office. Mr Sullivan purred after him. Mr Rosencrantz followed. Horrocks, aghast, caught Mr Sullivan by the sleeve.

'I say,' he said, 'look out. I think there's a mistake.'

'Wotcher mean, mistake?' retorted his employer in a fierce whisper. 'I dunno who he is, but he's got the goods, all right, so don't come butting in.'

'Ever played lead?' demanded Mr Rosencrantz of Wimsey.

Lord Peter paused in the inner doorway, raking the petrified audience right and left with impertinent eyes.

'I have played lead,' he announced, 'before all the crowned heads of Europe. Off with the mask! The Worm has Turned! I am Lord Peter Wimsey, the Piccadilly Sleuth, hot on the trail of Murder.'

He drew the two stout gentlemen into the room and shut the door behind them.

'That's a good curtain,' said somebody.

'Well!' gasped the Inspector. 'Well, I'll be damned!'

He made for the door, and this time Horrocks offered no resistance.

'Well, well, well,' said Mr Sullivan, 'Well, *well*!' He turned Wimsey's card over and stared at it. 'Dear, dear, what a pity. Such a waste, eh, Rosencrantz? With your face, you ought to be makin' a fortune.'

'There ain't nothing in this for me, anyhow,' said Mr Rosencrantz, 'so I'd better be pushin' along. The Vorm is a good Vorm, Sullivan, as Shakespeare says, but he ain't on the market. Unless Lord Peter has a fancy for the thing. It 'ud go vell, eh? Lord Peter Vimsey in the title rôle? The nobility ain't much cop these days, but Lord Peter is vell known. He does somethings. Nowadays, they all vant somebody as does somethings. A lord is nothing, but a lord that flies the Atlantic or keeps a hatshop or detects murders – there might be a draw in that, vot you think?'

Mr Sullivan looked hopefully at Wimsey.

'Sorry,' said his lordship. 'Can't be done.'

'Times are bad,' said Mr Rosencrantz, who seemed to grow more enthusiastic as the desired article was withdrawn from his grasp, 'but I make you a good offer. Vot you say to two hundred a veek, eh?'

Wimsey shook his head.

'Three hundred?' suggested Mr Rosencrantz.

'Sorry, old horse. I'm not selling.'

'Five hundred, then.'

'Excuse *me*,' said Mr Umpelty.

'It's no go,' said Mr Sullivan. 'Very sad, but it's no go. Suppose you are rich, eh? Great pity. It won't last, you know. Super-tax and death-duties. Better take what you can while you can. No?'

'Definitely, no,' said Wimsey.

Mr Rosencrantz sighed.

'Oh, vell – I'd best be moving. See you tomorrow, Sully. You have something for me then, eh?'

He retired, not through the antechamber, but through the private door on the opposite side of the room. Mr Sullivan turned to his visitors.

'You want me? Tell me what you want and make it snappy. I'm busy.'

The Inspector produced Olga's photograph.

'The Kohn girl, eh? Yes, what about her? No trouble, eh? A good girl. Works hard. Nothing against her here.'

The Inspector explained that they wanted to know whether Mr Sullivan had distributed any photographs of Olga recently.

'Well now, let me think. She hasn't been round here for a good time. Doing mannequin work, I rather think. Better for her. A good girl and a good-looker, but she can't act, poor child. Just a minute, though. Where's Horrocks?'

He surged to the door, set it cautiously ajar and bawled 'Horrocks!' through the crack. The secretary sidled in.

'Horrocks! You know this photograph of the little Kohn? Have we sent it out lately?'

'Why, yes, sir. Don't you remember? That fellow who said he wanted Russian types for the provinces.'

'That's right, that's right. I knew there was somebody. Tell these gentlemen about him. We didn't know him, did we?'

'No, sir. Said he was starting management on his own. Name of – wait a minute.' He pulled a book from a shelf and turned the leaves with a wetted finger. 'Yes, here we are. Maurice Vavasour.'

'Fine sort of name,' grunted Mr Sullivan. 'Not his own, naturally. Never is. Probably called Potts or Spink. Can't run a company as Potts or Spink. Not classy enough. I've got the fellow now. Little chap with a beard. Said he was casting for romantic drama and wanted a Russian type. We gave him the Livinsky girl and the little Petrovna and one or two more. He seemed struck with this photograph, I remember. I told him Petrovna had more experience, but he said he didn't mind about that. I didn't like the fellow.'

'No?'

'No. Never like 'em when they want pretty girls without experience. Old Uncle Sullivan may be a hard nut, but he ain't standing for anything of that sort. Told him the girl was fitted up with a job, but he said he'd have a shot at her. She never came to me about it, though, so I suppose she turned him down. If she had come, I'd have put her wise. I ain't that keen on my commission, and if you ask any of the girls they'll tell you so. What's the matter, eh? Has this Vavasour got her into a hole?'

'Not exactly,' said Wimsey. 'She's still in her mannequin job. But Vavasour – show Mr Sullivan that other photograph, Inspector. Is that the man?'

Mr Sullivan and Horrocks put their heads together over the photograph of Paul Alexis and shook them simultaneously.

'No,' said Horrocks, 'that's not the man.'

'Nothing like him,' said Mr Sullivan.

'Sure?'

'Nothing like him,' repeated Mr Sullivan with emphasis. 'How old's that fellow? Well, Vavasour was forty if he was a day. Hollow-cheeked beggar with a voice like Mother Siegel's Syrup. Make a good Judas, if you were wanting such a thing.'

'Or a Richard III,' suggested Mr Horrocks.

'If you read the part smarmy,' said Mr Sullivan. 'Can't see him in Act V, though. All right for the bit with the citizens. You know. Enter Richard above, reading, between two monks. Matter of fact,' he added, 'that's a difficult part to cast for. Inconsistent, to my mind. You mightn't think it, but I do a bit of reading and thinking now and again, and what I say is, I don't believe W. Shakespeare had his mind on the job when he wrote that part. Too slimy at the beginning and too tough at the end. It ain't nature. Not but what the play always acts well. Plenty of pep in it, that's why. Keeps moving. But he's made Richard two men in one, that's what I complain of. One of 'em's a wormy, plotting sort of fellow and the other's a bold, bustling sort of chap who chops people's heads off and flies into tempers. It don't seem to fit, somehow, eh?'

Inspector Umpelty began to scrabble with his feet.

'I always think,' said Wimsey, 'that Shakespeare meant Richard to be one of those men who are always deliberately acting a part – dramatising things, so to speak. I don't believe his furies are any more real than his love-making. The scene about the strawberries – that's clearly all put on.'

'Maybe. But the scene with Buckingham and the clock – eh? Maybe you're right. It ain't supposed to be my business to know about Shakespeare, eh? Chorus-ladies' legs are my department. But I been mixed up with the stage all my life one way and another, and it ain't all legs and bedroom scenes. That makes you laugh, um? To hear me go on like this. But I tell you what, it makes me sick, sometimes, bein' in this business. Half these managers don't want actors and actresses – they want types. When my old father was runnin' a repertory company it was actors he wanted – fellows who could be Iago one night and Brutus the next and do a bit of farce or genteel comedy in the intervals. But now! If a fellow starts out making his hit with a stammer and an eyeglass he's got to play stammers and eyeglasses till he's ninety. Poor old Rosencrantz! He sure was fed-up that you weren't thinking of playing his Worm for him. As for getting an experienced actor and giving him a show in the part – nix! I've got the man that could do it – nice chap – clever as you make 'em. But he made a hit as the dear old silver-haired vicar in *Roses Round the Door*, and nobody will look at him now, except for silver-haired vicars. It'll be the end of him as an actor, but who cares? Only old Uncle Sullivan, who's got to take his bread the side it's buttered and look pleasant about it, eh?'

Inspector Umpelty rose to his feet.

'I'm sure we're much obliged to you, Mr Sullivan,' he said. 'We won't detain you any longer.'

'Sorry I couldn't do more for you. If ever I see that Vavasour fellow again I'll let you know. But he's probably come to grief. Sure it ain't any trouble for little Kohn?'

'We don't think so, Mr Sullivan.'

'She's a good girl,' insisted Mr Sullivan. 'I'd hate to think of her going wrong. I know you're thinkin' me an old fool.'

'Far from it,' said Wimsey.

They were let out through the private door, and picked their way down a narrow staircase in silence.

'Vavasour, indeed!' grunted the Inspector. 'I'd like to know who he is and what he's up to. Think that fat idiot was in the game?'

'I'm sure he knows nothing about it,' said Wimsey. 'And if he says he knows nothing about Vavasour you may be pretty sure he's not really a producer or anything genuinely theatrical. These people all know one another.'

'Humph! Fat lot of help that is.'

'As you say. I wonder –'

'Well?'

'I wonder what made Horrocks think of Richard III.'

'Thought the man looked a bad egg, I suppose. Wasn't that the fellow who made up his mind to be a villain?'

'He was. But I don't somehow think Horrocks is quite the man to read villainy in someone's face. I should say he was quite satisfied with the regrettable practice of type-casting.

I've got something at the back of my mind, Inspector, and I can't seem to get it out.'

The Inspector grunted and tripped over a packing-case as they emerged into the purlieus of Wardour Street.

XXIV

THE EVIDENCE OF THE L.C.C TEACHER

'Such lily-livered, meek humanity.'
Death's Jest-Book

MONDAY, 29 JUNE
TUESDAY, 30 JUNE

PAUL ALEXIS was buried on the Monday, with many
flowers and a large crowd of onlookers. Lord Peter was
still in London with the Inspector, but he was suitably
represented by Bunter, who had returned from Huntingdonshire that morning and, ever efficient, had brought with
him a handsome wreath, suitably inscribed. Mrs Weldon
was chief mourner, supported by Henry in solemn black,
and the staff of the Resplendent sent a representative contingent and a floral emblem in the shape of a saxophone.
The leader of the orchestra, an uncompromising realist, had
suggested that the effigy of a pair of dancing-pumps would
have been more truly symbolic, but general opinion was
against him, and there was, indeed, a feeling that he had
been actuated by professional jealousy. Miss Leila Garland
made her appearance in restrained and modified weeds, and
affronted Mrs Weldon by casting an enormous bunch of
Parma violets into the grave at the most affecting moment
and being theatrically overcome and carried away in hysterics. The ceremony was fully reported, with photographs,
in the National Press, and the dinner-tables of the Resplendent were so crowded that evening that it became necessary
to serve a supplementary dinner in the Louis Quinze Saloon.

'I suppose you will be leaving Wilvercombe now,' said Harriet to Mrs Weldon. 'It will always have sad memories for you.'

'Indeed, my dear, I shall not. I intend to stay here until the cloud is lifted from Paul's memory. I know positively that he was murdered by a Soviet gang and it's simply a disgrace that the police should let this kind of thing go on.'

'I wish you would persuade my mother to leave,' said Henry. 'Bad for her health to hang on here. You'll be leaving yourself, I expect, before long.'

'Probably.'

There seemed, in fact, to be little for anyone to stay on for. William Bright applied to the police for leave to depart and was accorded it, subject to an undertaking that he would keep them informed of his whereabouts. He promptly retired to his lodgings at Seahampton, packed up, and started a trek northwards. 'And it's to be hoped,' said Superintendent Glaisher, 'that they'll keep an eye on him. We can't follow him through all the counties in England. We've nothing against him.'

Wimsey and the Inspector, returning to Wilvercombe on the Tuesday morning, were greeted with a piece of fresh information.

'We've pulled in Perkins,' said Superintendent Glaisher.

It appeared that Mr Julian Perkins, after leaving Darley and being driven to Wilvercombe in his hired car, had taken the train to Seahampton and resumed his walking-tour at that point. About twenty miles out he had been knocked down by a motor-lorry. As the result, he had lain speechless and senseless for nearly a week in the local hospital. There was nothing in his travelling-pack to indicate his identity, and it was only when he began to sit up and take notice that anything was known about him. As soon as he was well enough for desultory chat, he discovered that his fellow-patients were discussing the Wilvercombe inquest, and he mentioned, with a feeble sense of self-importance, that he had actually been in contact with the young lady who found the body. One of the nurses then called to mind that there had been a broadcast inquiry for somebody called Perkins in connection with that very case. The Wilvercombe police were communicated with, and P.C. Ormond had been sent over to interview Mr Perkins.

It was now clear enough, of course, why no reply to the S.O.S. message had been received from either Mr Perkins himself or from his associates at the time of broadcasting. It was now also made clear why nobody had made any inquiry about Mr Perkins's disappearance. Mr Perkins was a teacher in an L.C.C. School, and had been granted leave of absence for one term on account of his health. He was unmarried, and an orphan with no near relations, and he lived in a hostel in the neighbourhood of Tottenham Court Road. He had left the hostel in May, announcing that he was going on a tramping holiday and would have no settled address. He would write from time to time, telling the staff of the hostel where to forward letters. As it happened, no letters had arrived for him since the last time he had written (on the 29th May, from Taunton). Consequently, nobody had thought to make any inquiry about him, and the S.O.S. which mentioned only his surname had left it doubtful whether the Mr Perkins wanted by the police was the Mr Julian Perkins of the hostel. In any case, since nobody knew where he was supposed to be, there was no information that anybody could have supplied. The police got into touch with the hostel and had Mr Perkins's mail sent down. It consisted of an advertisement from a cheap tailor, an invitation to secure a last-minute chance in the Irish Sweep, and a letter from a pupil, all about Boy Scout activities.

Mr Julian Perkins seemed to be an unlikely sort of criminal, but one never knew. He was interviewed, propped up in bed in his little red hospital jacket, with his anxious and unshaven face surrounded with bandages, from which his large horn-rimmed glasses looked out with serio-comic effect.

'So you abandoned your trip and walked back to Darley with this young lady,' said Constable Ormond. 'Now, why did you do that, sir?'

'I wanted to do my best to help the young lady.'

'Quite so, sir, very natural. But as a matter of fact, of course, you couldn't help her much.'

'No.' Mr Perkins fumbled with the sheet. 'She said something about going along to look for the body, but of course – I didn't see that I was called upon to do that. I'm not a strong man; besides, the tide was coming in. I thought—'

P.C. Ormond waited patiently.

Mr Perkins suddenly relieved his mind with an outburst of confession.

'I didn't like to go on along that road, and that's the truth. I was afraid the murderer might be lurking about somewhere.'

'Murderer, eh? What made you think it was a case of murder?'

Mr Perkins shrank among his pillows.

'The young lady said it might be. I'm not a very courageous person, I'm afraid. You see, since my illness, I've been nervous – nervous, you know. And I'm not physically strong. I didn't like the idea at all.'

'I'm sure you can't be blamed for that, sir.' The policeman's bluff heartiness seemed to alarm Mr Perkins, as though he detected something false in the ring of it.

'So when you came to Darley you felt that the young lady was in good hands and needed no further protection. So you went away without saying goodbye.'

'Yes. Yes. I – I didn't want to be mixed up in anything, you know. In my position it isn't nice. A teacher has to be careful. And besides—'

'Yes, sir?'

Mr Perkins had another confessional outburst.

'I'd been thinking it over. I thought it was all rather queer. I wondered if the young lady – one hears of such things – suicide pacts and so on – You see? I felt that I didn't want to be associated with that kind of thing. I am rather timid by nature, I admit, and really *not* strong since my illness, and what with one thing and another—'

P.C. Ormond, who had a touch of imagination and a strong, though elementary, sense of humour, smothered a grin behind his hand. He suddenly saw Mr Perkins, terrified, hobbling on his blistered feet between the devil and the deep sea; fleeing desperately from the vision of a homicidal maniac at the Flat-Iron only to be pursued by the nightmare that he was travelling in company with a ruthless and probably immoral murderess.

He licked his pencil and started again.

'Quite so, sir. I see your point. Very disagreeable situation. Well, now – just as a matter of routine, you know, sir, we've got to check up on the movements of everybody who passed along the coast-road that day. Nothing to be alarmed at.' The pencil happened to be an indelible one and left an unpleasant taste in the mouth. He passed a pink tongue along his purple-stained lips, looking, to Mr Perkins's goblin-haunted imagination, like a very large dog savouring a juicy bone. 'Whereabouts might you have been round about two o'clock, sir?'

Mr Perkins's mouth dropped open.

'I – I – I –' he began, quavering.

A nurse, hovering near, intervened.

'I hope you won't have to be long, constable,' she said, acidly. 'I can't have my patient upset. Take a sip of this, No. 22, and you must try not to get excited.'

'It's all right,' Mr Perkins sipped and regained his colour. 'As a matter of fact I can tell you exactly where I was at two o'clock. It's very fortunate that that should be the time. Very fortunate. I was at Darley.'

'Oh, indeed,' said Mr Ormond, 'that's very satisfactory.'

'Yes, and I can prove it. You see, I'd come along from Wilvercombe. I bought some calamine lotion there, and I daresay the chemist would remember me. My skin is very sensitive, you know, and we had a little chat about it. I don't know just where the shop was, but you could find out. No; I don't know quite what time that would be. Then I walked on to Darley. It's four miles. It would take me a bit over an hour, you know, so I must have started from Wilvercombe about one o'clock.'

'Where did you stay the night before?'

'In Wilvercombe. At the Trust House. You'll find my name there all right.'

'Rather a late start, wasn't it, sir?'

'Yes, it was; but I didn't sleep very well. I was rather feverish. Sunburn, you know; it takes me that way. It does some people. I come out in a rash – most painful. I told you my skin was sensitive. It was the hot sun that last week. I hoped it would get better, but it got worse, and shaving was an agony, really an agony. So I stayed in bed till ten and had a late breakfast at eleven, and got to Darley about two o'clock. I know it was two o'clock, because I asked a man there the time.'

'Did you indeed, sir? That was very fortunate. We ought to be able to substantiate that.'

'Oh, yes. You'd find him easily enough. It wasn't in the village itself. It was outside. It was a gentleman that was camping in a tent. At least, I call him a gentleman, but I can't say he behaved like one.'

P.C. Ormond almost jumped. He was a young man, unmarried and full of enthusiasms, and he had fallen into a state of worshipping admiration for Lord Peter Wimsey. He worshipped his clothes, his car and his uncanny skill in prediction. Wimsey had said that the gold would be found on the body; and lo! it was so. He had said that, as soon as the inquest had established the time of death, Henry Weldon would turn out to have an alibi for two o'clock, and here was the alibi arriving as true to time as moon and tide. He had said that this new alibi would turn out to be breakable. P.C. Ormond set out with determination to break it.

He asked, rather suspiciously, why Mr Perkins had inquired the time of a casual stranger and not in the village.

'I didn't think about it in the village. I didn't stop anywhere there. When I got out of it I began to think about my lunch. I'd looked at my watch a mile or so back and it said five-and-twenty to two, and I thought I'd push along to the shore and have my meal there. When I looked at it again it still said five-and-twenty to two, and I found it had stopped, so I knew time must be getting on. I saw a kind of little lane going down towards the sea, so I turned down that way. There was an open space at the foot of it with a motor-car and a little tent, and a man doing something to the car. I hailed him and asked what the time was. He was a big man with dark hair and a red face, and he wore coloured spectacles. He told me it was five minutes to two. I set my watch going and thanked him and then I just said something pleasant about what a nice camping-place he had found. He grunted rather rudely, so I thought perhaps he was put out by his car being out of order, so I just asked him – most politely – whether there was anything wrong. That was all. I can't think why he should have taken offence but he did. I expostulated with him and said I only asked out of politeness and to know if I could help him in any way, and he called me a very vulgar name and –' Mr Perkins hesitated and blushed.

'Well?' said P.C. Ormond.

'He – I am sorry to say he forgot himself so far as to assault me,' said Mr Perkins.

'Oh! what did he do?'

'He – kicked me,' said Mr Perkins, his voice rising up into a squeak, 'on my – that is to say, from behind.'

'*In*deed!'

'Yes, he did. Of course, I did not retaliate. It would not have been – fitting. I just walked away and told him that I hoped he would feel ashamed of himself when he thought it over. I regret to say that he ran at me after that, and I thought it would be better not to associate with such a person any longer. So I went away and had my lunch on the beach.'

'On the beach, eh?'

'Yes. He had – that is to say, I was facing in that direction when the assault took place – and I did not wish to pass this unpleasant person again. I knew by my map that it was possible to walk along the shore between Darley and Lesston Hoe, so I thought it better to go that way.'

'I see. So you had your lunch on the shore. Whereabouts? And how long did you stay there?'

'Well, I stopped about fifty yards from the lane. I wished to let the man see that he could not intimidate me. I sat down where he could see me and ate my lunch.'

P.C. Ormond noted that the kick could not have been a painfully hard one. Mr Perkins could sit down.

'I think I stayed there for three-quarters of an hour or so.'

'And who passed you on the beach during that time?' demanded the constable sharply.

'Who passed me? Why, nobody.'

'No man, woman or child? No boat? No horse? Nothing?'

'Nothing whatever. The beach was quite deserted. Even the unpleasant man took himself off in the end. Just before I left myself, that would be. I kept an eye on him, just to see that he didn't try any more tricks, you know.'

P.C. Ormond bit his lip.

'And what was he doing all that time? Tinkering with his car?'

'No. He seemed to finish that quite quickly. He seemed to be doing something over the fire. I thought he was cooking. Then he went away up the lane.'

The constable thought for a moment.

'What did you do then?'

'I walked rather slowly on along the beach till I came to a lane that runs down between stone walls on to the beach. It comes out opposite some cottages. I got on to the road that way, and walked along in the direction of Lesston Hoe till I met the young lady.'

'Did you see the man with the dark spectacles again that afternoon?'

'Yes; when I came back with the lady, he was just coming up out of the lane. To my annoyance, she, quite unecessarily, stopped and spoke to him. I went on, as I did not wish to be subjected to any further incivility.'

'I see, sir. That's a very clear account. Now I want to ask you a very important question. When you next had an opportunity of regulating your watch, did you find it fast or slow, and how much?'

'I compared it with the clock in the garage at Darley. It was exactly right at 5.30.'

'And you had not altered it in the interval?'

'No – why should I?'

P.C. Ormond looked hard at Mr Perkins, shut up his note-book with a snap, thrust out his lower jaw and said, quietly but forcefully:

'Now, look here, sir. This is a case of murder. We *know* that somebody passed along that beach between two o'clock and three. Wouldn't it be better to tell the truth?'

Fear flashed up into Mr Perkins's eyes.

'I don't – I don't –' he began, feebly. His hands clawed at the sheet for a moment. Then he fainted, and the nurse, bustling up, banished P.C. Ormond from the bedside.

XXV

THE EVIDENCE OF THE DICTIONARY

' 'Tis but an empty cipher.'
The Brides' Tragedy

IT was all very well, thought Constable Ormond, to be sure that Perkins' evidence was false: the difficulty was to prove it. There were two possible explanations. Either Perkins was a liar, or Weldon had deliberately deceived him. If the former were the case, then the police would be faced with the notorious difficulty of proving a negative. If the latter, then a reference to Mr Polwhistle at the Darley Garage would probably clear the matter up.

Mr Polwhistle and his mechanic were ready and eager to help. They perfectly remembered Mr Perkins – which was not surprising, since the arrival of a complete stranger to hire a car was a rare event in Darley. Mr Perkins had pulled out his watch, they remembered, and compared it with the garage clock, mentioning as he did so that the watch had run down and that he had had to inquire the time of a passer-by. He had then said: 'Oh, yes, it seems to be just right,' and had further asked whether their clock was reliable and how long they would take to get to Wilvercombe.

'And *is* your clock reliable?'

'It was reliable that day all right.'

'How do you mean, that day?'

'Well, she loses a bit, and that's a fact, but we'd just set her on the Thursday morning, hadn't we, Tom?'

Tom agreed that they had, adding that 'she' was an eight-day clock, and that he was accustomed to wind and set her every Thursday morning, Thursday being an important day on account of Heathbury market, the centre about which all local business seemed to revolve.

There seemed to be no shaking this evidence. It was true that neither Mr Polwhistle nor Tom had actually seen the face of Mr Perkins' watch, but they both declared that he had said: 'It seems to be just right.' Therefore, if there was any discrepancy, Perkins must have been intentionally concealing the face. It was, perhaps, a little remarkable that Perkins should so insistently have drawn attention to the rightness of his watch. Constable Ormond remounted his motor-cycle and returned to Wilvercombe, more than ever convinced that Perkins was an unconscionable liar.

Inspector Umpelty agreed with him. ' 'Tisn't natural,' he said, 'to my mind, for a man all upset as he was to start bothering about the exact time the minute he gets into a place. Trouble is, if he says he saw Weldon, and we can't prove he didn't, what are we going to do about it?'

'Well, sir,' suggested Ormond, with deference, 'what I've been thinking is, if Weldon or whoever it was rode along the shore between Darley and the Flat-Iron, somebody ought to have seen him. Have we asked all the people who passed along the top of the cliffs round about that time?'

'You needn't think that hadn't occurred to me, my lad,' replied the Inspector, grimly. 'I've interrogated everyone that went past between one o'clock and two o'clock, and not a soul of 'em saw hide nor hair of a horse.'

'How about those people at the cottages?'

'Them?' The Inspector snorted. '*They* never saw anything, you bet your life – nor they wouldn't, not if old Pollock was concerned in it, as it's our belief he was – always supposing there was anything to be concerned in. Still, go and try your hand on them again if you like, young 'un, and if you get anything out of 'em I'll hand it to you. Old Pollock's got his back up, and neither him nor that brother-in-law of his, Billy Moggeridge, is out to give anything away to the police. Still, you trot along there. You're a comely bachelor, and there's no saying but you may be able to get something out of the women-folk.'

The blushing Ormond accordingly made his way to the cottages, where, much to his relief, he found the men-folk absent and the women employed at the wash-tub. At first he was none too cordially received, but, after he had stripped off his uniform tunic and given young Mrs Pollock a hand with the mangle and carried two buckets of water from the well for Mrs Moggeridge, the atmosphere became less frigid, and he was able to put his questions.

But the results were disappointing. The women were able to give very good reasons for having seen nothing of any horse or rider on Thursday, 18th. The family dinners had been eaten as usual at twelve o'clock, and after dinner there was the ironing to finish. There was a sight of washing, as Mr Ormond could see for himself, for Mrs Pollock and Mrs Moggeridge to deal with. There was Granpa Pollock and Granma Pollock and Jem, what was that particular about his shirts and collars, and young Arthur and Polly and Rosie and Billy Moggeridge and Susie and Fanny and little David and the baby and Jenny Moggeridge's Baby Charles what was a accident what Mrs Moggeridge was looking after, Jenny being out in service, all of which do make work and often the washing don't get finished till Saturday and you couldn't be surprised, what with the men's jerseys and stockings and one thing and another and every drop of water having to be fetched. Nobody hadn't been out of the house that afternoon, leastways, only at the back, not till after three o'clock for sure, when Susie took the potatoes out into the front garden to peel for supper. Susie see a gentleman then, dressed in shorts and carrying a knapsack, come up the lane from the shore, but it wouldn't be him as Mr Ormond wanted to know about, because he came in later on with a lady and told them about the body being found. Mr Ormond was quite pleased to hear about this gentleman, nevertheless. The gentleman was wearing horn-rimmed spectacles and he came up the lane 'somewhere between half-past three and four,' and went straight off along the road towards Lesston Hoe. This must, of course, have been Perkins, and a brief calculation showed that this time fitted in reasonably well both with his own story and Harriet's. Harriet had met him about half-a-mile further on at four o'clock. But that proved nothing, and the crucial period between 1.30 and three o'clock remained as obscure as before.

Puzzled and dissatisfied, Ormond chugged slowly back to Darley, noticing as he went how little of the beach could actually be seen from the road. It was, in fact, only for about a mile on either side of the Flat-Iron that the road ran actually close to the edge of the cliffs. Here there was the breadth of a wide field between them and the height of the cliff hid the sands from view. It would not really have been so risky a business as one might suppose to ride in broad daylight to commit a murder at the Flat-Iron, and it was hardly surprising that no traveller on the road had seen the bay mare pass. But had she passed? There was the horse-shoe to prove it and there was the ring-bolt on the rock to suggest it. It was the ring-bolt that was chiefly bothering Constable Ormond, for if it was not there to hold the horse, what was it for? And Wimsey's latest theory had made it necessary for the horse to be released and sent back before the Flat-Iron was reached.

And that was a very hit-or-miss theory, from the murderer's point of view. How could he be sure that the animal would go back and would not hang about the place attracting attention? In fact, after being galloped violently for four and a half miles, it was far more likely to take matters easy. If one was to ignore the ring-bolt, was it not possible that the bay mare had been tethered somewhere, to be picked up later? There were weighty objections to that. There was no post or groyne along the shore to which she could have been tied, and if the murderer had brought her close in under the cliff, then he would have had to leave two lines of footprints – the mare's in going and his own in returning. But he might have argued that this would not greatly matter if it was at some distance from the Flat-Iron. It might just be worth while to turn back and examine the shore from that point of view.

He did so, riding right up as far as the Flat-Iron itself, scrambling down by the same path that Harriet had used, and working his way along at the foot of the cliff in the direction of Darley. After about half-an-hour's search, he found what he was looking for. There was a recess in the cliff where at some time there had been a fall of rock. Jammed in among the boulders was a large wooden post, which had apparently formed part of a fence – erected, no doubt, to keep men or animals from straying upon the dangerous part of the cliffs. If the bay mare had been brought in there, she might easily have been tethered to the beam, while, owing to the overhang of the cliff and the accumulation of fallen stones, she would have been practically invisible, either from the sea or from the road above.

This discovery was gratifying, but it would have been more gratifying if Ormond could have found any positive indication that this had really happened. The sand was so loose and dry that no recognisable marks could be expected above high-water mark, nor, though he examined the wooden post very carefully with a lens, could he find any indications of its having been used as a horse-post. A strand of rope fibre, a horse-hair or two would have been better than a bank-note to Ormond at that moment, while a bunch of horse-droppings would have been worth its weight in rubies. But none of these simple, homely sights rewarded his anxious gaze. There was the piece of timber and there was the recess in the cliff, and that was all.

Shaking his head, he walked to the edge of the water and set out at a brisk trot for the Flat-Iron. He found that by pelting along as fast as a heavyish, fully-clothed young constable could be expected to pelt on a hot summer's day, he could reach the rock in twelve minutes exactly. It was too far. Five minutes' walk was the most that Weldon could possibly have allowed himself by Wimsey's calculation. Ormond again scrambled up the cliff, remounted his bicycle and began to do sums in his head.

By the time he arrived at the police-station, these sums had taken a definite form.

'The way I look at it is this, sir,' he said to Superintendent Glaisher. 'We've been going along the line that it was Perkins that was providing the alibi for Weldon. Suppose it was the other way round. Suppose Weldon is providing the alibi for Perkins. What do we know about Perkins? Only that he's a school-teacher and that nobody seems to have kept tabs on him since last May. Now, he says he slept at Wilvercombe and didn't start away that morning till one o'clock. That's a bit thick to start with. The only proof he offers of that is that he bought some stuff at a chemist's – he doesn't remember the chemist and he isn't clear about the time. Now we know that Weldon was in Wilvercombe that morning, and *his* time isn't altogether accounted for, either. Supposing those two had met and fixed it all up there. Perkins comes along to Darley and gets the horse.'

'We'll have to find out whether anyone saw him pass through the village.'

'That's so, sir. We must check that up, naturally. But say he really got there at about 1.15 or so. Then he'd have plenty of time to get along with the mare, tie her up where that there post is, and buzz along on foot to the rock and commit his murder.'

'Wait a moment,' said Glaisher. 'This place is fifteen minutes' quick walk from the rock.'

'More like fifteen minutes' run, sir.'

'Yes, but over wet sand; through water, actually. Shall we call it just over a mile? Right. Then that leaves three and a half miles for the mare. At eight miles an hour, that needs – eight miles in sixty minutes, one mile in sixty over eight' – Glaisher always had to work these rule-of-three problems out on the corners of blotting-pads; it had been the worst stumbling-block he had had to overcome on his way to promotion – 'thirty multiplied by seven over eight – oh, dear! divide by two – multiply – divide –'

Ormond, who had the gift of being able to add three columns of figures at once in his head, waited respectfully.

'I make it about twenty-six minutes,' said Glaisher.

'Yes, sir.'

'That means' – Glaisher gazed at the face of the station-clock with working lips. 'Fifteen minutes from two o'clock, 1.45; twenty-six minutes from that again – that's 1.19.'

'Yes, sir; and we can allow him four minutes to tie the mare up; 1.15 I make it he'd have to start out from Darley.'

'Just so; I was only verifying your figures. In that case he'd have had to be in the village at 1.10 or thereabouts.'

'That's right, sir.'

'And how and when did he pick the mare up again, Ormond?'

'He didn't, sir, not as I make it out.'

'Then what became of it?'

'Well, sir, I look at it like this. Where we've been making the mistake is in thinking as the whole job was done by one person. Supposing now as this Perkins commits his murder at two o'clock and then hides under the Flat-Iron, same as we thought. He can't get away till 2.30; we know that, because Miss Vane was there till that time. Well, then, at 2.30 she clears and *he* clears, and starts to walk back.'

'Why should he walk back? Why not go on? Oh, of course – he's got to fix up his time to fit in with Weldon's 1.55 alibi.'

'Yes, sir. Well, if he was to walk straight back to Pollock's cottage, which is two miles from the Flat-Iron, doing a steady three miles an hour, he'd be there at 3.10, but Susie Moggeridge says she didn't see him till between 3.30 and four o'clock, and I don't see that she's got any call to lie about it.'

'She may be in it too; we've got our doubts about old Pollock.'

'Yes, sir; but if she was lying she'd lie the other way. She wouldn't give him more time than he needed to come from the Flat-iron. No, sir, it's my belief Perkins had to stop on the way for something, and I fancy I know what that was. It's all right for the doctor to say that the man who cut this chap's throat *may* not have got blood on himself, but that's not to say he *didn't* get it – not by a long chalk. I think Perkins had to stop all that time to get his togs changed. He could easily take an extra shirt and pair of shorts in his kit. He may have given the one he was wearing a bit of a wash, too. Say he did that, and then got to Pollock's place about 3.45. He comes up by the lane, where Susie Moggeridge sees him and he goes along another half-mile or so, and he meets Miss Vane at four o'clock – as he did.'

'H'm!' Glaisher revolved this idea in his mind. It had its attractive points, but it left a great deal open to question. 'But the mare, Ormond?'

'Well, sir, there's only one person could have brought back the mare that we know of, and that's Weldon, and only one time he could have done it, and that's between four o'clock, when Polwhistle and Tom said good-bye to him, and 5.20, when Miss Vane saw him in Darley. Let's see how that works out, sir. It's three and a half miles from Hink's Lane to the place where the mare was left; he could start at four, walk there in an hour or a bit less, ride back quick, and just be back at 5.20 in time to be seen by them two. It all fits in, sir, doesn't it?'

'It fits, as you say, Ormond, but it's what I'd call a tight fit. Why do you suppose Perkins came back with Miss Vane instead of going on to Lesston Hoe?'

'It might be to find out what she was going to do, sir, or it might be just to look innocent-like. He'd be surprised to see her there, I expect – not knowing about her going up to Brennerton – and it's not wonderful he should have seemed a bit put about when she spoke to him. He might think going back with her was the boldest and best thing to do. Or he may have felt anxious and wanted to see for himself whether Weldon had got back with the nag all right. He was very careful not to speak to Weldon when they did meet – went out of his way to have nothing to do with him, as you might say. And as for his clearing off the way he did, that's natural if you come to think of it, supposing he had those pants and things all soiled with blood in his knapsack.'

'You've got an answer for everything, Ormond. Here's another for you. Why in the name of goodness, if all this is true, didn't Perkins ride the ruddy horse right up to the rock, while he was about it? He could have taken her back and tethered her up just the same.'

'Yes, sir, and I fancy, judging from the ring-bolt, that must have been the first idea. But I was looking at those cliffs today and I noticed that it's just about a mile from the Flat-Iron that the road comes so close to the edge of the cliff as to give you a proper view down on to the beach. When they came to think it over they may have said to themselves that a man riding along that open bit of beach would be conspicuous-like. So Perkins cached the gee where the cover ended and paddled the rest of the way, thinking it would be less noticable.'

'Yes; there's something in that. But all this depends on the time that Perkins passed through Darley. We'll have to get that looked into. Mind, Ormond, I'm not saying you haven't done a good bit of thinking over this, and I like to see you having initiative and striking out a line for yourself; but we can't go behind facts when all's said and done.'

'No, sir; certainly not, sir. But of course, sir, even if it wasn't Perkins, that's not to say it wasn't somebody else.'

'Who wasn't somebody else?'

'The accomplice, sir.'

'That's beginning all over again, Ormond.'

'Yes, sir.'

'Well, cut along and see what you can make of it.'

'Yes, sir.'

Glaisher rubbed his chin thoughtfully when Ormond was gone. This business was worrying him. The Chief Constable had been chivvying him that morning and making things unpleasant. The Chief Constable, a military gentleman of the old school, thought that Glaisher was making too much fuss. To him it was obvious that the rather contemptible foreign dancing-fellow had cut his own throat, and he thought that sleeping dogs should be left alone. Glaisher only wished he could leave the thing alone, but he felt a sincere conviction that there was more to it than that. He was not comfortable in his mind – never had been. There were too many odd circumstances. The razor, the gloves, Weldon's incomprehensible movements, the taciturnity of Mr Pollock, the horse-shoe, the ring-bolt, Bright's mistake about the tides and, above all, the cipher letters and the photograph of the mysterious Feodora – each one of these might, separately, have some ordinary and trivial explanation, but not all of them – surely, not all of them. He had put these points to the Chief Constable, and had received a grudging kind of permission to go on with his inquiries. But he was not happy.

He wondered what Umpelty was doing. He had heard the story of his excursion to town with Wimsey, and felt that this had only plunged matters into a still deeper obscurity. Then there was the tiresomeness about Bright. Bright was reported to be working his way towards London. It was going to be a job keeping an eye on him – especially as Glaisher was rather hard put to it to find a good reason for the surveillance. After all, what had Bright done? He was an unsatisfactory character and he had said it was high tide when it was, in fact, low tide – in every other respect he appeared to have been telling the exact truth. Glaisher realised that he was making himself unpopular with the police of half-a-dozen counties, on very insufficient grounds.

He dismissed the case from his mind and applied himself to a quantity of routine business connected with petty theft and motoring offences, and so got through the evening. But after his supper he found the problem of Paul Alexis gnawing at his brain again. Umpelty had reported the result of a few routine inquiries about Perkins, of which the only interesting fact was that Perkins was a member of the Soviet Club and was reported to have Communist sympathies. Just the sort of sympathies he would have, thought Glaisher: it was always these week, mild, timid-looking people who yearned for revolution and bloodshed. But, taken in connection with the cipher letters, the matter assumed a certain importance. He wondered how soon the photographs of the letters found on Alexis would come to hand. He fretted, was short with his wife, trod on the cat, and decided to go round to the Bellevue and look up Lord Peter Wimsey.

Wimsey was out, and a little further inquiry led Glaisher to Mrs Lefranc's, where he found, not only Wimsey, but also Inspector Umpelty, seated with Harriet in the bed-sitting-room that had once housed Paul Alexis, all three apparently engaged in a Missing Word Competition. Books were strewn about the place, and Harriet, with *Chambers*'s *Dictionary* in her hand, was reading out words to her companions.

'Hullo, Super!' exclaimed Wimsey. 'Come along! I'm sure our hostess will be delighted to see you. We are making discoveries.'

'Are you, indeed, my lord? Well, so have we – at least, that lad, Ormond, has been rummaging about, as you might say.'

He plunged into his story. He was glad to try it on somebody else. Umpelty grunted. Wimsey took a map and a sheet of paper and began figuring out distances and times. They discussed it. They argued about the speed of the mare. Wimsey was inclined to think that he might have underestimated it. He would borrow the animal – make a test – Harriet said nothing.

'And what do *you* think?' Wimsey asked her, suddenly.

'I don't believe a word of it,' said Harriet.

Glaisher laughed.

'Miss Vane's intuition, as they call it, is against it,' said he.

'It's not intuition,' retorted Harriet. 'There's no such thing. It's common sense. It's artistic sense, if you like. All those theories – they're all wrong. They're artificial – they smell of the lamp.'

Glaisher laughed again.

'That's beyond me, that is.'

'You men,' said Harriet, 'have let yourselves be carried away by all these figures and time-tables and you've lost sight of what you're really dealing with. But it's all machine-made. It cracks at every joint. It's like – like a bad plot, built up round an idea that won't work. You've got it into your heads that you must get Weldon and the horse and Perkins into it somehow or other; and when you come up against an inconsistency, you say: "Oh, well – we'll get over that somehow. We'll make him do this. We'll make him do that." But you can't make people do things to suit you – not in real life. Why are you obliged to bring all these people into it at all?'

'You won't deny that there's a good deal that needs explaining,' said Umpelty.

'Of course there's a lot that needs explaining, but your explanations are more incredible than the problem. It's not possible that anyone should plan a murder like that. You've made them too ingenious in one way and too silly in another. Whatever the explanation is, it must be simpler that that – bigger – not so cramped. Can't you see what I mean? You're simply making up a case, that's all.'

'I see what you mean,' said Wimsey.

'I daresay it is a bit complicated,' admitted Glaisher, 'but if we don't make up a case against Weldon and Bright and Perkins, or two of them, or one of them – whom are we to make up a case against? Against Bolshies? Well, but this Perkins is a Bolshie, or a Communist, anyhow, and if he's in it, then Weldon must be, because of their mutual alibi.'

'Yes, I know; but your whole case is like that. First you want Weldon to be guilty, because of getting his mother's money, so you say that Perkins must be his accomplice because he's giving an alibi for Weldon. Now you want Perkins to be guilty because he's a Communist, and so you say Weldon must be the accomplice, because he's giving an alibi for Perkins. But it's simply impossible that both those theories should be true. And how did Weldon and Perkins get to know one another?'

'We haven't finished making inquiries yet.'

'No; but it does seem unlikely, doesn't it? A Council School teacher from the Tottenham Court Road and a Huntingdonshire farmer. What form? What likelihood?

And as for Bright, you have nothing – *nothing* to connect him with either of them. And if his story's true, then there's not an atom of proof that Alexis didn't kill himself. And in any case, if you want to prove murder, you've got to connect Bright with whoever did it, and you certainly haven't found the least trace of communication between him and either Weldon or Perkins.'

'Has Bright been receiving any letters?' asked Wimsey of Umpelty.

'Not a line, not since he turned up here, anyway.'

'As for Perkins,' said Glaisher, 'we'll soon get a line on him. Of course, his getting knocked down and laid up like that must have puzzled his accomplices just as much as it puzzled us. There may be a whole correspondence waiting for him at some accommodation address, under another name, in some town or other.'

'You will insist on its being Perkins,' protested Harriet. 'You really think Perkins rode a horse bare-backed along the beach and cut a man's throat to the bone with a razor?'

'Why not?' said Umpelty.

'Does he look like it?'

' "Do I look like it? said the Knave. Which he certainly did not, being made entirely of cardboard." I've never seen the bloke, but I admit that his description isn't encouraging.' Wimsey grinned. 'But then, you know, friend Henry took *me* for something in the night-club line.'

Harriet glanced briefly at his lean limbs and springy build.

'You needn't fish,' she said, coldly. 'We all know that your appearance of langour is assumed and that you are really capable of tying pokers into knots with your artistic fingers. Perkins is flabby and has a neck like a chicken and those flipflop hands.' She turned to Glaisher. 'I can't see Perkins in the rôle of a desperado. Why, your original case against me was a better one.'

Glaisher blinked, but took the thrust stolidly.

'Yes, miss. It had a lot to be said for it, that had.'

'Of course. Why did you give it up, by the way?'

Some instinct seemed to warn Glaisher that he was treading on thin ice.

'Well,' he said, 'it seemed a bit too obvious, so to say – and besides, we couldn't trace any connection between you and the deceased.'

'It was wise of you to make inquiries. Because, of course, you had only my word for everything, hadn't you? And those photographs were evidence that I was pretty cold-blooded? And my previous history was rather – shall we say, full of incident?'

'Just so, miss.' The Superintendent's eyes were expressionless.

'Of whom did you make the inquiries, by the way?'

'Of your charwoman,' said Glaisher.

'Oh! you think she would know whether I knew Paul Alexis?'

'In our experience,' replied the Superintendent, 'charwomen mostly know things of that sort.'

'So they do. And you've really given up suspecting me?'

'Oh, dear me, yes.'

'On my charwoman's testimony to my character?'

'Supplemented,' said the Superintendent, 'by our own observation.'

'I see.' Harriet looked hard at Glaisher, but he was proof against this kind of third degree, and smiled blandly in response. Wimsey, who had listened with his face like a mask, determined to give the stolid policeman the first prize for tact. He now dropped a cold comment into the conversation.

'You and Miss Vane having made short work of each other's theories,' he said, 'perhaps you would like to hear what we have been doing this evening.'

'Very much, my lord.'

'We began,' said Wimsey, 'by making a new search for clues among the corpse's belongings, hoping, of course, to get some light on Feodora or the cipher letters. Inspector Umpelty kindly lent us his sympathetic assistance. In fact, the Inspector has been simply invaluable. He has sat here now for two hours, watching us search, and every time we looked into a hole or corner and found it empty, he has been able to assure us that he had already looked into the hole or corner and found it empty too.'

Inspector Umpelty chuckled.

'The only thing we've found,' went on Lord Peter, 'is *Chambers's Dictionary*, and we didn't find that this evening, because Miss Vane had found it before, while she was engaged in wasting her time on crosswords instead of getting on with her writing. We've found a lot of words marked with pencil. We were engaged in making a collection of them when you came in. Perhaps you'd like to hear a few specimens. Here you are. I'm reeling them off at random: Peculiar, diplomacy, courtesan, furnished, viscount, squander, sunlight, chasuble, clergyman, luminary, thousand, poverty, cherubim, treason, cabriolet, rheumatics, apostle, costumier, viaduct. There are lots more. Do these words say anything to you? Some of them have an ecclesiastical ring about them, but on the other hand, some of them have not. Courtesan, for example. To which I may add tambourine, wrestling and fashion.'

Glaisher laughed.

'Sounds to me as though the young fellow was a crossword fan himself. They're nice long words.'

'But not the longest. There are many longer, such as supralapsarian, monocotyledenous and diaphragmatic, but he hasn't marked any of the real sesquipedalians. The longest we have found is rheumatics, with ten letters. They all have two peculiarities in common, though, as far as we've gone – that are rather suggestive.'

'What's that, my lord?'

'None of them contains any repeated letter, and none of them is less than seven letters long.'

Superintendent Glaisher suddenly flung up one hand like a child at school.

'The cipher letters!' he cried.

'As you say, the cipher letters. It looks to us as though these might be key-words to a cipher, and from the circumstance that no letters are repeated in any of them, I fancy one might be able to make a guess at the type of cipher. The trouble is that we have already counted a couple of hundred marked words, and haven't finished the alphabet yet. Which leads me to a depressing inference.'

'What's that?'

'That they have been changing the key-word in every letter. What I think has happened is this. I think that each letter contained in it the key-word of the next, and that these marks represent a stock of words that Alexis looked up beforehand, so as to be ready with them when it came to his turn to write.'

'Couldn't they be the key-words already used?'

'Hardly. I don't believe he has sent out over two hundred code-letters since March, when they first began to be exchanged. Even if he wrote one letter a day, he couldn't have got through that number.'

'No more he could, my lord. Still, if the paper we found on him is one of these cipher letters, then the key-word will be one of those marked here. That narrows things a bit.'

'I don't think so. I think these are key-words for the letters Alexis sent out. In each letter he would announce *his* key-word for *his* next letter. But his correspondent would do the same, so that the key-word for the paper found on Alexis is much more likely to be one that isn't marked here. Unless, of course, the paper is one of Alexis' own writing, which isn't very likely.'

'We can't even say that, then,' moaned Glaisher. 'Because the correspondent might very well hit on some word that Alexis had marked in advance. It might be anything.'

'Perfectly true. Then the only bit of help we get from this is that the cipher used was an English word, and that the letters were probably written in English. That doesn't absolutely follow, because they might be in French or German or Italian, all of which have the same alphabet as English; but they can't be in Russian at any rate, which has an alphabet totally different. So that's one mercy.'

'If it's anything to do with Bolsheviks,' said Glaisher, thoughtfully, 'it's a bit surprising they didn't write in Russian. It would have made it doubly safe if they had. Russian by itself would be bad enough, but a Russian cipher would be a snorter.'

'Quite. As I've said before, I can't quite swallow the Bolshevik theory. And yet – dash it all! I simply can*not* fit these letters in with the Weldon side of the business.'

'What *I* want to know,' put in the Inspector, 'is this. How did the murderers, whoever they were, get Alexis out to the Flat-Iron? Or if it was Bolsheviks that got him there, how did Weldon & Co. know he was going to be there? It must be the same party that made the appointment and did the throat-cutting. Which brings us to the point that either Weldon's party wrote the letter or the foreign party did the murder.'

'True, O king.'

'And where,' asked Harriet, 'does Olga Kohn come in?'

'Ah!' said Wimsey, 'there you are. That's the deepest mystery of the lot. I'll swear that girl was telling the truth, and I'll swear that the extremely un-Irish Mr Sullivan was telling the truth too. Little flower in the crannied wall I pluck you out of the crannies, but, as the poet goes on to say, *if* I could understand I should know who the guilty man is. But I don't understand. Who is the mysterious bearded gentleman who asked Mr Sullivan for the portrait of a Russian-looking girl, and how did the portrait get into the corpse's pocket-book, signed with the name Feodora? These are deep waters, Watson.'

'I'm coming back to my original opinion,' grumbled the inspector. 'I believe the fellow was dotty and cut his own throat and there's an end of it. He probably had a mania for collecting girls' photographs and sending himself letters in cipher.'

'And posting them in Czechoslovakia?'

'Oh, well, somebody must have done that for him. As far as I can see, we've no case against Weldon and no case against Bright, and the case against Perkins is as full of holes as a colander. As for Bolsheviks – where are they? Your friend Chief-Inspector Parker has put out inquiries about Bolshevik agents in this country, and the answer is that none of 'em are known to have been about here lately, and as regards Thursday, 18th, they all seem to be accounted for. You may say it's an unknown Bolshevik agent, but there aren't as many of those going about as you might think. These London chaps know quite a lot more than the ordinary public realises. If there'd been anything funny about Alexis and his crowd, they'd have been on to it like a shot.'

Wimsey sighed, and rose.

'I'm going home to bed,' he declared. 'We must wait till we get the photographs of the paper. Life is dust and ashes. I can't prove my theories and Bunter has deserted me again. He disappeared from Wilvercombe on the same day as William Bright, leaving me a message to say that one of my favourite socks had been lost in the wash and that he had lodged a complaint with the management. Miss Vane, Harriet, if I may call you so, will you marry me and look after my socks, and, incidentally be the only woman-novelist who ever accepted a proposal of marriage in the presence of a superintendent and inspector of Police?'

'Not even for the sake of the headlines.'

'I thought not. Even publicity isn't what it was. See here, Superintendent, will you take a bet that Alexis didn't commit suicide and that he wasn't murdered by Bolsheviks?'

The Superintendent replied cautiously that he wasn't a sporting man.

'Crushed again!' moaned his lordship. 'All the same,' he added, with a flash of his old spirit, 'I'll break that alibi if I die for it.'

XXVI

THE EVIDENCE OF THE BAY MARE

'Hail, shrine of blood!'
The Bride's Tragedy

WEDNESDAY, 1 JULY

THE photographs of the paper found on the corpse duly arrived next morning, together with the original; and Wimsey, comparing them together in the presence of Glaisher and Umpelty, had to confess that the experts had made a good job of it. Even the original paper was far more legible than it had been before. The chemicals that remove bloodstains and the stains of dyed leather, and the chemicals that restore the lost colour to washed-out ink had done their work well, and the colour-screens that so ingeniously aid the lens to record one colour and cut out the next had produced from the original, thus modified, a result in which only a few letters here and there were irretrievably lost. But to read is one thing; to decipher, another. They gazed sadly at the inextricable jumble of letters.

XNATNX
RBEXMG
PRBFX ALI MKMG BFFY, MGTSQ JMRRY. ZBZE
FLOX P.M. MSIU FKX FLDYPG FKAP RPD KL DONA
FMKPC FM NOR ANXP.
  SOLFA TGMZ DXL LKKZM VXI BWHNZ MBFFY
MG, TSQ A NVPD NMM VFYQ. CJU ROGA K.C. RAC

RRMTN S.B. IF H.P. HNZ ME? SSPXLZ DFAX LRAEL TLMK XATL RPX BM AEBF HS MPIKATL TO HOKC-CI HNRY. TYM VDSM SUSSX GAMKR, BG AIL AXH NZMLF HVUL KNN RAGY QWMCK, MNQS TOIL AXFA AN IHMZS RPT HO KFLTIM. IF MTGNLU H.M. CLM KLZM AHPE ALF AKMSM, ZULPR FHQ – CMZT SXS RSMKRS GNKS FVMP RACY OSS QESBH NAE UZCK CON MGBNRY RMAL RSH NZM, BKTQAP MSH NZM TO ILG MELMS NAGMJU KC KC.

TQKFX BQZ NMEZLI BM ZLFA AYZ MARS UP QOS KMXBJ SUE UMIL PRKBG MSK QD.

NAP DZMTB N.B. OBE XMG SREFZ DBS AM IMHY GAKY R. MULBY M.S. SZLKO GKG LKL GAW XNTED BHMB XZD NRKZH PSMSKMN A.M. MHIZP DK MIM, XNKSAK C KOK MNRL CFL INXF HDA GAIQ.

GATLM Z DLFA A QPHND MV AK MV MAG C.P.R. XNATNX PD GUN MBKL I OLKA GLDAGA KQB FTQO SKMX GPDH NW LX SULMY ILLE MKH BEALF MRSK UFHA AKTS.

At the end of a strenous hour or two, the following facts were established:

1. The letter was written on a thin but tough paper which bore no resemblance to any paper found among the effects of Paul Alexis. The probability was thus increased that it was a letter received, and not written by him.

2. It was written by hand in a purplish ink, which, again, was not like that used by Alexis. The additional inference was drawn that the writer either possessed no typewriter or was afraid that his typewriter might be traced.

3. It was not written in wheel-cipher, or in any cipher which involved the regular substitution of one letter of the alphabet for another.

'At any rate,' said Wimsey, cheerfully, 'we have plenty of material to work on. This isn't one of those brief, snappy "Put goods on sundial" messages which leave you wondering whether E really is or is not the most frequently-recurring letter in the English language. If you ask me, it's either one of those devilish codes founded on a book – in which case it must be one of the books in the dead man's possession, and we only have to go through them – or it's a different kind of code altogether – the kind I was thinking about last night, when we saw those marked words in the dictionary.'

'What kind's that, my lord?'

'It's good code,' said Wimsey, 'and pretty baffling if you don't know the key-word. It was used during the War. I used it myself, as a matter of fact, during a brief interval of detecting under a German alias. But it isn't the exclusive property of the War Office. In fact, I met it not so long ago in a detective story. It's just –'

He paused, and the policemen waited expectantly.

'I was going to say, it's just the thing an amateur English plotter might readily get hold of and cotton on to. It's not obvious, but it's accessible and very simple to work. It's the kind of thing that young Alexis could easily learn to encode and decode; it doesn't want a lot of bulky apparatus; and it uses practically the same number of letters as the original message, so that it's highly suitable for long epistles of this kind.'

'How's it worked?' asked Glaisher.

'Very prettily. You choose a key-word of six letters or more, none of which recurs. Such as, for example, SQUANDER, which was on Alexis' list. Then you make a diagram of five squares each way and write the key-word in the squares like this:

S	Q	U	A	N
D	E	R		

'Then you fill up the remaining spaces with the rest of the alphabet in order, leaving out the ones you've already got.'

'You can't put twenty-six letters into twenty-five spaces,' objected Glaisher.

'No; so you pretend you're an ancient Roman or a medieval monk and treat I and J as one letter. So you get this.'

S	Q	U	A	N
D	E	R	B	C
F	G	H	IJ	K
L	M	O	P	T
V	W	X	Y	Z

'Now, let's take a message – What shall me say? "All is known, fly at once" – that classic hardy perennial. We write it down all of a piece and break it into groups of two letters, reading from left to right. It won't do to have two of the same letters coming together, so where that happens we shove in Q or Z or something which won't confuse the reader. So now our message runs AL QL IS KN OW NF LY AT ON CE.'

'Suppose there was an odd letter at the end?'

'Well, then we'd add on another Q or Z or something to square it up. Now, we take our first group, AL. We see that they come at the corners of a rectangle in which the other corners are SP. So we put down SP for the first two letters of the coded message. In the same way QL becomes SM and IS becomes FA.'

'Ah!' cried Glaisher, 'but here's KN. They both come on the same vertical line. What happens then?'

'You take the letter next below each – TC. Next comes OW, which you can do for yourself by taking the corners of the square.'

'MX?'

'MX it is. Go on.'

'SK,' said Glaisher, happily taking diagonals from corner to corner, 'PV, NP, UT –'

'No, TU. If your first diagonal went from bottom to top, you must take it the same way again. ON = TU, NO would be UT.'

'Of course, of course. TU. Hullo!'

'What's the matter?'

'CE come on the same horizontal line.'

'In that case you take the next letter to the *right* of each.'

'But there isn't a letter to the right of C.'

'Then start again at the begininning of the line.'

This confused the Superintendent for a moment, but he finally produced DR.

'That's right. So your coded message stands now: SP SM FA TC MX SK PV NP TU DR. To make it look prettier and not give the method away, you can break it up into any lengths you like. For instance. SPSM FAT CMXS KPV NPTUDR. Or you can embellish it with punctuation at hapazard. S.P. SMFA. TCMXS, KPVN, PT! UDR. It doesn't matter. The man who gets it will ignore all that. He will simply break it up into pairs of letters again and read it with the help of the code diagram. Taking the diagonals as before, and the next letter *above*, where they come on the same vertical line, and the next to the *left* where they come on the same horizontal.'

The two policemen pored over the diagram. Then Umpelty said:

'I see, my lord. It's very ingenious. You can't guess it by way of the most frequent letter, because you get a different letter for it each time, according as it's grouped to the next letter. And you can't guess individual words, because you don't know where the words begin and end. Is it at all possible to decode it without the key-word?'

'Oh dear, yes,' said Wimsey. 'Any code ever coded can be decoded with pains and patience – except possibly some of the book codes. I know a man who spent years doing nothing else. The code diagram got so bitten into him that when he caught measles he came out in checks instead of spots.'

'Then he could decode this,' said Glaisher, eagerly.

'On his head. We'll send him a copy if you like. I don't know where he is, but I know those that do. Shall I bung it off? It would save us a lot of time.'

'I wish you would, my lord.'

Wimsey took a copy of the letter, pushed it into an envelope and enclosed a brief note.

'DEAR CLUMPS, – Here's a cipher message. Probably Playfair, but old Bungo will know. Can you push it off to him and say I'd be grateful for a construe? Said to hail from Central Europe, but ten to one it's in English. How goes?

'Yours,
'WIMBLES.'

'Seen anything of Trotters lately?'

He addressed the envelope to an official at the Foreign Office, and picked up another copy of the cipher.

'I'll take this if I may. We'll try it out with some of Alexis' selected words. It'll be a nice job for Miss Vane, and a healthy change from crosswords. Now, what's the next item?'

'Nothing very much yet, my lord. We haven't found anybody who saw Perkins pass through Darley at any time, but we've found the chemist who served him in Wilvercombe. He says Perkins was there at eleven o'clock, which gives him ample time to be at Darley by 1.15. And Perkins has had a bad relapse and can't be interrogated. And we've seen Newcombe, the farmer, who corroborates finding the mare wandering on the shore on Friday morning. He says, too, that she was in the field O.K. when his man was down there on the Wednesday, and that he is quite sure she couldn't have got through the gap in the hedge by herself. But then, naturally, nobody ever believes his own neglect is to blame for anything.'

'Naturally not. I think I'll run over and see Farmer Newcombe. In the meantime, Miss Vane is going to do her damnedest with the cipher – trying out all the marked words on it. Aren't you?'

'If you like.'

'Noble woman! It would be fun if we got ahead of the official interpreter. I suppose the Weldons show no signs of moving.'

'Not the slightest. But I haven't seen much of them since the funeral. Henry seems a bit stand-offish – can't get over the snake episode, I suppose. And his mother –'

'Well?'

'Oh, nothing. But she seems to be trying to get fresh information out of Antoine.'

'Indeed?'

'Yes. Antoine is being very sympathetic.'

'Good luck to him. Well, cheerio!'

Wimsey drove over to Darley, interviewed the farmer and asked for the loan of the bay mare and a bridle. Mr Newcombe not only granted the loan most cordially, but expressed his intention of accompanying Wimsey to watch the experiment. Wimsey was at first not best pleased; it is perhaps easier to wallop another man's horse over a four-mile course if the owner is not looking on. On reflection, however, he thought he saw a use to which he could put Mr Newcombe. He asked that gentleman to be good enough to precede him to the Flat Iron, and make a note of the exact moment at which he himself should come into view, and thence time his progress. The farmer, surmising with a wink that the loosing of the mare and the tragedy at the Flat-Iron had some connection with one another, readily agreed, and, himself mounting a sturdy white nag, took his departure along the shore, while Wimsey, glancing at his watch, set out in pursuit of the bay mare.

She came up to be caught with remarkable readiness, no doubt connecting Wimsey in her simple equine mind with oats. The gap in the hedge had been opened again, by permission, and Wimsey, having bridled her, rode her through it and stirred her up to a canter.

The mare, though willing enough, had, as he expected, no exceptional turn of speed, and since their progress had to be made actually through the water, it was a trifle impeded and remarkably noisy. As he rode, Wimsey kept his eye on the cliffs above. Nobody and nothing was in sight, with the exception of a few grazing animals. The road was hidden. He made good time to the cottages, and then began to look about for Ormond's break in the cliff. He recognised it when he came to it by the fallen rocks and the fragments of broken fence above, and looked at his watch. He was a little ahead of time. Glancing along the shore, he saw the Flat-Iron well in view, with Farmer Newcombe seated upon it, a little dark lump at a mile's distance. He left the break in the cliff to be explored on the return journey, and urged the mare to her best pace. She responded vigorously, and they made the final mile in fine style, the water spraying about them. Wimsey could see the farmer clearly now; he had the white horse tethered to the famous ring-bolt and was standing on the rock, watch conscientiously in hand, to time them.

It was not till they were within a few score paces of the rock that the bay mare seemed to realise what was happening. Then she started as if she had been shot, flung up her head and slewed round so violently that Wimsey, jerked nearly on to her neck by the plunge, was within an ace of being spun off altogether. He dug his knees into her bare sides and hauled hard upon the bridle, but, like many farm nags, she had a mouth of iron, and the snaffle made little impression upon her. She was off, tearing back in her tracks as if the devil was after her. Wimsey, cynically telling himself that he had under-estimated her power of speed, clung grimly to her withers and concentrated on shortening his left-hand rein so as to wrench her head round to the sea. Presently, finding it hard to go forward against this determined drag, she slacked pace, skirmishing sideways.

'Bless and save you, my girl,' said Wimsey, mildly, 'what's the matter with you?'

The mare panted and shuddered.

'But this'll never do,' said Wimsey. He stroked her sweaty shoulder reassuringly. 'Nobody's going to hurt you, you know.'

She stood quietly enough, but shook as she stood.

'There, there,' said Wimsey.

He turned her head once more in the direction of the Flat-

Iron, and was aware of the hurried approach of Mr New-combe on the white horse.

'Lord a'mighty,' exclaimed Mr Newcombe, 'what's come to the mare? I thought she'd have you off surely. Done a bit of riding, ain't you?'

'Something must have frightened her,' said Wimsey. 'Has she ever been there before?'

'Not as I know on,' said the farmer.

'You weren't waving your arms or anything, were you?'

'Not I. I was looking at my watch – and there! Dang me if I haven't clean forgot what time I made it. I was fair mazed with her taking fright so all of a sudden.'

'Is she given to shying?'

'Never known her take and do such a thing before.'

'Queer,' said Wimsey. 'I'll try her again. Keep behind us, and we'll know it wasn't you that startled her.'

He urged the mare back towards the rock at a gentle trot. She moved forward uneasily, chucking her head about. Then, as before, she stopped dead and stood trembling.

They tried her half-a-dozen times, cajoling and encouraging her, but to no purpose. She would not go near the Flat-Iron – not even when Wimsey dismounted and led her step by step. She flatly refused to budge, standing with her shaking legs rooted to the sand, and rolling white and terrified eyes. Out of sheer mercy for her they had to give up the attempt.

'I'll be damned,' said Mr Newcombe.

'And so will I,' said Wimsey.

'What can have come over her –' said Mr Newcombe.

'I know what's come over her all right,' said Wimsey, 'but – Well, never mind, we'd better go back.'

They rode slowly homeward. Wimsey did not stay to examine the break in the cliff. He did not need to. He knew now exactly what had happened between Darley and the Flat-Iron Rock. As he went, he put the whole elaborate structure of his theories together, line by line, and like Euclid, wrote at the bottom of it:

WHICH IS IMPOSSIBLE

In the meantime, Constable Ormond was also feeling a little blue. He had suddenly bethought him of the one person in Darley who was likely to have kept tabs on Mr Perkins. This was old Gaffer Gander who, every day, rain or shine, sat on the seat of the little shelter built about the village oak in the centre of the green. He had unaccountably overlooked Gaffer Gander the previous day, owing to the fact that – by a most unusual accident – the Gaffer had not been in his accustomed seat when Ormond was making his inquiries. It turned out that Mr Gander had actually been in Wilvercombe, celebrating his youngest grandson's wedding to a young woman of that town, but now he was back again and ready to be interviewed. The old gentleman was in high spirits. He was eighty-five come Martinmas, hale and hearty, and boasted that, though he might perhaps be a trifle hard of hearing, his eyes, thank God, were as good as ever they were.

Why, yes, he remembered Thursday, 18th. Day as the poor young man was found dead at the Flat-Iron. A beautiful day, surely, only a bit blowy towards evening. He always notices any strangers that came through. He remembered seeing a big open car come past at ten o'clock. A red one it was, and he even knew the number of it, because his great-grandson, little Johnnie – ah! and a bright lad he was – had noticed what a funny number it was. OI 0101 – just like you might be saying Oy, oy, oy. Mr Gander could call to mind the day when there wasn't none o' them things about, and folks was none the worse for it, so far as he could see. Not that Mr Gander was agin' progress. He'd always voted Radical in his young days, but these here

Socialists was going too far, he reckoned. Too free with other folks' money, that's what they were. It was Mr Lloyd George as give him the Old Age Pension, which was only right, seeing he had worked hard all his life, but he didn't hold with no dole for boys of eighteen. When Mr Gander was eighteen, he was up at four o'clock every morning and on the land till sunset and after for five shillings a week and it hadn't done him no harm as he could see. Married at nineteen he was, and ten children, seven of them still alive and hearty. Why, yes, the car had come back at one o'clock. Mr Gander had just come out from the Feathers after having a pint to his dinner, and he see the car stop and the gentleman as was camping in the lane get out of it. There was a lady in the car, very finely rigged out, but mutton dressed as lamb in Gaffer's opinion. In his day, women weren't ashamed of their age. Not that he minded a female making the best of herself, he was all for progress, but he thought they were going a bit too far nowadays. Mr Martin, that was the gentleman's name, had said good morning to him and gone into the Feathers, and the car had taken the Heathbury road. Why, yes, he'd seen Mr Martin leave. Half-past one it were by the church clock. A good clock, that was. Vicar, he'd had it put in order at his own expense two years ago and when they turned the wireless on, you might hear Big Ben and the church clock striking together quite beautiful. There hadn't been no wireless in Mr Gander's day, but he thought it was a great thing and a fine bit of progress. His grandson Willy, the one that was married on a woman over to Taunton, had give him a beautiful set. It was that loud, he could hear it beautiful, even though his hearing was getting a little hard. He'd heard tell as they were going to show you pictures by wireless soon, and he hoped the Lord might spare him long enough to see it. He hadn't nothing against wireless, though some people thought it was going a bit far to have the Sunday services laid on like gas, as you might say. Not but what it might be a good thing for them as was ailing, but he thought it made the young folks lazy and disrespectful-like. He himself hadn't missed going to Sunday church for twenty year, not since he broke his leg falling off the hayrick, and while he had his strength, please God, he would sit under vicar. Why, yes, he did remember a strange young man coming through the village that afternoon. Of course he could describe him; there wasn't nothing wrong with his eyes, nor his memory neither, praise be! It was only his hearing as wasn't so good but, as Mr Ormond might have noticed, you had only to speak up clear and not mumble as these young people did nowadays and Mr Gander could hear you well enough. One of these rickety-looking town-bred fellows it was, in big glasses, with a little bag strapped to his back and a long stick to walk with, same as they all had. Hikers, they called them. They all had long sticks, like these here Boy Scouts, though, as anybody with experience could have told them, there was nothing like a good crutch-handled ash-plant to give you a help along when you were walking. Because, it stood to reason, you got a better holt on it than on one of they long sticks. But young folks never listened to reason, especially the females, and he thought they was going a bit far, too, with their bare legs and short pants like football players. Though Mr Gander wasn't so old neither that he didn't like to look at a good pair of female legs. In his days females didn't show their legs, but he'd known men as would go a mile to look at a pretty ankle.

Constable Ormond put all his energy into his last question.

'What time did this young man go through?'

'What time? You needn't shout, young man – I may be a bit hard of hearing, but I'm not deaf. I says to vicar only last Monday, "That was a good sermon you give us yesterday," I says. And he says, "Can you hear all right where you sit?"

And I says to him, "I may not have my hearing as good as it was when I was a young man," I says, "but I can still hear you preach, vicar," I says, "from My Text is taken to Now to God the Father." And he says, "You're a wonderful man for your age, Gander," he says. And so I be, surely.'

'So you are, indeed,' said Ormond. 'I was just asking you when you saw this fellow with the glasses and the long stick pass through the village.'

'Nigh on two o'clock it was,' replied the old gentleman, triumphantly, 'nigh on two o'clock. Because why? I says to myself, "You'll be wanting a wet to your whistle, my lad," I says, "and the Feathers shuts at two, so you'd better hurry up a bit." But he goes right on, coming from Wilvercombe and walking straight through towards Hinks's Lane. So I says "Bah!" I says, "you're one o' them pussy-footin' slop-swal-lowers, and you looks it, like as if you was brought up on them gassy lemonades, all belch and no body" (if you'll excuse me), that's what I says to myself. And I says, "Gander," I says, "that comes like a reminder as you've just got time for another pint." So I has my second pint, and when I gets into the bar I see as it's two o'clock by the clock in the bar, as is always kept five minutes fast, on account of getting the men out legal.'

Constable Ormond took the blow in silence. Wimsey was wrong; wrong as sin. The two o'clock alibi was proved up to the hilt. Weldon was innocent; Bright was innocent; Perkins was innocent as day. It now only remained to prove that the mare was innocent, and the whole Weldon-theory would collapse like a pack of cards.

He met Wimsey on the village green and communicated this depressing intelligence.

Wimsey looked at him.

'Do you happen to have a railway time-table on you?' he said at last.

'Time-table? No, my lord. But I could get one. Or perhaps I could tell your lordship—'

'Don't bother,' said Wimsey. 'I only wanted to look up the next train to Colney Hatch.'

The constable stared in his turn.

'The mare is guilty,' said Wimsey. 'She was at the Flat-Iron, and she saw the murder done.'

'But I thought, my lord, you proved that that was impossible.'

'So it is. But it's true.'

Wimsey returned to report his conclusions to Superintendent Glaisher, whom he found suffering from nerves and temper.

'Those London fellows have lost Bright,' he remarked, curtly. 'They traced him to the *Morning Star* office, where he drew his reward in the form of an open cheque. He cashed it at once in currency notes and then skipped off to a big multiple outfitters – one of those places all lifts and exits. To cut a long story short, he diddled them there, and now he's vanished. I thought you could rely on these London men, but it seems I was mistaken. I wish we'd never come up against this qualified case,' added the Superintendent bitterly. 'And now you say that the mare was there and that she wasn't there, and that none of the people who ought to have ridden her did ride her. Are you going to say next that she cut the bloke's throat with her own shoe and turned herself into a sea-horse?'

Saddened, Wimsey went home to the Bellevue and found a telegram waiting for him. It had been despatched from a West End office that afternoon, and ran:

DOING BRIGHT WORK HERE. EXPECT RESULTS SHORTLY. COMMUNICATING CHIEF INSPECTOR PARKER. HOPE FIND OPPORTUNITY DESPATCH LOVAT TWEEDS FROM FLAT. – BUNTER.

XXVII

THE EVIDENCE OF THE FISHERMAN'S GRANDSON

> 'Has it gone twelve? –
> This half-hour. Here I've set
> A little clock, that you may mark the time.'
> *Death's Jest-Book*

WEDNESDAY, X JULY

'THERE'S one thing that stands out a mile,' said Inspector Umpelty. 'If there was any hanky-panky with that horse round about two o'clock at the Flat-Iron, Pollock and his precious grandson must have seen it. It's not a mite of use saying they didn't. I always did think that lot was in it up to the eyes. A quiet, private, heart-to-heart murder they might have overlooked, but a wild horse careering about they couldn't, and there you are.'

Wimsey nodded.

'I've seen that all along – but how are you going to get it out of them? Shall I have a go at it, Umpelty? That young fellow, Jem – he doesn't look as surly as his grandpa – how about him? Has he got any special interest or hobbies?'

'Well, I don't know, my lord, not without it might be football. He's reckoned a good player, and I know he's hoping to get taken on by the Westshire Tigers.'

'H'm. Wish it had been cricket – that's more in my line. Still, we can but try. Think one might find him anywhere about this evening? How about the Three Feathers?'

'If he's not out with his boat, you'd most likely find him there.'

Wimsey did find him there. It is always reasonably easy to

get conversation going in a pub, and it will be a black day for detectives when beer is abolished. After an hour's entertaining discussion about football and the chances of various teams in the coming season, Wimsey found Jem becoming distinctly more approachable. With extreme care and delicacy he then set out to work the conversation round to the subject of fishing, the Flat-Iron and the death of Paul Alexis. At first, the effect was disappointing. Jem lost his loquacity, his smile vanished, and he fell into a brooding gloom. Then, just as Wimsey was deciding to drop the dangerous subject, the young man seemed to make up his mind. He edged a little closer to Wimsey, glanced over his shoulder at the crowd about the bar, and muttered:

'See here, sir, I'd like to have a word with you about that.'

'By all means. Outside? Right! Dashed interesting,' he added, more loudly. 'Next time I'm down this way I'd like to come along and see you play. Well, I must be barging along. You going home? I can run you over in the car if you like – won't take a minute.'

'Thank'ee, sir. I'd be glad of it.'

'And you could show me those photographs you were talking about.'

The two pushed their way out. Good-nights were exchanged, but Wimsey noticed that none of the Darley inhabitants seemed particularly cordial to Jem. There was a certain air of constraint about their farewells.

They got into the car, and drove in silence till they were past the level crossing. Then Jem spoke:

'About that business, sir. I told Grandad he'd better tell the police how it were, but he's that obstinate, and it's a fact there'd be murder done if it was to get out. None the more for that, he did ought to speak, because this here's a hanging matter and there's no call as I see to get mixed up with it. But Grandad, he don't trust that Umpelty and his lot, and he'd leather the life out of Mother or me if we was to let on.

Once tell the police, he says, and it 'ud be all about the place.'

'Well – it depends what it is,' said Wimsey, a little mystified. 'Naturally, the police can't hide anything – well, anything criminal, but—'

'Oh, 'tis not that, sir. Leastways, not as you might take notice on. But if they Bainses was to hear tell on it and was to let Gurney know – but there! I've always told Grandad as it wur a fool thing to do, never mind if Tom Gurney did play a dirty trick over them there nets.'

'If it's nothing criminal,' said Wimsey, rather relieved, 'you may be sure *I* shan't let anybody know.'

'No, sir. That's why I thought I'd like to speak to you, sir. You see, Grandad left a bad impression, the way he wouldn't let on what he was doing off the Grinders, and I reckon I did ought to have spoke up at the time, only for knowing as Grandad 'ud take it out of Mother the moment my back was turned.'

'I quite understand. But, what was it you were doing at the Grinders?'

'Taking lobsters, sir.'

'Taking lobsters? What's the harm in that?'

'None, sir; only, you see, they was Tom Gurney's pots.'

After a little interrogation, the story became clear. The unfortunate Tom Gurney, who lived in Darley, was accustomed to set out his lobster-pots near the Grinders, and drove a very thriving trade with them. But, some time previously, he had offended old Pollock in the matter of certain nets, alleged to have sustained wilful damage. Mr Pollock, unable to obtain satisfaction by constitutional methods, had adopted a simple method of private revenge. He chose suitable moments when Tom Gurney was absent, visited the lobster-pots, abstracted the greater part of their live contents and replaced the pots. It was not, Jem explained, that Mr Pollock really hoped to take out the whole value of the damaged nets in lobsters; the relish of the revenge lay in the thought of 'doing that Gurney down' and in hearing 'that Gurney' swearing from time to time about the scarcity of lobsters in the bay. Jem thought the whole thing rather foolish and didn't care for having a hand in it, because it would have suited his social ambitions better to keep on good terms with his neighbours, but what with one thing and another (meaning, Wimsey gathered, what with old Pollock's surly temper and the possibility of his leaving his very considerable savings to some other person, if annoyed), Jem had humoured his grandfather in this matter of lobster-snatching.

Wimsey was staggered. It was as simple as that, then. All this mystification, and nothing behind it but a trivial local feud. He glanced sharply at Jem. It was getting dark, and the young man's face was nothing but an inscrutable profile.

'Very well, Jem,' he said. 'I quite see. But now, about this business on the shore. Why did you and your grandfather persist in saying you saw nobody there?'

'But that was right, sir. We didn't see nobody. You see, it was like this, sir. We had the boat out, and we brings her along there round 'bout the slack, knowin' as the other boats 'ud be comin' home with the tide, see? And Grandad says, "Have a look along the shore, Jem," he says, "and see as there's none o' them Gurneys a-hangin' about." So I looks, an' there weren't a soul to be seen, leaving out this chap on the Flat-Iron. And I looks at him and I sees as he's asleep or summat, and he's none of us by the looks of him, so I says to Grandad as he's some fellow from the town, like.'

'He was asleep, you say?'

'Seemingly. So Grandad takes a look at him and says, "He's doin' no harm," he says, "but keep your eyes skinned for the top of the cliffs." So I did, and there wasn't a single soul come along that there shore before we gets to the Grinders, and that's the truth if I was to die for it.'

'Now, see here, Jem,' said Wimsey. 'You heard all the evidence at the inquest, and you know that this poor devil was killed round about two o'clock.'

'That's true, sir; and as sure as I'm sitting here, he must ha' killed himself, for there was nobody come a-nigh him – barring the young lady, of course. Unless it might be while we was taking them pots up. I won't say but what we might a-missed summat then. We finished that job round about two o'clock – I couldn't say just when it were, not to the minute, but the tide had turned nigh on three-quarters of an hour, and that's when I looks at this fellow again and I says to Grandad, "Grandad," I says, "that chap there on the rock looks queer-like," I says, "I wonder if there's summat wrong." So we brings the boat in-shore a bit, and then, all of a sudden, out comes the young lady from behind them rocks and starts caperin' about. And Grandad, he says, "Let un bide," he says, "let un bide. Us have no call to be meddlin' wi' they," he says. And so we puts about again. Because, you see, sir, if we'd gone a-meddling and it was to come out as we was thereabouts with the boat full of Tom Gurney's lobsters, Tom Gurney'd a-had summat to say about it.'

'Your grandfather said you saw Alexis first at about 1.45.'

'It 'ud be before that, sir. But I'll not say as we kept our eyes on un all the time, like.'

'Suppose someone had come along, say, between 1.45 and two o'clock, would you have seen him?'

'Reckon so. No, sir; that poor gentleman made away with himself, there's no doubt of it. Just cut his throat quiet-like as he sat there. There's no manner of doubt about that.'

Wimsey was puzzled. If this was lying, it was done with a surprising appearance of sincerity. But if it was truth, it made the theory of murder still harder to substantiate than before. Every fragment of evidence there was pointed to the conclusion that Alexis had died alone upon his rock and by his own hand.

And yet – why wouldn't the bay mare go near the Flat-Iron? Was it possible – Wimsey was no friend to superstition, but he had known such things happen before – was it possible that the uneasy spirit of Paul Alexis still hung about the Flat-Iron, perceptible to the brute though not to self-conscious man? He had known another horse that refused to pass the scene of an age-old crime.

He suddenly thought of another point that he might incidentally verify.

'Will anybody be up and about at your home, Jem?'

'Oh, yes, sir. Mother's sure to be waiting up for me.'

'I'd like to see her.'

Jem offered no objection, and Wimsey went in with him to Pollock's cottage. Mrs Pollock, stirring soup for Jem in a saucepan, received him politely, but shook her head at his question.

'No, sir. We heard no horse on the beach this afternoon.'

That settled that, then. If Wimsey could ride past the cottages unnoticed, so could any other man.

'The wind's off-shore today,' added Mrs Pollock.

'And you're still sure you heard nothing of the sort last Thursday week?'

'Ah!' Mrs Pollock removed the saucepan. 'Not in the afternoon, what the police was asking about. But Susie have called to mind as she did hear something like a trampling round about dinner-time. Happen it might be twelve o'clock. But being at her work, she didn't run out to look.'

'Twelve o'clock?'

'Thereabout, sir. It come back to her all of a sudden, when we was talkin' over what that young Ormond wur askin' about.'

Wimsey left the cottage with his ideas all in disorder. If someone had been riding on the shore at twelve o'clock it accounted for the horseshoe, but it did not account for the murder. Had he, after all, been quite wrong in attaching so much importance to the horseshoe? Might not some mischievous lad, finding the bay mare at large, have ridden her along the beach for a lark? Might she not even have strayed away on her own account?

But that brought him back to her strange behaviour of that afternoon, and to the problem of the ring-bolt. Had the ring-bolt been used for some other purpose? Or suppose the murderer had come to the rock on horseback at twelve o'clock and remained talking there with Alexis till two o'clock? But Jem said that there had been only the one figure on the Flat-Iron. Had the murderer lurked hidden in the rocky cleft till the time came to strike the blow? But why? Surely the sole reason for riding thither could only have been the establishment of an alibi, and an alibi is thrown away if one lingers for two hours before taking advantage of it. And how had the mare got home? She was not on the shore between one o'clock and two o'clock if – again – Jem was to be trusted. Wimsey played for a few moments with the idea of two men riding on one horse – one to do the murder and one to take the animal back, but the thing seemed far-fetched and absurd.

Then an entirely new thought struck him. In all the discussions about the crime, it had been taken for granted that Alexis had walked along the coast-road to the Flat-Iron; but had this been proved? He had never thought to ask. Why might not Alexis have been the rider?

In that case, the time of the mare's passing might be explained, but other problems bristled up thick as thorns in a rose-garden. At what point had he taken horse? He had been seen to leave Darley Halt by road in the direction of Lesston Hoe. Had he subsequently returned and fetched the mare from the field, and so ridden? If not, who had brought her and to what rendezvous? And again, how had she returned?

He determined to hunt out Inspector Umpelty and face him with these problems.

The Inspector was just going to bed, and his welcome was not a hearty one, but he showed signs of animation on hearing Wimsey's fresh information.

'Them Pollocks and Moggeridges are the biggest liars in creation,' he observed, 'and if there's been murder done, it's good proof that they're all concerned in it,' said he. 'But as to how Alexis got there, you can set your mind at rest. We've found six witnesses who saw him at various points along the road between 10.15 and 11.45, and unless there's some other fellow been going about in a black beard, you can take it as proved that he went by the coast-road and no other way.'

'Did none of the witnesses know him personally?'

'Well, no,' the Inspector admitted, 'but it isn't likely there'd be more than one young fellow in a blue suit and a beard going about at that time, unless somebody was deliberately disguised as him, and where'd be the point of that? I mean to say, the only reasons for anybody impersonating him would be to make out either that he was in that neighbourhood at that particular time when he was really elsewhere, or that he was really alive some time after he was supposed to be killed. Now, we know that he was in that neighbourhood all right, so that disposes of number one; and we know that he really was killed at two o'clock and not earlier, and that disposes of number two. Unless, of course,' said the Inspector, slowly, 'the real Alexis was up to some funny business between 10.15 and two o'clock, and this other fellow was making an alibi for him. I hadn't thought of that.'

'I suppose,' said Wimsey, 'that it really *was* Alexis who was killed. His face was gone, you know, and we've only the clothes and a photograph to go upon.'

'Well, it was somebody else with a real beard, anyhow,' said the Inspector. 'And who would Alexis be wanting to kill, do you suppose?'

'Bolsheviks,' suggested Wimsey, lightly. 'He might make an appointment with a Bolshevik who meant to murder him, then murder the Bolshevik.'

'So he might – but that doesn't make things any easier. Whoever it was did the murder, he had to get away from the Flat-Iron. And how could he have managed to change clothes with the victim? There wasn't time.'

'Not after the murder, certainly.'

'Then where are you? It's only making things more complicated. If you ask me, I think your notion of the mare having been ridden down there at some other time by some mischievous young fellow is a good one. There's nothing against it except that ring-bolt, and that might quite well have been put there for a quite different purpose. That washes the mare out of the thing altogether and makes it all a lot easier. Then we can say that either Alexis did away with himself or else he was murdered by some person we don't know of yet, who just walked along the coast on his two feet. It doesn't matter that those Pollocks didn't see him. He could have been hiding under the rock, like you said. The only trouble is, who was he? It wasn't Weldon, it wasn't Bright, and it wasn't Perkins. But they're not the only people in the world.'

Wimsey nodded.

'I'm feeling a bit depressed,' he said. 'I seem to have fallen down a bit over this case.'

'It's a nuisance,' said Umpelty, 'but there! We've only been at it a fortnight, and what's fortnight? We'll have to be patient, my lord, and wait for the translation of that letter to come through. The explanation may be all in that.'

XXVIII

THE EVIDENCE OF THE CIPHER

'I know not whether
I see your meaning: if I do, it lies
Upon the wordy wavelets of your voice,
Dim as an evening shadow in a brook.'

Fragment

FRIDAY, 3 JULY

THE letter from 'Clumps' at the Foreign Office did not
arrive till the Friday, and then was a disappointment. It ran:

'DEAR WIMBLES,

'Got your screed. Old Bungo is in China, dealing with
the mess-up there, so have posted enclosure off to him as
per instructions. He may be up-country, but he'll probably
get it in a few weeks. How's things? Saw Trotters last week
at the Carlton. He has got himself into a bit of a mess with
his old man, but seems to bear up. You remember the
Newton-Carberry business? Well, it's settled, and Flops
has departed for the Continent. What-ho!

'Yours ever,

'CLUMPS.'

'Young idiot!' said Wimsey, wrathfully. He threw the letter
into the waste-paper basket, put on his hat and went round to
Mrs Lefranc's. Here he found Harriet industriously at work
upon the cipher. She reported, however, total failure.

'I don't think it's a scrap of good going on with these
marked words,' said Wimsey. 'And Bungo has failed us.

Let's put our great brains to the business. Now, look here. Here is a problem to start with. What is in this letter, and why wasn't it burnt with the rest?'

'Now you mention it, that is rather odd.'

'Very. This letter came on the Tuesday morning. On the Wednesday, bills were settled up, and on the Wednesday night, papers were burned. On Thursday morning, Alexis set out to catch his train. Is it too much to suppose that the instructions to do all this were in the letter?'

'It looks likely.'

'It does. That means that this letter probably made the appointment for the meeting at the Flat-Iron. Now why wasn't this letter burnt with the rest?'

Harriet let her mind range over the field of detective fiction, with which she was moderately well acquainted.

'In my own books,' she remarked, 'I usually make the villain end up by saying "Bring this letter with you." The idea is, from the villain's point of view, that he can then make certain that the paper is destroyed. From *my* point of view, of course, I put it in so that the villain can leave a fragment of paper clutched in the victim's stiffened hand to assist Robert Templeton.'

'Just so. Now, suppose our villain didn't quite grasp the duplicity of your motives. Suppose he said to himself: "Harriet Vane and other celebrated writers of mystery fiction always make the murderer tell the victim to bring the letter with him. That is evidently the correct thing to do." That would account for the paper's being here.'

'He'd have to be rather an amateur villain.'

'Why shouldn't he be? Unless this is really the work of a trained Bolshevik agent, he probably is. I suggest that somewhere in this letter, perhaps at the end, we shall find the words "Bring this letter with you" – and that will account for its presence.'

'I see. Then why do we find it tucked away in an inner pocket and not in the victim's hand as per schedule?'

'Perhaps the victim didn't play up?'

'Then the murderer ought to have searched him and found the paper.'

'He must have forgotten.'

'How inefficient!'

'I can't help that. Here *is* the paper. And no doubt it's full of dangerous and important information. If it made an appointment, it must be because it would then almost amount to a proof that Alexis didn't commit suicide but *was* murdered.'

'Look here, though! Suppose the letter was brought simply because it contained instructions for reaching the Flat-Iron and so on, which Alexis didn't want to forget.'

'Can't be that. For one thing, he'd have had it handy, in an outer pocket – not tucked away in a case. And besides—'

'Not necessarily. He'd keep it handy till he got to the place and then he'd tuck it away safely. After all, he sat at the Flat-Iron alone for an hour or so, didn't he?'

'Yes, but I was going to say something else. If he wanted to keep on referring to the letter, he'd take – not the cipher, which would be troublesome to read, but the de-coded copy.'

'Of course – but – don't you see, that solves the whole thing! He did take the copy, and the villain said: "Have you brought the letter?" And Alexis, without thinking, handed him the copy, and the villain took that and destroyed that, forgetting that the original might be on the body too.'

'You're right,' said Wimsey, 'you're dead right. That's exactly what must have happened. Well, that's that, but it doesn't get us very much farther. Still, we've got some idea of what must have been in the letter, and that will be a great help with the de-coding. We've also got the idea that the villain may have been a bit of an amateur, and that is borne out by the letter itself.'

'How?'

'Well, there are two lines here at the top, of six letters

apiece. Nobody but an amateur would present us with six isolated letters, let alone two sets of six. He'd run the whole show together. There are just about two things these words might be. One: they might be a key to the cipher – a letter-substitution key, but they're not, because I've tried them, and anyway, nobody would be quite fool enough to send keyword and cipher together on the same sheet of paper. They might, of course, be a key-word or words for the *next* letter, but I don't think so. Six letters is very short for the type of code I have in mind, and words of twelve letters with no repeating letter are very rare in any language.'

'Wouldn't any word do, if you left out the repeated letters?'

'It would; but judging by Alexis' careful marking of his dictionary, that simple fact does not seem to have occurred to these amateurs. Well, then, if these words are not keys to a cipher, I suggest that they represent an address, or, more probably, an address and date. They're in the right place for it. I don't mean a whole address, of course – just the name of a town – say Berlin or London – and the date below it.'

'That's possible.'

'We can but try. Now we don't know much about the town, except that the letters are said to have come from Czechoslovakia. But we might get the date.'

'How would that be written?'

'Let's see. The letters may just represent the figures of the day, month and year. That means that one of them is an arbitrary fill-up letter, because you can't have an odd number of letters, and a double figure for the number of the months is quite impossible, since the letter arrived here on June 17th. I don't quite know how long the post takes from places in Central Europe, but surely not more than three or four days at the very outside. That means it must have been posted after the 10th of June. If the letters do not stand for numbers, then I suggest that RBEXMG stands either for somethingteen June or June somethingteen. Now, to represent figures our codemerchant may have taken 1 = A, 2 = B, 3 = C, and so on, or he may have taken 1 as the first letter of the code-word and so on. The first would be more sensible, because it wouldn't give the code away.* So we'll suppose that 1 = A, so that he originally wrote A? JUNE or JUNE A? and then coded the letters in the ordinary way, the ? standing for the unknown figure, which must be less than 5. Very good. Now, is he more likely to have written June somethingteen or somethingteen June?'

'Most English people *write* the day first and the month second. Business people at any rate, though old-fashioned ladies still stick to putting the month first.'

'All right. We'll try somethingteen June first and say that RBEXMG stands for A? June. Very good. Now we'll see what we can make of that. Let's write it out in pairs. We'll leave out RB for the moment and start with *EX*. Now EX = JU. Now there's one point about this code that is rather helpful in decoding. Supposing two letters come next door to one another in the code-diagram, either horizontally or vertically, you'll find that the code pair and the clear pair have a letter in common. You don't get that? Well, look! Take our old key-word SQUANDER, written in the diagram like this:

S	Q	U	A	N
D	E	R		

* The hypothesis that RBEXMG represented a date written entirely in numerals proved to be untenable, and for bravity's sake, the calculations relating to this supposition are omitted.

If you're coding the pair of letters DE, then, by taking the letters to the right of them (by the horizontal rule) you get DE = ER; the letter E appears both in code and clear. And the same for letters that *immediately* follow one another in a vertical line. Now, in our first pair EX = JU, this doesn't happen, so we may provisionally write them down in diagonal form

J	E
X	U

Taking these letters as forming the corners of a parallelogram, we can tell ourselves that JX must come on the same line in the diagram either vertically or horizontally; the same with JE, the same with EU, and the same with UX.'

'But suppose JN follows the horizontal rule or the vertical rule without the two letters actually coming together?'

'It doesn't matter; it would only mean then that *all four of them* come on the same line, like this: ? J E U X, or X U E? J or some arrangement of that kind, So, taking all the letters we have got and writing them in diagonals we get this:

J	E	N	M	A	R
X	U	G	E	B	?

Unfortunately there are no side-by-side letters at all. It would be very helpful if there were, but we can't have everything.

'Now the first striking thing is this: that U and X have to come on the same line. That very strongly suggests that they both come in the bottom line. There are five letters that follow U in the alphabet, and only four spaces in which to put them. One of them, therefore, must be in the key-word. We'll take a risk with it and assume that it isn't Z. If it is, we'll have to start all over again, but one must make a start somewhere. We'll risk Z. That gives us three possibilities for our last line: UVXYZ with W in the key-word, or UWXYZ with V in the key-word, or UVWXZ with Y in the key-word. But in any case, U must be in the bottom left-hand corner. Now, looking again at our diagonals, we find that E and U must come in the same line. We can't suppose that E comes immediately above U, because it would be a frightful great key-word that only left us with four spaces between E and U, so we must put E in one of the top three spaces of the left-hand column, like this:

'That's not much, but it's a beginning. Now let's tackle X. There's one square in which we know it *can't* be. It can't come next to U, or there would be two spaces between X and Z with only one letter to fill them; so X must come in either the third or the fourth square of the bottom line. So now we have two possible diagrams.

Zc   (1)   (2)

'Looking at our diagonal pairs again, we find that J and X come in the same line and so do J and E. That means that J can't come immediately above X, so we will again enter it on both our diagrams in the top three squares in the X line. Now we come to an interesting point. M and N have got to come in the same line. In Diagram 1 it looks fearfully tempting to put them into the two empty spaces on the right of J, leaving K and L for the key-word; but you can't do that in Diagram 2, because there's not room in the line. If Diagram 1 is the right one, then M or N or both of them must come in the key-word. M and E come in the same line, but N can't come next-door to E. That warns us against a few arrangements, but still leaves a devil of a lot of scope. Our key-word can't begin with EN, that's a certainty. But now, wait! If E is rightly placed in the third square down, then N can't come at the right-hand extremity of the same line, for that would bring it next to E by the horizontal rule; so in Diagram 1 that washes out the possibility of JMN or JLN for that line. It would give us JLM, which is impossible unless N is in the key-word, because N can't come next to E and yet must be in the same line with it and also with M.'

Wimsey clawed a little at his hair and sat muttering.

'It looks as though we'd sucked our five letter rather dry,' said Harriet. 'How about trying the rest of the message? I've got it all ready sorted out into pairs. Hullo! Here's our old friend EXMG appearing again in the body of it.'

'Is there?' Wimsey sat up. 'Then, if we're right, that will be another date in June. I can't believe it's part of two words, one of which ends in J, or I, or JU or IU or IUN or JUN. If the letter was making an appointment for June 18th, why shouldn't the two letters before it be the letters for 18, that is AH? We'll try it, anyway; what are they?'

'O.B.'

'OB=AH. That's a fat lot of use. Well, we'll stick 'em down.

O	A
H	B

O and A in the same line, O and H in the same line, and A and B we knew about before. That looks as though we might be on the right track, but it doesn't help us much, because none of the letters we've already placed comes into it.'

'Just a moment,' put in Harriet. 'I've got a brainwave. That town in the heading – it's supposed to be something in Central Europe. It's got six letters, and the last two are the first two reversed. How about Warsaw?'

'By jove! that's bright! We can but try it. Let's see – that gives us this He wrote down the new pairs of diagonals.

W	X		R	A
N	A		T	S

'W and X come in the same line,' he observed, 'and it's terribly tempting to imagine that W comes in the last line, next door to X. Otherwise, of course, it must be in the keyword. Just for fun, let's enter it in the last line in both our diagrams. Now, this becomes interesting. W and N are also in the same line. We can't place N in the fourth line down, because it's got to be in line with E. Nor can we put it in the third line down, because there are only six letters that come between N and U, and we should have eight spaces left to put them in. Therefore, if W is rightly placed, N has got to go in the top two lines, which means that it definitely does belong to the key-word.'

Harriet filled the letters in tentatively.

e	n	i		
e	n	i		
e				
U	W	X	Y	Z

(1)

e		n	i	
e		n	i	
e			i	
U		W	X	Z

(2)

'That makes Diagram 1 took wrong,' she said. 'Why? What have we done? Oh, I know. E and N can't come together, so if that's the right diagram, E must come in the third line. I *say!* That would mean a key-word of eleven letters!'

'Not necessarily. E may be in its proper alphabetical place. But if Diagram 1 is right, then the beginning of Line 3 is the only place for it. Let's get on. S and T come in one line, and so do R and T, but RST don't follow one another, or RS would become ST, which it doesn't. I should like ST to go in the two places next before U, but we can't be sure that that is the right place for them. Well, dash it! stick 'em down – if we're wrong we must do it again, that's all. There! Now, in that case, R must be in the key-word and therefore in one of the top two spaces on the right of the diagram. That means that RS will be something-T.'

'But we know RS! If AT = RS, then RS = AT.'

'Good lord! so it does! That's fine! That practically proves that our S and T are correct. And now we know that AR must come next to one another in the key-word.'

Harriet pored over the diagrams again.

'Can't we do something now with NX = AW? Yes – look!

If we put A into either of the squares in Diagram 1, so as to make NX = AW, then A won't come next to R! So either we're all wrong, or we can wash our Diagram 1 altogether.'

'Hurray! Brilliant woman! I always hated Diagram 1, so we'll stash it. That leaves us with a very hopeful-looking Diagram 2.'

e		N	ia	r
e		N	ia	r
e			i	
			S	T
U	V	W	X	Z

'I'm glad you think it's hopeful! How about this business of M and N coming in the same line? Can we do anything with that now?'

'Why not? Let's try. Put M immediately below the N spaces. That leaves five spaces between it and S and only three letters to fill them, because we know that N and R are in the key-word. So that M must come in one of the four spaces in the top left-hand corner. Now we do know that NE = MG. Obviously G can't come immediately between E and N anywhere, because that would give us a key-word with MNG in it, which sounds almost incredible. But that still leaves us with several possible arrangements. Is there anything else we can do?'

'We can fill in Q in the space before S. It isn't likely to be in the key-word without its U, and we know roughly what has become of R.'

'Yes. All right. There it is. Do any of these pairs of letters make sense in the letter itself, by the way?'

'No. I've been trying to fit them in, but they're remarkably unhelpful. There's a group AT GM which works out as RS EN, but that might be anything. And quite near the beginning there's TS followed by QJ. TS = SQ, and you'd expect the next group to be U-something, but it isn't. QJ must be S-something.'

'So it is; that shows we're on the right track. Q is an arbitrary letter stuck in to separate the two S's. It's curious how little one can get out of the actual text at this stage. Shows what an ingenious beast of a code it is, doesn't it? Wait a jiff – the group before that is MG = NE – that gives us NESS. Perfectly possible and even probable, but it might be anything. Here it comes again! Whatever it is, it appears to be important – its the same word, BFFY followed by NESS, but BFFY is simply baffling, I can see nothing for it but to go on struggling with the top left-hand corner. Let's write out all the possible positions for NE = MG.'

(1)   (2)   (3)

'I can see one thing,' said Harriet, 'and that is that we have got to have a vowel of some kind between M and N, and that vowel can't be A, E, I, or U, because we've placed those elsewhere. Therefore it's got to be either O or Y.'

'O for preference. The number of words with MYN in them must be limited. But Y has got to be in the key-word somewhere. The end would be the likeliest place for it. perhaps it ends in MONY. That gives us MONY in Diagram (1), and a word of nine letters. That's quite plausible. And it's got to begin with E – G. That's less pleasant. EBG, ECG – let's run through the alphabet. EHG – I think not.

EIG – pronounceable, but we got I elsewhere. ELG – where's the dictionary? Nothing there. ENG is impossible, we know where N is – same with ERG. My child, you can wash out all words ending in MONY – they won't work on Diagram (1) or on Diagram (3), and as for Diagram (2), I refuse to believe in a fourteen-letter word until I'm absolutely forced to.'

'In that case, you can wash out Diagram (2) altogether.'

'Right-ho! I don't mind, though a thirteen-letter word ending in MON is not absolutely inconceivable. In that case, either our word begins with Mon, or it doesn't.'

'But it does! We couldn't find any words beginning E – G.'

'Nor we could. *Now* then! We've got our E and our G fixed as well as our MON. Now we shan't be long! Fill them in! Oh! and look here! I'm sure the F must go between the E and the G – it's so obviously the place for it.'

Harriet filled the diagram in with a quivering pencil.

M	O	N	ia	r
			ia	r
E	F	G	i	
		Q	S	T
U	V	W	X	Z

'That *does* look better,' she admitted. 'Now, let's see if it helps to get any sense out of the letter. Bother! What a lot of groups that we still haven't got! Still no sense for BFFY. Oh! wait! Here's something! MZ TS XS RS. Now, MZ is something-U, and quite possibly RU; it's a 50–50 chance, anyway. TS is SQ and XS is S-something, which means that the Q is just a fill-in letter. Now suppose XS = SI – there's no reason why it shouldn't. Then RS might quite likely be AT –

there's nothing against it. And suppose – suppose all these supposes are right, then MZTSXSRS is RUSQSIAT. Knock out the Q and we've got RUSSIAT. *Why* couldn't that be RUSSIA?'

'Why not, indeed? Let's make it so. Write the letters down. M O N A R – oh, Harriet!'

'Don't joggle!'

'I must joggle! We've got the key-word. MONARCH. Wait a jiff. That leaves three spaces before E, and we've only got B and D to put in. Oh, no, I forgot! Y – dear old Y! MONARCHY! Three loud cheers! There you are! All done by kindness! There! There's your square complete. And jolly pretty it looks, I must say.'

M	O	N	A	R
C	H	Y	B	D
E	F	G	Ij	K
L	P	Q	S	T
U	V	W	X	Z

'Oh, Peter! How marvellous! Let's dance or do something.'

'Nonsense! Let's get on with the job. None of your frivolling now. Start away. PR BF XA LI MK MG BF FY MG TS QJ – and let's get to the bottom of this BF FY business, once and for all. I'll read out the diagonals and you write 'em down.'

'Very well. T – O – H – I – "To His Serene" – can that be right?'

'It's English. Hurry up – let's get BFFY.'

'"To His Serene Highness" – Peter! what *is* all this about?'

Lord Peter turned pale.

'My God!' he exclaimed, melodramatically, 'can it be? Have we been wrong and the preposterous Mrs Weldon right? Shall I be reduced, at my time of life, to hunting for a Bolshevik gang? Read on!'

XXIX

THE EVIDENCE OF THE LETTER

'In one word hear, what soon they all shall hear:
A king's a man, and I will be no man
Unless I am a king.'

Death's Jest-Book

FRIDAY, 3 JULY

'To His Serene Highness Grand-Duke Pavlo Alexeivitch heir to the throne of the Romanovs.

'Papers entrusted to us by your Highness now thoroughly examined and marriage of your illustrious ancestress to Tsar Nicholas First proved beyond doubt.'

Harriet paused. 'What does that mean?'

'God knows. Nicholas I was no saint, but I didn't think he
ever *married* anybody except Charlotte-Louise of Prussia.
Who the deuce is Paul Alexis' illustrious ancestress?'

Harriet shook her head and went on reading.

'All is in readiness. Your people groaning under oppres-
sion of brutal Soviets eagerly welcome return of imperial
rule to Holy Russia.'

Wimsey shook his head.

'If so, that's one in the eye for my Socialist friends. I was
told only the other day that Russian Communism was doing
itself proud and that the Russian standard of living, mea-
sured in boot-consumption, had risen from zero to one pair
of boots in three years per head of population. Still, there

may be Russians so benighted as not to be content with that state of things.'

'Alexis did always say he was of noble birth, didn't he?'

'He did, and apparently found somebody to believe him. Carry on.'

'Treaty with Poland happily concluded. Money and arms at your disposal. Your presence alone needed.'

'Oho!' said Wimsey. 'Now we're coming to it. Hence the passport and the three hundred gold sovereigns.'

'Spies at work. Use caution. Burn all papers all clues to identity.'

'He obeyed that bit all right, blow him!' interjected Wimsey. 'It looks as though we were now getting down to brass tacks.'

'On Thursday 18 June take train reaching Darley Halt ten-fifteen walk by coast-road to Flat-Iron Rock. There await Rider from the Sea who brings instruction for your journey to Warsaw. The word is Empire.'

'The Rider from the Sea? Good gracious! Does that mean that Weldon – that the mare – that –?'

'Read on. Perhaps Weldon is the hero of the piece instead of the villain. But if so, why didn't he tell us about it?'

Harriet read on.

'Bring this paper with you. Silence, secrecy imperative. BORIS.'

'Well!' said Wimsey. 'In all this case, from beginning to end, I only seem to have got one thing right. I said that the letter would contain the words: "Bring this paper with you" and it does. But the rest of it beats me. "Pavlo Alexeivitch, heir to the throne of the Romanovs." Can your land-lady produce anything in the shape of a drink?'

After an interval for refreshment, Wimsey hitched his chair closer to the table and sat staring at the decoded message.

'Now,' he said, 'let's get this straight. One thing is certain. This is the letter that brought Paul Alexis to the Flat-Iron. Boris sent it, whoever he is. Now, is Boris a friend or an enemy?'

He rumpled his hair wildly, and went on, speaking slowly.

'The first thing one is inclined to think is that Boris was a friend and that the Bolshevik spies mentioned in the letter got to the Flat-Iron before he did and murdered Alexis and possibly Boris as well. In that case, what about Weldon's mare? Did she bring the "Rider from the Sea" to his appointment? And was Weldon the rider, and the imperialist friend of Alexis? It's quite possible, because – no, it isn't. That's funny, if you like.'

'What?'

'I was going to say, that in that case Weldon could have ridden to the Flat-Iron at twelve o'clock, when Mrs Pollock heard the sound of hoofs. But he didn't. He was in Wilvercombe. But somebody else may have done so – some friend to whom Weldon lent the mare.'

'Then how did the murderer get there?'

'He walked through the water and escaped the same way, after hiding in the niche till you had gone. It was only while Weldon or Bright or Perkins was supposed to be the murderer that the time-scheme presented any real difficulty. But who was the Rider from the Sea? Why does he not come forward and say: "I had an appointment with this man. I saw him alive at such a time?"'

'Why, because he is afraid that the man who murdered Alexis will murder him too. But it's all very confusing. We've now got two unknown people to look for instead of one: the Rider from the Sea, who stole the mare and was at the Flat-Iron about midday, and the murderer, who was there at two o'clock.'

'Yes. How difficult it all is. At any rate, all this explains Weldon and Perkins. Naturally they said nothing about the mare, because she had gone and come again long before either of them was at the camping-ground. Wait a moment, though; that's odd. How did the Rider from the Sea know that Weldon was going to be away in Wilvercombe that morning? It seems to have been pure accident.'

'Perhaps the Rider damaged Weldon's car on purpose.'

'Yes, but even then, how could he be sure that Weldon would go away? On the face of it, it was far more likely that Weldon would be there, tinkering with his car.'

'Suppose he knew that Weldon meant to go to Wilvercombe that morning in any case. Then the damaged H.T. lead would be pure bad luck for him, and the fact that Weldon did, after all, get to Wilvercombe, a bit of compensating good luck.'

'And how did he know about Weldon's plans?'

'Possibly he knew nothing about Weldon at all. Weldon only arrived at Darley on the Tuesday, and all this business was planned long before that, as the date of the letter shows. Possibly whoever it was was horrified to find Weldon encamped in Hinks's Lane and frightfully relieved to see him barge off on the Thursday morning.'

Wimsey shook his head.

'Talk about coincidence! Well, maybe so. Now let's go on and see what happened. The Rider made the appointment with Alexis, who would get to the Flat-Iron about 11.45. The Rider met him there, and gave him his instructions – verbally, we may suppose. He then rode back to Darley, loosed the mare and went about his business. Right. The whole thing may have been over by 12.30 or 12.45, and it must have been over by 1.30, or Weldon would have seen him on his return. Meanwhile, what does Alexis do? Instead of getting up and going about *his* business, he sits peacefully on the rock, waiting for someone to come along and murder him at two o'clock!'

'He may have been told to sit on a bit, so as not to leave at the same time as the Rider. Or here's a better idea. When the Rider has gone, Alexis waits for a little bit – say five minutes – at any rate, till his friend is well out of reach. Then up pops the murderer from the niche in the rock, where he has been eavesdropping, and has an interview with Alexis. At two o'clock, the interview ends in murder. Then I turn up, and the murderer pops back into hiding. How's that? The murderer didn't show himself while the Rider was there, because he didn't feel equal to tackling two men at once.'

'That seems to cover the facts. I only wonder, though, that he didn't murder you too, while he was about it.'

'That would make it look much less like suicide.'

'Very true. But how was it you didn't see these two people talking animatedly on the Flat-Iron when you arrived and looked over the cliff at one o'clock?'

'Goodness knows! But if the murderer was standing on the seaward side of the rock – or if they both were – I shouldn't have seen anything. And they may have been, because it was quite low tide then, and the sand would have been dry.'

'Yes, so it would. And as the discussion prolonged itself, they saw the tide turn, so they scrambled up on to the rock to keep their feet dry. That would be while you were asleep. But I wonder you didn't hear the chattage and talkery going on while you were having your lunch. Voices carry well by the sea-shore.'

'Perhaps they heard me scrambling down the cliff and shut up.'

'Perhaps. And then the murderer, knowing that you were there, deliberately committed his murder under your very nose, so to speak.'

391

'He may have thought I had gone. He knew I couldn't see him at the moment, because he couldn't see me.'

'And Alexis yelled, and you woke up, and he had to hide.'

'That's about it. It seems to hang together reasonably well. And that means we've got to look for a quite new murderer who had an opportunity of knowing about the appointment between Boris and Alexis. And,' added Harriet, hopefully, 'it needn't be a Bolshevik. It might be somebody with a private motive for doing away with Alexis. How about the da Soto gentleman who got the reversion of Leila Garland? Leila may have told him some nasty story about Alexis.'

Wimsey was silent; his thoughts seemed to be wandering. Presently he said:

'Yes. Only we happen to know that da Soto was playing at the Winter Gardens all that time. But now I want to look at the thing from a quite different point of view. What about this letter? Is it genuine? It's written on ordinary sort of paper, without a water-mark, which might come from anywhere, so that proves nothing, but if it really comes from a foreign gentleman of the name of Boris, why is it written in English? Surely Russian would be safer and more likely, if Boris was really a Russian imperialist. Then again – all that opening stuff about brutal Soviets and Holy Russia is so vague and sketchy. Does it look like the letter of a serious conspirator doing a real job of work? No names mentioned; no details about the Treaty with Poland; and, on the other hand, endless wasted words about an "illustrious ancestress" and "His Serene Highness". It doesn't ring true. It doesn't look like business. It looks like somebody with a very sketchy idea of the way revolutions really work, trying to flatter that poor boob's monomania about his birth.'

'I'll tell you what it does look like,' said Harriet. 'It's like the kind of thing I should put into a detective story if I didn't know a thing about Russia and didn't care much, and only wanted to give a general idea that somebody was a conspirator.'

'That's it!' said Wimsey. 'You're absolutely right. It might have come straight out of one of those Ruritanian romances that Alexis was so fond of.'

'Of course – and now we know why he was fond of them. No wonder! They were all part of the mania. I suppose we ought to have guessed all that.'

'And here's another thing. Do you notice that the first two paragraphs of the letter are very casually coded. The sentences are all run together anyhow, as though the writer didn't much care whether Alexis got them right or wrong. But the minute the good Boris gets down to specific instructions, he starts marking off the ends of his sentences with extra Q's and X's, so as to make sure there will be no mistake in decoding. The Flat-Iron loomed much larger in his mind than Holy Russia and disgruntled Poland.'

'In fact, you think the letter looks like a lure.'

'Yes. But it's difficult to be quite sure, even then, who sent it and why. If Weldon is at the bottom of it, as we originally thought, then we are still bothered by all these alibis. If it isn't Weldon, who is it? If we're really investigating a political plot, then who was Alexis? Why should anybody want to get rid of him? Unless, of course, he genuinely was somebody important, which seems hard to believe. He can't ever have imagined himself to be one of the Russian Imperial house – his age is all wrong. I know we're always hearing tales about the Tsarevitch's having survived the Revolution, but *his* name was Alexei Nicholaivitch, not Pavlo Alexeivitch. And his age would be quite different – and besides, there never was any doubt about *his* descent from Nicholas I. There isn't any note in any of Alexis' books anywhere, is there? – that would tell us who he imagined he might have been.'

'Not a thing.'

Wimsey gathered up the papers from the table and rose to his feet.

'I shall hand these over to Glaisher,' he said. 'They will give him something to think about. I like to see other people doing a spot of work from time to time. Do you realise that it's nearly tea-time and we haven't had any lunch?'

'Time passes when one is pleasantly occupied,' said Harriet, sententiously.

Wimsey put his hat and papers down on the table, opened his mouth to speak, changed his mind, took up his belongings again and marched to the door.

'Cheerio!' he said, amiably.

'Cheerio!' replied Harriet.

He went out. Harriet sat looking at the closed door.

'Well,' she said, 'thank goodness he's given up asking me to marry him. It's much better he should put it out of his mind.'

She must have felt strongly about it, for she repeated the remark several times.

Wimsey absorbed an anomalous meal in the Grill Room, went round to the police-station, handed the decoded letter to the Superintendent, whom it surprised very much, and then ran his car out to Darley. He was still worried by the coincidence about Weldon and his absence from Hinks's Lane during the crucial period. He approached Mr Polwhistle.

'Why, yes, my lord,' said that worthy. 'The fault was in the H.T. leads all right. We tried the mag, and she was working top-hole, and there wasn't nothing wrong with the plugs, so after we'd fiddled about a bit more, young Tom here says, "Well," he says, "only thing I can think of is the leads," he says. Didn't you, Tom?'

'That's right. Me having a motor-bike, and having had trouble with the leads before, on account of the insulation

394

having got worked through, like, against the radiator-fins, I said, "How about the H.T. leads?" And Mr Martin, he says, "That's an idea," and before I could say "knife" he whips the leads out of the clip and gets them off. "Let's have a look, sir," I says. "Never mind looking at the blasted things," he says, "you can't do no bloody good" – begging your pardon – "by looking at 'em," he says. Shove a new pair in and look smart." So I got a bit of H.T. wire out of my bag and I fixes up a new pair of leads and connects 'em up, and no sooner I done so than up she starts, sweet as a nut. What I think, my lord, there must have been a fault in the insulation, see? – what were giving an intermittent short the day before when Mr Martin complained of bad running and starting, and somehow or other the wires might ha' got fused together, and that made a dead short on the Thursday.'

'Very likely,' said Wimsey. 'Did you actually examine the leads afterwards?'

Tom scratched his head.

'Now you ask me,' he said, 'I don't rightly know what happened to them leads. I recollect seein' of Mr Martin a-dangling of them in his hand, but whether he took 'em away or whether he left 'em I couldn't say for certain.'

'Ah!' said Mr Polwhistle, triumphantly, 'but I can, though. When Mr Martin went to start up the engine, he pushed them leads into his pocket, careless-like, and when he pulled out his handkercher to wipe the oil off of his fingers, them leads falls out on the grass. And I picks 'em up, seeing as he wasn't likely to be a-wantin' of 'em and I drops 'em into my little bag, what I always carried, being a tidy-minded man and thinkin' as a bit on 'em might come in useful one day for a motor-bike or such-like. And there they lays to this day, if they ain't been used for nothin' since.'

'I'd like to have a look at them.'

'Nothing easier,' said Mr Polwhistle, producing a small

tool-bag and rooting among a quantity of miscellaneous odds and ends. 'Nothing easier, and here they do be, which just shows you what it is to be a tidy-minded man.'

Wimsey took the pair of leads from his hands.

'H'm – yes – they seem to be fused together just where they pass under the clip.' He jerked the wires apart. 'Nothing wrong with the insulation, though, apparently. Hullo! hullo!'

He ran a finger lightly along one of the leads.

'Here's your trouble,' he said.

Mr Polwhistle also ran his finger along and then withdrew it with a hasty exclamation.

'That's pretty sharp,' he muttered. 'What is it?'

'I suggest that it's the business end of a sewing-needle,' said Wimsey. 'Give us a sharp pen-knife, and we'll soon see.'

When the insulation was opened up the cause of the short-circuit was abundantly plain. A needle had been passed through the lead and broken off short, so as to leave no visible trace of its presence. When the two leads were in place side by side, it was clear that the needle would pass through both, thus effectively bridging the circuit and shorting the spark.

'Well, there now!' said Mr Polwhistle. 'To think of that! That's a nice, dirty trick to play on a gentleman. Who could a-done it beats me. How was it you missed seeing them two leads skewered together that way, Tom?'

'Nobody could positively see it when it was in place,' said Wimsey. 'It would be pushed up under the clip.'

'And Mr Martin jerking the leads out that sudden,' put in Tom, 'it stands to reason I couldn't a-seen it. Of course, if I'd had 'em in my hands afterwards –'

He gazed reproachfully at Mr Polwhistle, who ignored the gaze.

'It's a wonder to me,' said Mr Polwhistle, 'how you came to think of such a thing, my lord.'

'I've seen it done before. It's a very handy way of holding up a motor-cyclist at the beginning of a race, for example.'

'And when you came here asking about them leads, did you expect to find that needle there, my lord?'

'I didn't, Tom. I'd made sure I shouldn't find it. I came here on purpose to prove it wasn't there. Look here, you two, don't say a word about this to anybody.'

'Not, my lord? But we did surely ought to find out what young devil it is that was monkeying about with the gentleman's car.'

'No. I'll take the thing up myself if it's necessary. But it's possible that this – trick may have been played by somebody connected with that business up at the Flat-Iron, and it's best not talked about. You see? Somebody who didn't want Mr Martin to go to Wilvercombe that morning.'

'I see, my lord. Very good. We won't say a word. But that's a queer thing, none the more for that.'

'It is,' said Wimsey, 'very queer.'

It was rather queerer than Mr Polwhistle quite realised, though a peculiar glint in Tom's eye suggested that he at least was beginning to appreciate its full oddity. A needle thrust through the H.T. leads of a two-cylinder car does not produce intermittent firing or erratic running: it stops the ignition dead. Yet on the Wednesday, Mr Martin's Morgan had been running (though not well) up to the moment of his return to Hinks's Lane. And to Wimsey, who knew that Martin was Weldon, the whole thing seemed doubly in-explicable. Why had Weldon gone out of his way to hire a Morgan for his little trip when, with a tent and luggage to carry, he would surely have found a larger vehicle more convenient? Was it another coincidence that he should have particularly asked for a two-cylinder vehicle, which could be put completely out of action with one sewing-needle? True, a Morgan pays a smaller tax than a four-wheeled car, but then, Weldon was not paying the tax. It might cost a little less to hire, but, under the circumstances, why should Weldon skimp himself on a week's carhire?

And yet – and yet – whichever way you took it, it was obviously to everybody's interest to get Mr Weldon away to Wilvercombe, and not keep him hanging about Hinks's Lane. Could it be a coincidence that some practical joker had chosen to put the Morgan out of action at that particular moment? Surely not. But then, who had done it? Somebody who wanted a witness at Darley? Somebody who did not want Weldon to carry out his investigations in Wilvercombe? And why had Weldon complained of bad running the day before? Another coincidence? An intermittent choke, perhaps, which had blown itself out since? Perhaps.

One thing was certain: that Henry Weldon, arriving incognito in dyed hair and dark spectacles to carry on a bit of detective work on his own, had contrived to involve himself in a tangle of coincidence and conjecture which looked almost like the work of a malignant and interfering demon.

Another thing seemed certain, too: that every theory Wimsey had so far formed about the case was utterly and madly wide of the mark.

XXX

THE EVIDENCE OF THE
GENTLEMAN'S GENTLEMAN

'Just so they crossed, and turned, and came again.'
The Second Brother

SATURDAY, 4 JULY

MR. MERVYN BUNTER sat in the bedroom of a cheap hotel in Bloomsbury, keeping his eye on a rather dusty window, adorned with a rather grubby curtain, which he could see just across a very dingy courtyard. It was Mr Bunter's fourth residence in as many days, and he felt that, if this went on much longer, it would be very difficult for him to keep out of view. His first night had been spent in the street, watching the door of a common lodging-house in the Whitechapel district. Thence he had followed his quarry to a gloomy little boarding-house in Brixton. On this occasion he had found a night's lodging over a tobacconist's opposite, and by dint of returning very late and getting up very early, had contrived to keep on Mr Bright's trail the following morning. The chase had then led him all round the more dreary parts of London, following a continual succession of trams and omnibuses. This had been very difficult. Once or twice he had ventured on the same vehicle with Bright, but a dread of being spotted had obliged him to do most of his sleuthing in taxis, which, in that part of the town, were apt to be hard to find and painfully conspicuous when found. The night had been dismally spent in the crypt of St Martin's-in-the-Fields. Now here they were, and Bunter hoped that the ordeal would not last much longer.

He had bought himself a suit of horrible cheap serge, which it gave him acute agony to wear, and he had also purchased a disgusting bowler of curly shape and heavy quality – also a check cap, a soft hat and a subfusc overcoat. Each day he had endeavoured to alter his appearance by successively assuming these repellent garments, carrying the others about with him in paper parcels, until at last he had felt that the perpetual presence of a man with a paper parcel would alarm the fugitive, and had relieved his arm and his mind by depositing the loathly bowler under the table in an eating-house and leaving it to its fate. Now, with a pair of pyjamas in one pocket of the overcoat and a razor and tooth-brush in the other along with the cap, he sat, felt hat in hand, ready to dart out as soon as Bright showed any signs of moving.

During these last four hours, Bright had merely wandered. He had entered no hairdresser's shop and had made no attempt to get work. He seemed to be merely filling in time, or else deliberately confusing his trail. He had gone to a Talkie once or twice, had visited the British Museum, sat for a whole afternoon on a bench in Hyde Park. He had spoken to nobody, except to bus-conductors, tram-conductors, waitresses and other harmless, necessary persons. At present he was sitting at his bedroom window, reading a book by Edgar Wallace which Bunter had seen him purchase the day before at Leicester Square Tube Station.

Suddenly, as Bunter watched him, he shut up the book and stepped back from the window. Peering across the courtyard, Bunter saw him stooping, moving about, raising and lowering his arms in a familiar series of actions. Bunter, who had performed these actions many hundreds of times, was not at a loss. The man was folding and packing pyjamas and other wearing apparel. Bunter hastened down to the office, handed over the key of his room (there was no bill for, being without luggage, he had paid for his bed and breakfast in advance), and stepped out into the street. Here he was fortunate enough to find a cruising taxi with an intelligent-looking driver, who was ready enough to engage in a little detective work. The street was a cul-de-sac and Bunter, getting into the taxi, was driven out into the main road. Here he got out and entered a newspaper shop, leaving the taximan to watch the entrance to the cul-de-sac. Presently, while Bunter, standing just within the doorway, pretended to be absorbed in the morning paper, he saw the driver raise his hand as a signal. A green taxi had driven into the cul-de-sac. So far, so good.

'Go slowly along to the corner,' said Bunter, 'and stand there till the taxi comes out again. If it's the right man, I'll tap on the glass. Then follow him, but not too close. Only don't lose him in the traffic.'

'Right you are. Divorce, eh?'

'Murder,' said Bunter.

'Crikey!' said the driver. 'Police, eh?'

Bunter nodded.

'Gorblimey,' said the driver. 'You don't look it. P'raps you don't mean to. Here we are. Taxi's at the 'otel door. Keep your 'ed down – I'll tell you when 'e comes out.'

So saying, the taximan descended in a leisurely way from his perch and pulled open the bonnet of his machine. A passing policeman gave him a glance, nodded and strode heavily by.

'Just a-coming out now,' said the driver, thrusting his head in at the window, and then, in a louder tone: 'All right, guv'nor – jest a loose connection. She'll start first swing now.'

He crawled up, just as the green taxi swung out of the cul-de-sac. Bunter, peering from behind his newspaper, recognised the pale face of Mr Bright and tapped on the glass. The green taxi passed within a foot of them. Bunter's taxi circled in the road and swung in thirty yards behind.

The green taxi wriggled through some dismal by-streets, emerged into Judd Street and went ahead through Brunswick Square into Guilford Street and down Lamb's Conduit Street and Red Lion Street. It turned to the right into Holborn, then to the left again into Kingsway, and then circled across into Great Queen Street and Long Acre. The following taxi kept it in view without very great difficulty till at last it turned to the left down one of the narrow streets, encumbered with huge drays and stationary carts, which lead down into Covent Garden. At the entrance to the market the green taxi pulled up.

Bunter's taxi was one of the new and superior sort, which have an electric speaking-tube which really works. Bunter pressed the button and addressed his driver.

'If he gets out here, drive past very slowly round that big cart. I shall slip out. Don't look round or take any notice. I'm leaving a ten-bob note on the seat. Go straight on through the market.'

The driver's head nodded assent. From the left-hand window, Bunter saw Bright standing on the pavement settling his fare. Bunter went on his way, and as the taxi passed on the far side of the big cart, he slipped quickly to the pavement. A fruiterer's man, observing this manoeuvre, turned sharply to shout to the driver that his fare was bilking him, but at that moment the hand of the faithful taximan came round and slammed the door shut. The fruiterer's man stood staring, while Bunter, who had exchanged the felt hat for the cap in the taxi, dodged round in front of the cart to look for Bright.

To his great delight he saw Bright standing on the kerb, watching with a pleased air the steady retreat of Bunter's taxi. After a quick scrutiny of his sourroundings, the man appeared satisfied that he was not being followed and set off, briskly, suit-case in hand, towards the market. Bunter took up the trail, squelching his way among the oddments of fruit and cabbage-leaves. The chase led through the market, out into Tavistock Street and down towards the Strand. Here Bright took a bus going West, Bunter pursuing in a fresh taxi. The new trail led only as far as Charing Cross, where Bright got out and hastened into the station-yard. Bunter, hurriedly flinging a florin to his driver, dived in after him.

Bright led the way into the Charing Cross Hotel; Bunter was forced this time to follow closely, lest he should lose his prey. Bright went up to the desk and spoke to the reception-clerk. After a short pause and the display of a visiting-card, a parcel was handed over. Upon receiving it and putting it away in his suit-case, Bright turned sharp round and walked back to the door, passing Bunter within a couple of feet. Their eyes met, but Bright's showed no recognition. He went straight out into the station-yard again.

From now onwards it was hit or miss for Bunter. He had been seen once and it was now more than ever his business to keep out of sight. He waited for a few agonising moments before following, and was just in time to see Bright vanishing down the subway to the Underground.

At this moment, Bunter would have given much for his trusty bowler. He did his best, by again exchanging the cap for the hat as he ran across the yard, and struggling into the subfusc overcoat. It is not necessary to pursue the involved underground journey that occupied the next hour. At the end of it, hare and hound emerged in good order at Piccadilly, having boxed the compass pretty successfully in the interval The next move was to the Corner House, where Bright took the lift.

Now, at the Corner House there are three large floors, and each large floor has two doorways. Yet to get into the same lift as Bright was to challenge disaster. Bunter, like a baffled cat that sees its mouse vanish down a hole, stood and watched the ascending lift. Then he moved to the centre counter and stood, apparently inspecting the array of cakes and sweetmeats, but in reality keeping a sharp look-out on all the lift-doors and the two marble staircases. After ten minutes he felt that he might assume Bright's purpose to be genuinely that of getting refreshment. He made for the nearest staircase and went up it like a lamp-lighter. The lift passed him on a downward journey before he reached the first floor, and he was assailed by a horrible conviction that it was bearing Bright away with it. No matter, the die was cast now. He pushed open the swing door on the first floor and began his slow stroll among the crowded tables.

The sight of bewildered customers looking for a seat is no unusual one in the Corner House. Nobody paid any attention to Bunter until he had made the circuit of the big room and satisfied himself that Bright was not among those present. He went out by the farther door, where he was challenged by the inquiry whether he had been served. He replied that he was looking for a friend and ran on up to the second floor.

This room was the exact twin of the first, except that, instead of a male orchestra in evening dress playing *My Canary has Circles under His Eyes*, it possessed a female orchestra in blue playing excerpts from *The Gondoliers*. Bunter pushed his way slowly through the throng until – his staid heart giving a sudden leap beneath the deplorable blue serge waistcoat – he caught sight of a familiar sandy head and crooked pair of shoulders. Bright was there, seated at a table containing three elderly women, and peacefully eating a grilled chop.

Bunter gazed desperately about him. At first it seemed hopeless to find a seat anywhere near, but at length he espied a girl making-up her face and dabbling at her hair preparatory to leaving. He made a dart for the table and secured the reversion of her chair. He was some time catching the eye of the waitress and ordering a cup of coffee; fortunately Bright seemed to be in no particular hurry with his chop. Bunter asked for the bill as soon as the coffee was brought, and sat patiently, his useful newspaper well spread out before him.

After what seemed an interminable delay, Bright finished his lunch, looked at his watch, called for his bill and rose. Bunter was four behind him in the queue at the pay-desk, and squeezed through the door in time to see the sandy head disappearing down the stairs. At this happy moment, the lift arrived. Bunter bundled into it, and was shot out on the ground floor well ahead of the quarry. He watched Bright out, took up the trail and, after a few minutes of hectic traffic-dodging, found himself in a cinema in the Haymarket, purchasing a ticket for the stalls.

Bright took a seat in the third row of the three-and-sixpennies. Bunter, hastily whispering to the attendant that he didn't care to be too far forward, managed to slip in a couple of rows behind him. Now he could breathe again. From where he sat, he could see the top of Bright's head, outlined against the comparative brightness at the foot of the screen. Ignoring the drama of Love and Passion which shimmered and squeaked its mechanical way from the first misunderstanding to the last lingering kiss, Bunter fixed his eyes on that head with such concentration that the tears stole down his cheeks.

The film shuddered to its close. The lights went up. Bright stood suddenly upright and pushed his way out into the gangway. Bunter prepared to follow, but Bright, instead of making for the nearest exit, merely walked across and passed behind a discreet curtain over which was blazoned in blue fire the legend 'GENTLEMEN.'

Bunter sank down again and waited. Other gentlemen passed in and out, but no Bright returned. Fear smote Bunter. Was there a way out through the cloak-room? The lights dimmed and blacked out, and a Comic started.

Bunter rose up, tripping over the feet of three sniggering girls and an irritable old man, and sneaked gently down the gangway.

As he did so the curtain leading to 'GENTLEMEN' was drawn aside and a man came out. Bunter stared at him as he passed in the soft, thick twilight, but the sharp peak of the silhouette told him that this was a bearded man. He passed Bunter with a muttered apology and went on up the gangway. Bunter proceeded on his way down but, by some instinct, turned at the curtained door and looked back.

He saw the back of the bearded man, outlined against the sudden blue daylight, passing through an exit, and remembered how Wimsey had once said to him: 'Any fool can disguise his face, but it takes a genius to disguise a back.' He had not followed that back through London for five days without knowing every line of it. In a moment he was hurrying up the gangway and out through the exit. Beard or no beard, this was his man.

Two more taxis and then a clear run out to Kensington. This time, Bright appeared to be really going somewhere. His taxi drew up at a neat house in a good quarter; he got out and let himself in with a latch-key. Bunter went on to the next corner and there interrogated his driver.

'Did you see the number of the house they stopped at?'

'Yes, sir. Number 17.'

'Thanks.'

'Divorce, sir?' asked the man, with a grin.

'Murder,' said Bunter.

'Crikey!' This appeared to be the natural reaction to murder. 'Well,' said the taximan, ' 'ope 'e swings for it.' and drove off.

Bunter glanced about him. He dared not pass Number 17. Bright might still be on the watch, and both the cap and the felt hat were now, he felt, war-worn veterans of whom nothing more could be asked in the way of disguise. He saw a chemist's shop and went in.

'Can you tell me,' he asked, 'who lives at No. 17?'

'Why, yes,' said the chemist, 'gentleman of the name of Morecambe.'

'Morecambe?' A great piece of jig-saw seemed to fall into place in Bunter's mind with an almost audible click. 'Littlish gentleman with one shoulder a bit higher than the other?'

'That's right.'

'Reddish hair.'

'Yes, sir; reddish hair and beard.'

'Oh, he wears a beard?'

'Oh, yes sir. Gentleman in the City, he is. Lived here as long as I can remember. Very pleasant gentleman. Did you want to know—?'

'Yes,' said Bunter. 'The fact is, I heard there might be a vacancy for a gentleman's personal attendant at No. 17, and I thought I'd like to know what the family was like before applying for it.'

'Oh, I see. Yes, You'd find it a nice family. Quiet. No children. Mrs Morecambe is a nice lady. Good-looking in her time, I should say. Used to be on the stage, I'm told, but that must have been a good long time ago. Two maids kept and everything quite as you might wish to find it.'

Bunter expressed his gratitude and left the shop to send a telegram to Lord Peter.

The chase was ended.

XXXI

THE EVIDENCE OF THE
HABERDASHER'S ASSISTANT

'Ha! well! what next?
You are the cupbearer of richest joy—
But it was a report, a lie.'
The Second Brother

MONDAY, 6 JULY

'I LOOK at it this way,' said Superintendent Glaisher. 'If this here Bright is Morecambe, and Mrs Morecambe is in cahoots with Weldon, then, likewise, Weldon and Bright – so to call him – are in cahoots together.'

'Undoubtedly,' said Wimsey, 'but if you think that this identification is going to make life one grand, sweet song for you, you are mistaken. All it has done so far is to bust up every conclusion we have so far come to.'

'Yes, my lord; undoubtedly the thing still has a hitch in it. Still, every little helps, and this time we've got more than a little to go on with. Suppose we work out where we stand. First of all, if Bright is Morecambe, he isn't a hair-dresser; therefore he had no legitimate call to buy that razor; therefore his tale about the razor is all eyewash, like we always thought it was; therefore, humanly speaking there's not much doubt that Paul Alexis didn't commit suicide, but was murdered.'

'Exactly,' said Wimsey, 'and since we have devoted a great deal of time and thought to the case on the assumption that it was a murder, it's a convenience to know that the assumption is probably correct.'

'So it is. Well, now, if Weldon and Morecambe are both in this together, it's likely that the motive for the murder is what we thought – getting hold of Mrs W.'s money – or isn't it?'

'It's likely,' agreed Wimsey.

'Then what's all this Bolshevik business got to do with it?' demanded Inspector Umpelty.

'Lots,' said Wimsey. 'Look here; I'm going to offer you two more identifications. First of all, I suggest that Morecambe was the bearded friend who came to stay with Weldon at Fourways Farm at the end of February. And secondly, I suggest that Morecambe was the bearded gentleman who approached Mr Sullivan of Wardour Street and asked him for the photograph of a Russian-looking girl. It is interesting that Mr Horrock's cultivated theatrical mind should have associated him immediately with Richard III.'

Inspector Umpelty looked puzzled, but the Superintendent smacked his hand on the table.

'The hunchback!' he cried.

'Yes – but they seldom play Richard as a real hunch-back nowadays. A slight suggestion of crookedness is what they usually give you – just that scarcely perceptible twistiness of shoulder that Morecambe has about him.'

'Of course, that's plain enough, now we know about the beard,' said Glaisher. 'But why the photograph?'

'Let's try and put the story together in the right order, as far as we've got it,' suggested Wimsey. 'First of all, here is Weldon, over head and ears in debt, and raising money against his expectations from his mother. Very well. Now, early this year, Mrs Weldon comes to Wilvercombe, and begins to take a great deal of interest in Paul Alexis. In February, she definitely announces that she means to marry Alexis, and possibly she is foolish enough to admit that, if she does marry him, she will leave him all her money. Almost immediately after this announcement, Morecambe comes to stay at Weldon's farm. And within a week or two, the strange coded letters with the foreign stamps begin to arrive for Alexis.'

'That's clear enough.'

'Now, Alexis has always hinted to people that there is a mystery about his birth. He fancies that he is of noble Russian descent. I suggest that the first letter —'

'One minute, my lord. Who do you suppose wrote those letters?'

'I *think* Morecambe wrote them, and got them posted by some friend in Warsaw. As I see it, Morecambe is the brains of the conspiracy. He writes his first letter, no doubt in plain English, hinting at Imperialist activities in Russia and grandiose prospects for Paul Alexis, if he can prove his descent – but, of course, there must be complete secrecy about the whole thing.'

'Why the secrecy?'

'To preserve the romantic atmosphere. Alexis, poor egg, swallows this, hook, line and sinker. He promptly writes back telling the so-called Boris everything he knows or imagines about himself. The code is henceforth used, of course, to keep Alexis in the proper frame of mind and give him a nice toy to play with. Then, from the little bits of family tradition that Alexis supplies, "Boris" (that is, Morecambe) builds up a suitable genealogical fantasy to fit in with these data, and outlines a marvellous plot to place Alexis on the Imperial throne of Russia. Meanwhile, Alexis reads books about Russian history, and obligingly assists his murderer to bait and arm the trap. Eventually, Boris tells him that the conspiracy is nearly ready to take effect; and that is when we find Alexis indulging in mysterious hints and prophecies of his forthcoming apotheosis.'

'Just a minute,' said Glaisher. 'I should have thought that the simplest way for Morecambe would have been to get Alexis to break off with Mrs Weldon on the grounds that he had to go to Russia and be a Tsar. Surely that would have attained the object of the plot without bumping off the poor little blighter.'

'Well, would it?' said Wimsey. 'In the first place, I rather imagine that Mrs Weldon's romantic reaction to a notion of that kind would have been to hand over large sums of money to Alexis for the Imperial war-chest, which would hardly have suited Messrs Weldon and Morecambe. Secondly, if Alexis did break off the engagement and they trusted to that – what would happen next? They couldn't go on for the remainder of all their lives writing code-letters about imaginary conspiracies. Some time or other, Alexis would wake up to the fact that the plot was never going to materialise. He would tell Mrs Weldon and in all probability the *status quo* would be restored. And the lady would be keener than ever on the marriage if she thought her fiancé really was the unacknowledged Tsar of all the Russias. No; the safest way was to tell Alexis to keep the whole thing absolutely secret, and then, when the time came, they could wipe him out finally and completely.'

'Yes – I see that.'

'Now we come to Leila Garland. I don't think there is any doubt that Alexis deliberately pushed her off on to our conceited young friend, da Soto – though naturally neither da Soto nor she would admit that possibility for a moment. I fancy Antoine has got the right idea about that; he is probably an observer of considerable experience in these matters. Leila would be a very dangerous person if she were allowed to know anything about the pretended plot. She would be bound to talk, and they didn't want talk. We've got to remember that the object of all this business was to stage a suicide. Young emperors on the point of leading successful revolutions do not commit suicide. To tell Leila about the plot was to tell the world: therefore, Leila must be got rid of, because, if she remained closely in contact with

Alexis, it would be almost impossible to keep her in ignorance.'

'Sounds as though young Alexis was a bit of a blackguard,' said Inspector Umpelty. 'First, he chucks his girl. Secondly, he leads poor old Mrs Weldon up the garden, by pretending to go in with an engagement he doesn't mean to carry out.'

'No,' said Wimsey. 'You don't allow for the Imperial outlook. A prince in exile may form irregular attachments, but, when the call comes to him to take up his imperial station, all personal ties must be sacrificed to his public duty. A mere kept woman, like Leila, can be simply dismissed or handed over to somebody else. A person to whom he is bound by more honourable ties will also have to be sacrificed, but with more ceremony. We do not know, and we never shall know, exactly what Alexis meant to do about Mrs Weldon. We have her word for it that he tried to prepare her for some grand and surprising development in the near future, though, naturally, she put the wrong interpretation on the thing. I imagine that what Alexis intended to do was to write her a letter, after his departure for Warsaw, telling her what had happened to him and offering her his hospitality at his Imperial court. The whole affair would have been surrounded with a halo of romance and splendour and self-sacrifice, and no doubt Mrs Weldon would have enjoyed it down to the ground. There's one thing: although, before all this Russian business started, Alexis had Mrs Weldon completely under his thumb, he apparently always refused to take any large sums of money from her – and that, I think, is greatly to his credit, and shows that he had the instincts of a gentleman, if not necessarily of a prince.'

'That's true,' said Glaisher. 'I suppose, if the plot had never been started, he would have married her.'

'Oh, yes, I should think so. He'd have married her and

done his duty by her according to his own lights, which were probably – well, continental. He would have been a charming husband to her and kept a mistress in a discreet and decent manner.'

Inspector Umpelty seemed disposed to quarrel with the term 'decent,' but Wimsey hurried on with his argument.

'I fancy, too, that Alexis may have shown a little reluctance to take this course with Leila and Mrs Weldon. He may have been really fond of Leila; or he may have felt uncomfortable about letting Mrs Weldon down. So that was why they invented Feodora.'

'And who *was* Feodora.'

'Feodora was no doubt supposed to be the lady of lofty lineage destined to be the bride of the new Tsar Pavlo Alexeivitch. What was easier than to go to a theatrical agent, find the photograph of a not-too-well-known lady of Russian extraction, and send it to Alexis as the portrait of the Princess Feodora, the lovely lady who was waiting and working for him in exile until the time should come for her to take her place beside him on the Imperial throne? Those blessed romances that Alexis was so fond of are full of that kind of thing. There would be letters, perhaps, from Feodora, full of tender anticipation. She would be already in love with the Grand-Duke Pavlo from all she had heard of him. The glamour of the whole idea would bewitch him. And besides, it would be his duty to his people to marry Feodora. How could he hesitate? A glance at that very beautiful face, crowned with its regal head-dress of pearls—'

'Oh!' said Glaisher. 'Yes, of course. That would be one reason why they hit on that particular photograph.'

'Of course. No doubt the pearls were merely the best Woolworth, like the whole pathetic illusion, but these things serve their purpose, Glaisher, they serve their purpose. My God, Glaisher – when you think of that poor silly devil, going to his death on a lonely rock, with his brain spinning with the idea of being crowned Emperor—'

Wimsey broke off, shaken by an unwonted vehemence of feeling. The two policemen shuffled their feet sympathetically.

'Well, it does seem a shame, my lord, and that's a fact,' said Glaisher. 'Let's hope he died quick, without knowing any better.'

'Ah!' said Wimsey, 'but how did he die? That's the snag, you know. Well, never mind that for the moment. What next? Oh, the three hundred pounds in gold. That's a funny little incident, and very nearly upset the conspiracy altogether.

'I can't believe that that was any part of the plot as originally worked out. Morecambe couldn't have foreseen the opportunity of collecting that gold. I think that must have been Paul Alexis' own contribution to the romance. He had probably read in books about gold – about its passing current everywhere, and all that – and thought it would somehow be a fine thing to set out to conquer a throne with a beltful of gold. It was ridiculous, of course – an absurd little sum, bulky and awkward to carry about – but it was gold. Gold has its glitter, you know. As somebody says, "the glitter is the gold". That sounds like relativity physics, but it's psychological fact. If you were a romantic young prince, Glaisher, or thought you were, would you rather pay your bills with a few dirty bits of paper, or with this?'

He put his hand in his pocket and drew out a handful of gold sovereigns. They rolled ringing over the table as he threw them down, and Glaisher and Umpelty flung out eager hands to catch them as they spun away in the lamplight. They picked them up and weighed them in their palms; they held them between their fingers, passing inquisitive fingers along the milled edges and over the smooth relief of the gleaming George and Dragon.

414

'Yes,' said Wimsey, 'they feel pleasant, don't they? There are ten of them there, and they're worth no more than paper pounds,* and to me they're actually worth nothing, because, being a tom-fool, I can't bring myself to spend them. But they're gold. I wouldn't mind possessing £300 worth of them, though they might weigh five pounds avoirdupois and be an infernal nuisance. But the queer thing is this – that that extra five pounds of weight just disturbed the very delicate balance between the corpse and the water. The specific gravity of a dead body is *just* less than sufficient to sink it – but only just. A very heavy pair of boots or a belt stuffed with gold is enough to carry it down and wedge it among the Grinder rocks – as you know to your cost, Umpelty. It would have been uncommonly awkward for the conspirators if Alexis had never been found. In time Mrs Weldon would have come to believe in his death, I daresay – but she might have squandered a fortune first, in hunting for him.'

'It's a queer story altogether,' said Glaisher, 'and what nobody that hadn't been through it all from the beginning as you might say would hardly be disposed to believe. But now, my lord, allowing that it was all worked out as you say, how about the murder?'

'Exactly. As regards the murder I frankly admit we're not much further on than before. The preliminaries are all easy enough. First of all, somebody must have come along to have a look at the place. I don't quite know who that was, but I think I can guess. Somebody who already knew the lie of the land, from having stayed here before. Somebody who had a car to spin about the country in. Somebody who had a very good excuse for being in the neighbourhood and respectable friends whose guests were above suspicion.'

'Mrs Morecambe!'

* The acute reader will discern that at the date of this story, Great Britain had not yet gone off the Gold Standard.

'Just so. Mrs Morecambe. Possibly Mr Morecambe also. We can soon find out whether that delightful couple spent a week-end at Heathbury Vicarage any time within the last few months.'

'Yes, they did,' put in Umpelty. 'The lady was here for a fortnight at the end of February and her husband came down for one weekend. They told us that when we made our inquiries, but we didn't attach any importance to it at the time.'

'Of course not. Very well. Then, at the moment when everything is ready to poop off, the rest of the gang arrive. Morecambe gets himself up as a hairdresser and establishes his identity round about the neighbourhood. He has to do that, because he wants to purchase a razor in a way which it is difficult to trace. You may say, why a razor at all, when they must have known that Alexis didn't shave? Well, I can imagine why. It's quieter than a pistol and it's a typical suicide's weapon. And it's very safe and sure, and much handier to carry about than, say, a carving-knife. And if any question was raised about it, Morecambe could always come forward with a convincing story about how he had given the razor to Alexis.'

'Ah! I was thinking about that. Would he have come forward, do you suppose, if you hadn't put that bit in the paper?'

'Difficult to say. But I imagine that he would have waited to see how things went. He would probably have attended the inquest, as a casual spectator, and then if the coroner showed any signs of not accepting the suicide theory, he would have risen up and put the matter beyond doubt with a few well-chosen words. You see, the beauty of his itinerant hairdresser impersonation was that it afforded him an excellent excuse for appearing and disappearing like a Cheshire cat, and also changing his name. By the way, I think we shall find that he really did live in Manchester at some time or another, and so knew just how much dope to dole out about derelict streets and departed hairdressers' shops in that city.'

'I take it, then, that he wears a beard in ordinary life.'

'Oh, yes. He just shaved it off when he began his impersonation. Then, when he went back to London, he had only to get a false beard sent to him at a hotel under a different name, and wear it for the brief period of his taxi-ride to Kensington. If the attendant at the picture-palace happened to notice a gentleman putting on a false beard in the cloak-room – which he may not have done – it would not be his business to interfere, and Morecombe had done his very best to throw off any shadowers. If Bunter hadn't been uncommonly persevering and uncommonly quick, he'd have lost the trail twenty times over. As it was, he very nearly missed Morecombe in the cinema. Supposing Bunter had followed Morecambe into the cloak-room. Morecambe would have postponed the beard business and there would have been another chase, but by having the wits to keep outside, he gave Morecambe the impression that the coast was clear. Scotland Yard is keeping an eye on Morecambe's house now, but I expect they will find that the gentleman is ill in bed, being attended by his devoted wife. When his beard has grown again, he will emerge; and meantime, Mrs Morecambe, who was an actress and knows something about make-up, will see to it that there is always a beard fit for inspection when the maid comes in to do the room.'

'So much for Morecambe,' said Glaisher. 'Now, how about Weldon? We'd pretty well put him out of the thing. Now we've got to bring him back. He comes along in his Morgan, two days before the murder is due to take place, and he camps in Hinks's Lane, which somebody's been good enough to find out all about beforehand. Mrs Morecambe, I suppose – very good. He accounts for his presence on the scene by a cock-and-bull tale about keeping an eye on his mother's love-affairs. All right. But what I want to know is, why did he come and mix himself up in the thing at all, taking all those risks? He wasn't there to do the murder, because we know where he was at 1.30, if not at 1.55, and we can't fit the times in anyhow, even supposing Perkins is a liar, which we can't prove. And he wasn't there to ride the mare down to the Flat-Iron, because we know where he was at twelve o'clock—'

'Do we?' said Harriet, gently.

She had joined the committee-meeting half-way through the session, and had been sitting quietly in an armchair, smoking, with her hat on her knee.

'Yes, do we?' said Wimsey. 'We thought we did when Mrs Morecambe was supposed to be an unimpeachable witness, but do we now? I think I see a gleam in Miss Vane's eye that suggests she is about to put one over on us. Speak. I am bound to hear! What has Robert Templeton been discovering?'

'Mr Weldon,' said Harriet, 'was not doing anything nefarious in Wilvercombe on Thursday, 18th. He wasn't doing anything in Wilvercombe. He never was in Wilvercombe. He didn't buy collars. He didn't go to the Winter Gardens. Mrs Morecambe arrived alone and she left alone, and there's no evidence that Mr Weldon was with her at any point of the journey.'

'O my prophetic soul! There goes my reputation! I said that the two o'clock alibi would be broken, and it's standing like the Flat-Iron Rock. I said the Wilvercombe alibi would stand, and it has broken in pieces like a potter's vessel. I'll go no more a-sleuthing with you, fair maid. O, now, for ever farewell the tranquil mind! Farewell content! Farewell, Othello's occupation's gone. Are you sure about it?'

'Pretty well. I went to the men's outfitting and asked for collars like the ones my husband bought on the 18th. Had I the bill? No. What kind of collars? Well, collars, just ordinary collars. What was my husband like? I described Henry Weldon and his dark spectacles. Nobody remembered him. Would they look up the day-book? Well, they looked up the paper thing that twizzles round in the till, and found the item. Oh, yes – the assistant remembered *those* collars. Sold to a lady. A lady? Oh, yes, my sister-in-law, no doubt. I described Mrs Morecambe. Yes, that was the lady. Was that the only sale of collars that morning? It was. Then those must be the collars. So I bought six of them – here they are – and asked whether the gentleman had been outside in the car. Gentlemen are *so* funny about going into shops. No, no gentleman. The assistant had taken the parcel out to the car, which was empty. So then I went to the Winter Gardens. I knew, of course, that they had been asked about Weldon, but *I* asked them about Mrs Morecambe, and I found an attendant who remembered her by her appearance and get-up, and by the fact that she had taken notes of the programme. For Weldon, naturally. After that I tried the bobby on point-duty in the Market Square. Such a nice, intelligent bobby. He remembered the car, because of the funny number, and he'd noticed that there was no one in it except the lady who was driving. He'd noticed it again when it came away: still only the lady in it. So that's that. Of course, Mrs Morecambe may have dropped Henry Weldon at some point between Darley and Wilvercombe, but as for being *in* Wilvercombe – that I'll swear he wasn't; at any rate, he didn't arrive in the Square with her, as he said.'

'No,' said Glaisher. 'And it's pretty clear now where he was. He was riding that damned mare along the beach – out at eleven o'clock and back at 12.30, or thereabouts. But why?'

'That's clear, too. He was the Rider from the Sea. But he still didn't kill Paul Alexis. Who did?'

'Well, my lord,' said Umpelty, 'we'll have to go back to

our first idea. Weldon brought bad news about this here conspiracy, and Alexis killed himself.'

'With Morecambe's razor? No, it's all wrong, Inspector. It's all *wrong*.'

'Hadn't we better ask Weldon what he knows about it all? If we confront him with what we know about Morecambe and the letter and all that, he may come clean. If he was along there at 12.15, he must have seen Alexis, anyhow.'

Wimsey shook his head.

'Deep waters,' he said, 'deep waters. Look here! I've an idea we've been working this thing from the wrong end. If only we knew more about those papers that Alexis sent to "Boris", they might tell us something. Where do you suppose they are? You may say, in Warsaw – but I don't think so. I fancy Warsaw was only an accommodation address. Everything that went there probably came back to Morecambe.'

'Then perhaps we'll find them in London,' suggested Glaisher, hopefully.

'Very much perhaps. The man who planned this show is no fool. If he told Alexis to destroy all his papers, he'll hardly have risked keeping anything of that sort himself. But we could try. Have we enough evidence against him to justify a search-warrant?'

'Why, yes.' Glaisher pondered. 'If Morecambe's identified as Bright, then he's been giving false information to the police. We could detain him on suspicion and go through his place in Kensington. The London fellows are keeping tabs on him now, but we didn't want to be in too much of a hurry. We thought, maybe, the real murderer might be getting in touch with him. You see, there must be another party to the business – the chap who did the actual job, and we don't know who he is from Adam. But of course, there's this to it – the longer we leave Morecambe to himself, the more time he's got to make away with the evidence. It may be you're right, my lord, and we ought to pull him in. Only you'll bear in mind, my lord, that if we do detain him, we'll have to make a charge. There's such a thing as Habeas Corpus.'

'All the same,' said Wimsey, 'I think you'll have to risk that. I don't suppose you'll find any papers, but you may find something else. The paper and ink used to write the letters, perhaps, and books of reference about Russia. Books aren't as easy to get rid of as papers. And we've got to find out the exact connection between Morecambe and Weldon.'

'They're working on that now, my lord.'

'Good. After all, people don't conspire to commit murder for the fun of the thing. Does Mrs Weldon know anything about the Morecambes?'

'No,' said Harriet. 'I asked her. She's never heard of them.'

'Then the connection won't go too far back. It'll belong to London or Huntingdonshire. What *is* Morecambe, by the way?'

'Described as a Commission Agent, my lord.'

'Oh, is he? That's a description that hides a multitude of sins. Well, go to it, Superintendent. As for me, I'll have to do something drastic to restore my self-respect. Seeking the bubble reputation even in the cannon's mouth.'

'Oh yeah?' Harriet grinned impishly. 'When Lord Peter gets these fits of quotation he's usually on to something.'

'Sez you,' retorted Wimsey. 'I am going, straight away, to make love to Leila Garland.'

'Well, look out for da Soto.'

'I'll chance da Soto,' said Wimsey. 'Bunter!'

'My lord?'

Bunter emerged from Wimpeys' bedroom, looking as prim as though he had never sleuthed in a bad bowler through the purlieus of South London.

'I wish to appear in my famous impersonation of the perfect Lounge Lizard – *imitation très difficile.*'

'Very good, my lord. I suggest the fawn-coloured suit we do not care for, with the autumn-leaf socks and our outsized amber cigarette-holder.'

'As you will, Bunter; as you will. We must stoop to conquer.'

He kissed his hand gallantly to the assembly and vanished into his inner chamber.

XXXII

THE EVIDENCE OF THE FAMILY TREE

'A hundred years hence, or, it may be, more,
I shall return and take my dukedom back.'
                                        Death's Jest-Book

MONDAY, 6 JULY

THE conquest of Leila Garland followed the usual course. Wimsey pursued her into a tea-shop, cut her out neatly from the two girl-friends who accompanied her, fed her, took her to the pictures and caried her off to the Bellevue for a cocktail.

The young lady showed an almost puritanical discretion in clinging to the public rooms of that handsome hotel, and drove Wimsey almost to madness by the refinement of her table-manners. Eventually, however, he manoeuvred her into an angle of the lounge behind a palm-tree, where they could not be overlooked and where they were far enough from the orchestra to hear each other speak. The orchestra was one of the more infuriating features of the Bellevue, and kept up an incessant drivel of dance-tunes from four in the afternoon till ten at night. Miss Garland awarded it a moderate approval, but indicated that it did not quite reach the standard of the orchestra in which Mr da Soto played a leading part.

Wimsey gently led the conversation to the distressing publicity which Miss Garland had ben obliged to endure in connection with the death of Alexis. Miss Garland agreed that it had not been nice at all. Mr da Soto had been very much upset. A gentleman did not like his girl-friend to have to undergo so much unpleasant questioning.

Lord Peter Wimsey commended Miss Garland on the discretion she had shown throughout.

Of course, said Leila, Mr Alexis was a dear boy, and always a perfect gentleman. And most devoted to her. But hardly a manly man. A girl could not help preferring manly men, who had *done* something. Girls were like that! Even though a man might be of very good family and not *obliged* to do anything, he might still *do* things, might he not? (Languishing glance at Lord Peter.) That was the kind of man Miss Garland liked. It was, she thought, much finer to be a noble-born person who *did* things than a nobly-born person who only *talked* about nobility.

'But was Alexis nobly born?' inquired Wimsey.

'Well, he *said* he was – but how is a girl to know? I mean, it's easy to talk, isn't it? Paul – that is, Mr Alexis – used to tell wonderful stories about himself, but it's *my* belief he was making it all up. He was such a boy for romances and story-books. But I said to him, "What's the good of it?" I said. "Here you are," I said, "not earning half as much money as some people I could name, and what good does it do, even if you're the Tsar of Russia?" I said.'

'Did he say he was the Tsar of Russia?'

'Oh, no – he only said that if his great-great-grandmother or somebody had married somebody he might have been somebody very important, but what I said was, "What's the good of saying If," I said. "And anyhow," I said, "they've done away with all these royalties now," I said, "so what are you going to get out of it anyway?" He made me tired, talking about his great-grandmother, and in the end he shut up and didn't say anything more about it. I suppose he tumbled to it that a girl couldn't be terribly interested in people's great-grandmothers.'

'Who did he think his great-grandmother was, then?'

'I'm sure *I* don't know. He did go on so. He wrote it all down for me one day, but I said to him, "You make my head ache," I said, "and besides, from what you say, none of your people were any better than they should have been," I said, "so I don't see what you've got to boast about. It doesn't sound very respectable to me," I said, "and if princesses with plenty of money can't keep respectable," I said, "I don't see why anybody should put any blame on girls who have to earn their own living." That's what I told him.'

'Very true indeed,' said Wimsey. 'He must have had a bit of a mania about it.'

'Loopy,' said Miss Garland, allowing the garment of refinement to slip aside for a moment. 'I mean to say, I think he must have been a little silly about it, don't you?'

'He seems to have given more thought to the thing than it was worth. Wrote it all down, did he?'

'Yes, he did. And then, one day he came bothering about it again. Asked me if I'd still got the paper he'd written. "I'm sure I don't know," I said. "I'm not so frightfully interested in it as all that." I said. "Do you think I keep every bit of your handwritting?" I said, "like the heroines in story-books?" I said. "Because," I said, "let me tell you I don't," I said. "Anything that's *worth* keeping, I'll keep, but not rubbishing bits of paper."'

Wimsey remembered that Alexis had offended Leila towards the end of their connection by a certain lack of generosity.

' "If you want things kept," I said, "why don't you give them to that old woman that's so struck on you?" I said. "If you're going to marry her," I said, "she's the right person to give things to," I said, "if you want them kept," And he said he particularly didn't want the paper kept, and I said, "Well, then, what are you worrying about?" I said. So he said, if I hadn't kept it, that was all right, then, and I said I

425

reely didn't know if I'd kept it or not, and he said, yes, but he wanted the paper burnt and I wasn't to tell anybody about what he'd said – about his great-grandmother, I mean – and I said. "if you think I've nothing better to talk to my friends about than you and your great-grandmother," I said, "you're mistaken," I said. Only fancy! Well, of course, after that, we weren't such friends as we had been – at least, I wasn't, though I will say he always was very fond of me. But I couldn't stand the way he went on. Silly, I call it.'

'And *had* you burnt the paper?'

'Why, I'm sure I don't know. You're nearly as bad as he is, going on about the paper. What does the stupid paper matter, anyhow?'

'Well,' said Wimsey, 'I'm inquisitive about papers. Still, if you've burnt it, you've burnt it. It's a pity. If you could have found that paper, it might be worth–'

The beautiful eyes of Leila directed their beams upon him like a pair of swivelling head-lamps rounding a corner on a murky night.

'Yes?' breathed Leila.

'It might be worth having a look at,' replied Wimsey, coolly. 'Perhaps if you had a hunt among your odds-and-ends, you know –'

Leila shrugged her shoulders. This sounded troublesome.

'I can't see what you want that old bit of paper for.'

'Nor do I, till I see it. But we might have a shot at looking for it, eh, what?'

He smiled. Leila smiled. She felt she had grasped the idea.

'What? You and me? Oh, *well!* – but I don't see that I could exactly take you round to my place, *could* I? I mean to say –'

'Oh, that'll be all right,' said Wimsey, swiftly. 'You're surely not afraid of *me*. You see, I'm trying to *do* something, and I want your help.'

'I'm sure, anything I can do – provided it's nothing Mr da

Soto would object to. He's a terribly jealous boy, you know.'

'I should be just the same in his place. Perhaps he would like to come too and help hunt for the paper?'

Leila smiled and said she did not think that would be necessary, and the interview ended, where it was in any case doomed to end, in Leila's crowded and untidy apartment.

Drawers, bags, boxes, overflowing with intimate and multifarious litter which piled itself on the bed, streamed over the chairs and swirled ankle-deep upon the floor! Left to herself, Leila would have wearied of the search in ten minutes, but Wimsey, bullying, cajoling, flattering, holding out golden baits, kept her remorselessly to her task. Mr da Soto, arriving suddenly to find Wimsey holding an armful of lingerie, while Leila ferreted among a pile of crumpled bills and picture postcards which had been bundled into the bottom of a trunk, thought the scene was set for a little genteel blackmail and started to bluster. Wimsey told him curtly not to be a fool, pushed the lingerie into his reluctant hands and started to hunt through a pile of magazines and gramophone records.

Curiously enough, it was da Soto who found the paper. Leila's interest in the business seemed rather to cool after his arrival – was it possible that she had had other designs upon Lord Peter, with which Luis' sulky presence interfered? – whereas da Soto, suddenly tumbling to the notion that the production of the paper might turn out to be of value to somebody, gradually became more and more interested.

'I wouldn't be that surprised, honey-bunch,' he observed, 'If you left it in one of those story-books you're always reading, same like you always do with your bus-tickets.'

'That's an idea,' said Wimsey, eagerly.

They turned their attention to a shelf stacked with cheap fiction and penny novelettes. The volumes yielded quite a surprising collection, not only of bus-tickets, but also of cinema-ticket counterfoils, bills, chocolate-papers, envelopes, picture-cards, cigarette-cards and other assorted book-markers, and at length da Soto, taking *The Girl who gave All* by the spine and administering a brisk shake, shot out from between its passionate leaves a folded sheet of writing-paper.

'What do you say to that?' he inquired, picking it up quickly. 'If that isn't the fellow's handwriting you can call me a deaf-and-dumb elephant with four left feet.'

Leila grabbed the paper from him.

'Yes, that's it, all right,' she observed. 'A lot of stuff, if you ask me. *I* never could make head or tail of it, but if it's any good to you, you're welcome to it.'

Wimsey cast a rapid glance at the spidery lines of the family tree which sprawled from top to bottom of the sheet.

'So that's who he thought he was. Yes – I'm glad you didn't chuck this away, Miss Garland. It may clear things up quite a lot.'

Here Mr da Soto was understood to say something about dollars.

'Ah, yes,' said Wimsey. 'It's lucky it's me and not Inspector Umpelty, isn't it? Umpelty might run you in for suppressing important evidence.' He grinned in da Soto's baffled face. 'But I won't say – seeing that Miss Garland has turned her place upside-down to oblige me – that she mightn't get a new frock out of it if she's a good girl. Now, listen to me, my child. When did you say Alexis gave you this?'

'Oh, ages ago. When him and me were first friends. I can't remember exactly. But I know it's donkey's years since I read that silly old book.'

'Donkey's years being, I take it, rather less than a year ago – unless you knew Alexis before he came to Wilvercombe.'

'That's right. Wait a minute. Look! Here's a bit of a cinema-ticket stuck in at another page, with the date on it. Ooh, yes! November 15th – that's right. I remember now.

We went to the pictures and then Paul came round to see me afterwards and told me a lot about himself. It was the same evening. He expected me to be terribly excited about it all.'

'November; you're sure?'

'Yes, sure.'

'At any rate, it was some time before those funny letters started to come for him?'

'Oh, yes, ages. And after the letters started to come, he shut up about it, and wanted his silly old paper back. I told you that before.'

'I know you did. All right. Now, sit down. I want to look at this.'

This was the paper:

FRANCIS JOSIAS
D. of Saxe-Coburg-Gotha (1678–1735)
|

Charles Marie Levannier = Anastasia (illegitimate)
(of the French Legation) | b. 1728
|

Nicholas I = Charlotte, *b.* 1770
Tsar of Russia | (youngest of seven children)
(morganatically in
1815)
|

Nicolaevna (Nicole) = Gaston, natural son
of Louis-Philippe,
b. 1820, *m.* 1847
|

Capt. Stefan Ivanovitch Krasky = Louise, *b.* 1848
m. 1871
|

Alexis Gregorovitch Vorodin = Mélanie, *b.* 1883
|

Pavlo Alexeivitch Vorodin, *b.* 1909

'H'm!' said Wimsey. 'I wonder where he got this from. I never knew that Nicholas I married anybody but Charlotte-Louise of Prussia.'

'I remember about that,' said Leila. 'Paul said that that marriage couldn't be proved. He kept on about that. He said, if only it could be proved he'd be a prince or something. He was always worrying over that Charlotte-person – horrid old wretch she must have been, too. Why, she was forty-five if she was a day, and then she went and had a baby. I wonder it didn't kill her. It ought to have, I'm sure.'

'Nicholas I must have been quite a kid at the time. Let's see – 1815 – that would be when he was in Paris after the Waterloo business. Yes, I see – Charlotte's father was something to do with the French legation; that fits in all right. I suppose he had this illegitimate daughter of Duke Francis pushed off on to him when he was in Saxe-Coburg. She went back and lived with him in Paris and had seven children, and the youngest of them was Charlotte, who, I suppose, somehow got hold of the young Emperor and cradle-snatched him.'

' "The old beast!" I said to Paul, when he took up with this Mrs Weldon. "Well," I said, "marrying old hags must run in your family," I said. But he wouldn't hear anything against Great-Great-Grandma Charlotte. She was something quite out of the way, by his account of it. A sort of what's-her-name.'

'Ninon de l'Enclos?'

'Yes, I daresay – if that's the old wretch who went on having lovers till she was about a hundred and fifty. I don't think it's nice at all. I can't think what the men were thinking about. Potty, they must have been, if you ask me. Anyway, what you said is about right. She was a widow several times over – Charlotte, I mean. She married some Count or other or General Somebody – I forget – and had something to do with politics.'

'Everybody in Paris in 1815 had to do with politics,' said Wimsey. 'I can see Charlotte all right, playing her cards carefully among the new nobility. Well, this elderly beauty marries, or doesn't marry, the young Tsar and produces a daughter and calls her Nicolaevna after her illustrious papa. Being in France, they call the child Nicole. What happens next? Old Charlotte goes on playing her cards well, and, having tasted royal blood, so to speak, thinks she'll worm herself in on the Bourbons. There are no legitimate princes she can bag for her daughter, but she thinks the wrong side of the blanket better than being left out in the cold, and marries the girl off to some little accident of Louis-Phillippe's.'

'A nice set of people they must have been in those days!'

'So-so. I daresay Charlotte may really have thought she *was* married to Nicholas, and been frightfully disappointed at finding her claims set aside. They must have been one too many for her there – Nicholas and his diplomats. Just when she thought she had hooked her fish so well – the fading beauty, with her wit and charm, pulling off the biggest coup of her life – making herself Empress. France was in confusion, the Empire broken, and those who had climbed to power on the eagle's wings falling with his fall – who knew what would happen to the intriguing widow of one of Napoleon's counts or generals? – but Russia! The double-headed eagle still had all his pinions –'

'How you do go on!' said Miss Garland, impatiently. 'It doesn't sound a bit likely to me. If you ask me, I think Paul made it all up out of those books he was so fond of.'

'Very probably,' admitted Wimsey. 'I only mean that it was a good story. Colourful, vivid stuff, with costume effects and plenty of human interest. And it fits in reasonably well from the historical point of view. You're quite sure you heard all about it in November?'

'Yes, of course I'm sure.'

'My opinion of Paul Alexis' powers of invention is going up. Romantic fiction should have been his line. Anyhow, we'll pass all that. Here's Charlotte, still clinging to this idea about morganatic marriages and thrones, and marrying her daughter Nicole to this Bourbon fellow, Gaston. Nothing unlikely about that. He'd come in between the Prince de Joinville and the Duc d'Aumale as regards age, and there's no reason why he shouldn't. Now, what happens to Nicole? She has a daughter – the family seems to have run to daughters – called Mélanie. I wonder what happened to Gaston and Nicole under the second Empire. Nothing is said about Gaston's profession. Probably he accepted the fait accompli and kept his royalist leanings and origin quiet. At any rate, in 1871, his daughter Louise marries a Russian – that's a throw-back to the old stock. Let's see – 1871. What do I connect with 1871? Of course – the Franco-Prussian War, and Russia's behaving rather unkindly to France about the Treaty of Paris. Alas! I fear Louise went over, horse, foot and artillery, to the enemy! Possibly this Stefan Ivanovitch came to Paris in some diplomatic connection about the time of the Treaty of Berlin, Goodness knows!'

Leila Garland yawned dreadfully.

'Louise has a daughter, anyhow,' pursued Wimsey, wrapped up in his speculation. 'And she marries another Russian. Presumably they are living in Russia again now. Mélanie is the daughter's name, and the husband is Alexis, Gregorovitch, and they are the parents of Paul Alexis, otherwise Goldschmidt, who is rescued from the Russian revolution, brought over to England and naturalised, becomes a hotel gigolo and is murdered on the Flat-Iron Rock – why?'

'Goodness knows,' said Leila, and yawned again.

Wimsey, making sure that Leila had really told him all she knew, gathered up his precious piece of paper and carried the whole problem away to Harriet.

'But it's simply silly,' said that practical young woman when she saw it. 'Even if Alexis' great-great-grandmother had been married to Nicholas I fifty times over, he wouldn't have been the heir to the throne. Why, there are heaps and heaps of people nearer than he was – the Grand-Duke Dmitri, for instance, and all sorts of people.'

'Oh? Of course. But you can always persuade people into believing what they want to, you know. Some sort of tradition about it must have been handed down in the family from old Charlotte – you know what people are when they get these genealogical bugs in their heads. I know a fellow who's a draper's assistant in Leeds, who very earnestly told me once that he ought really to be King of England, if he could only find the record of somebody's marriage to Perkin Warbeck. The trifling accident of a few intervening changes of dynasty didn't worry him at all. He really thought he had only to state his case in the House of Lords to have the crown handed to him on a gold plate. And as for all the other claimants, Alexis would probably be told that they'd all abdicated in his favour. Besides, if he really believed in this family tree of his, he'd say that his claim was better than theirs, and that his great-great-grandmother was the only legitimate descendant of Nicholas I. I don't think there was a Salic Law in Russia to prevent his claiming through the female line. Anyhow, it's perfectly clear now how the trap was baited. If only we could get hold of the papers that Alexis sent to "Boris"! But they'll have been destroyed, as sure as eggs is eggs.'

Inspector Umpelty, accompanied by Chief Inspector Parker, of Scotland Yard, rang the bell at No. 17 Popcorn Street, Kensington, and was admitted without difficulty. It was obliging of Chief Inspector Parker to be taking a personal interest in the matter, though Umpelty felt he could have done with a less distinguished escort – but the man was

Lord Peter's brother-in-law and no doubt felt a peculiar interest in the case. At any rate, Mr Parker seemed disposed to leave the provincial inspector a free hand with his inquiries.

Mrs Morecambe tripped into the room, smiling graciously.

'Good morning. Won't you sit down? Is it something about this Wilvercombe business again?'

'Well, yes, madam. There appears to be some slight misunderstanding.' The Inspector brought out a notebook and cleared his throat. 'About this gentleman, Mr Henry Weldon, to whom you gave a lift on the Thursday morning. I think you said that you drove him in to the Market Square?'

'Why, yes. It is the Market Square, isn't it? Just outside the town, with a sort of green and a building with a clock on it?'

'Oh!' said Umpelty, disconcerted. 'No; that's not the Market Square – it's the fair-ground, where they have the football matches and the flower show. Was that where you put him down?'

'Why, yes. I'm sorry. I quite thought it was the Market Square.'

'Well, it's called the Old Market. But what they call the Market Square now is the square in the centre of the town, where the point-constable stands.'

'Oh, I see. Well, I'm afraid I've been giving you misleading information.' Mrs Morecambe smiled. 'Is that a very dreadful offence?'

'It might have serious consequences, of course,' said the Inspector, 'but nobody can't help a genuine mistake. Still, I'm glad to have it cleared up. Now, just as a matter of routine, madam, what did you yourself do that morning in Wilvercombe?'

Mrs Morecambe considered, with her head on one side.

'Oh, I did some shopping, and I went to the Winter Gardens, and I had a cup of coffee at the Oriental Café – nothing very special.'

'Did you happen to buy any gentleman's collars?'

'Collars?' Mrs Morecambe looked surprised. Really, Inspector, you seem to have been going into my movements very thoroughly. Surely I'm not suspected of anything?'

'Matter of routine, madam,' replied the Inspector, stolidly; he licked his pencil.

'Well, no, I didn't *buy* any collars. I looked at some.'

'Oh, you looked at some?'

'Yes; but they hadn't the sort my husband wanted.'

'Oh, I see. Do you remember the name of the shop?'

'Yes – Rogers & something – Rogers & Peabody, I think.'

'Now, madam.' The Inspector looked up from his notebook and stared sternly at her. 'Would it surprise you to learn that the assistant at Rogers & Peabody's says that a lady dressed in the same style as yourself and answering your description, bought the collars there that morning and had the parcel taken out to the car?'

'It wouldn't surprise me at all. He was a very stupid young man. He did take a parcel out to the car, but it wasn't collars. It was ties. I went in twice – once for the ties, and then I remembered the collars and went back; but as they hadn't got what I wanted, I left them. That would be about half-past twelve, I think, if the time is of any importance.'

The Inspector hesitated. It might – it might *just* be true. The most honest witness makes a mistake sometimes. He decided to let it go for the moment.

'And you picked Mr Weldon up at the Old Market again?'

'Yes. But when you say it was this Mr Weldon, Inspector, you're putting words into my mouth. I picked up somebody – a man with dark spectacles – but I didn't know his name till he told me, and I didn't recognise the man afterwards when I saw him without the spectacles. In fact I thought then, and I still think, that the man I picked up had dark hair. The other man's voice sounded much the same – but, after all, that isn't a lot to go upon. I thought it must be he, because he seemed to remember all about it, and knew the number of my car, but of course, if it came to swearing to his identity – well!' She shrugged her shoulders.

'Quite so, madam.' It was clear enough to the Inspector what was happening. Since the discovery of the real time of the murder had made the morning alibi more dangerous than useful, it was being ruthlessly jettisoned. More trouble, he thought sourly, and more checking-up of times and places. He thanked the lady politely for her helpful explanation, and then asked whether he might have a word with Mr Morecambe.

'With my husband?' Mrs Morecambe registered surprise. 'I don't think he will be able to tell you anything. He was not staying at Heathbury at the time, you know.'

The Inspector admitted that he was aware of the fact, and added, vaguely, that this was a purely formal inquiry. 'Part of our system,' he explained, and obscurely connected with the fact that Mr Morecambe was the legal owner of the Bentley.

Mrs Morecambe smiled graciously. Well, Mr Morecambe was at home, as it happened. He had not been very well, lately, but no doubt he would be ready to assist the Inspector if it was really necessary. She would ask him to come down.

Inspector Umpelty indicated that this was not really necessary. He would be happy to accompany Mrs Morecambe to her husband's room. At which precaution Chief Inspector Parker smiled: any necessary arrangements between the Morecambes would surely have been perfected by this time.

Mrs Morecambe led the way to the door, followed by Mr

Umpelty. She glanced round as though expecting Parker to follow, but he kept his seat. After a momentary hesitation, Mrs Morecambe went out, leaving her second guest to his own devices. She went upstairs, with the Inspector padding behind her, murmuring apologies and trying to keep his boots from making a noise.

The room they entered on the first floor was furnished as a study, and beyond it, another door, half-open, led into a bedroom. At a table in the study sat a small, red-bearded man, who turned sharply to face them at their entrance.

'My dear,' said Mrs Morecambe, 'this is Inspector Umpelty of the Wilvercombe police. He wants to know something about the car.'

'Oh, yes, Inspector, what is it?' Mr Morecambe spoke genially, but his geniality was as nothing compared to the geniality of the Inspector.

'Hullo, Bright, my man!' said he. 'Risen a bit in the world since I last saw you, haven't you?'

Mr Morecambe raised his eyebrows, glanced at his wife, and then broke into a hearty laugh.

'Well done, Inspector!' said he. 'What did I tell you, dear? You can't deceive our fine British police-force. With his usual acumen, the man has spotted me! Well, sit down, Inspector and have a drink, and I'll tell you all about it.'

Umpelty cautiously lowered his large form into a chair and accepted a whisky-and-soda.

'First of all, congratulations on your sleuthing,' said Mr Morecambe, cheerfully. 'I thought I'd got rid of that fellow in Selfridge's, but I suppose the other fellow with the quick-change headgear managed to keep on the scent, in spite of my artistic camouflage in the Cinema. Well, now, I suppose you want to know why Alfred Morecambe, commission-agent of London, was going about at Wilvercombe disguised as William Bright, that seedy and unsatisfactory tonsorial artist. I don't blame you. I daresay it does look queerish. Well, to start with – here's the explanation.'

He gathered up a number of sheets of paper from his writing-table and pushed them across to Umpelty.

'I'm writing a play for my wife,' he said. 'You have no doubt discovered that she was the famous Tillie Tulliver before she married. I've written a play or two before, under the name of Cedric St Denis – spare-time work, you know – and this new one deals with the adventures of an itinerant hairdresser. The best way to pick up local colour is to go and get it personally.'

'I see, sir.'

'I ought to have told you all this at the time,' said Mr Morecambe, with a frank air of apology, 'but it really didn't seem necessary. As a matter of fact, I felt it would make me look a bit of a fool in the City. I was supposed to be taking a holiday for my health, you see, and if my partner had known what I was really up to, he might have been a little annoyed. In any case, you had my evidence, which was all that was really necessary – and I must admit that I rather enjoyed playing the ne'er-do-well to all you people. I did it rather well, don't you think? Thanks to my wife's coaching, of course.'

'I see, sir.' Inspector Umpelty fastened promptly on the salient point of all this. 'Your account of your meeting with Paul Alexis was a fact, then?'

'Absolutely true in every particular. Except, of course, that I never really had the slightest intention of committing suicide. As a matter of fact, the idea of passing the night in one of the lodging-houses appropriate to my impersonation didn't greatly appeal to me at that moment, and I was putting off the evil hour as long as possible. It's quite true that I made up a hard-luck story for Alexis – though I didn't actually take any money from the poor fellow. I drew the line at that. The pound-note I paid out that night was my own. But you nearly tied me up over that business about the tide. I rather over-reached myself there with all that picturesque detail.' He laughed again.

'Well, well,' said the Inspector. 'You've led us a fine dance, sir.' He glanced at the manuscript sheets in his hands, which appeared, so far as he could make out, to substantiate Morecambe's story. 'It's a pity you didn't take us into your confidence, sir. We could probably have arranged for nothing to come out about it in the press. However – if I take a fresh statement from you now, that will clear that up all right.'

He cocked his head for a moment as though listening, and then went on rapidly:

'I take it, that statement will just confirm the evidence you gave at the inquest? Nothing to add to it in any way?'

'Nothing at all.'

'You never, for instance, came across this Mr Henry Weldon at any time?'

'Weldon?'

'The man I gave the lift to,' prompted Mrs Morecambe, 'whose mother was engaged to the dead man.'

'Oh, him? Never saw him in my life. Don't suppose I'd recognise him now if I saw him. He didn't give evidence, did he?'

'No, sir. Very good, then. If you like, I will take a statement from you now. I'll just call in my colleague, if you don't mind, to witness it.'

The Inspector threw open the door. Chief Inspector Parker must have been waiting on the landing, for he marched in at once, followed by a respectable-looking working-woman and a large, stout man smoking a cigar. The Inspector kept his eye on the Morecambes. The wife looked merely surprised, but Morecambe's face changed.

'Now, Mrs Sterne,' said Parker, 'have you ever seen this gentleman before?'

'Why, yes, sir; this is Mr Field, as was staying with Mr Weldon down at Fourways in February. I'd know him anywhere.'

'That's who he is, is he?' said the stout gentleman. 'I thought it might be Potts or Spink. Well, Mr Maurice Vavasour, did you give the little Kohn girl a show after all?'

Mr Morecambe opened his mouth, but no sound came. Inspector Umpelty consulted the Scotland Yard man by a glance, cleared his throat, took his courage in both hands, and advanced upon his prey:

'Alfred Morecambe,' he said, 'alias William Bright, alias William Simpson, alias Field, alias Cedric St Denis, alias Maurice Vavasour, I arrest you for being concerned in the murder of Paul Alexis Goldschmidt, otherwise Pavlo Alexeivitch, and I warn you that anything you say may be taken down and used in evidence at your trial.'

He wiped his forehead.

Alibi or no alibi, he had burnt his boats.

XXXIII

EVIDENCE OF WHAT SHOULD HAVE HAPPENED

'Now see you how this dragon egg of ours
Swells with its ripening plot?'
Death's Jest-Book

WEDNESDAY, 8 JULY

'TURNING my hair grey, that's what it is,' said Inspector Umpelty.

'Not a book, not a scrap of paper, not as much as a line on the blotting pad . . .

'No, not even a bottle of purple ink . . .

'He's an artful one if you like. Always posted his own letters, or so the girl says . . .

'Yes, I know, it's all very well saying he must have been up to mischief – the job is to prove it. You know what juries are . . .

'Weldon's the fool of the two, but he's not talking. And we shan't find anything at his place – Morecambe never trusted *him* with anything . . .

'No; we haven't traced his friend in Warsaw – not yet . . .

'Oh, I know; but meantime we've got to charge them with something that looks like something. And do it quick. There's such a thing as Habeas Corpus . . .

'It's absolutely positive that neither of them could have been at the Flat-Iron cutting throats, nor yet the lady. And it's a bit awkward to fetch up three people and charge 'em with being accomplices to a murder which you can't even prove *is* a murder . . .

441

'Thank you, my lord, I don't mind if I do.'

'I freely admit,' said Wimsey, 'that it's the queerest case I ever struck. We've got all the evidence – at least, not all, but overwhelming evidence – of an elaborate conspiracy to do something or the other, And we've got a corpse which looks like the victim of a conspiracy to murder. But when we come to put the two together, they don't fit. Everything in the garden is lovely except the melancholy fact that none of the people engaged in the conspiracy could possibly have done the murder. Harriet! It's your business to work out problems of this sort – how do you propose to tackle this one?'

'I don't know,' said Harriet. 'I can only suggest a few methods and precedents. There's the Roger Sheringham method, for instance. You prove elaborately and in detail that A did the murder; then you give the story one final shake, twist it round a fresh corner, and find that the real murderer is B – the person you suspected first and then lost sight of.'

'That's no good; the cases aren't parallel. We can't even plausibly fix anything on A, let alone B.'

'No; well, there's the Philo Vance method. You shake your head and say: "There's worse yet to come," and then the murderer kills five more people, and that thins the suspects out a bit and you spot who it is.'

'Wasteful, wasteful,' said Wimsey. 'And too slow.'

'True. There's the Inspector French method – you break the unbreakable alibi.'

Wimsey groaned.

'If anybody says "alibi" to me again, I'll – I'll—'

'All right. There are plenty of methods left. There's the Thorndyke type of solution, which, as Thorndyke himself says, can be put in a nut-shell. "You have got the wrong man, you have got the wrong box, and you have got the wrong body." Suppose, for instance, that Paul Alexis is really—'

'The Emperor of Japan! Thank you.'

'Well, that might not be so far off. He thought he was an Emperor, or next door to it, anyhow. Though even if he had fifty kinds of Imperial blood in his veins instead of only two or three, it wouldn't help us to explain how he managed to get killed with nobody near him. The real difficulty—'

'Wait a moment,' said Wimsey. 'Say that again.'

Harriet said it again. 'The real difficulty,' she persisted, 'is that one can't see how *anybody* – let alone Morecambe or Henry Weldon – could have done the murder. Even if Pollock—'

'The real difficulty,' interrupted Wimsey, in a suddenly high-pitched and excited voice, 'is the time of the death, isn't it?'

'Well, yes, I suppose it is.'

'Of course it is. If it wasn't for that, we could explain everything.' He laughed. 'You know, I *always* thought it was funny, if Henry Weldon did the murder, that he shouldn't seem to know what time he did it at. Look! Let's pretend we've planned this murder ourselves and have timed it for twelve o'clock, shall we?'

'What's the good of that? We know it wasn't actually done till two o'clock. You can't get round that, my lord.'

'Ah! but I want to look at the original murder as it was planned. It's true that the murderers later on found themselves faced with an unexpected alteration in the time-scheme, but just for the moment we'll work out the time-scheme as it originally stood. Do you mind? I want to.'

The Inspector grunted, and Wimsey sat for a few minutes, apparently thinking hard. Then he spoke, without any trace of his former excitement.

'It's February,' he said. 'You're Henry Weldon. You have just heard that your elderly and foolish mother is going to marry a dancing dago thirty-five years younger than herself, and disinherit you. You are badly in need of money and you want to stop this at all costs. You make yourself unpleasant, but you find it's no good: you'll only lose all the money instead of only part. You are not an inventive man yourself, but you consult – yes, why do you consult Morecambe, Inspector?'

'Well, my lord, it seems that when Weldon came down here to see his mother, he picked up with Mrs Morecambe somewhere or other. He's a great man with the ladies, and she probably thought there was money to be made out of him, seeing his mother was a rich woman. He pretty soon put her right about that, I fancy, and she got the idea of bringing her husband in on the job. That's all speculative, as you might say, though we've checked up that Mrs M. was staying at Heathbury about the time Weldon was in Wilvercombe. Anyhow, we have made sure of one thing, and that is that Morecambe's "Commission Agency" is a pretty vague sort of affair and uncommonly rocky on its pins. Our idea was that the lady brought the two men together, and that Morecambe promised to do what he could for Weldon on a fifty-fifty basis.'

'Fifty-fifty of what?' asked Harriet.

'Of his mother's money – when he raked it in.'

'But that wouldn't be till she died.'

'No, miss, it wouldn't.'

'Oh – do you think—?'

'I think those two might have been in it for what they could get out of it, miss,' said the Inspector, stolidly.

'I agree,' said Wimsey, 'Anyway, the next thing that happens is that Mr Morecambe goes to Leamhurst and stays a few days with Weldon. All through this business, Morecambe has been far too smart to put anything on paper, except all that rubbish in cipher, so I imagine the plot was more or less worked out then. Weldon mentions to Morecambe the romantic tale of Alexis' Imperial descent, and that gives them the idea for luring their victim to the

Flat-Iron. Immediately after this, the mysterious letters begin to go out. I wonder, by the way, what was the excuse for not writing that first letter in Russian. Because, of course, that must have gone out in clear and not in code.'

'I've got an idea about that,' said Harriet. 'Didn't you say you knew of an English novel that had an explanation of the Playfair cipher?'

'Yes – one of John Rhode's. Why?'

'I suggest that the first letter merely gave the title of the book and the chapters concerned and added the code-word for the next message. Since the book was English it would be quite natural to make the whole message English.'

'Ingenious beast,' said Wimsey. 'Meaning you. But it's quite a possible explanation. We needn't go into all that story again. Obviously, Mrs Morecambe was the source of information about the topography and fauna of Wilvercombe and Darley. Weldon was chosen to do the throat-cutting and horse-riding part of it, which needed brawn only, while Morecambe buzzed about despatching letters and photographs and working Alexis up to the top-notch of excitement. Then, when everything is about ready, Morecambe goes off to take up his rôle of travelling hairdresser.'

'But why all that incredible elaboration?' demanded Harriet. 'Why didn't they just buy an ordinary razor or knife in an ordinary way? Surely it would be less traceable.'

'You'd think so. In fact, I daresay it might have been. But it's surprising how things do get traced. Look at Patrick Mahon and the chopper, for instance. The plan was to make the thing really impregnable by double and triple lines of defence. First, it was to look like suicide; secondly, if that was questioned and the razor traced, there was to be a convincing origin for the razor; thirdly, if by any chance Morecambe's disguise was seen through, there was to be an explanation for that.'

'I see. Well, go on. Morecambe had the courage of his

own convictions, anyhow – he did the thing very thoroughly.'

'Wise man. I admit that he took me in absolutely. Well, now – Weldon. He had his character of Haviland Martin all ready to slip into. Acting under instructions, he hired a Morgan, crammed it uncomfortably with a small tent and his personal belongings, and went to camp at Darley, next door to Farmer Newcombe's field. Morecambe arrived at Wilvercombe the same day. Whether and when those two met I don't know. It's my impression that the whole thing was scheduled beforehand as far as possible, and that there was next to no communication after the plot had once got going.'

'Very likely,' said Umpelty. 'That would account for its getting hitched-up over the times.'

'Possibly. Well, on the Thursday, Alexis starts off for the Flat-Iron according to instructions. By the way, it was necessary that the body should be found and recognised – hence, I fancy, the fact that Alexis was told to go openly to the rock by the coast-road. In case the body got lost, there would be witnesses to say that he had been last seen going in that direction, and to suggest a possible area for search. It would never have done for him simply to disappear like snow upon the desert's dusty face.

'So Alexis goes off to look for a crown. Meanwhile, Henry Weldon has run a needle through the H.T. leads of the Morgan, so as to provide a very good reason for asking for a lift into Wilvercombe. And now you see why a Morgan. It had to be something with only two cylinders, if the whole ignition was to be put out of action with one needle: that is, a Morgan, a Belsize-Bradshaw or a motor-bike. He probably avoided the bike on the ground of exposure to weather, and chose the Morgan as the next most handy and numerous two-cylinder bus.'

Inspector Umpelty smacked his thigh, and then, remembering that none of all this did away with the central snag in the case, blew his nose mournfully.

'Shortly after ten o'clock, along comes Mrs Morecambe in the Bentley with the conspicuous number-plate. That number-plate was pure bunce for them – they can scarcely have picked or wangled it on purpose, but it came in very convenient as a means of identifying the bus. What more natural than that Weldon, if questioned, should remember a number so screamingly funny as that? Oi, oi, oi! Highly humorous, wasn't it, Inspector?'

'Where did she put him down, then?' asked Umpelty, scowling.

'Anywhere, out of sight of the village and the passing throng. At some point where he can cut across the fields to the shore again. The road turns in rather sharply from the coast between Darley and Wilvercombe, which doubtless accounts for their having left him so much time for his walk back. In any case, by, say, 11.15, he has walked back to Darley and is cocking an eye over the fence at Farmer Newcombe's bay mare. He pulls a stake out of the hedge and goes into the field, with oats in one hand and a rope-bridle in the other.'

'What did he want to take oats for? Surely the horse would have come up to him if he just said "Coop" or whatever it is and shaken his hat about? It seems silly of him to scatter oats all over the place like that.'

'Yes, my child,' said Wimsey. 'But there was a reason for that. I think the oats he scattered were from the day before, when he first started to make friends with the mare. Teach an animal to come for food once and it'll come twice as fast the second time; but once disappoint it, and it won't come at all.'

'Yes, of course. You're quite right.'

'Now,' said Wimsey, 'I *think*, I can't prove it, but I *think*, our hero left most of his clothes behind him. I'm not certain, but it seems an obvious precaution. At any rate, he bridled the mare and mounted her and rode off. You've got to remember that between Darley and Pollock's cottage the shore is hidden from the road, so that the only risk he ran of being seen was by somebody straying on the edge of the cliff itself. And they would probably not worry much about a man exercising a horse along the shore. His real awkward moment was the passing of the cottages, but he had carefully chosen the very time when the working-classes have their dinner. I fancy he went past there just before midday.'

'They heard hoofs about that time.'

'Yes. And a little later, Paul Alexis heard them too, as he sat on his rock and dreamed of the Imperial Purple. He looked and saw the Rider from the Sea.'

'Quite so,' said Umpelty, unmoved. 'And what then?'

'Ah! – you recollect that we are merely describing an ideal crime, in which everything works out as planned.'

'Oh, yes – of course.'

'Then – in the ideal crime – Weldon rides up to the rock through the water – and by the way, you will bear in mind that it is fully an hour before low tide and that there is a foot and a half of water at the foot of the Flat-Iron. He ties the mare close by the head to the ring-bolt put there the day before, and he climbs up on to the rock. Alexis may or may not have recognised him. If he did . . .'

Wimsey paused, and his eyes grew angry.

'Whether he did or not, he hadn't much time for disappointment. Weldon asked him to sit down, I think; emperors sit, while respectful commoners stand behind them, you see. Weldon asked for the letter, and Alexis gave him the decoded translation. Then he leaned over him from behind with the razor . . .

'Weldon, of course, was a fool. He did everything wrong that he could do. He ought to have removed those gloves, and he ought to have seen to it that he had the original letter. Perhaps he ought to have searched the body. But I think that would have been worse still. It might have destroyed the suicidal appearance. Once move a body and you never can recapture the first, fine, careless rapture, don't you know. And besides, the mare was struggling and nearly breaking away. That would have been fatal . . .

'Do you know, I rather take my hat off to Weldon about this. Ever seen a horse that has suddenly had fresh blood splashed all over it? Not pretty. Definitely not. Cavalry horses have to get used to it, of course – but the bay mare could never have smelt blood before. When I realise that Weldon had to mount that squealing, plunging, terrified brute bareback from the top of a rock, and ride her away without letting her once plunge on to the sand, I tell you, I take off my hat.'

'You mean, you would have had to, if it had happened that thick way.'

'Exactly. A man who could seriously contemplate bringing that scheme off knew something about horses. He may even have known too much. I mean . . . there are ways and ways of subduing violent animals, and some ways are crueller than others . . .

'We'll suppose he did it. That he somehow got the mare untied from the rock and forced her straight out to sea. That would be the best way. That would tire her out, and at the same time wash the blood away. Then, having got control of her, he rides back as he came. But she has loosened a shoe in her frantic plunging and kicking, and on the way back she wrenches it off altogether. Probably he doesn't notice that. He rides on past his camp to wherever he left his clothes, looses the mare, gets dressed and hurries out to flag the Bentley on the return journey. I don't suppose he gets there much before, say 12.55. He's picked up and set down at the Feathers at one o'clock. Here we leave romance and come back to the facts. Then, after lunch, he goes down to his own place, burns the rope-bridle, which is bloody, and kicks out our friend Perkins, who seems disposed to take too much interest in the rope.'

'He hadn't the rope with him at the Feathers, had he?'

'No; I expect he threw it down in some handy spot on his way back from the Flat-Iron – somewhere near the stream, I should imagine. Well, all he has to do after that is to get Polwhistle to come along and deal with the Morgan. He made another mistake there, of course. When he was putting those leads in his pocket he should have *put* them in his pocket and seen that they stayed put.

'But you see that he, too, was intended to have three lines of defence. First, of course, the death was to look like suicide; secondly, the camper at Darley Halt was to be Mr Martin of Cambridge, having no connection with anybody; and thirdly, if Mr Martin was proved to be Henry Weldon, there was the alibi in Wilvercombe, with all the details about Bach and shirt-collars, and an absolutely independent witness in a Bentley car to swear to the story.'

'Yes, but –' said Umpelty.

'I know, I know – bear with me. I know the plan went all wrong, but I want you to realise what it was meant to be. Suppose all this had worked properly – what would have happened? The body would have been left on the rock at about noon, with the razor lying below it. By 12.30, the murderer was well away, nearly at Darley. By one o'clock, he was at the Feathers, eating and drinking, with a witness to swear that he had spent the whole morning in Wilvercombe. If the body was found before the tide turned, there would be no footprints, other than those of the corpse, and suicide would probably be presumed without a second thought – especially when the razor turned up. If the body was not found till later, the footprints would be less important, but the medical evidence would probably establish the time of death, and then the alibi would come in.

'It sounds a very risky plan, but it sounds riskier than it was. Its boldness was its strength. From the Flat-Iron and for a mile or more before you come to it, the coast-road is visible from the shore. He could keep an eye on it and bide his time. If it looked dangerous, he could put it off to a more convenient season. Actually, the only real risk he ran was of being seen at the very moment of the murder and chased by car along the coast. Otherwise, even if it turned out later that a horseman had been seen on the shore about noon, who could prove who the horseman was? It could certainly not be Mr Haviland Martin, who had no connection with anybody and had spent the morning musically in Wilvercombe. And in any case, how many people did pass along that road? What were the odds that the body would be discovered under a few hours? Or that the death would be supposed to be anything except suicide?'

'What are the odds now that it wasn't suicide?' said Inspector Umpelty. 'By your own showing it can't have been anything else. But I see what you mean, my lord. You mean that all this plan was made out, and then, when Weldon got along to the Flat-Iron, something made him change his mind. How's this? When Alexis sees his Rider from the Sea, he recognises Weldon and asks him to explain, Weldon tells him how they've made a fool of him and somehow gets him to promise to chuck Mrs Weldon. Maybe he threatens him with the razor. Then Weldon goes away and Alexis is so disappointed that, after thinking it over a bit, he cuts his throat.'

'Weldon having thoughtfully armed him with the razor for that purpose?'

'Well, yes – I suppose so.'

'And what did the bay mare see?' asked Harriet.

'Ghosts,' replied Inspector Umpelty, with a snort of incredulity. 'Anyhow, you can't put horses in the witness-box.'

'Weldon made a mistake afterwards in coming to Wilvercombe,' went on Wimsey. 'With that identification mark on his arm, he should have kept away, mother or no mother. But he *had* to poke his nose in and see what was happening. And Morecambe – well, his possible appearance as a witness was foreseen, of course. I wonder, though, if he was really wise to answer that advertisement of ours. I suppose it was the best thing he could do – but he ought to have smelt the trap, I think. But my private impression is that he wanted to keep an eye on Weldon, who was blundering about all over the place.'

'Excuse me, my lord,' said Inspector Umpelty, 'but we've wasted a good hour now speculating about what these people might have done or meant to do. That's very interesting to you, no doubt, but meanwhile we're no nearer to knowing what they did do, and here's three people in prison for doing something they can't have done. If Alexis cut his own throat, we've either got to release these people with apologies, or get up a case against them for conspiring to procure by menaces or something. If some accomplice of theirs killed him, we've got to find that accomplice. In either case, I mustn't waste any more time about it. I only wish I'd never touched the bleeding case.'

'But you're so hasty, Inspector,' bleated Wimsey. 'I only said the plan went wrong; I never said they didn't carry it out.'

Inspector Umpelty looked sadly at Wimsey, and his lips silently formed the word 'loopy'. But aloud he merely observed:

'Well, my lord, whatever they did, they didn't murder Alexis at two o'clock, because they weren't there to do it; and they didn't murder him at twelve o'clock, because he didn't die till two. Those are facts, aren't they?'

'No.'

'No?'

'No.'

'You mean, one or other of them was there at two o'clock?'

'No.'

'You mean, they did murder Alexis at twelve o'clock?'

'Yes.'

'By cutting his throat?'

'Yes.'

'Right through?'

'Right through.'

'Then how is it he didn't die till two o'clock?'

'We have no evidence at all,' said Wimsey, 'as to the time Alexis died.'

XXXIV
EVIDENCE OF WHAT DID HAPPEN

'Take thou this flower to strew upon *his* grave,
A lily of the valley; it bears bells,
For even the plants, it seems, must have their fool,
So universal is the spirit of folly;
And whisper, to the nettles of *his* grave,
"King Death hath asses' ears." '

Death's Jest-Book

WEDNESDAY, 8 JULY

'Do you mean to say,' demanded Inspector Umpelty, with slow indignation, 'that the young lady finds herself mistaken all this time?'

Harriet shook her head, and Wimsey said, 'No.'

'Well, my lord, I don't think you can go against the doctor. I've asked other doctors about it, and they say there's no doubt about it.'

'You didn't tell them the whole of the facts,' said Wimsey. 'I don't blame you,' he added, kindly, 'I've only just thought of the rest of the facts myself. Something you said about blood put it in my head, Harriet. Suppose we put down a few things we know about this supposed heir of the Romanovs.'

1. He is known to have been very ill as a child, through being knocked down in the playground.
2. At the age of twenty-one he wore a beard, and had never used a razor. He was also

3. Extraordinarily timid about using sharp weapons or visiting the dentist.
4. Moreover, he had had at least one molar crowned – the last resort to avoid extraction.
5. On Thursday 18th, when scrambling over rocks, he wore gloves.
6. Periodic pains in the joints caused him acute suffering.
7. He used antipyrin to relieve this condition.
8. In no circumstances would he see a doctor, though he anticipated that the trouble would eventually cripple him.
9. Lack of the usual post-mortem stains were remarked on at the inquest.
10. Inquest also established that the great vessels were almost completely drained of blood.
11. And, finally, one may inherit other things besides Imperial crowns through the female line.

Harriet and the Inspector stared at this for a moment or two. Then Harriet laughed:

'Of course!' she said. 'I thought your style was a little laboured in places! But as an impromptu effort it's creditable.'

'I don't see what you get from all that,' said Umpelty. And then, suspiciously: 'Is it a joke? Is it another of these ciphers?' He snatched up the paper and ran a large thumb down the lines. 'Here!' he said, 'what are you playing at? Is it a riddle?'

'No, it's the answer,' said Harriet. 'You're right, Peter, you're right – you must be. It would explain such a lot. Only I didn't know about antipyrin.'

'I'm almost sure that is right; I remember reading about it somewhere.'

'Did it come through the Romanovs?'

'Possibly. It doesn't prove that he really was a Romanov, if you mean that. Though he may have been, for young

Simons recognised something familiar in his face, which may have been a family resemblance. But it may quite likely have been the other way: the fact that he had it may have lent colour to the tradition. It often occurs spontaneously.'

'What *is* all this?' asked the Inspector.

'Don't tease him, Peter. Try the initial letters, Mr Umpelty.'

'Ah – oh! You *will* have your fun, my lord! H, A, E – Haemophilia. What in the name of blazes is that, when it's at home?'

'It's a condition of the blood,' said Wimsey, 'due to a lack of something-or-the-other, calcium or what not. It is inherited, like colour-blindness, through the female, and shows itself only, or practically only, in the male, and then only in alternate generations. That is to say, it might lie hidden in generation after generation of daughters, and then, by some malignant chance, pop suddenly up in a son born of a perfectly healthy father and an apparently quite healthy mother. And so far as is known it is incurable.'

'And what is it? And why do you think Alexis had it? And what does it matter if he did?'

'It's a condition in which the blood doesn't clot properly; if you get even a tiny little scratch, you may bleed to death from it. You may die of having a tooth drawn or from cutting your chin with a razor, unless you know how to deal with it – and in any case, you will go on bleeding like a stuck pig for hours. And if you get a fall or a blow, you have internal bleeding, which comes out in great lumps and swellings and is agonisingly painful. And even if you are terribly careful, you may get internal bleeding at the joints for no reason at all. It comes on from time to time and is horribly painful and gives you a hell of a fever. Hence, if I remember rightly, the antipyrin. And what's more, it generally ends up by ankylosing your joints and making you a permanent cripple.'

'The Tsarevitch had it, of course,' and Harriet. 'I read

about it in those books of Alexis – but like a fool, I never thought about it in connection with the murder.'

'I don't know that I see it now,' said the Inspector, 'except that it explains why Alexis was such a namby-pamby and all that. Do you mean it proves that Alexis really was a royalty of sorts and that the Bolshies –?'

'It may or may not prove any of that,' said Wimsey. 'But don't you see, my dear old goat, that it completely busts up and spifficates the medical evidence? We timed the death for two o'clock because the blood hadn't clotted – but if Alexis was a haemophilic, you might wait till Kingdom Come, and his blood would never clot at all. Therefore, he may have died at noon or dawn for all we know. As a matter of fact, the blood might end by clotting very slightly after some hours – it depends how badly he had the disease – but as evidence for the time of death, the blood is a simple washout.'

'Good lord!' said Umpelty.

He sat open-mouthed.

'Yes,' he said, when he'd recovered himself a little, 'but here's a snag. If he might have died any time, how are we to prove he died at twelve o'clock?'

'Easy. First of all, we know it must have been then, because that's the time these people have an alibi for. As Sherlock Holmes says somewhere: "Only a man with a criminal enterprise desires to establish an alibi." I must say, this case is really unique in one thing. It's the only one I have ever known in which a murderer didn't know the time he was supposed to have done the murder at. No wonder the evidence at the inquest gave Henry Weldon such a jolt!'

'Yes – but –' the Inspector seemed worried. 'That's all right for us, but I mean to say, that doesn't prove it was a murder – I mean, you've got to prove it was a murder first, before you prove anything else. I mean to say –'

'Quite right,' said Wimsey. 'Unlike Mr Weldon, you can spot the *petitio elenchi*. But look here, if Alexis was seen alive on the road between half-past ten and half-past eleven and was dead at two o'clock, then he must have died during the period covered by the alibis; that's certain. And I think we can get it down a bit closer. Jem Pollock and his grandad puzzled us by saying that they thought they saw the man lying down on the rock well before two o'clock. In that case, he was probably dead already. We now know that they were in all likelihood speaking the truth, and so we need not now imagine them to be accomplices in the crime. You can whittle the period during which death must have occurred down to about two hours – say from 11.30, when Alexis could have reached the rock, to about 1.30, when the Pollocks first set eyes on the body. That ought to be near enough for you – especially as you can trace the weapon quite definitely to the hands of one of the accomplices. I suppose you can't find that the razor was sent anywhere by post for Weldon to get hold of?'

'We've tried that, but we couldn't find anything.'

'No. I shouldn't wonder if Weldon's trip to Wilvercombe on the Wednesday was made for the purpose of picking up the razor. It could so easily have been left somewhere for him. Of course, Morecambe took good care not to be in Wilvercombe that day himself, the cunning devil – but what could be easier than to deposit a little parcel at a tobacconist's or somewhere to be called for by his friend Mr Jones? I suggest that you look into that, Inspector.'

'I will, my lord. There's just one thing. I can't see why Weldon and Morecambe should have been so surprised about the inquest evidence. Wouldn't Alexis have told them about this disability of his? If he thought it proved his descent from the Romanovs, you'd think he'd have mentioned it first thing.'

'Oh, no, you wouldn't. It's pretty clear that Alexis disguised that little matter very jealously. It's not a recommendation to a man who wants to lead a successful revolution that he is liable to be laid up at any moment by a painful and incurable disease. Nor would it be exactly an inducement to "Feodora" to marry him, if he was known to be a "bleeder". No, poor devil, he must have been terrified the whole time for fear they should find it out.'

'Yes, I see. It's natural, when you come to think of it.'

'If you exhume the body,' said Wimsey, 'you will very likely find the characteristic thickening of the joints that accompanies haemophilia. And I daresay you might get conclusive evidence by inquiring among the people who knew Alexis in London and America. I'm pretty sure he had the disease.'

'It's funny,' said Harriet, 'the way all this worked out for Weldon & Co. They had such good luck in one way and such bad luck in another. I mean: first of all they laid a fairly good plot, which turned on an alibi and a disguise. Then I came along unexpectedly and bust up the disguise. That was bad luck. But at the same time I produced a lot of unnecessary cleverness and observation which gave them a far better alibi for a totally different time, which was good luck. Then they lost the body, owing to the £300 in gold, which would have been a beastly nuisance for them. But again I barged in with evidence and photographs, and so drew attention to the death and got the body found again. Then, when, to their horror, their original lovely alibi turned out to be useless and dangerous, along comes poor little Perkins – who of course is as innocent as any sucking-pig – to give them a cast-iron alibi for the wrong time. We found the horseshoe, which would have pretty well cooked their goose, but for the astonishing bit of luck over the blood-clotting affair. And so on. It's been an incredible muddle. And it's all my fault, really. If I hadn't been so bright and brainy nobody would ever have known anything about the condition of the blood at all, and we should have taken it for granted that Alexis had died long before I came on the scene. It's so complicated, I really don't know whether my being there helped or hindered.'

'It's so complicated,' said the Inspector with a groan, 'that I don't believe we'll get any jury to believe it. Besides there's the Chief Constable. I'll bet you anything you like he'll pooh-pooh the whole thing. He'll still say that after all we haven't *proved* it wasn't suicide, and we'd better let it go at that. He's as mad as a dog with us for arresting those people anyhow, and if I come along with this story about haemo-what-you-call, he'll have fifty thousand fits. See here, my lord, if we do prosecute, d'you really think we've a hope in Hades?'

'I'll tell you this,' said Harriet. 'Last night, Mrs Weldon consented to dance with M. Antoine, and Henry didn't like it at all. If you let Henry Weldon and Morecambe loose again, what premium would you take on those two lives – Antoine's and Mrs Weldon's?'

There was silence after the Inspector left them.

'Well!' said Harriet at last.

'Well,' said Wimsey, 'isn't that a damned awful, bitter, bloody farce? The old fool who wanted a lover and the young fool who wanted an empire. One throat cut and three people hanged, and £130,000 going begging for the next man who likes to sell his body and soul for it. God! What a jape! King Death has asses' ears with a vengeance.'

He got up.

'Let's clear out of this,' he said. 'Get your things packed and leave your address with the police and come on up to town. I'm fed to the back teeth.'

'Yes, let's go. I'm terrified of meeting Mrs Weldon. I don't want to see Antoine. It's all frightening and disgusting. We'll go home.'

'Right-ho! We'll go home. We'll dine in Piccadilly. Damn it,' said Wimsey, savagely, 'I always did hate watering-places!'

WIMSEY, Peter Death Bredon, d.s.o.; *born* 1890, *2nd son of* Mortimer Gerald Bredon Wimsey, 15th Duke of Denver, and of Honoria Lucasta, *daughter of* Francis Delagardie of Bellingham Manor, Hants.

Educated: Eton College and Balliol College, Oxford (1st class honours, Sch. of Mod. Hist 1912); served with H.M. Forces 1914/18 (Major, Rifle Brigade). *Author of:* 'Notes on the Collecting of Incunabula', 'The Murderer's Vade-Mecum', etc. *Recreations:* Criminology; bibliophily; music; cricket.

Clubs: Marlborough; Egotists'. *Residences:* 110A Piccadilly, W.; Bredon Hall, Duke's Denver, Norfolk.

Arms: Sable, 3 mice courant, argent; crest, a domestic cat couched as to spring, proper; motto: As my Whimsy takes me.

A short biography of Lord Peter Wimsey, brought up to date (May 1935) and communicated by his uncle Paul Austin Delagardie.

I AM asked by Miss Sayers to fill up certain lacunae and correct a few trifling errors of fact in her account of my nephew Peter's career. I shall do so with pleasure. To appear publicly in print is every man's ambition, and by acting as a kind of running footman to my nephew's triumph I shall only be showing a modesty suitable to my advanced age.

The Wimsey family is an ancient one – too ancient, if you ask me. The only sensible thing Peter's father ever did was to ally his exhausted stock with the vigorous French-English strain of the Delagardies. Even so, my nephew Gerald (the present Duke of Denver) is nothing but a beef-witted English squire, and my niece Mary was flighty and foolish enough till she married a policeman and settled down. Peter, I am glad to say, takes after his mother and me. True, he is all nerves and nose – but that is better than being all brawn and no brains like his father and brother, or a mere bundle of emotions, like Gerald's boy, Saint-George. He has at least inherited the Delagardie brains, by way of safeguard to the unfortunate Wimsey temperament.

Peter was born in 1890. His mother was being very much worried at the time by her husband's behaviour (Denver was always tiresome, though the big scandal did not break out till the Jubilee year), and her anxieties may have affected the boy. He was a colourless shrimp of a child, very restless and mischievous, and always much too sharp for his age. He had nothing of Gerald's robust physical beauty, but he developed what I can best call a kind of bodily cleverness, more skill than strength. He had a quick eye for a ball and beautiful hands for a horse. He had the devil's own pluck, too: the intelligent sort of pluck that sees the risk before he takes it. He suffered badly from nightmares as a child. To his father's consternation he grew up with a passion for books and music.

His early school-days were not happy. He was a fastidious child, and I suppose it was natural that his schoolfellows should call him 'Flimsy' and treat him as a kind of comic turn. And he might, in sheer self-protection, have accepted the position and degenerated into a mere licensed buffoon, if some games-master at Eton had not discovered that he was a brilliant natural cricketer. After that, of course, all his eccentricities were accepted as wit, and Gerald underwent the salutary shock of seeing his despised younger brother become a bigger personality than himself. By the time he reached the Sixth Form, Peter had contrived to become the fashion – athlete, scholar, *arbiter elegantiarum – nec pluribus impar*. Cricket had a great deal to do with it – plenty of Eton men will remember the 'Great Flim' and his performance against Harrow – but I take credit to myself for introducing him to a good tailor, showing him the way about Town, and teaching him to distinguish good wine from bad. Denver bothered little about him – he had too many entanglements of his own and in addition was taken up with Gerald, who by this time was making a prize fool of himself at Oxford. As a matter of fact Peter never got on with his father, he was a ruthless young critic of the paternal misdemeanours, and his sympathy for his mother had a destructive effect upon his sense of humour.

Denver, needless to say, was the last person to tolerate his own failings in his offspring. It cost him a good deal of money to extricate Gerald from the Oxford affair, and he was willing enough to turn his other son over to me. Indeed, at the age of seventeen, Peter came to me of his own accord. He was old for his age and exceedingly reasonable, and I treated him as a man of the world. I established him in trustworthy hands in Paris, instructing him to keep his affairs upon a sound business footing and to see that they terminated with goodwill on both sides and generosity on his. He fully justified my confidence. I believe that no woman has ever found cause to complain of Peter's treatment; and two at least of them have since married royalty (rather obscure royalties, I admit, but royalty of a sort). Here again, I insist upon my due share of the credit; however good the material one has to work upon it is ridiculous to leave any young man's social education to chance.

The Peter of this period was really charming, very frank, modest and well-mannered, with a pretty, lively wit. In 1909 he went up with a scholarship to read History at Balliol, and here, I must confess, he became rather intolerable. The world was at his feet, and he began to give himself airs. He acquired affectations, an exaggerated Oxford manner and a monocle, and aired his opinions a good deal, both in and out of the Union, though I will do him the justice to say that he never attempted to patronise his mother or me. He was in his second year when Denver broke his neck out hunting and Gerald succeeded to the title. Gerald showed more sense of responsibility than I had expected in dealing with the estate; his worst mistake was to marry his cousin Helen, a scrawny, over-bred prude, all county from head to heel. She and Peter loathed each other cordially; but he could always take refuge with his mother at the Dower House.

And then, in his last year at Oxford, Peter fell in love with a child of seventeen and instantly forgot everything he had ever been taught. He treated that girl as if she was made of gossamer, and me as a hardened old monster of depravity who had made him unfit to touch her delicate purity. I won't deny that they made an exquisite pair – all white and gold – a prince and princess of moonlight, people said. Moonshine would have been nearer the mark. What Peter was to do in twenty years' time with a wife who had neither brains nor character nobody but his mother and myself ever troubled to ask, and he, of course, was completely besotted. Happily, Barbara's parents decided that she was too young to marry; so Peter went in for his final Schools in the temper of a Sir Eglamore achieving his first dragon; laid his First-Class Honours at his lady's feet like the dragon's head, and settled down to a period of virtuous probation.

Then came the War. Of course the young idiot was mad to get married before he went. But his own honourable scruples made him mere wax in other people's hands. It was pointed out to him that if he came back mutilated it would be very unfair to the girl. He hadn't thought of that, and rushed off in a frenzy of self-abnegation to release her from the engagement. I had no hand in that; I was glad enough of the result, but I couldn't stomach the means.

He did very well in France; he made a good officer and the men liked him. And then, if you please, he came back on leave with his captaincy in '16, to find the girl married – to a hardbitten rake of a Major Somebody, whom she had nursed in the V.A.D. hospital, and whose motto with women was catch 'em quick and treat 'em rough. It was pretty brutal; for the girl hadn't had the nerve to tell Peter beforehand. They got married in a hurry when they heard he was coming home, and all he got on landing was a letter, announcing the *fait accompli* and reminding him that he had set her free himself.

I will say for Peter that he came straight to me and admitted that he had been a fool. 'All right,' said I, 'you've had your lesson. Don't go and make a fool of yourself in the other direction.' So he went back to his job with (I am sure) the fixed intention of getting killed; but all he got was his majority and his D.S.O. for some recklessly good intelligence work behind the German front. In 1918 he was blown up and buried in a shell-hole near Caudry, and that left him with a bad nervous breakdown, lasting, on and off, for two years. After that, he set himself up in a flat in Piccadilly, with the man Bunter (who had been his sergeant and was, and is, devoted to him), and started out to put himself together again.

I don't mind saying that I was prepared for almost anything. He had lost all his beautiful frankness, he shut everybody out of his confidence, including his mother and me, adopted an impenetrable frivolity of manner and a dilettante pose, and became, in fact, the complete comedian. He was wealthy and could do as he chose, and it gave me a certain amount of sardonic entertainment to watch the efforts of post-war feminine London to capture him. 'It can't,' said one solicitous matron, 'be good for poor Peter to live like a hermit.' 'Madam,' said I, 'if he did, it wouldn't be.' No; from that point of view he gave me no anxiety. But I could not but think it dangerous that a man of his ability should have no job to occupy his mind, and I told him so.

In 1921 came the business of the Attenbury Emeralds. That affair has never been written up, but it made a good deal of noise, even at that noisiest of periods. The trial of the thief was a series of red-hot sensations, and the biggest sensation of the bunch was when Lord Peter Wimsey walked into the witness-box as chief witness for the prosecution.

That was notoriety with a vengeance. Actually, to an experienced intelligence officer, I don't suppose the investigation had offered any great difficulties; but a 'noble sleuth' was something new in thrills. Denver was furious; personally, I didn't mind what Peter did, provided he did something. I thought he seemed happier for the work, and I liked the Scotland Yard man he had picked up during the run of the case. Charles Parker is a quiet, sensible, well-bred fellow, and has been a good friend and brother-in-law to Peter. He has the valuable quality of being fond of people without wanting to turn them inside out.

The only trouble about Peter's new hobby was that it had to be more than a hobby, if it was to be any hobby for a gentleman. You cannot get murderers hanged for your private entertainment. Peter's intellect pulled him one way and his nerves another, till I began to be afraid they would pull him to pieces. At the end of every case we had the old nightmares and shell-shock over again. And then Denver, of all people – Denver, the crashing great booby, in the middle of his fulminations against Peter's degrading and notorious police activities, must needs get himself indicted on a murder charge and stand his trial in the House of Lords, amid a blaze of publicity which made all Peter's efforts in that direction look like damp squibs.

Peter pulled his brother out of that mess, and, to my relief, was human enough to get drunk on the strength of it. He now admits that his 'hobby' is his legitimate work for society, and has developed sufficient interest in public affairs to undertake small diplomatic jobs from time to time under the Foreign Office. Of late he has become a little more ready to show his feelings, and a little less terrified of having any to show.

His latest eccentricity has been to fall in love with that girl whom he cleared of the charge of poisoning her lover. She refused to marry him, as any woman of character would. Gratitude and a humiliating inferiority complex are no foundation for matrimony; the position was false from the start. Peter had the sense, this time, to take my advice. 'My boy,' said I, 'what was wrong for you twenty years back is right now. It's not the innocent young things that need gentle handling – it's the ones that have been frightened and hurt. Begin again from the beginning – but I warn you that you will need all the self-discipline you have ever learnt.'

Well, he has tried. I don't think I have ever seen such patience. The girl has brains and character and honesty; but he has got to teach her how to take which is far more difficult than learning to give. I think they will find one another, if they can keep their passions from running ahead of their wills. He does realise, I know, that in this case there can be no consent but free consent.

Peter is forty-five now, it is really time he was settled. As you will see, I have been one of the important formative influences in his career, and, on the whole, I feel he does me credit. He is a Delagardie, with little of the Wimseys about him except (I must be fair) that underlying sense of social responsibility which prevents the English landed gentry from being a total loss, spiritually speaking. Detective or no detective, he is a scholar and a gentleman; it will amuse me to see what sort of shot he makes at being a husband and father. I am getting to be an old man, and have no son of my own (that I know of); I should be glad to see Peter happy. But as his mother says, 'Peter has always had everything except the things he really wanted,' and I suppose he is luckier than most.

PAUL AUSTIN DELAGARDIE.